MADE to be BROKEN

Kelley Armstrong lives in rural Ontario, Canada, with her husband, three children and far too many pets. She is the author of the supernatural Women of the Otherworld series, *Exit Strategy*, the first in the Nadia Stafford adventure series, and *The Summoning*, the first in a new young adult trilogy.

ALSO BY KELLEY ARMSTRONG

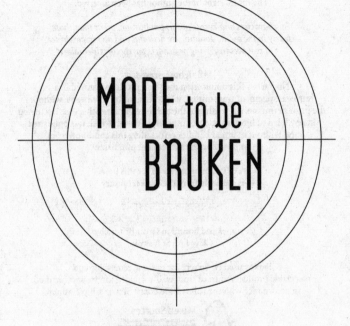

MADE to be BROKEN

KELLEY ARMSTRONG

sphere

SPHERE

First published in Great Britain in 2009 by Sphere

ISBN 978-0-7515-3813-7

Printed and bound in Great Britain by
Clays Ltd, St Ives plc

Papers used by Sphere are natural, renewable and
recyclable products sourced from well-managed forests and certified
in accordance with the rules of the Forest Stewardship Council.

Mixed Sources
Product group from well-managed
forests and other controlled sources
www.fsc.org Cert no. SGS-COC-004081
© 1996 Forest Stewardship Council

Sphere
An imprint of
Little, Brown Book Group
100 Victoria Embankment
London EC4Y 0DY

An Hachette UK Company
www.hachette.co.uk

www.littlebrown.co.uk

ACKNOWLEDGEMENTS

Much thanks to the usual group of folks who do their damnedest to make me look good: my agent, Helen Heller, and my editors, Anne Groell of Bantam, Anne Collins of Random House Canada, and Antonia Hodgson of Little, Brown & Co.

Thanks, too, to my first Nadia series beta readers, Chris Wagner and Sharon.

One

Below the belfry, the city sparkled, the late afternoon sun glinting off the skyscrapers, every surface dripping from a brief shower. A spectacular view... even through the scope of a sniper's rifle.

A pigeon landed on the ledge beneath the belfry, squawking about the rain. My eye still fixed to the scope, I reached into my pocket and tossed a handful of dried corn into the courtyard below. A flapping of wings told me he'd gone for it. The pigeons were the one drawback to this perch. Fortunately, I'd noticed them when scouting and came prepared. I didn't want a sudden flurry of birds from the belfry telling onlookers exactly where the shot had come from.

The doors below opened onto the quiet side street and at exactly five-thirty, out walked Grant Beecham. A creature of habit, like most people. He was alone. I expected that, but found myself instinctively looking for bodyguards or well-armed friends. I was used to Mafia thugs who knew there was a mark on their heads and never set foot outside alone.

But Beecham had no reason to think his life was in danger. He was just a pharmaceutical company researcher. Yes, he'd suppressed reports of fatalities in a new multiple sclerosis drug study. But his confession came only after evidence was found in an illegal search, so it'd been ruled inadmissible, the case thrown out. He hadn't even been fired; he was too valuable.

Sure, there were devastated families who'd lost loved

ones, but this wasn't the Wild West. Injured parties seek financial restitution through the courts, and you take the money and shut up. You don't use your payoff to hire a hitman.

Beecham's car rounded the corner. A Lincoln with a driver to take him to his big house in Forest Hill, maybe with a stop along the way to convince another desperate family that he could provide—under the table and for the right price—the suppressed miracle drug.

I pulled the trigger. The bullet passed through the base of his skull, killing him instantly.

I didn't wait to see him crumple to the sidewalk. Or to watch passersby look over warily, assessing the cut of his suit before deciding he hadn't just fallen down drunk. By the time someone took out a cell phone, I'd be halfway down the belfry stairs.

I moved as quickly and silently as I could. Not easy when the steps were so ancient each one protested under my weight.

Dust whirled in my wake. I was wearing disposable booties, the kind considerate furniture deliverers wear. They'd eliminate prints, but did nothing for the dust reaching my nose and eyes. At my second stifled sneeze, a head popped around the bottom flight. Quinn, aka the Boy Scout—though the latter wasn't used by anyone who wanted to get on his good side.

Beecham was Quinn's job. Vigilante work was the only kind he did, hence the unflattering alternate nom de guerre. Among professional killers, a vigilante—even one as solid as Quinn—is viewed with the same disdain a veteran beat cop has for an idealistic, college-educated young detective. A prissy boy who wants to do a man's job without getting his hands dirty.

At six foot two, with a solid linebacker's physique, square face, stubborn jaw, and piercing eyes, Quinn didn't fit anyone's image of a "prissy boy." But few of the hitmen who scorned him had ever seen him. Like me, Quinn kept to himself, and for good reason. Killing criminals wasn't the only way Quinn pursued justice. He was a federal agent. What branch, I had no idea. I didn't ask.

Most people in my profession would have a problem partnering with a cop, even one moonlighting as a hitman. I didn't. I came from a long line of law-enforcement officers. My life goal had been to join that family tradition. And I had . . . until seven years ago, when I shot a suspect point-blank, made national headlines, and saw my life crash and burn.

As I rounded the last flight, Quinn backed inside. Gaze still fixed on the trash-cluttered courtyard, he unbuttoned his dark overcoat to reveal a suit. I passed him the fake briefcase that housed my takedown rifle. As I tugged off my shoes, he backed in another step and gave me his arm for support. Off with the sneakers, and on with pumps more suited to my slacks and blazer. There was more to our disguises than clothing, but that was all we changed.

I let go of his arm, then slung the leather knapsack with my gear onto my shoulder. Quinn took my hand. We walked quickly through a narrow alley, then slowed to a stroll as we stepped into a paved passage between office towers. At the end, we merged with the commuter crowd heading to the subway.

As we stepped onto the subway stairs, the distant wail

of sirens was almost swallowed by the roar of rush-hour traffic.

There are many names for what I do. Want to channel your inner Godfather? Go for hatchet man or hired gun. Prefer an air of legitimacy? Try professional killer or contract killer. Add an air of mystery and intrigue? Use assassin. I like it plain and simple. Hitman. Hitwoman or even hit-person, if one wants to be PC, but if you ask me, "politically correct" and "killer" are two terms never meant to go together.

I moonlight as a hitman to keep my business—a wilderness lodge—open. After the crash of my life seven years ago, the lodge is my lifeline to sanity, and if killing traitors for a small New York crime family keeps it running, then that's fine with me. I know it shouldn't be. But it is.

Quinn doesn't need the money; he needs to scratch the itch that can come with immersing yourself in a justice system that doesn't always see justice done. I exploded on the job and watched my career implode. Quinn found a better way.

I met him six months ago. My mentor, Jack, put together a team to go after a hitman whose foray into serial-killer-hood put us at risk. He'd invited Quinn to keep us abreast of the federal investigation.

Quinn and I had exchanged almost weekly e-mails since. Then, two weeks ago, he said he had a job in Toronto, could use a second pair of hands and eyes, and, knowing I lived somewhere in Ontario, would I be interested.

I'd insisted on taking the shot. I'd been distance shooting since high school and narrowly missed being on the Olympic team. Quinn had started three years ago. When he balked, I'd reminded him that he was risking my safety on his marksmanship. That made him back down.

"Hey, there's the CN Tower," he said as we emerged from the subway. "Earlier it was hidden in the fog."

"Smog."

"I didn't think you got that up here."

"We get everything up here. Except HBO."

He peered up at the tower as we moved away from the commuter crowd. "Nice and clear now, though. Good night to eat in that revolving restaurant."

I made a face. "Overpriced tourist food."

He went quiet. I looked over to see him scratching his chin.

"Unless you want to, of course," I said quickly. "You *are* a tourist. It might be tough without reservations..." I caught his look. "You made reservations."

"Kind of. Yeah."

"Shit. I'm sorry. Really, I'd love to try it. I've just never had the cash to go."

"I should have asked you first. You're the local. I wanted to take you someplace nice, to say, you know..."

"Thanks for pulling my hit?"

A sharp laugh. "Yeah. I tried finding a Hallmark. They say they have a card for every occasion, but they seem to have missed that one. I thought we could have a quiet dinner, maybe talk about that thing I mentioned."

"Sure."

When I'd arrived, Quinn had announced he needed to

talk to me about something personal. It was almost certainly about where our relationship was heading. Now, even as he mentioned it, my heart thumped double time. With anticipation or dread? I honestly wasn't sure. Fear probably covered it either way.

Last year, Quinn had made it clear he was interested in me. Very clear and very interested. Stoked by the case, I'd reciprocated. He was fun and sexy and we had a lot in common. And, yes, I'll admit it, I'd been flattered. I'm a thirty-three-year-old wilderness lodge proprietor. The closest thing I get to a pass these days is married guys with beer breath cornering me in the boathouse and saying they think I'm "kinda cute."

After the job ended, we had to go our separate ways, so we'd stepped back into friendship.

Months passed and, as much as we communicated, there'd been no whiff of anything but friendship. Maybe I should have been disappointed. But I wasn't. I was almost . . . relieved.

I have an odd relationship with risk. I grew up looking each way twice before crossing the road. Then, after my life-crash, one day I found myself perched at the hatch of an airplane, parachute on my back. Today, I couldn't live without the adrenaline rush of white-water rafting or rappelling down a cliff. But I still look both ways—twice—before crossing. I have tidy boxes for the risk in my life, and Quinn doesn't fit into them.

I like him. I think we could have something. As weird as it sounds, he could be exactly what my life needs. But even now—walking with him, enjoying his company, sneaking peeks and liking what I see—I can't feel what I want to feel. I'm sure it will come. I just don't want to rush into a decision. So I'm praying that whatever he needs to talk about, it isn't that.

We were still in disguise at dinner. That's the downside of socializing with colleagues in this job. You can never just be yourself. Quinn had briefly seen me without a disguise last fall accidentally, but that was no excuse to leave it off now. With Quinn, I wasn't Nadia, I was "Dee." Yes, that was my nom de guerre. I'd have preferred one with a little more flair, but Jack had picked it. Jack didn't do flair.

We'd just stepped inside the base of the CN Tower when Quinn's cell phone buzzed. I wandered over to read one of the displays while he took the call. Likely business—the legitimate kind. He'd arranged the Beecham hit to coincide with a work trip. I wasn't sure that was wise, but trusted he knew what he was doing.

When he was done with his call, we went up the tower, where I was pleasantly surprised to find that the "revolving restaurant" didn't revolve very fast. I don't know what I expected: a merry-go-round? It moved so slowly you didn't notice until you looked up and realized the view had changed. And it was a good thing the motion didn't cause queasiness, because the prices certainly did. After I choked on the thought of paying fourteen dollars for a Caesar salad, Quinn confiscated my menu and read me the choices.

Through the appetizers and into the entrees we talked about our ski seasons, comparing stories and injuries.

"I have to admit," Quinn said. "When I first mentioned getting together, that's what I had in mind. A ski trip. I had a place in Vermont picked out. Even scanned a brochure to e-mail you. Then I chickened out."

"How come?"

He stabbed a pearl onion with his fork, his gaze fixed on his plate. "I guess I took another look at the brochure—couples in hot tubs, couples sipping hot chocolate, couples in front of blazing fires—and it just seemed so . . . couple-ish."

"Which isn't what you had in mind."

"I know I rushed things last time. The job was intense, and that spilled over."

"No kidding, huh?" I gave a small laugh. "Look, I totally understand—"

I broke off as his cell rang again. A murmured apology to me and he pulled it out. A matron at the next table shot me a glare, as if to say I shouldn't tolerate such behavior. Obviously she'd never dated a cop.

"Work," he said as he glanced at the display.

"I'll go to the washroom while you—"

He laid his hand on my arm as I rose. "Sit. Eat while it's warm. If I need to, I'll step outside, but it's probably the same as last time. He can't find a file."

I'd rather have had the excuse to leave for a minute, gather my thoughts, prepare for what was coming. Because I knew now that it wasn't good.

Since we'd met that morning, Quinn hadn't flirted with me, hadn't even given me one of his sexy grins. That was *not* the Quinn I remembered. I'd thought he was just trying to play it cool until after the job, having been chewed out by Jack last year for acting unprofessional. But now, with his admission about the ski lodge, I knew I was about to get the infamous "Maybe we should just be friends" speech.

I should have been happy. Hadn't I been thinking the same thing? But it still stung. To have a guy be interested, then back off once he got to know me better? I only wish I could say it was the first time that ever happened.

Quinn's brows furrowed as he listened to his call. "What?"

Pause.

"When?"

Pause.

"Goddamn it!"

A furtive look my way, then a slight rise in color as he caught the glower of the woman beside us. He mouthed an apology.

I tried not to eavesdrop, focusing my attention on his free hand, drumming the table. He had square hands, big and broad. Smooth, but with ghosts of calluses and tiny scars, as if he'd worked with them once, maybe teen summers in construction.

He'd stopped drumming now, fingers gone still, tips raised a quarter-inch above the table, as if halted midtap. His fingers curled under, clenching as his voice went brittle before his fingers unfolded and collapsed, palm flat, to the tablecloth.

It took a moment to realize he'd hung up and was watching me, waiting until he had my attention. When I looked over, the crease between his brows was still there, now joined by faint lines at the corners of his mouth.

"You have to go," I said.

He nodded. "It's a case. I'm booked on a flight in two hours."

"Should we get the bill?"

"No, no. We're finishing. I get through security a little faster than the average tourist."

We ate for another five minutes before I said, "So what did you want to talk to me about?"

He moved a mushroom aside. "It wasn't important."

Before I could prod, he launched into the story of getting snowbound driving to a ski hill, and I realized I wasn't getting a better answer. Not tonight.

Two

My lodge is in the Kawarthas, north of Peterborough. A little over two hours from Toronto. I got back just past midnight. I could have stayed in Toronto—I'd paid cash for a room already—but with Quinn gone, there wasn't any reason to linger.

By the time I pulled in, the only light was a guest room reading lamp, barely visible through the blinds. We hadn't had any bookings, so it must be a drop-in. I stared up at that window a moment, thinking about the unknown guest, wondering what guide services they'd expect in the morning. It didn't matter—that was my job and I was always ready to accommodate a guest—but thinking about it let me mentally switch from Dee, contract killer, to Nadia Stafford, wilderness lodge proprietor.

It would take more than that tonight. Normally I had a long drive, maybe even a night's rest before I came home after a job, and that gave me time to shift personas. Tonight I was still thinking about Quinn and about Grant Beecham, and neither of them belonged here. I watched the window for another minute, then went down to the dock and did a few laps of the lake in my kayak. By the time I was done, I was me again.

I headed up to the lodge. On the outside, its weathered, rough-hewn wood suggested a true wilderness experience, with blazing fires for heat, lanterns for light, and an outhouse around the corner. It's an illusion, of course. We have a furnace, electricity, running water, even Jacuzzi tubs in two bedrooms. At a place like Red Oak, it's the illusion that matters—the feeling that you're getting back to nature. Roughing it without actually roughing it.

Most of our clientele need lessons in everything from holding a canoe paddle to using binoculars, meaning the trails winding through the property are so well marked you could find your way in the dark. Yet we still provide maps and, if you'd like, I'll take you out, just to be safe. I'll also take you biking, canoeing, kayaking, white-water rafting, spelunking, rappelling, and shooting, though you'll have to sign a three-page waiver for that last one.

If you want bonfires and beer or a picnic lunch in the wildflowers or coffee and fresh muffins while watching the sun rise, then Red Oak Lodge is the place for you. If you're looking for gourmet meals, big-screen TVs and Jet Skis, I can recommend a lovely place thirty minutes northwest . . . at double the cost.

Because no one expected me back, no one had signed up for the 6 a.m. jog. So I could have skipped it. But no sign-ups meant I could go alone.

The morning air was still so cold it was like sucking ice cubes, the endless silence broken only by the rhythmic thump of my feet. When I'm running with guests, I usually do only five kilometers. Today, I went twice that, through White Rock and back.

At this hour, the town was even quieter than the forest. As I jogged down the main street, the only sound was the lone stop sign creaking in the wind.

White Rock is a nowhere town. Every kid who lives there can't wait to get out. For tourists, it's a stopover, not a destination. The town survives as a service center for hunters and snowmobilers and cottagers, a place where you can buy everything you need for survival and nothing that isn't essential to it.

As down home and comfortable as an old pair of sneakers—my kind of town.

Back at the lodge, I detoured to the lake for a dip. Crazy on a May morning, but it certainly knocked any remaining dream cobwebs from my mind. By the time I headed up to the lodge, it was nearly nine. Waiting on the back deck was Emma Walden, the lodge's live-in housekeeper/cook. Her husband, Owen, takes care of the grounds and buildings. They're both past retirement age and were when they came to work for me. As Emma says, this *is* their retirement.

"Anyone up yet?" I called.

"I made cinnamon buns."

The smell of Emma's rolls woke guests faster than a dunk in the frigid lake.

"You look like a drowned rat. I hope you're planning on drying off before our guests see you."

I leaned over and squeezed a rivulet from my hair onto her clogs. She snapped her dishtowel at me. I snatched it and quick-dried my shoulder-length curls.

"You know where that towel's been?" she asked.

"No worse than where my hair's been. Has Sammi started work yet?"

"She's here all right. But working?" Emma snorted.

I tried not to sigh too loudly. Sammi Ernst was Emma's part-time assistant, hired two months ago.

"About Sammi, Nadia, we had a problem with the York

couple. They didn't mention it until they were checking out, after you left."

Emma explained that they'd complained about Sammi's baby, Destiny. They'd left their kids with their parents, and hadn't appreciated hearing a crying baby on their romantic getaway. I could point out that Destiny rarely cried—Sammi didn't put her down long enough for her to fuss—but I could see the couple's point.

"I know you feel sorry for the girl, Nadia. No job, no man, no one to help with the baby. But that baby is all she cares about. Stella Anderson offered to look after Destiny for free, just because she likes having little ones around, but Sammi won't do it."

"Maybe if I rework Sammi's schedule..."

"Maybe if you fired her pretty little butt—" Emma bit off the remark. "I'm sorry, but it burns me up, seeing you being so nice to her, and how does she repay you? Complains like you're her mother giving her chores."

"She's seventeen. At that age, my work ethic sucked, too. To get decent help from town, I'd need to pay more than ten bucks an hour, so I'm stuck with Sammi."

"We don't need the help. I just hate seeing you pay for nothing. She doesn't appreciate it. Save your charity for someone who does."

"I'll talk to her." I checked my hair. Dry enough for a few more minutes outside. I handed Emma back her towel. "I'm going to check the hot-tub chemicals before I come in."

She pulled a piece of paper from her pocket. "Your messages. Mostly regulars, looking to book for summer, and wanting to talk to you directly."

None of the names on the list was my brother's. Not

that I really expected Brad to call. Last time I heard from him was December 2002, when he'd wondered whether his little sister had two grand he could borrow. I didn't, but I'd scraped it together anyway. Wired him the cash. Never got so much as a thank-you.

Because Brad never called, Jack used his name when he needed to get in touch with me. It had been four months now since I'd heard from him.

After our joint job with Quinn, I'd realized that Jack himself had been financing it. So I'd refused payment. He insisted I take it and buy the gazebo and hot tub I dreamed of for the lodge. I'd said he could use my share to take me to Egypt, something we'd joked about. To my surprise, he'd agreed. He still wanted me to take some money, but the rest would go toward our trip.

As fall had dragged on, I'd heard from him only once, in November. He said exactly five words. "Everything okay?" and "All right then" when I said it was. No mention of Egypt. No mention of when he'd call again.

In early December, he'd shown up, bringing me the money. Twenty thousand. I took half, for the gazebos, but refused the rest. When I mentioned Egypt, still jokingly, sensing he'd changed his mind, he'd said his schedule was tight and that it might be a while. I said that was fine, I'd wait.

Then, at Christmas, a ten-person hot tub arrived at my door and I knew we weren't going to Egypt.

When he called a couple of weeks later, he'd muttered something about getting a good deal on the tub and we'd "work it out." That was the last I heard from him.

* * *

I found Sammi in the kitchen, rocking in a chair she'd dragged in from the front room. The best chair from the front room, I might add. She was cuddling Destiny and crooning to her. Mother and child. A scene to warm the heart . . . if the mother in question wasn't currently being paid to clean the guest rooms.

I'd let Sammi bring Destiny to her job, even picked up a secondhand playpen. But the baby was never in it. Sammi worked holding Destiny on her hip, which made for very sloppily made beds and crudely chopped vegetables.

With her long blond hair, trim figure, and big violet eyes, Sammi Ernst was the prettiest girl in White Rock. When I walked in, her face was glowing with an inner beauty that would have made Revlon sign her up on the spot. Then she saw me and the light went out.

"I heard we had a complaint," I said.

"Emma couldn't wait to tattle, could she? Mr. and Mrs. Toronto Yuppies abandoned their kids, then bitched 'cause I'm taking care of mine."

"I hear Mrs. Anderson offered to look after Destiny for you."

"That old bag? She's so fucking senile she'd probably put Destiny out with the recycling and feed her milk to the cat."

Inhale. Exhale.

I reached down to pat Destiny on the head. Sammi swatted my hand away.

"That's her soft spot, you know."

"No, I don't know. I don't have kids, as you're quick to remind me. I don't understand babies. But I do understand this business. Whether or not that couple should have complained doesn't matter because the customer—"

"—is always right," she muttered, rolling her eyes. "You take too much of their shit, Nadia. You wouldn't see me letting people walk over me like that."

"No? Maybe you're right. The next time I've just sat down to a meal and a guest demands after-dinner drinks served by the lake, I'll hand them a beer and point them to the path. Then they'll write an online review complaining about the lousy service. After a few of those, our bookings will drop, and I won't be able to keep a house-keeping assistant on the payroll."

She said nothing, but that told me I'd made my point.

"Do you want this job, Sammi?"

"Fuck, yeah. You think I'd take everyone's shit if I didn't need the money?"

"You don't need to take anyone's shit. You could apply for welf—social assistance—until Destiny is old enough to go to school."

She glowered up at me. "No fucking way. I am not winding up like *her*." From the venom in her voice, I knew she meant her mother. "I'm going to show Destiny how a real mother acts. I'm going to work for a living and look after us."

"All right then, tell me if this would work out . . ."

I outlined some changes to her schedule, bringing her in later and having her leave before dinner. Most of her hours would be midday, when guests were out.

"That means fewer hours a day, but you'll be working five days instead of four. And if we have a full house, I may need you for serving at dinner hour and cleanup after. You'll need someone to pick up Destiny during that time."

A long pause. Then, "I guess Tess or Kira could..."

"I also want to see Destiny in her playpen now and then. And when I was in Toronto, I saw someone wearing this sling for carrying babies. It would keep your hands free—"

"I can't afford any more stuff."

"I'll buy it. If you want to take it home, you can pay me back. How's that?"

She complained more about accepting "charity" than my other conditions, but eventually we came to an agreement. I prayed it would work out.

In the brochure for the Red Oak Lodge, there are four seasons. "Summer Sizzle" runs mid-June through August. "Fall Foliage" goes until mid-November. Then "Winter Wonderland" runs through March. The lowest priced one is "Spring Savings," so named because "Dismal, Muddy, and Black-Fly Infested" really doesn't have the same marketing oomph.

Being early May, we were in the "Muddy" section of that season, with the damp chill fading and the black-flies moving in, but slowly. For people wanting a deal or looking for a break after a long winter, May is a decent enough month. On weekdays we were lucky to have any guests, but weekends we usually ran close to capacity. The lodge has a dozen rooms—including mine—so at full occupancy we can host twenty-two. By Friday evening, we had seventeen, enough to keep one elderly couple, one hostess/guide, and one teen girl busy.

For once, Sammi pulled her weight. She didn't turn into a cleaning dynamo, but she did her "chores" with less complaining and even put Destiny in the playpen for her naps, snapping at me that I'd better not wake her with my "thumping around" or it'd be my own fault if Sammi had to rock her when she should be working.

Even on a staff of three, Sammi was never going to make Employee of the Month. But living out here meant Sammi didn't have a lot of life choices. Having Destiny at sixteen meant no high school diploma. With her family reputation, no one would hire her. Even if they did, there wasn't any day care in town. She couldn't even move out of her mother's home; there were no rental units around. If I could help her make enough money and get enough job experience to leave White Rock, it was the best thing anyone could do for her.

Three

Quinn e-mailed me Sunday. Just a quick note to apologize again for taking off early and to thank me again for helping him...and to ask whether I'd have time for an IM chat that evening.

I said yes to the chat...and spent the rest of the day mentally preparing for the "Let's just be friends" speech. But it never came. We chatted as we always did. There was a case in the U.S. that week of a man charged after beating to death a guy he'd found raping his girlfriend. Quinn wanted to know if I'd heard about it and what I thought. We talked about that for a while, debating the circumstances and the ethics. Then he asked a few spelunking questions and we got into that, swapping stories until I had to sign off.

So nothing had changed. Maybe "the speech" was still coming. Or maybe he'd decided, since I hadn't seemed disappointed that nothing romantic happened in Toronto, that I was okay sticking with friendship and there was no need to discuss it.

Was I okay with friendship? I *did* feel a pang of disappointment. Was that because I'd wanted to be seduced? To feel what I had last fall, Quinn's enthusiasm sweeping aside my reservations? To enjoy the passionate, reckless affair I'd imagined?

Or was that pang just bruised ego? Maybe more than that—a slap to a still-tender part bruised when I'd been rejected by friends, family, and lover after I shot Wayne Franco.

But I'd been thinking the same thing about Quinn—that we'd be better off as friends—and it didn't mean there was anything wrong with *him*. There just wasn't enough of a spark to take the risk. Normally when a potential lover says "let's just be friends," it really means "I don't actually like you that much," and the promised friendship never materializes. Quinn still sought my company, still wanted to chat . . . and chat and chat.

Maybe it would deepen into more someday, when both of us were ready. For now, I could use a friend more than I could use a lover.

Tuesday morning, I was returning from a walk with our only guests—an elderly couple—and saw Emma on the porch, ostensibly filling the bird feeders. That was Owen's job, meaning she was waiting to talk to me.

"Did you let Sammi go?" she asked after our guests had gone inside.

"What? No. What'd she say?"

"Nothing. She hasn't shown up, and whatever her faults, she's punctual."

My first thought was that she'd messed up her new schedule and thought she had Mondays *and* Tuesdays off. But before she left Sunday afternoon, she'd double-checked with me on what time to be in today. "Have you called her place yet?"

"Yes, and I got a mouthful of Janie's cussing for my trouble. She hung up before I could even say why I was calling."

"Maybe the baby's sick. You know what Sammi's like. If Destiny's temperature hits a hundred, she's off to the hospital. It would be nice if she called to say she couldn't make it, but I'm sure she'll be here tomorrow."

My elderly guests had forgone the campfire Monday night—in early May, I don't blame them—but they'd helped themselves to the beer and drunk more than I would expect for a lovely pair of schoolteachers in their seventies. Fresh air does that to people. I didn't notice that the beer case was empty until late afternoon. We had only two rooms booked that night, and I wasn't sure either would want the bonfire, but if they did, they wouldn't appreciate a dry one.

The White Rock liquor store closed at six on Tuesdays in the off-season. I got there at five minutes past, just as the manager, Rick Hargrave, was backing out of the parking lot.

When he saw my pickup tear around the corner, mud flying behind me, he pulled back into his spot, opened the store, and gave me a case of beer to be paid for next time I was in town. You don't get that kind of service in a big city.

Before I left, Hargrave mentioned that his daughter, Tess, wanted to hold her eighteenth birthday party out at the lodge next month. Tess was Sammi's best friend, which reminded me that I hadn't heard from my errant employee.

The Ernst place was just around the corner. Technically, I should say the "Ernst *house*," but that elevated the structure to a status it didn't deserve. For my first six months in White Rock, I thought the Ernst place was deserted. No one could possibly live in a hovel so dilapidated that a rumble of thunder would surely reduce it to toothpicks and dust.

Driving by one day, I'd seen a preteen girl walk out and had assumed the local kids were using the place as a hideout. I'd mentioned this to the grocer, expressing my concern that the roof could fall in and hurt them. When he told me that the girl, Sammi, lived there, I'd walked out without remembering what I'd come for.

I parked on the road, walked up the weed lawn, and rapped at the door. When it opened, the stench of garbage and unwashed dishes nearly made me gag. Janie parked herself in the gap. If she had once possessed an iota of her daughter's beauty, it had long since vanished. Her leathery skin was enough to make me want to slather on SPF 60 every time I so much as sat in a sunny window. Add a lifetime of booze and cigarettes, and Janie Ernst didn't look like she was about to keel over; she looked like she'd risen from the grave.

"What the fuck do you want, cop?"

The words flew out in a hail of booze-drenched spittle. To someone like Janie, the biggest problem with me wasn't the circumstances surrounding my departure from law enforcement, but the fact that I'd been a cop at all.

"Sammi didn't come to work—"

"And now you're her parole officer?"

"I was concerned because she didn't call. May I speak to her, please?"

"May I speak to her, please?" Janie mimicked.

"Whoa, that's good. Taking insult lessons from third graders, Janie?"

"Bitch."

"What you say is what you are. Oh, wait, what's that other one? 'I'm rubber and you're glue. Whatever you say bounces off me and sticks to you.'"

The door hit my hand. I grabbed the edge, holding it fast as I leaned inside.

"Why don't I just come in and talk to Sammi?"

"You got a warrant, cop?"

She threw her weight against the door, catching me off guard. It hit my nose and I jumped back, eyes watering. The door slammed shut.

I stepped off the crumbling cement slab and tried peering through the front window, but grime as thick as a blackout blind blocked my view. A blare of noise from within made me jump. I stepped closer to the door. Gunfire rang out. The television.

I returned to my pickup. Even with the doors closed, I could still hear Janie's TV. I glanced at the house one last time, but there was no sign of Sammi, so I started the engine and pulled away.

When Sammi came back to work, I'd make sure we worked something out. Sure, she was smart-mouthed and resentful, but what did I expect? The kid had been raised by dust bunnies.

The next morning, I came in from helping Owen in the boathouse and found Emma stripping the beds, alone.

"Sammi's not here again?" I said.

She shook her head.

"Did she call?"

Another head shake.

Now this was really bugging me. Sammi had said she didn't want to lose her job, then after we'd come to an agreement on better hours, she stopped showing up—giving me just the excuse I needed to fire her. Something was wrong. Time for another run at Janie.

Four

Twenty minutes later, I was banging on Janie's front door. I didn't expect her to answer—she wasn't known for getting up before noon. But I was reasonably certain babies didn't sleep that late, so Sammi should have been awake.

"Sammi? If you're in there, open up! We need to talk."

I jumped down to the dirt patch in front of the window, a garden that likely hadn't been a garden in fifty years. I rapped on the dirt-encrusted glass.

"Sammi! It's Nadia. Look, I'm not here to chew you out. I just need to know if you're coming back to work."

Silence. I put my ear to the window, but couldn't hear so much as a baby gurgling. I rapped harder.

Nothing. I stalked back to the pickup. As I was getting in, I heard a soft voice behind me.

"She's not there. She's gone."

I turned to see Tess Hargrave. Her face was wan and splotchy, eyes rimmed with red.

"Where is she?" I asked.

Tess cast a nervous glance at the Ernst place. After a series of bounced checks years ago, her dad had stopped serving Janie, so Tess was no more welcome at the hovel than I was, even if she was Sammi's friend.

"Climb in," I said. "Let's grab a coffee."

"I can't. Stock arrived this morning and Dad needs my help. Can I catch up with you later?"

"Lunch?"

She nodded. Again, her gaze flickered toward the Ernst place. "I told Don about it, but he doesn't seem to care."

Staff Sergeant Don Riley was commander of the local Ontario Provincial Police detachment.

"What'd you tell him?" I asked.

"That Sammi and Destiny are gone."

"Gone? When?"

"Sunday night. My dad says—" Her eyes brimmed with tears. "I gotta go. Meet me at Larry's? At noon?"

"Sure, but—"

She sprinted away, long hair flapping behind her. I thought of following, but the animosity between Janie and Rick Hargrave extended to Hargrave's opinion of Sammi, and I knew Tess wouldn't feel comfortable discussing her friend in front of him.

I glanced down the street at the OPP office. Most cops don't have a problem with me. In fact, the "public safety" occupations—cops, military, firefighters, paramedics—form a large part of my lodge clientele. They might not agree with what I did, but they understand how it could happen. Don Riley and his sergeant, Rudy Graves, were among the exceptions. The first time we met, Riley told me I was a murdering bitch, no better than the man I'd killed. Our relationship had deteriorated from there. Yet, given the choice between spinning my wheels at the lodge and going a few rounds with Riley, I chose the latter.

When I walked into the tiny station that housed the White Rock OPP detachment, I bypassed the desk clerk, Maura, who wisely pretended she didn't see me. There were three officers in the main room: Riley, Graves, and a new guy. Riley was in his usual place, leaning against the pillar in the center of the room. One of these days, after years of straining to hold him up, it's going to give way. With any luck, it'll take him and Graves with it.

"Get out of my station, Stafford," Riley said as I entered. "You aren't welcome here."

"It's a public building," I said. "Paid for by my tax money."

The new guy scrambled for the door, saying something about fresh coffee. I stepped aside to let him pass, and murmured a greeting. He gave me a half-smile as he brushed past.

"What do you want, Stafford?" Riley said.

His hand moved to the butt of his gun, stance widening. I hummed the theme to *The Good, the Bad, and the Ugly*. He turned on his heel and stomped into his office, slamming the door behind him.

Graves took his boss's place, planting himself in my path.

"What do you want, Stafford?" he said, parroting his boss.

"I hear Sammi and her baby are missing."

"No, they're not!" Riley thundered from the back.

"You know, Don, you can eavesdrop better if you put a glass to the door. Come on, guys. Let's cut the crap. I'm not here to cause trouble—"

"You wouldn't dare," Riley said, striding out. "Not in my town."

I bit my tongue to keep from humming the Western theme again. "I'm worried about Sammi. Tess says she's disappeared."

"Really? Wow. Kid's had a record since she was thirteen, gets herself knocked up at sixteen, and now she's disappeared? There's a shocker, eh, Rudy?"

Riley lumbered to Graves's desk and thudded his bulk into the chair. He picked up a car magazine and thumbed through it.

"So you think she ran away?" I said. "How did she get out of town? Taxi? No, wait, we don't have one. Bus? Train? Limo service? Hmmm, don't have those, either."

"She probably hot-wired a car," Graves said. "That's what she did the last time. Stole a cottager's SUV and rolled it."

"She went joyriding in a car with the keys left in the ignition. That was four years ago, and she hasn't been in trouble since. Has someone reported a car stolen?"

"That's privileged information."

"In other words, no. Or else you'd be saying Sammi *did* steal a car." I perched on an empty desk. "Look, I'm concerned, okay? Don't turn this into a pissing match. My employee has disappeared and I want to know if there's any reason to worry. Have you spoken to Janie?"

"Why?" Graves said, crossing the room to stand in front of me. "Sammi Ernst is gone, big deal. The Ernsts don't breed nothing but trash. Never have. If you were from around here, you'd know that. You feel sorry for that little baby? Look at Janie Ernst. I remember when she was a little baby herself, everyone saying how cute she was, how she'd be the one to break the cycle. But she wasn't, was she? Just passed it on to her brat, who passed it on to hers."

"Is that how you guys work around here? Decide who deserves help and who doesn't?"

"You think we got nothing better to do than chase runaway kids?" Riley said. "We've got two cottage B&Es, a cougar on the loose—"

"Cougar?"

"Cougar, mountain lion, whatever. The point is—"

"We don't have cougars around here."

"No fucking kidding. Why do you think it's a problem? It must have escaped from that zoo over on 55 and now we've got campers calling in, freaking out about hearing a cougar in the woods. You think we need that kind of trouble?"

"Is the zoo missing a cougar?"

"How the hell should I know?" Graves said.

I bit my tongue—hard—and stood. "If there's a big cat out there, I'd like to know about it. I take guests into those woods and I've got enough trouble worrying about—"

"Had enough trouble with Sammi, too, didn't you, Stafford? I think we've solved the case, Don. Sammi pissed Stafford off and she gave the kid permanent walking papers." He pointed his forefinger between my eyes, cocking his hand into a gun. "Pow. The Stafford Special."

I stared at his finger. Thought about breaking it.

I let myself savor the fantasy for ten seconds. Then I turned and walked out.

I walked back to Janie's place and spent another ten minutes banging on the doors and windows. She didn't answer. Big surprise there. Next I popped into the liquor store, paid Hargrave for yesterday's beer, and told Tess I was heading to the diner. I had a half hour before she'd be off for lunch, but I went early and ordered coffee.

Of the half dozen people in Larry's Diner that morning, two worked there and four spent so much time there that Larry should have charged them rent. I sat at the counter with everyone else.

After the initial greetings, I lapsed into listening mode, hoping to hear something about Sammi so I could join the conversation rather than instigate it. After fifteen minutes of listening to the Myers brothers bitch about native land rights, I realized no easy segue was coming.

"Anyone hear what happened to Sammi?" I asked when Jason Myers paused for a caffeine refill. "She hasn't been to work in two days."

"Took off," Jason said.

Everyone nodded.

His brother, Eric, leaned forward, jabbing his finger at the countertop in front of Larry, the diner owner. "Now, these Indians, we paid them for their land. If I sell my house to someone, my grandkids can't come back fifty years later and say they got a bum deal and want it back."

I could have pointed out the fallacy of this argument but, during my years in White Rock, I'd learned there were certain issues you didn't debate with the locals.

"About Sammi," I said. "Did she really run away?"

The Myers brothers shrugged in unison.

"Hey, Nadia," Brett Helms called down the counter. "You see any sign of that cougar up your way?"

I shook my head. "Heard about it, though. It's for real, then?"

"Guess so. Some kids camping over by the Potter place heard it. Came racing in here just before closing, huh, Larry?"

Larry nodded and poured fresh grinds into the coffee-maker.

"Scared shitless," Brett said, laughing. "City kids. Said

they'd heard cougars on some wildlife show and they were sure that's what it was."

"Man, that'd be a trophy," Eric said. "Think Don'll let us hunt it?"

I tuned them out and sipped my coffee. Seventeen-year-old girl goes missing and no one even wonders why. But an escaped cougar? Now that's news.

Five

Tess arrived ten minutes early. She only had a half hour before she needed to begin the drive to school. Tess was in her last year and had crammed in enough credits that she only needed to attend afternoon classes. Mornings were spent working with her dad to save for college.

We took a booth at the back and ordered burgers. When lunch arrived, Tess nibbled the crispy end off one fry, then stared down at the overflowing plate.

"Sorry," she said. "I'm not very hungry."

"That's okay. So the last time you saw Sammi was ...?"

"Sunday. I was driving home from my grandma's, saw her walking to town from your place and gave her a lift. Kira and I usually stop by Sammi's around ten, after Destiny's asleep. That night, Sammi didn't come out, so Kira snuck in the back door. Janie was passed out on the couch, and Sammi and Destiny weren't home. Yesterday morning, I went back, 'cause I was worried, but Janie ran me off, said Sammi was gone and good riddance."

"Did Sammi say anything unusual when you gave her a ride?"

Tess shook her head and blew her nose on the napkin.

"New boyfriend?" I asked.

Another head shake.

"What about Trent? Did they get back in contact? Maybe she followed him out to Vancouver."

Tess made a noise of disgust. "That asshole couldn't get away from here fast enough, get on with his new college life where no one knew he'd had a kid. Sammi would *never* lower herself to going after him. And even if he asked her to, she'd tell him where to stuff it."

"Did she make a new friend? Acquaintance?"

"No."

"Did she say she wanted to leave?"

"No more than usual. She mentions it, but it's the same old 'God, I hate this town' shit that we all say."

"Had she said it more often recently?"

She shook her head. "Since she's been working for you, she hasn't said it as much. She has a plan now. Her mom makes her pay rent, but almost all the rest goes in the bank and she figures by the time Destiny's ready for school, she'll have enough to move to Oshawa or Kingston."

She circled a fry through her ketchup, then set it down and looked at me. "She's grateful, for the job and all. I'm sure she's never said so, but she is. It's just really hard on her. She wants to work, but she doesn't want to leave Destiny with a sitter. Sammi . . . she pretty much raised herself and I tell her it's not the same thing if she finds a good sitter, but to her it still feels like abandoning Destiny."

"Maybe she saw your point and decided the problem was that she couldn't find good child care *here*. In the city, that wouldn't be as much of a problem."

"I just . . . I don't think she left."

"Did she give you anything recently? An unexpected gift? Something she owned? Maybe seem more sentimental than usual?"

Tess paused to think, then shook her head.

"Did she start taking an interest in other places? Buying the city papers, looking for an apartment or a job?"

"No, she hates reading. She—" Tess lowered her voice. "She's not very good at it."

"Okay, so—"

"Wait. There was something. Not a job, really, but something she didn't want anyone else to know."

I leaned onto my elbows. "What?"

Tess glanced around, but no one was within ten feet of our booth. "There was this guy, a tourist, a few weeks ago when we had that warm spell. He saw Sammi and Destiny at the park. He worked for some modeling agency in Toronto. He told Sammi—"

"—she could be a model," I finished.

"No, not Sammi. Destiny. His agency works with babies. He took a bunch of pictures of her, then wrote down Sammi's number and said he'd call in a few days. Only he never did. She was real broken up about it. She'd hoped it might be a way to make extra money and get out of here even sooner."

"Maybe she went to Toronto looking for him."

"If she did, she would have taken her mom's truck. But that's not like Sammi, anyway. She doesn't go begging." She twisted her napkin. "I think someone took her."

"Took her?"

"You know. A serial killer. A rapist. I told her she shouldn't go walking the back roads at night, but she always laughed, you know. Said no one would grab a girl with a baby."

My gut went cold. "When did Sammi do this?"

"Every night, around dusk. Said it was good for Destiny. The fresh air helped her sleep."

"But we don't know that Sammi went out Sunday night."

Tess shot up straight, eyes gleaming fierce. "Yes, we do. That's what I told Don. Kira's mom saw Sammi walk past their place around eight. She went for her walk and she never came back. That's what I've been trying to tell everyone."

After lunch, I dropped Tess off at her car and told her I'd keep in touch. Then I drove the route she'd said Sammi usually took on her evening walk, and found nothing.

Next stop: talk to the person who'd last seen Sammi.

Meredith Desmond was Kira's mother. They lived in a tidy bungalow outside town. Meredith and I got on fine. I'd decorated the lodge with her watercolors and made a point of sending guests to her home-based studio.

According to Meredith, Sammi had walked past around eight, roughly the same time she had every night this month. Meredith and her husband had been on the front swing, reading and enjoying the sunset. When Sammi walked past, Meredith called out a greeting, as usual. Sammi waved back, as usual. Then she kept going.

Unlike the other adults I'd spoken to so far, Meredith was concerned. Sammi was a good kid, she said. Pissed off at the world, but who'd blame her?

As for Tess's theory, that Sammi had been picked up by a sexual predator, Meredith conceded anything was possible. But we hadn't had such a killer around here since . . . well, since never. In this region, stranger rape wasn't unheard of. *Murder* by a stranger, though, was so rare that neither of us could recall the last one.

Most likely, Meredith thought, Sammi had used her nightly routine as a launch pad for a planned disappearance. She'd taken Destiny on her usual walk, planning either to meet a ride or to swipe a summer car left at one of the big cottages over by the nearby Potter place. Maybe she'd hoped to stir up a little trouble with her sudden disappearance, make people sit up and take notice. Maybe even, for the first time in her life, she'd make her mother worry about her. If that was the case, I hoped she never learned the truth—that except for her friends, nobody seemed to care.

Still, something about that scenario rankled. If Sammi had trusted Tess with the secret about the photographer, wouldn't she have at least hinted that she was leaving?

I didn't like the "modeling photographer" idea, either. As a cop, I'd seen that routine too often. Pervert approaches teenage girl and asks her to "model" for him. So why target Destiny instead? Because anyone who'd spent five minutes with Sammi knew her world revolved around her baby. She was streetwise enough to see through any guy who offered to make *her* a star. But Destiny? That would be hard to resist. Maybe the guy had called and asked Sammi to meet him that night.

I wanted to walk Sammi's route, but only made it as far as parking on the roadside, where I sat staring out the windshield.

Before Tess left, she'd cursed herself for not being more forceful with Sammi and insisting she stop her nighttime rambles. I'd reassured her that there'd been nothing she could do except give her advice. It had been up to Sammi to take it. But now, sitting here, Tess's words came back. "I should have done something. It was my job, you know? That's the way we were, Sammi and me. She was the fun one, always getting into trouble. I followed along, and made sure that didn't get out of hand. I kept her safe."

I kept her safe.

It was my job.

How many times had I thought that about my cousin Amy? A year older than me, Amy had been my best friend from the time I was born, to hear our parents tell it. She was the one who knew how to have fun, and I was the one who kept it from getting out of hand.

I'd been thirteen the summer she'd decided we were old enough to take the train to the CNE, back in the days when it made a special stop at the big Toronto fair. My father thought we were too young. My uncle had laughed and slapped him between the shoulders.

"Nadia will keep them out of trouble. She always does."

Dad had resisted, but I'd begged, and everyone told him he was being silly, my mother finally snapping in annoyance.

"Stop coddling the girl, Bill. How do you expect her to grow up when you're always hovering over her? Are you going to drive her on dates, too?"

"Nah, he'll order one of the new recruits to do it. In full uniform, with a squad car." Uncle Eddie slapped my dad again. "Come on, Bill, let the girls have their fun."

So we went. And we had fun. Innocent fun. Amy flirted with the carnies too much, but I managed to drag her attention elsewhere before they could ask for her phone number. I was interested in boys, too, but with me, the operative word was *boy*. Amy's tastes ran dangerously close to *men*, though none of her boyfriends yet had been more than a high school senior.

Afterward, when we got to the train station, Amy's father wasn't there yet. My dad had wanted to pick us up, but he'd been called last night to switch shifts.

Still riding high from the day of freedom, Amy wanted to start walking. It was dark, but the road was lit, so I said okay. We'd gone about a kilometer when Drew Aldrich pulled over in his pickup, and asked if we needed a ride.

Aldrich lived down the road from Amy. He was twenty-four, with dark hair, a leather jacket, and bushy brows over eyes that always seemed to be laughing at you. Amy swore he was the spitting image of Matt Dillon in *The Outsiders,* and swooned every time he stopped to talk to her . . . which he did often enough to make me nervous. I'd wanted to tell my dad. She'd blown up when I suggested it—one of the few real fights we'd ever had. After a week of not talking, I'd promised to mind my own business when it came to Drew Aldrich.

But he made me nervous. So when he offered us a ride that night, my answer was no. Amy cajoled. Amy pleaded. I stood my ground, anxiously scanning the road, praying to see Uncle Eddie's big white car. It was only when Amy threatened to go alone that I got into the truck.

I had to keep her safe.

It was my job.

I spent the next few hours walking Sammi's route. Like most roads up here, this one was heavily wooded on both sides, with endless twists and hills and valleys. Stand at any point and you couldn't see more than a hundred feet in either direction.

Every few steps, I'd look around and ask myself "If I found a mark here, could I make a safe hit?" In every case, the answer was yes. The few times that I heard a car coming, it took at least three minutes for it to come into view, more than enough time to pull a body—and a stroller—into the ditch and hide.

Yet if someone had attacked Sammi, I was sure it would have been a sexual predator. That meant he wouldn't have a corpse to dispose of. He'd have a live teenager and baby to deal with. Sammi would put up a fight and it would take more than three minutes to get her into the woods.

There were no signs of struggle in the gravel, no broken bushes to suggest that anyone had been dragged into the forest.

The more I thought about it, the more I suspected that Meredith, and everyone else, was right. Sammi had run off. There was only one thing I needed to do to set my mind at rest. Break into Janie's place and search for proof that Sammi had packed and left.

Six

I returned to the lodge ten minutes late for a scheduled shooting lesson. That wouldn't do. While the disappearance of a teen and a baby might seem more important than explaining basic gun safety to four guys who just wanted to shoot something, I made my living by my reputation, and my reputation was that of a conscientious hostess who put her guests first.

After the lesson and some target practice, I sent the men in to dinner while I stayed behind, ostensibly to lock up. In my experience, putting guns in the hands of newbies has a strange effect on hormones. I'd warded off more wandering hands postshooting than after the most beer-drenched bonfires.

I took the shortcut back to the lodge, avoiding the men, and slipped in the kitchen door. The wail of an electric carving knife greeted me. Emma looked up from her chicken and motioned to the message pad by the phone. On the top sheet was a note that my aunt Evie had called.

Aunt Evie?

It had to be Evelyn. She'd never contacted me here before because Jack forbade it. The only excuse she'd have was if Jack wasn't around to pass along a message.

I told Emma to start serving dinner without me, then I hurried upstairs.

"It's about Jack," Evelyn said, skipping any pleasantries.

As I lowered myself to the edge of the bed, she bitched

about his rule against calling me. I could picture her, in her designer shirt and slacks, white hair cut in a sleek bob, cussing like a sailor as she chewed out her favorite student. Evelyn was probably closing in on seventy, if not past it, and was supposed to be retired, but she still lived and breathed the business, pulling strings, manipulating players, delighting in watching them dance.

"Is he okay?" I asked finally, cutting her rant short.

"He's an idiot, that's what he is. Acts like he's still twenty, like he can still do the things he did at twenty, then gets himself hurt—"

"Hurt?" My fingers clenched the plastic tighter. I should have called. Goddamn it, I should have called when that first month passed without any word—

"He broke his ankle."

"Ankle?" I said. "Is that … it?"

"Other than cuts and bruises, and wounded pride, which, let me tell you, is stinging worst of all. Serves him right. The fucking stubborn Mick. I told him—"

"When did it happen?"

"A couple of weeks ago."

Only a couple of weeks? So much for "that explains everything."

"I'm sorry to hear it," I said. "I hope he's on the mend and I appreciate you telling me—"

"I'm not calling so you can send him a get-well card, Nadia."

I tensed at the use of my real name. With Evelyn, it was always a dig—reminding me how much she knew. But I suppose I wouldn't want her calling me "Dee" on my personal line, either.

"He's holed up in Buffalo," Evelyn continued.

"Holed up?"

"There was a problem. Nothing critical, but with his ankle, he's not in any condition to jaunt off to Europe until things cool down. He needs a place to stay, and someone to watch his back—such as a friend who lives in a backwoods cabin in the middle of nowhere."

"He wants to come here?"

Silence, so long I thought we'd lost the connection.

"You know Jack, Nadia. He never wants anything. Never admits to it, anyway. Goddamned—"

"So this is your idea."

"Only because he's too stubborn to ask. God forbid he should ask for help. Gotta be fair and square, all debts paid up. Thirty years I've known him, and you saw the shit he pulled last fall, when he wanted my help. Dangled the fucking case in front of my nose until I jumped, then hemmed and hawed about letting me join, when the whole goddamned reason he came to my house—"

"He doesn't even know you're asking me, does he?"

More silence as she tried to figure out another way to bluster and divert. After a moment, she sighed. "This is how you have to deal with Jack, Nadia. You go to him, make the offer, listen to him mutter about how he doesn't need help, doesn't want to *inconvenience* you, but the minute you turn to walk away, he'll be on your tail, following you home. Just so long as it's your idea."

"I don't think he's going to follow me anywhere."

She snorted. "How much you betting, girl? Name your wager, because surer odds I've never—"

"I haven't heard from him in four months."

"What?" The word came sharp with genuine surprise. "Did you two have another fight? I told you the last time, *you* have to go to *him*. You know what it's like getting him to talk, one fucking word at a time, dragged out like teeth, but—"

"There wasn't a fight. He called in January, we chatted, and that was the last I heard from him."

"So call him! The man has zero people skills, Nadia, in case that somehow escaped your notice. He once went six months without contacting me and when I lit into him for nearly giving me a heart attack, he acted like—"

"He didn't just forget to call. I could feel the cold front moving in for months. He doesn't want to see me, and I'm not driving to Buffalo so he can give me the brush-off in person."

"You owe him."

"I repaid him last fall. Now, apparently, we're square. He made sure of that before he—"

"For God's sake, stop sulking, Nadia. Jack's hurt your feelings—"

"I'm not hurt; I'm pissed off."

"Then tell him to his face. It's the Blue Sky motel, room 18, off the—"

I hung up.

From what Tess had said, Janie would be dead drunk by ten, meaning I could safely enter at midnight. Tess had also mentioned that the back door was usually unlocked. If there had ever been anything of value in the place, it was long gone. One could argue that having a beautiful teenage daughter meant you *did* have something to protect, but Janie would see the price sticker on even a cheap deadbolt and decide the money was better spent on a bottle of rye.

I arrived at eleven-thirty, parked behind the grocery store, and waited. I tried to plan my break-in, but there wasn't much strategy involved with an open door. That meant I had nothing to think about except the one topic I'd been avoiding.

Evelyn was right. I was hurt. What pissed me off was the implication that, in being hurt, I was acting immature. That I had no right to be upset.

Three years ago, Jack had come to me. He'd appeared one night, sent—as I now knew—by Evelyn to assess my suitability as a new student. He'd returned and told her I wouldn't do, then kept coming himself.

At first, I thought he was taking my measure as a security risk, deciding whether to kill me. Maybe he had been. Whatever tests he'd applied, though, I must have passed. Eventually he considered me not only a colleague worthy of continued existence, but one worth his interest.

I won't flatter myself into thinking he was impressed by my skills. I was nowhere near Jack's league and had no intention of applying for membership. Maybe that was part of the attraction. I wasn't competition.

Whatever the reason, that attraction was purely platonic—another aspect that made it easy to let my guard down. Still I'd resisted. Jack was no vigilante or Mafia thug killer. He was a hitman. You paid him, he killed. While I got the feeling it wasn't that simple these days, he was motivated more by economics than by ethics.

He'd said once that if I'd known him years ago, I'd have sooner shot him than talked to him. But talk we did, long nights in the woods behind the lodge. Admittedly I carried most of the conversation—Jack wasn't the chatty type—but he'd seemed to enjoy those visits, passing on tips and tricks to me, listening to me chatter about the lodge. He'd kept coming back, so it couldn't have been too painful.

I hadn't known how important those nights were to me until they stopped. With Jack, I had something I didn't get these days: an honest relationship. He knew who I was—both sides of my life. On the job last fall, I'd realized he'd even seen the parts I'd congratulated myself on keeping hidden. At this point in my life, no one knew me better than Jack.

Now, apparently, he'd decided he didn't care to know me at all.

And it hurt like I'd never imagined it could.

At the stroke of midnight, I was creeping around Janie's home. The back door was indeed open and, as expected, she was asleep on the couch. From the rough rise and fall of her chest, she was snoring loud enough to bring down the rotted rafters, but the sound was drowned out by the booming television. That was a problem.

One might think I'd appreciate loud noise to cover my own sounds, but I've learned to open doors, windows, drawers, even shuffle through papers in silence. If a house is quiet, I can work with confidence, knowing that a key in the front door lock or the creak of bedsprings will resonate like thunder, giving me time to clean up and clear out.

The blaring television meant I wouldn't hear Janie if

she woke. I considered turning it off, but even if Janie somehow did wake and catch me, the only thing she could do was call the police, who hated her as much as they hated me. By the time an officer bothered to stop by, I'd be home in bed, having left not so much as a shoe print to support her story.

To be safe, I unplugged the old rotary phone. That'd give me a few extra minutes. Hell, she'd probably spend an hour pounding on the plunger before realizing it was disconnected.

I looked down at Janie. If I wanted information, my best source was lying right here, drunk and helpless. I fingered the gun under my jacket, and thought of how easy it would be to make Janie talk to me. Throw her onto the carpet, pin her down, let her sputter in a puddle of her own vomit for a few minutes, and she'd decide maybe she could spare the time to answer my questions after all.

Don Riley would love to have me up on an assault charge, but not if it meant dealing with Janie. And he'd be setting the word of the town drunk against that of a hard-working member of the business community.

I could put Janie Ernst into a six-foot hole and most people would say exactly the same thing she'd said about Sammi's disappearance: good riddance. In the end, that's why I didn't do it. If I asked Janie about her daughter and granddaughter, and saw that sneer of hers again, heard her say she didn't give a damn what had happened to them, as long as they didn't come back, I'm not sure I could stop with a beating.

I found Sammi's bedroom. Not exactly a feat of brilliant deduction when there were two bedrooms and only one held a crib. Sammi's room was half the size of her mother's with a twin bed pushed against the wall, crates stacked for storage, a crib, and nothing more. The walls were covered with what might once have been rose-dotted wallpaper, but now was a dingy yellow backdrop with pinkish-brown splotches.

The only decorations were pages ripped from parenting magazines—checklists for infant development, tips on breast-feeding, ads for baby gear. I imagined Sammi in here, ripping down all the signs of her teenage years and putting up all these symbols of motherhood, then surveying the results, not with regret but with satisfaction, the knowledge that she was recentering her world in a worthy direction.

I found their clothing in two crates, one for Sammi and one for Destiny. Having seen them wear the same outfits several times a week, I knew they hadn't owned much, and it all seemed to be there.

There was very little else to search. No diary, no journal. There were no novels or textbooks in which she might have hidden a letter. As Tess said, Sammi was barely literate. The only books I found were a baby memory book, a dog-eared copy of *What to Expect the First Year*, and a few back issues of parenting magazines with the local doctor's name on the mailing label.

Under the bed was an empty cigarette carton stuffed with photographs of Sammi, Tess, and Kira growing up. Under the pictures lay Destiny's hospital bracelet. Sammi's treasures. Her friends and her baby. That was all she had, all she cared about. If she *had* run away, would she have left these things behind?

I flashed my light around the rest of the room. A baby carrier and folded playpen were stacked in the corner, both things that could be replaced once Sammi resettled. Wait. I shone the light back at the carrier. It doubled as a car seat, and fit on top of the stroller.

Sammi always walked to the lodge with the stroller and the car seat attached, in case the weather turned ugly and she needed a lift home. One gorgeous cloud-free day, she'd decided to leave the seat at home. Then, just before she was to leave work, it started pouring. I'd offered her a lift, saying she could hold Destiny on her lap and I'd drive slow. She'd freaked. Her baby did *not* travel in a car without a proper infant seat. She'd sat in the lodge for two hours until the weather cleared enough for her to walk.

So now, when Sammi had supposedly run off and stolen a car or met someone, she'd taken Destiny in the stroller *without* the car-seat attachment? Never. When Sammi left for her walk that evening, she'd been planning to come home.

Seven

By 3 a.m. I was on the 401 heading toward Toronto and, ultimately, Buffalo. I figured I could make it back before lunch, so I'd call Emma around eight and claim I'd zipped out early to get the ATV parts Owen needed from Peterborough. All of our guests were leaving in the morning, meaning there were no activities scheduled and no one had signed up for the morning jog.

I had a long night of driving ahead, but if I went home, I'd only lie awake waiting for morning so I could resume the hunt for Sammi. Since I had no idea *where* to resume that hunt, I might as well spend the time driving and thinking, while accomplishing another task.

Evelyn was right. I had to look Jack in the eye and hear him tell me that he wasn't coming around anymore. A reason would be even better, but probably too much to hope for.

My first thought on arriving at the Blue Sky motel was that Janie Ernst would feel right at home. The sign was the only thing visible from the highway, probably hoping to lure in tired travelers who'd round the bend into the driveway, see the building, and be unable to muster up the energy to escape. I parked between two cars so rusted that I opened my door with extreme caution, afraid a bump would reduce them to a pile of scrap metal. For the first time in years, I locked my old pickup's doors.

I tried to find a front walk, gave up, and cut across

the grass. The motel was long and squat. Robin's-egg-blue paint peeled from the stucco...in the places where the stucco was still affixed to the backboard. I stayed on the grass, to avoid walking under the eaves. Portions were held on with duct tape; the remainder crackled in the wind, threatening to fall. In the distance I could see the shiny new sign by the highway, promising "clean, affordable rooms," the vacancy sign blinking with a note of desperation.

No doubt the Blue Sky qualified as affordable, though Jack could afford better—much better. At his tier, he was probably pulling in a hundred grand a hit, tax free, with no dependents and no bad habits to spend it on. His tastes were utilitarian. Working class, Evelyn sniffed. But it meant he had money—lots of it, I was sure—and while the Hilton really wasn't his style, this was well below it. Still, this was the kind of place where you could plunk down cash for a week and no one would ask for a name, much less ID, which was likely its chief attraction.

For the last half hour, I'd been rehearsing these next few minutes. Walking to his door, knocking... "Hey, Jack, sorry to bother you, but Evelyn was concerned. She seemed to think you need a place to hunker down, maybe the lodge— That's what I thought. No, that's fine. I had to go into Toronto today, so this wasn't that far out of my way. Just thought I'd check— No, I understand. Believe me, I'm not here to drag you anywhere you don't want to go. Just making the offer. So I'll be on my way. Oh, and I know you haven't been coming around— No, no, that's okay. Time to move on, for both of us. I just wanted to say thanks, and if you ever need anything..."

I still wasn't sure about the last part. I wanted to end

on a civil note, but when I heard myself saying that, it sounded as quietly desperate as that blinking vacancy sign.

I stepped around a tower of beer cases—empties. Room fifteen, sixteen...eighteen must be on the end. That would be Jack's choice—easiest to escape.

As for my parting words, I shouldn't leave them so open-ended. Close the relationship door gently but firmly.

"Don't worry about me calling you up for anything, Jack. Better to cut ties completely."

Too defiant? Angry? Hurt?

Shit, I didn't want to sound hurt. Maybe I should stick with open-ended.

The last door was number eighteen, the eight sleeping on its side. I circled wide around the window, so he wouldn't see my shadow pass the drawn drapes, though I doubted Jack was sitting up at 5 a.m. watching for trouble.

I checked the end of the unit. No window or other escape route. Not that Jack would run. If he thought he'd been cornered, he'd greet his guest with a gun to the skull. I'd prefer to avoid that kind of drama so early in the morning.

I returned to the door and took one last survey of my surroundings. The only noise came from the highway.

I knocked, counted to five, and knocked again. The first would wake him. The second would confirm he really had heard a knock. I listened, heard nothing, but didn't knock again. He'd be up. Sitting on the edge of the bed now, listening as he pulled out his gun. Then making his way across the room as silently as he could with his injured foot. A peek through the curtain crack. A whispered curse when he couldn't see who was at the door. Circling around to the other side of that door, so he could watch the window at the same time. Reaching for the dead-bolt . . .

"It's me, Jack."

A muffled "Fuck" from exactly where I'd pictured him. The chain rattled, but when the door opened, it stopped short, the anchor still in place. The aura of calm I'd spent four hours gathering slipped away.

"Na— Dee."

I could only see a sliver illuminated by the porch light through the door crack. One dark eye. A slice of stubbled cheek. A bare chest. I pulled my gaze back up to the eye.

Jack leaned against the door frame, his gun clacking as it brushed the wall.

"What's up?" he said.

"Not much. I was just driving by and thought I'd stop in, say hi . . ." I lowered my voice. "What the hell do you *think* I'm doing here, Jack? Who else knows where you are?"

"Evelyn. Fuck."

He shifted, his hand splaying over the crack, moving not to open the door but to block that gap.

"Look," I said. "If you've got someone in there, just come outside—"

"Someone—? Fuck, no."

"Then open the damned door. I just drove four hours because Evelyn called me last night, freaking out, and I'm not going to stand on the sidewalk whispering."

"Hold on." He undid the chain, opened the door another six inches, but only moved into the gap. "Diner down the road. We'll grab coffee. Talk. Meet me in ten min—"

I slammed my palm against the door hard enough to startle him into letting go.

"I don't want coffee, Jack," I said and pushed my way past him.

I stared at the room, fighting the urge to flinch as my gaze tripped from the pizza box to the tossed beer cans to the piles of newspapers to the overflowing ashtrays. My shoulders tightened. I tried to ignore the mess, but it was like spiders creeping up my spine, making my skin itch, stopping only when I scooped up the nearest pile of papers.

"Don't—" Jack began.

"I see housekeeping wasn't included in the rent." I tried to laugh, but it came out tight. I grabbed another stack of newspapers.

"Leave it." The thump of his cast on the floor. A hand gripped my elbow. "Nadia."

"I've got it."

"That's why I said 'wait,' " he muttered. "Just—"

"I've got it. Go get dressed so we can talk."

A grumbling sigh, underlain with another oath. Then the thump of his retreat. I snuck a glance over my shoulder. It didn't look like he was wearing a walking cast, but that wasn't stopping him. A single crutch rested against the door, as if he only used it for going out. From the looks of this room, he hadn't been doing much of that.

The place wasn't dirty, just untidy. Not like Jack. Still, it wasn't as if there was a crate of empty whiskey bottles. Alcoholic binges required relinquishing control, and Jack couldn't abide that.

He dealt with stress another way, and evidence of it rested in every overflowing ashtray. Jack had almost quit, but got stuck at one cigarette a day. The only time he smoked more than one was when something was bothering him. As an ex-smoker myself, I know that urge all too well.

Dumping the ashtrays, I noticed they were all American brands. Jack smoked a very specific brand—Irish, hard to find. He only resorted to American cigarettes when the need outweighed his distaste.

I stacked a couple of crossword puzzle books, and couldn't resist thumbing through them. Most were done. Surprising. I'd never known Jack to do crosswords. But then, I'd never known him to do anything that qualified as recreational.

A noise from the bathroom. I looked up to see Jack in the doorway, surveying the room, shaking his head.

"All cleaned up," I said.

"I see that."

He scratched his jaw, wincing as he hit a fresh shaving nick. His hair glistened from a quick shower. He wore the sweatpants from earlier, but had pulled on a T-shirt, showing lean muscled arms with no scars, no tattoos, no distinguishing features—those he added only with a disguise.

When Jack had started coming to see me at the lodge, I'd always presumed he was in disguise. He hadn't been. The darkness had been disguise enough, though it also had the effect of making him look younger, leading to a stellar foot-in-mouth moment when I first saw him in the light and commented on his aging techniques . . . only to realize later he hadn't been using any.

Like his arms, the rest of him—the visible parts at least—bore no distinguishing features. There was little distinguishing about Jack at all. Average build, average height. He had an angular face that couldn't quite be called handsome, with lines deepening by his mouth and between his eyes, threatening to become creases. His wavy black hair was shot through with silver. Midforties, maybe creeping toward fifty.

Jack's eyes were the only feature a witness might remember, not for any unusual color or shape, but for his gaze—that piercing, unnerving way of watching, as if tracking everything around him. Even that, though, he could turn off with a blink and retreat into unadulterated ordinariness. Perfect for a hitman.

"Evelyn thinks you should lie low with me for a while, at the lodge."

"Nah."

He hobbled to the bed. I resisted the impulse to help.

"So you're fine," I said as he sat.

"Yeah."

"All right, then."

I headed for the door.

"Shouldn't have called," he said.

I turned. "What?"

"Evelyn. Bothering you. Shouldn't have."

"She's concerned."

A grunt. He scratched his chin again. The conversation, such as it was, was over. I wanted to turn and walk out, made it forty-five degrees, then stopped.

"I have the room, Jack. It's a slow time of the year. One more guest wouldn't be a problem." I managed a small laugh. "Free housekeeping, if that's any incentive. And meals, of course. You've had Emma's cooking, and you know it's better than take-out pizza." I heard an edge of desperation creep into my voice and choked it back. "I'm just saying that the offer's genuine. Evelyn isn't twisting my arm."

"Nah."

He reached for the cigarette pack on the bedside table, as if I'd already left.

I made it as far as the door, hand on the knob.

"How's it going?" he asked.

I looked over my shoulder. "How's what going?"

A shrug. "Stuff. The lodge. The job. You. Things okay?"

"Everything's fine."

He nodded and struck a match. I waited five seconds. Then I left.

Eight

Self-delusion is grand, ain't it? I'd convinced myself I'd only wanted to see Jack, and make sure he was okay. Like when I'd started high school and told my mother I didn't expect a Santa stocking anymore. Of course I'd still *wanted* one. But if I'd expected my mother to get me anything she didn't need to, I'd been delusional.

I *had* continued to get stockings, but from my father, on the sly, so neither of us would have to deal with my mother's "you spoil her" tirades. I'd gotten them every year, even after I graduated from police college and moved to Toronto. Then the next year, there'd been no one to give it.

I hadn't seen my mother in three years. Or spoken to my brother in four. And now Jack...I was starting to sense a pattern. After Amy's death twenty years ago, my relationships with others had changed. I was still as sociable as ever, but it was like with my guests at the lodge. I gave generously; expected nothing; accepted nothing.

I'd say it's my personality. I'm a people-pleaser. But buried in that is the other side of the equation. If you take nothing, you owe nothing. Keep the account square.

Like Jack...

Only I would never let someone travel four hundred kilometers to help me out, then brush her off with a "nah."

As I backed out, a *crack* made my stomach drop as my foot smacked the brake. I twisted in my seat to look behind me. All was as clear as it had been when I'd shoulder-checked.

Another sharp rap, clearly now coming from the front end. I whipped around to see Jack, his open palm over the hood as he hobbled across the front of the truck, crutch under his arm.

He motioned for me to lower the window. I cranked it halfway down. He leaned against my door. Twenty seconds of silence passed.

"Yes, Jack?" I said finally.

"Could use a place. Lodge'd be good. I'll pay."

"You don't have to—"

"I want to."

"Okay." I rattled off the price. "That's a room, all activities, breakfast, dinner, snacks, and beverages. Lunch is available for ten more, eight for a picnic basket—"

"That's fine." If he caught the sarcasm in my recital, he gave no sign. "Probably be two weeks. That okay?"

I nodded.

"Gimme five minutes."

He stumped off. I opened the door to follow and help him pack, then forced myself to close it. Better to take a few minutes and figure out how I was going to swing this past Emma. I'd decided on a story, and was jotting notes in my "Sammi casebook," when Jack rapped on the driver's window. When I looked up, he beckoned me out.

I rolled the window down. "We have to go, Jack. I have work waiting. If there's a problem—"

"Gonna drive. Up all night. Should sleep."

Out of practice with Jack's habit of dropping pronouns—and any other words he deemed nonessential—it took a minute to realize he meant that *I'd* been up all night so *I* should get some sleep while *he* drove.

"Have you forgotten your broken ankle?" I said.

"Left foot. Truck's automatic."

"You aren't driving my truck with a cast on. It may be a piece of crap but—"

"Out."

I shifted into reverse. The truck lunged back.

Jack swore, eyed me, as if trying to figure out how serious I was, then cursed again, slung his bag into the pickup bed, and hobbled to the passenger side.

I used my real ID at the border. I suspect Jack wasn't thrilled with that, but if I was using my own vehicle, it was silly to pull a fake passport. I presumed his was fake. I didn't take a good look.

Jack didn't say much on the drive, maybe because I kept the radio cranked up. When I pulled over in Oakville for a washroom break and coffees, I came back to find him in the driver's seat. Arguing would have required energy, and I was asleep before we reached the highway.

When I woke up, we'd already gone through Toronto and were passing Whitby. I stretched, reached for my coffee, and found it cold and bitter.

"Got time for breakfast?" Jack asked.

I checked my watch. Almost eight. I needed to call Emma and explain, but with that explanation came the excuse for being as late as I wanted. I directed him off the highway and made the call.

I told Emma that Jack was my dad's cousin. When Aunt Evie called the night before, it had been about him, stranded in Buffalo with a broken ankle in the midst of a cross-country job-hunting move. He really needed a place to stay while he recuperated and Aunt Evie thought the lodge would be perfect.

I'd started worrying about him, stuck in a strange city, and took off last night to pick him up. For most people this might seem odd, but Emma didn't question it from me. She'd only grumbled that she hoped I wasn't being taken advantage of by family that otherwise couldn't be bothered with me. I assured her he was paying and that cheered her up.

For a name, I went with John. That way, if I slipped and called him Jack, I'd just say that's what family called him.

We stopped at one of the rare Canadian Denny's, the lot filled with trucks. My dad always said that was the best way to look for food on the road—go where the truckers go. Not true. Truckers go where it's cheap and filling, but he always took me to places like this for breakfast on a road trip, so that's where I instinctively turned in.

These truckers must have been pretty hungry, because they'd all grabbed the first table they reached, leaving the other end empty. Jack chose the farthest table, next to a window, earning a sour look from the servers, who'd probably hoped to keep the mess contained to one side.

Getting our coffees and placing our orders consumed a few minutes. A few more disappeared as I scrubbed up in the bathroom. But then, after I returned, the silence became too obvious to ignore. Jack folded a paper napkin and creased it with his thumbnail, intent on that task until, finally, even he could bear it no longer.

"Been meaning to call," he said.

Coffee churned in my stomach. My own fault for not being my usual chatty self, making him think the emptiness meant I was waiting for those obligatory words. Empty words. Like when a friend you haven't seen in years calls, and the lie comes naturally: I was going to call you.

"You've been busy," I said.

"Yeah."

He sipped his coffee long enough to drain half of it.

"Money," he said. "You okay?"

In other words, did I need any jewels fenced? On Jack's advice, the Tomassinis paid me in uncut jewels, which were easier than cash to transfer over the border, easier to store, and safer to liquidate, with Jack as middleman, putting an extra layer between me and the cash. He was supposed to keep a cut for himself, and I presumed he did, though I had no way of knowing.

Jack fenced only what I needed. As wonderful as it would be to pay off the mortgage and fully renovate the lodge, it would be a little hard to explain to Revenue Canada since the business barely broke even. It already took some creativity to inject just enough extra cash to keep the lodge in good repair.

"I'm fine," I said.

"Sure?"

I nodded. "I got some money this week. Quinn cut me in on a job in Toronto and he had cash, so it seemed safe enough to take that."

Jack lowered his mug to the table. "You're working with Quinn?"

"Just that one job."

The lines around his mouth deepened.

"You know we kept in contact," I said.

"Know you're seeing him. Not working with him."

"Actually, it's the other way around. Last week was the first time I'd seen him since Wilkes. But you knew we were in contact, and you didn't have a problem with that..."

"Social contact? None of my business. Working with him?" He rubbed his hand over his mouth. "Shoulda run it by me."

And how was I supposed to do that? I didn't say the words. They'd only sound like petulance, and he could remind me that he *had* provided a way for me to initiate contact, if I needed him.

"This job. Tell me about it."

"It went fine."

His gaze met mine, holding it. "Details. Later."

I could have balked at the suggestion that I needed Jack to vet my jobs, even in retrospect, but that would be like taking offense if a ski buddy wanted to double-check my equipment before a killer hill. When your life is at stake, it's no time for pride.

Jack preferred for me to stick to my semiannual Tomassini hits. When it came to contract killing, that was like skiing on the bunny hill. I could take offense at the implication, but I was new and a part-timer with an outside life. A mistake could mean the end of the life I'd rebuilt so carefully.

We relapsed into silence until breakfast arrived. Jack had ordered the "Lumberjack Grand Slam": three pancakes, ham, bacon, sausage links and two eggs, hash browns, and toast. As he attacked it, I wondered how long it'd been since he'd ventured from the motel for a meal. I remembered the overflowing ashtrays.

"I know this isn't the place to discuss it," I said, "but just a heads-up—we're going to need to talk about what kind of trouble you're in. If you're staying at the lodge—"

He swallowed a mouthful of egg. "Trouble?"

"The reason you need a place to stay."

"Ah, fuck." He lowered his fork. "What'd Evelyn say?"

"Just that you need someone to watch your back. Something to do with the job you broke your ankle on. Or, at least, that's what she seemed to be—"

"—suggesting." He chomped down on a slice of bacon, crispy bits flying, then chewed it as he shook his head. "Nothing happened on the job. Except that." He waved the remainder of the bacon slice at his cast, stretched into the aisle.

"So you aren't lying low?"

He finished his bacon slice, chewing slower. "Yeah, I am. Kinda. Nothing serious. Same shit, different day. You know."

I didn't, but asking wouldn't fix that.

"So I don't need to worry about anyone gunning for you at the lodge?"

He met my gaze, giving me a look that straddled reproach and indignation. "Wouldn't do that to you."

I nodded and sliced into my egg.

Nine

We were almost in Peterborough when Jack said, "What's this?" and I looked over to see my Sammi notes on his lap. I took them and slid the book down beside me.

"Just something I'm working on."

"Job?"

I shook my head, signaled, and moved into the left lane. When I was past the transport, I moved back.

"Gonna tell me?"

The truth was that I was dying to tell someone, to get a second opinion, and no one was safer than Jack. So I filled him in.

"I know," I said when I finished. "I should leave it to the police, but they've made it very clear that—"

"They aren't interested."

"That's just it. No one's interested. Her mother's a piece of work, so no big shock there, but nobody in town seems to care. These *aren't* bad people. If it was Tess or Kira or any of the other girls in town, there would be search teams combing the forests. But with Sammi it seems like, even if something did happen, it's..." I fumbled for the words.

"Expected."

I nodded. "Like she was heading that way all her life. Made to be broken."

The last words came out as a whisper, echoing through the years.

"Hmmm?" Jack said.

I picked up the notes. "Would you mind looking them over? Tell me if I'm... I don't know. Being paranoid."

* * *

Part of me hoped Jack would say that all signs indicated Sammi had run off and I was making a big deal out of nothing. But he agreed there were too many factors arguing against it.

We discussed it as I headed up Highway 55. I was in the middle of telling him more about Janie when the faded highway sign for *Bob's Wild Kingdom* flew past, and I hit the brakes.

"Cougar."

"Huh?"

I turned onto the exit ramp. "There's something I need to check out."

Sometime in the last week, kids camping near the Potter place said they'd heard a cougar in the forest. Sunday night, Meredith had watched Sammi and Destiny walk heading toward the road that led past the Potter place.

"The only cougars within an hour's drive are the ones in this roadside zoo," I told Jack. "A big cat raised in captivity wouldn't know how to hunt normal prey, meaning if one did escape, it would get very hungry and it wouldn't be afraid of humans."

He nodded slowly. "It could kill the girl. Drag her off. Come back for the baby."

He said it without emotion. Not coldly, just matter-of-fact. I tried to keep my thoughts as logical, not to picture the scenario he'd described.

"I didn't see any signs of a struggle near the road," I

said. "But it had been a few days and there was rain…
Still, it doesn't account for the missing stroller."

"Could have fallen into the ditch. Or been dragged.
Cat trying to get the baby out."

I looked out the passenger window.

"Or maybe it wasn't a cat," he said after a moment.

"Maybe."

I made a cell phone call before we reached the zoo. Kira's
mother, Meredith, was a member of Zoocheck Canada,
an animal protection agency that monitored the conditions of circuses and roadside zoos. Meredith had been
trying to get *Bob's Wild Kingdom* closed for years. Every
few months, I signed her petition.

Before storming in there, I needed to know how many
cougars they had. If one did escape, the owner obviously
hadn't reported it. And if I didn't know my facts, he could
bullshit me from here to Newfoundland.

The first time we drove by, I took one look at the haphazard maze of mesh wire enclosures and dismissed it as
an abandoned farm. At the next intersection, another
sign for *Bob's Wild Kingdom* pointed back the way we'd
come and I realized that the "abandoned farm" had been
the zoo.

It was certainly no kingdom. Those wire mesh enclosures housed deer, ostriches, llamas, two mangy camels,
and one yak with matted fur. Each fenced area was no
larger than fifteen feet square. The ground was bare dirt

and muddy straw. For food and water dishes, they had plastic buckets and ice cream pails.

Meredith had said that Bob wasn't a Robert, but Roberta MacNeil, as the crooked sign on her trailer proclaimed. In the spring, the zoo was open from Friday to Sunday only, so I went up to the trailer and rapped on the door. No answer. Jack knocked louder. Still nothing. He peered into a window.

"Dark," he said.

I walked to the gate. No sign of anyone. I glanced up at the six-foot chain-link fence. Easy to scale.

"Slow down," Jack murmured, though I hadn't taken a step toward it.

"Meredith said there are two cougars here," I said as I walked to the fence and put my fingers through the links. "All I have to do is find them, and this place is so small it'll only take a minute. Just stand guard for five minutes while—"

Curses rang out from one of the buildings.

Jack gave me a "told you" look. I pretended not to see it.

"Hello?" I called. "Hello!"

A short, stocky woman emerged from a rusty metal shed.

"We're closed."

"I just wanted—"

"Bill Bryson, SPCA, Investigations Department," Jack said, flashing his wallet too fast for her to see more than a card. He didn't introduce me, which, I admitted, was wiser than my plan. Roberta and I had never met, but if she bumped into me around town after this, I could claim I'd been escorting "Bill."

Jack continued, his faint brogue swallowed as he affected what I called his "national newscaster" voice, no trace of any regional accent. "I need to talk to you about your big cats."

"I didn't lose no cougars." She opened the gate and ushered us through. "Look around all you want. Tex and Mex are right where they should be. In their cage back here." She started walking, then turned and gestured to Jack's cast. "Watch your step. It's mud season. Damned slippery."

We passed cages of monkeys, foxes, and one lynx that lay draped over a branch like it'd died there. Judging by the smell, it had. All the other animals moved to the edge of their cages and stared out at us with the hardened bitterness of lifers.

People *paid* to come in here. In summer, kids raced along these rows, parents scurrying after them, and they had a good time. What kept them from taking one look, one sniff, and running to the nearest exit?

"Here they are," Roberta said. "Tex and Mex. My cougars."

One of the tawny big cats lay in the lone beam of sunlight that filtered past the heavy bars. The other paced the shadows at the back. Both were old, with rotting teeth and mangy fur, just as Meredith had said. I couldn't imagine either having the strength to cover the twenty kilometers between here and the Potter place, let alone kill a healthy teenager.

I glanced at Jack, but he was watching the cat pace in its dirty cage. It turned to look at him, a haunted, half-mad emptiness in its eyes.

I checked the cage. No broken door bound shut with

rope. No recent welds on the bars. No signs of any recent repairs. The pacing cat slumped into an exhausted heap and fell asleep almost as soon as it hit the floor.

The cat lying in the sun turned its empty eyes on me. I shivered. Even if Roberta left the door open, I doubted these cougars would get farther than the front gate.

"Everything seems to be in order," Jack said.

"Like I told those cops when they called last night, I run a tight ship. Nothing gets in or out."

"A life sentence," I murmured. "No chance of parole."

Roberta frowned and scratched her head hard, as if something was nibbling at her scalp.

"That's all I needed to see," Jack said. "Thank you for your time."

"No trouble."

As we turned away, the one cougar stood and stretched, sniffing the air.

"You'll get fed soon enough, Mex," Roberta said. "Don't start your complaining now."

Roberta escorted us to the gate and held it open. As we exchanged good-byes, an unearthly scream ripped through the morning quiet.

Roberta laughed when I jumped. "That's just Mex, bitching for her food."

"It sounded like—"

"A woman screaming, I know. That's what everyone says. When I lived out West, tourists used to call the cops all the time, saying some poor woman was screaming in the forest."

Now I knew what those city kids had heard out near the Potter place. And it hadn't been a cougar.

Ten

At the lodge, I settled details for Jack's stay with Emma while she rolled dough for apple strudel.

"So make sure he's comfortable, show him around," I said as I snatched a sugarcoated apple slice from the bowl. "You probably won't see much of him anyway. He keeps to himself. I need to zip into town—"

"Still looking for Sammi?"

I stopped chewing.

"Did you think I wouldn't figure it out? You've been gone more in the last week than you have in months. You're worried about her. At least someone is." She peeled the rolled dough from the board and laid out another ball. "I asked around myself when I went shopping this morning. Everyone thinks she just ran off."

"Which she probably did."

"But something's telling you otherwise, so you keep looking. Did you get anything from Janie?"

"Do insults count?"

"You want me to take a run at her?"

I indulged in the fantasy for a moment. A killer ex-cop might not faze Janie, but Emma was a different story. Last month, in town, when Janie had tried to hit me up for an advance on her daughter's pay, Emma had come around the corner, eyes blazing as fiercely as her red-dyed hair, and Janie had skittered off so fast you'd think she'd spotted an unopened rye bottle in the ditch.

"Not yet," I said. "Let me check around a bit more on my own."

"Should I expect you for lunch?"

"I have to stop at the diner. I'll grab something there."

I parked in town and went to Canadian Tire for supplies. Better to walk into the diner carrying a shopping bag, to prove that I'd come to town for a reason. If Riley got wind of my snooping, he'd slap an interference charge on my ass so fast he'd be winded for days. Then, having accused me of buggering up his investigation, he'd actually need to start one, and probably balls it up to spite me.

Pretty much every town up here has a Canadian Tire, which carries everything from spark plugs to coffeemakers to paper towels. I suppose they carry tires, too, if you can find them. In White Rock, the Canadian Tire has everything from building supplies to inflatable rafts shoved into a store hardly big enough for fishing lures (aisle two, top shelf, behind the china mugs). Shopping there is great, if you like scavenger hunts. I'd developed a near-perfect system. Find an item that has absolutely nothing in common with the item you want, move it aside, and, bingo, there's what you came for.

After twenty minutes, I had everything I needed: a monster-sized ball of string, a box of disposable plastic gloves, and a pocket-sized Maglite with extra batteries. Then I grabbed a handful of other items the lodge could always use, like ant traps, dish towels, and a copy of *Chatelaine* for Emma. At the checkout, I stifled the itch to ask for news of Sammi. If there was any, I'd hear it soon enough.

*   *   *

Outside Larry's Diner I grabbed a copy of the local weekly paper. Then I went inside and ordered a coffee. My stomach wouldn't consider lunch.

Reading the newspaper front to back took ten minutes, and I'm no speed reader. As I'd hoped, there was an article on the cougar, one that confirmed my fear—the "scream" had indeed been heard Sunday night, between eight and nine, soon after Sammi was last seen walking in the same area.

According to Liz Bowles—the owner, editor, and sole reporter of the *White Rock Times*—the "cougar story" was nothing more than further proof that city living destroys brain cells. How many times, she ranted, did cottagers from southern Ontario mistake boulders for bears, garter snakes for Massasauga rattlers, local dogs for wolves? Americans were even worse, wandering around looking for reindeer and polar bears. Those kids probably heard a tomcat yowl, then expected the police to investigate, wasting our tax dollars with their ignorance.

Liz was pleased to report that our local OPP detachment, as efficient as ever, had cleared the matter up with a phone call, confirming that *Bob's Wild Kingdom* was not, in fact, missing a cougar. Did I mention that Liz's maiden name was Riley? As in sister to Don Riley, head of our efficient OPP detachment?

"So they cleared up that cougar thing," I said as Larry refilled my coffee.

"Well, that's what they seem to be saying."

"You don't believe it?"

Larry shrugged.

"Well," I said, folding the paper. "If there is a big cat out there, I, for one, would sure like to know."

"If I were you, I'd tell your guests to stay out of the wood for a while."

"Damn. That's not good." I added cream to my coffee. "You know, I hear cougars are territorial, stick mostly to one spot." I'd heard nothing of the sort, but it worked for me. "Maybe it'll be enough to keep people away from that particular area. Those kids were over by the Potter place, weren't they?"

Larry put the pot back on the burner. "Yep. The lot next to it, where that cottage burned down a few years back. If folks want to camp before the MicMac opens for the season, Eric sends them over there."

"Any idea from which direction they heard the cat? North, south?"

"East, away from your place. It was close to the campsite, though. They came tearing in here like the devil was on their tail. They said it sounded like the cougar was right beside 'em. I told Eric not to go telling any more folks to camp over there. Cougar or not, we don't need that kind of trouble."

"No kidding. I'll make sure none of my guests go hiking that way. Thanks."

I lingered for the minimum amount of time, engaging in the minimum amount of small talk, then hurried to my truck.

I went to the makeshift campsite, still hoping those kids had indeed heard a cat. But there's a point at which optimism crosses over into denial.

So I took precautions. If I found something, I couldn't let the police know I'd been first on the scene. I had to treat this search as if I was looking for a place to hide a body myself.

I wore the spare rubber boots I kept in the truck, two sizes larger than my own feet, so they could be worn by anyone who borrowed the pickup and got stuck in the spring mud. If I found anything, I'd dispose of them. I tied my hair back with an elastic, then donned the Raptors ball cap I stored in the truck for hair emergencies, and tucked every strand of hair under it. The Maglite and batteries went into my coat pocket, along with three pairs of clear plastic gloves and a big ball of string. I was ready.

I parked on a logging road several kilometers away, so neither my truck nor its tire tracks would be near a potential crime scene. Then I walked the roadway stretch, hoping to see signs of a struggle or a disturbance on the forest's edge that I might have missed two days ago. Nothing. When I reached the campsite, I started my search.

I began with the stretch from the east edge of the campsite to the road Sammi had traveled. I footmeasured a meter into the forest, then tied the end of the string to a tree to mark my starting point. As I walked, I stretched the string behind me, marking my path and giving me a one-meter strip. Once I neared the road, I tied the string off, measured another strip, started a new string on the other side, and searched that strip. Then I cut the first string, removed it, and started a fresh one.

A temporary grid system. It seemed like a waste of time in the early stages, when the road marked my starting point, but once I got farther into the forest, it'd all start to look alike and it was too easy to drift and miss areas.

I found a sizable walking stick and started searching the grid, using the stick to clear the path in front of me, so I wouldn't miss anything beneath the cushion of dead leaves. When I came to low bushes or thick undergrowth, I used a smaller stick to poke around and shone the high-powered Maglite into dark crevices. It was excruciatingly slow work.

It might seem as if I was making this more complicated than it needed to be. Surely if anything had happened to Sammi, the signs would be there. You can't drag a teenage girl and baby stroller into the forest without leaving marks, right?

It's not that easy. Just because people hadn't been tramping through the woods didn't mean other creatures hadn't. Herds of deer made herds of human-sized trails through the undergrowth. I saw plenty of trampled grass and broken twigs, but, unlike in Sherlock Holmes stories, that didn't necessarily mean a person had been this way. I had to search inch by inch.

After four hours, all I had was a sore back.

Time to break for dinner. Eating was the last thing on my mind, but I didn't want to do anything out of the ordinary. Not with Jack around. I'd considered letting him know what I was doing, but he might offer to help. If I found what I most feared, I wanted to do it alone.

Jack was here to recuperate. A guest. Not a friend, not a colleague, not a mentor. I wasn't going to bring him into this any more than I had to, and when I did, it would be as a calm, detached professional investigating a case. If I found Sammi's body, I would not be calm, detached, or professional, no matter how hard I tried. So he was staying out until I had something to report.

I found Emma in the kitchen, taking a casserole from the oven.

"How's John?" I asked.

"They should be back any minute. He went out fishing with Owen."

I tried to picture that, and failed. "I didn't know John fished."

"He doesn't, apparently, but Owen offered to show him how and he agreed to give it a shot." She pulled the foil from the dish, steam billowing up. "Actually, it was more like: 'You fish?' 'Nah.' 'Wanna try?' 'Sure.' At least they won't scare the fish away with their chattering."

"Any last-minute check-ins?"

She shook her head. "Empty again tonight unless someone comes by late. But we have two more bookings for the weekend, so it looks like we'll have a full house."

I imagined a weekend stuffed with kayaking and bird-watching, no time for Sammi. My stomach fluttered. I reminded myself *this* was my priority. My gut didn't agree.

"I'll be heading out again after dinner, if that's okay. Just a few things I need to wrap up, make sure I'm clear for the weekend."

Emma studied me. "Is everything okay, Nadia?"

I forced a smile. "Sure. Why?"

Another long look that I struggled not to squirm under. Then she said, "You do whatever you have to do."

* * *

Jack and Owen appeared before dinner reached the table. I ate like a race car stuck in a fifty-kilometer zone—wolfing a few bites, forcing myself to slow down, gulping some more, slamming on the brakes...

I told myself Jack wasn't really a guest, so I didn't need to play hostess. But it was the looks he kept shooting that slowed me down—his intense gaze swinging my way every time I gulped a mouthful or responded with one-word answers to Emma's efforts to strike up conversation.

I even had a slice of strudel... or at least cut it up and pushed pieces around on my plate. Then I cleared the table for Emma, loaded the dishwasher, and fled by way of the kitchen door.

I found Jack leaning against my truck's fender, one elbow braced on the hood, the crutch in front of him, resting against his chest. He didn't say a word, just watched my approach with that unwavering gaze.

I shoved my hands into my pockets, going for casual. Even managed a smile. "Hey. Everything going okay? All settled in?"

"Same as last time you asked."

"Right, well, if you need anything, Emma's around. She's officially on duty until ten." I pulled out my keys and had to flip through the ring twice to find the right one. "I hate to eat and run, but with no guests around, I have to take advantage of it. Got some work to do on the other side of the property."

"That where you think she's buried?"

The keys slipped and I fumbled to grab the ring before it fell. "B-buried?"

"Sammi. You're looking for her body."

I tried to laugh. "In these woods? If Sammi's out there, I don't have a hope in hell of finding—"

"Cut the shit, Nadia. We both know that cougar scream was a girl. You found out where. Now you're searching."

"No, I—"

"You're gonna tell me you're not? What's the big deal?"

He had a point. So why did my stomach clench at the thought of admitting it? I supposed I just didn't want him saying that hunting for a live girl was fine, but digging up a dead one could get me in trouble, and I couldn't afford anyone taking too close a look at my life. And if he *did* say that, he'd have another point. But I didn't want to hear it.

He swung the crutch under his arm and pulled open the driver's door. "You can drive."

"You aren't coming, Jack. I appreciate the offer, but you're injured and I really need to be thorough—"

"And careful. So I'm going. Make sure you are."

"Are you suggesting—?"

"Not suggesting. *Saying.* You aren't yourself. Haven't been since you picked me up. Quiet. Tense. Your mind's someplace else. I thought it was just me. Us. Then you run off. Come back. Inhale dinner. All you can think about is getting back. Back to *her.*"

The keys bit into my palm. I loosened my grip. "I'm not running off half-cocked. I'm being careful and I have my priorities straight. I need to search for Sammi now, so I don't have to run off when guests arrive tomorrow."

"So if you had guests, you'd slow down? Fuck, no. Be climbing the walls." He paused and met my gaze. "I've seen you like this before. With Wilkes."

"Don't—"

"You get single-minded. Obsess—" He cut the word off by rubbing his mouth. "Not trying to stop you. Just want to watch your back. Cover your tracks."

He headed around to the passenger side. I got in and waited for him.

Eleven

Having searched the east side of the campsite, I started a fresh grid on the west. It seemed unlikely that anyone would have taken Sammi more than a half kilometer into the dense woods.

After almost two hours, I found a patch of disturbed earth less than a hundred feet from the main road. The sun was setting, as it would have been when Sammi walked by, good enough to see, but not to see well. I fought the urge to start digging and simply marked the location by sticking the string roll over a tree branch.

I headed back for the truck.

"Need something?" Jack asked.

I headed at the sound of his voice. In the last two hours, he'd said maybe a dozen words, as he silently poked around, letting me work.

"Need something?" he repeated.

"Stuff."

I retrieved my larger flashlight, and came back to find Jack hunkered down by the disturbed earth.

"Something dug here," he said. "Be careful. Remember—"

I slapped the flashlight into his hand, cutting him short. "Shine it on me, so I don't miss anything."

I pulled on a pair of gloves, crouched, and examined the spot under the glare of the Maglite. It wasn't a large area—less than six square inches of bare earth where something had cleared away the layer of rotting leaves. Claw marks scored the ground, each the size of fork tines. The animal had dug down an inch or two, then given up.

There was a dark, wet-looking patch in the center of the spot. I picked up a clump of dirt, crushed it between my gloved fingers, and looked closer. It was dry, just darker than the surrounding earth. I ground another clump between my thumb and forefinger. Jack shone the Maglite on it.

"Blood," Jack said. "Here, let me—"

"Got it."

I gently swept aside the disturbed earth. Beneath the thin layer the animal had scraped through, the ground was hard. You can pack a hole as tightly as you want, but you can never cover the signs of disturbance. Blood had seeped into the ground here, but nothing was buried beneath it.

I took a moment to wipe off my hands, gaze down, not letting Jack see how relieved I was.

Then I shifted onto my haunches and looked around. Something had come through here, damaging bushes and low-hanging branches to the north, the direction of the road, and to the southwest. I knew the disturbance couldn't have taken place more than a week or so ago because the exposed wood of each break was fresh, and new leaves hung from the broken end of the twigs, still surviving on stored food.

Despite the obvious signs of passage, the site showed no ground-level indication that anyone had passed this way. Fallen leaves carpeted the ground beneath the broken twigs. Not a single inch of bare earth was exposed. Perfectly undisturbed. *Too* perfect. All around this patch, dead and fallen leaves lay in heaps and clumps, the earth peeking through. Someone had covered his tracks here.

I proceeded southwest. I didn't need to search for broken branches and twigs. The too-perfect layer of leaves stretched out before me like a red carpet. Less than fifty feet later, it ended at a clearing.

I flexed my hands, inhaling to calm my galloping heart, then crept on my hands and knees to the middle and began clearing leaves. Without a word, Jack set up the flashlight to shine on the patch, then started working at the other side.

Within minutes we'd found a tightly packed patch of upturned earth.

Staying on my knees, I cleared the area and marked the perimeter of the hole. Two feet wide. Just over five feet long. Once it was clear, I eased back and sat there, staring at it.

I stood, hands shaking as I brushed dirt from my pants.

"I need—" The words snagged in my throat. I'd been working so long in silence it was hard to speak. I cleared my throat. "I have to go back to the truck and get—"

Jack stepped up beside me, holding a shovel. I hadn't even noticed he'd left.

"Here," he said. "You sit. Rest. I'll—"

"No."

I took the shovel and scraped off layers of dirt, rather than digging. If Sammi was here, I'd need to replace everything as it had been and find a way to lead the police search in the right direction.

About nine inches down, the tip of my shovel revealed a pale nub, glowing in the reflected flashlight beam. I bent and, working with my gloves on, finger-scooped around the object until I could see it. A toe. A small toe with chipping purple nail polish.

I moved back, drawing in a ragged breath.

"Want me to—?" Jack began.

"No."

I crawled to the other end of the hole and began scraping away at the earth. Soon, yet another pale nub showed through the inky earth. A nose. Using my fingers, I cleared away the final layer of dirt. Then I leaned back and sat there, looking down at Sammi. A bloody gag covered her mouth. Her eyes were open, those beautiful violet orbs streaked with dirt and filled, not with shock or fear, but rage. A last snarl at the world that had ignored her.

Jack's fingers brushed my arm. I instinctively pulled back, then stopped, letting his fingertips rest there, warm against my cold skin, my jacket long since discarded.

"I didn't even like her," I whispered, staring down, trapped by the force of Sammi's final rage.

"You gave her a job."

"Because I felt sorry for her. She knew that and she hated it. Hated me for it. Can I blame her? That's all she ever got in her life. Pity and antipathy."

"First is better than the second."

"Is it?" I glanced up at him. "I could have helped her. Really helped her. Not just given her handouts and patted myself on the back for it. Girls like Sammi . . ." I shook my head and looked back at that paint-chipped toenail, unable to look at her eyes again. "People see a pretty girl with a short skirt and a big attitude, and they think they know her. They think they know the *type*. Girls like

Sammi...like Amy...People think they've got them all figured out."

His fingers wrapped around my forearm. "She's not Amy, Nadia."

"I know that," I snapped, yanking away. "I just meant that I knew better. I knew, from Amy, what it must have been like for Sammi. I could have done more."

"Didn't have to do anything."

I looked at him.

He shrugged. "Just saying..."

I knelt and started digging again.

"Nadia..."

"I need to find her."

He lowered himself beside me, awkwardly, struggling with the cast. "You know it's her. You don't need to—"

"Not Sammi. Her baby. I need to find her baby."

He nodded, straightened, and started scraping at the earth as I dug with my hands.

To Sammi's killer, the baby would have been inconsequential, a minor obstacle to be removed. Before he had his fun with Sammi, he'd have killed Destiny to silence her cries. To minimize effort, it would make sense to bury the baby's body in the same grave.

I dug down within an inch of Sammi's body, still wary of disturbing her, in case someone later found her. When I uncovered nothing on top of her, I dug on either side, going down until the earth went hard, less than a foot lower.

"Baby's not here," Jack said.

I stood and looked around.

"Nadia—"

I shook off his restraining hand. "There's only one

thing in the world Sammi cared about, Jack, and I'm not leaving until I give that back to her. Yes, I know, that doesn't make a lot of sense. But I need to, okay?" I tossed him the truck keys. "You go on, and I'll walk back."

He handed them back. "Let me help search."

I followed the killer's trail back to the road, being careful to watch for cars as we neared it, dousing the light when we heard one. We checked for disturbed earth, both on and beside his route. We hunted until the ground blurred and the trees shimmied, and I started stumbling over my own feet.

When I tripped over a fallen tree, Jack grabbed my arm, jerking me back to my feet.

"Baby's not here," he said.

"She has to—"

"Think about it. Already dug one hole. Why dig two? She's here? Gotta be in that hole."

"But I looked—" I stopped. "Under Sammi."

He nodded.

We returned to the site. Checking beneath Sammi meant fully uncovering and moving her body. I crawled over the hole, keeping my knees on opposite sides of her body and, wearing a fresh pair of gloves, I brushed away the final layer of dirt. When I was done, I backed off the shallow grave and looked down at her.

"What's wrong with this picture?" I murmured.

"You tell me," Jack said. "You're the cop. Were."

I jumped at the sound of his voice, having forgotten, yet again, that he was there. I told myself it was just that he was so quiet. The truth was, it wouldn't have mattered if he'd kept up a running commentary for the past few hours. My attention was focused entirely on Sammi.

"She's dressed," I said. "Fully dressed."

Some sexual predators did reclothe their victims. Behavioral experts saw that as a sign of remorse, the killer's twisted attempt to put everything back together, give their victims some final dignity. It was also often a sign of an opportunistic kill, where an inexperienced killer saw the perfect victim and acted on impulse. Yes, a beautiful teenage girl walking down a wooded road at dusk did make the perfect victim. But one with a baby stroller? A baby whose screams could give him away? And no inexperienced killer would have covered his tracks so well.

"Pants zipped, button done up, belt fastened," I mused. "I don't think he ever undressed her. So this isn't what it seems."

Jack only grunted.

I shook my head. Questions could wait.

When I reached to turn Sammi, Jack got on the other side, wordlessly helping. We lifted her and laid her to the side. I sifted through the disturbed earth.

"Destiny isn't here," I said.

Another grunt.

I turned to Sammi. Her hands were tied behind her with rope. I checked her feet. As I expected, there was no signs of binding. She'd been gagged, her hands bound, then shoved into the forest to the killing site. A gun at her head. Her killer forcing compliance by threatening to hurt Destiny? I pushed the scene from my head.

"Just because she wasn't raped, doesn't mean it wasn't sexual," I said, working it through. "He could get off on torture, mutilation . . . But there's no sign of that."

I lifted Sammi's shirt and saw only a bruise on her

shoulder. The splotches of blood on her shirtfront probably came from her nose, judging by the blood-soaked gag.

"Her nose looks broken. He hits her, she goes down, she's crouched over, nose streaming blood into the dirt back there. Then he subdues her and drags or carries her here. But why punch her in the nose? That's a fighting blow."

"Incapacitating."

I glanced back at Jack.

He shrugged. "Gotta stop someone from fighting back? Three spots. Two for a woman."

I nodded. "Nose, solar plexus, or, on a man, the groin. One sharp wallop and you deliver blinding pain. But if it's sexual, he'd pull a knife or beat the crap out of her. Maybe when she attacked him, he lashed out on impulse, right hook going straight for her nose. Point is, if that's where all the blood comes from, there wasn't any torture or mutilation. And how did he kill her?"

"How's her throat?"

Strangulation. Right. I checked.

"No marks, which doesn't completely rule it out, but..."

My gaze kept sliding back to her broken nose. Something wasn't right. Yes, it was definitely broken, but the angle was wrong. It was almost as if—

Using a tissue from my pocket and dew from the grass, I cleaned the strip of skin between Sammi's nose and her gag. There it was, an undeniable bullet hole, complete with muzzle burns. A gun pressed to her upper lip, trigger pulled.

"CNS shot," Jack grunted.

A bullet through the central nervous system. "But that's— That's not a thrill kill. That's . . . a professional hit."

A line of sweat dribbled down the side of my face. I swiped at it.

Why would anyone want Sammi dead?

In a passionless, efficient murder like this, the reason had to be equally cold and calculated. A professional hit is done for two reasons. First, you've wronged some very powerful people. But Sammi was just a kid living in small-town Ontario. She couldn't possibly have pissed off anyone with the clout to order a hit.

The second most common reason for hiring a professional killer is more common, and the one I won't deal with. Murder for personal gain. Have your wife killed for the insurance money. Your business partner for his shares. Your parents for your inheritance. Your romantic rival for a woman. But Sammi had nothing. The killer hadn't even emptied her wallet. Then, the truth hit me so hard I gasped.

Something *was* missing.

"The baby," I whispered.

Twelve

After we reburied Sammi the same way the killer had left her, Jack drove us back to the lodge. If I thought there was any chance he'd let me walk, I would have tried. Riding with him might mean having to talk about what we'd found, and I couldn't bear that.

I didn't need to worry. He never opened his mouth. Yet somehow that silence was worse. It sat, between us, a vacuum of words unsaid, sucking up the air in the cab. I inched as close to the door panel as I could get, staring out the side window, ticking off the seconds until the drive ended.

The landscape flew past so fast I wasn't even sure what road we were on. The truck jerked and swayed, struggling to keep a grip in the dirt. My head slammed into the seat as the tires found every rut. I knew if I looked over at Jack, I'd see him clutching the wheel, praying he could get us back before I broke down into tears, wondering how in God's name he'd been stupid enough to get mixed up with me again.

When we reached the lodge parking lot, he slammed on the brakes so hard, I'd have a seat belt bruise come morning. Then he just sat there, the engine idling, making no move to turn it off.

I reached for the door handle.

"You're not gonna call the cops," he said.

A statement, not a question. Informing the police was a perfectly logical next step, but my chest tightened at the very thought. Excuses rose to my lips. Maybe I'd left some trace evidence. An anonymous call was too risky—they'd figure the killer had an attack of conscience. And it'd fall under the White Rock OPP jurisdiction. Those guys couldn't find a killer if he left a blood trail to his house.

Excuses, and poor ones. Jack had made sure I'd left nothing. As for the call, he could make it, using any accent from a pay phone in Peterborough. And whatever I thought of the White Rock OPP, they wouldn't ignore a body.

What stopped me from making that call was the memory of Amy's death. My father and the other police thought they had an airtight case. They'd arrived on the scene moments after Amy died, before Drew Aldrich had a chance to run or hide evidence. And they had me, an eyewitness. They'd been so confident of a guilty verdict that they hadn't allowed me to testify in court, saving me from the hell of cross-examination.

Aldrich's defense had ripped their airtight case to shreds. My father and Amy's had rushed to the scene not as cops, but as grief-crazed relatives of the victim. They'd tried to follow procedure, but emotions had been running high and mistakes were made. What really happened, the attorney had argued, was kinky teen sex turned tragic.

Amy and Drew had sex. She'd wanted him to choke her—the jury got a lesson on breath control sex play. The innocent younger cousin looked in, saw what looked like her cousin being strangled and raped, and ran for help. Amy realized she'd been seen and, fearing punishment, lashed out, explaining cuts on Aldrich. He'd instinctively tightened his grip and accidentally killed her. Then her father and uncle, believing the younger cousin's story, fabricated evidence to support it.

Years later, examining the evidence, I couldn't believe the jury bought it. But they had. It fit their view of the world. Drew Aldrich was a decent young man who'd gotten mixed up with a wild teen seductress and let his hormones override his common sense. If he'd been the sadistic rapist killer the crown portrayed, surely he'd have done *something* to me. They just weren't buying the argument that he'd been planning to rape me, too, and I escaped before he could.

I'd watched Drew Aldrich walk away. I'd seen Amy denied justice. I wasn't letting that happen with Sammi. I didn't trust the White Rock police not to let their views of Sammi color their investigation. I *would* turn over this case, just as soon as I had the evidence needed to point them in the right direction and give them no excuse to shelve it.

I told Jack that—about needing evidence, not about Amy. He listened, then nodded, "Yeah. Probably a good idea."

I went for the door handle again.

"Wanna walk?" he said. "To the lake? Sit? Talk?"

"I've made up my mind, Jack—"

"Not about the cops. Just... talk. About what happened."

My shoulders tightened. The obligatory offer, made at the last possible moment so, if I hesitated, he could escape before I said "actually, that sounds good..."

"No, thank you," I said.

I opened the door.

"Nadia..."

I stopped.

"Think you should. *We* should. Take a walk. Talk or don't. Just . . . do something."

I looked over my shoulder, expecting to see him gripping the door handle, ready to make his escape. But he was turned my way, one hand on the wheel, the other a few inches from my leg. The offer sounded genuine and his eyes said it was. Hope fluttered.

"How about shooting? Grab a bottle. Make some bets." A crooked half-smile. "Chance to win back your fifty bucks?"

That flicker of hope folded in on itself and curled up in the pit of my stomach. Last fall, after a hellish night when Wilkes had escaped us—only to kill another victim—Jack had taken me shooting at night, some anonymous strip of forest in Illinois, just the two of us, skeet-shooting beer cans as we chugged whiskey. Supposedly he'd been teaching me how to compensate for being intoxicated. An excuse—one that had fallen through quickly the drunker we got, goofing around, joking and betting, blowing off steam.

No one had ever done something like that for me before. No one had ever known me well enough to know it was exactly what I'd needed. Over the next few days, Jack had let down his guard enough to give me glimpses into his past, and I realized he'd already seen beyond my barriers, looked at that part of myself I kept so carefully hidden.

He'd seen the worst in me, and it didn't change anything. Or so it seemed at the time. Later I realized he'd only tried to help me that night because he'd needed me focused and on track, watching his back. The minute the job was over, he couldn't get away fast enough.

Now, here again was that same Jack, considerate and understanding, ready to do whatever it took to snap me out of this. But this time, I knew it wasn't because he gave a rat's ass how Sammi's death affected me, but because he was trapped. He was hiding out at the lodge, and he needed me focused and on track, watching his back.

Without a word, I opened the door and climbed out. He didn't follow.

I sat on my bed, hugging my knees, still dressed, watching the hours flip past. I didn't dare lie down for fear I'd sleep. With sleep would come the nightmares.

I'd woken Jack with them twice last fall and wouldn't risk it again. I considered sneaking downstairs for a roll of duct tape. I'd done that once, when I'd been desperate, but the off-chance that Jack might catch me made me stop. Sleeping with duct tape over your mouth? Crazy woman behavior.

The nightmares were always the same. I was running through an endless forest, trying in vain to get home, get my dad, save Amy. I hear Drew Aldrich right behind me, getting closer as the forest's edge stretched ever farther away.

That part never happened—he didn't chase me; he'd been too busy raping Amy in the cabin. I'd peered around the corner, seen him on her, heard her muffled screams, and I'd run. Left her there and run away. Left her to die. Saved myself.

A parade of therapists have tried to tell me otherwise. I'd been going for help, as I'd been taught, and that was the right thing to do. Everyone told me I'd done the smart thing—my father, Amy's father, even my mother had snapped, "Of course, you should have run. Don't be stupid."

I'd done what my father and every cop in our family had taught me from the time I was old enough to set foot outside alone. If anything happens, try to get away. Don't fight unless you absolutely have to. Run for help. Let us look after the rest.

I'd gotten help, but not in time. In the aftermath of Amy's death, I'd clung to that promise: let us look after the rest. Justice would be done, one way or another. Only it wasn't. Aldrich went free and all those cops who'd made me that promise let him walk away.

And justice for none.

Even as I considered ways to anonymously alert someone to Sammi's body, I heard the whispers of the past.

Is anyone really surprised?

Oh, I don't mean Amy brought this on herself, but . . .

Did you see the way she dressed? Only fourteen, flirting with everything in pants. And a cop's daughter no less. A Stafford. If they couldn't teach her better, no one could.

Some girls . . .

I'm not saying she brought it on herself . . .

I don't think Drew ever meant to hurt her. Things just got out of hand.

Now if it had been Nadia . . .

Yes, if it had been Nadia . . . There's a good girl. So polite. So helpful. A Stafford through and through. But he never touched her. That says something right there, doesn't it? Amy, with her tight skirts and her makeup . . .

Some girls . . .

Made to be broken.

I could drag Don Riley to Sammi's grave, show him her body, and it wouldn't change what he—and all of White Rock—thought of her. If there was any investigation, it would be quick, halfhearted at best.

As for Destiny, they'd claim she was somewhere in those woods. No one in White Rock was going to waste investigative efforts finding another Ernst brat. Right now, the only person who cared who killed her was the one who'd discovered her body.

Finding justice for Sammi wouldn't change what I'd done to Amy. But I could try.

At six, as my exhausted mind skated the border between reality and dreamland, the answer hit me and I jolted awake, certain I knew what had happened to Destiny.

The identity of Destiny's father was no mystery in White Rock. Sammi had been far from the perfect teen, but she could be counted on never to repeat her mother's mistakes, which meant she didn't screw every boy who looked her way. She had one boyfriend the year she got pregnant: Trent Drayton, whose parents owned the best land in the White Rock area.

When Destiny was born, it didn't take a genius to count back nine months and realize she'd been conceived when Trent had been spending Christmas holidays at the cottage. Even Mr. and Mrs. Drayton knew who Destiny's daddy was, though they'd spent all year threatening to sic their lawyer on anyone who said so. The family never paid a cent in support, and I suppose Sammi was too proud to claim Destiny's birthright. As for Trent, he'd been shipped off to UBC last fall after his father had found him a summer job in Vancouver.

The story sounds terribly romantic: rich boy, poor girl, star-crossed lovers...Not Sammi. She'd been raised to survive, not fantasize. When she met Trent, I'm pretty sure what she saw wasn't a prep-school Romeo, but her meal ticket out of White Rock. It's equally likely that Destiny's conception was no accident.

I'm not speaking ill of the dead. I could imagine being in Sammi's shoes, living in that house, a lifetime of Janie and her abuse, trapped in a nowhere town where everyone expects you to end up a drunken whore like your mother and her mother before her. God gave Sammi one asset: beauty. She'd be a fool not to use it, and Sammi was no fool—just a screwed-up kid with dreams of escaping the future everyone predicted for her.

So who would want Destiny? Trent Drayton's parents. After all, she was their granddaughter, white-trash mommy or not. How many times had they been to town since last fall and accidentally bumped into Sammi and their granddaughter? Seen her in worn hand-me-downs and a rusty stroller? Seen her going in and out of that hovel Sammi called home? With Sammi, Destiny had the most loving and attentive mother a child could want, but people like Frank and Lauren Drayton wouldn't see that. They'd see their flesh and blood growing up in poverty.

Sure, they could give Sammi some money and set her up in Peterborough, where they lived. But that would mean dealing with Sammi herself, treating her like a real person.

Taking Destiny legally was tricky. They'd need to prove Sammi was an unfit mother, which she wasn't. In the end, the Draytons would probably blow a huge wad of cash on legal fees only to be court-ordered to follow option one: providing for Sammi and her baby.

Why not spend that money on a more permanent solution? Get rid of Sammi for good, make it look like she'd run away, then tell the authorities that she'd handed Destiny to them on her way to a new life. Get some legal documents quietly drawn up, pay Janie to sign over her rights, and, boom, Frank and Lauren Drayton have adopted a beautiful baby girl.

I'd like to think no one would ever do such a thing. But I know better. There are people out there right now trying to find out how they can hire a hitman for jobs just like this. Got a problem? Put a bullet through it.

By seven, I was pulling out of the driveway heading to Peterborough.

Thirteen

Finding the Drayton home required nothing more than locating an area phone book. At a population of 130,000, Peterborough was still the kind of city where its wealthiest residents didn't fear putting their full names and addresses in the White Pages.

Locally, the Draytons were a big name. They owned Drayton Windows and Doors—a manufacturing plant that was one of the city's leading employers. By leading, I mean in terms of number of residents employed, not in wages or working conditions. I had a regular guest who worked at Drayton's factory and, for him and his wife, a weekend at the Red Oak was their only vacation. The nonunionized plant paid ten bucks an hour, a mere two dollars over the provincial minimum wage. Benefits included a discount on factory seconds and not much else.

Given the working conditions, one could assume that business was struggling and their only choice was to pay these low wages or shut down and put everyone out of work. But, having seen the Draytons' cottage, I strongly suspected their year-round residence wasn't going to be a modest bungalow.

The address led me a few kilometers beyond the official city limits. A stone wall marked the boundary between road and estate, but it wasn't more than three feet high—for show, not for privacy. No gate blocked the driveway. A metal grille was embedded at the end of the cement drive to keep the free-roaming horses in. On either side of the drive, a large brass plaque proclaimed The

Draytons. If I lived in a place like this and kept my employees hovering on the poverty line, I'd be ashamed to put my name on the mailbox. But that's just me.

Beyond the gates, a lawn stretched over several acres. In the middle were two ponds, separated by a wooden bridge. In one, a fountain jetted into the sky. The other had a gazebo and a wooden dock with a paddle boat. Yes, the pond was big enough for a paddle boat.

Horses roamed free in the yard. Seeing that, I felt the first sting of envy. Not that I'm a horse person. I ride now and then, and have even considered rescuing a couple of dog-food-bound nags for the lodge, but I wouldn't count horse-ownership among my lifelong dreams. And, being practical, I'm not sure I'd want horses—and horse shit—in my front yard. Still, seeing the horses roaming free, it was like the picture-perfect image of wealthy country living, the kind you only see in Lotto 6/49 ads.

Behind the ponds, at the end of the winding concrete driveway, stood the house—a two-story stone country manor with a wraparound porch and huge bay windows. L-shaped, it was set at a forty-five-degree angle to the road, so the full size was proudly displayed to anyone drooling from his car.

To be fair, I should point out that the Draytons were renowned philanthropists in Peterborough. Every year, their company donated an entire thousand dollars to the United Way. And at Christmas, according to my guests, they held an employee skating party on their ponds and served free hot chocolate and day-old donuts. For this event, they rented Port-a-Poos, so no snowy-booted kids traipsed through the house. I understood the precaution. If I was an employee, I'd find as many excuses as possible to use the indoor washroom, accidentally spill hot chocolate on the Oriental carpet, and mash jelly donut on the spa towels.

Next door to the Drayton estate, a gravel driveway led to an empty lot separated from the estate by a stand of pines. I drove up it and parked behind the trees. From here, you could see that the driveway had once led to a house. The bones of the foundation poked up beneath a blanket of sod, like a prehistoric skeleton waiting to be unearthed. A small house, not more than a thousand square feet. Not exactly the Draytons' ideal neighbors, I'm sure. They'd probably bought out the residents and demolished the house.

My plan was simple: break in and look for signs of a baby. Like I've said, I didn't know much about babies, except that they needed their own special everything, from car seats to beds to bathing products. Breaking into the Drayton home, though, would be a big step up from illegally entering the Ernst residence. You spend this kind of money on a house and you might as well advertise in the *Thieves Home Journal*: "Hey, we got stuff, and lots of it," meaning the Draytons probably couldn't even get insurance without an alarm system.

Whatever the security features, though, I couldn't wait until dark. At night, Frank Drayton and the kids would be home. I needed to get in now and see proof that they had Destiny.

The house and garage backed onto forest, remnants of the former conservation area. All the lawn was up front, where people could admire it. The problem with this, as any security-conscious person could tell you, was that all an intruder had to do was cut through the forest and come out within a few feet of the Draytons' back door.

Minutes later, I was behind their garage, which was a miniature of the house, complete with large windows along the sides and back. Security tip number two: do not put windows on a garage. Why would you? Do you read the morning paper in there? All you've done is provide window-shopping for the casual thief. One glimpse inside the garage assured me that there were no cars present, which meant no one was home, the Draytons not being a one-car kind of family.

Getting past the security system was easy. They had one that kept people from opening the doors, but didn't do jack shit for the big bay windows at the back, left open on this sunny spring day.

I selected the back window farthest from the garage-side door and pulled on a pair of latex gloves. When the screen was out, I pushed the window up as far as it would go, hoisted myself inside, then replaced the screen and closed the window to the six-inch opening.

I inhaled and looked around. I was in a main-floor laundry, with the kitchen to my right.

On the drive, I'd compiled a mental list of all the baby items I could think of. If the Draytons hadn't gone public with their new baby yet, they might hide the obvious things like a crib or baby toys, but could easily slip up when it came to dirty clothing or bottles. A quick flip through the laundry baskets revealed no obvious baby clothes, so I moved on to the kitchen.

I checked the dishwasher for bottles, and the fridge and cupboards for baby food.

From the kitchen I moved through the dining room,

doing a quick visual scan for any kind of feeding chair, then into the living room and family room, searching for toys or a playpen. In the center of the family room I stopped and inhaled. For someone unaccustomed to babies, the scent is obvious, be it spit-up or a wet diaper or baby shampoo and talcum powder. Here I smelled only wood cleaner, potpourri, and stale popcorn.

Next stop: the home office. I shuffled through papers, memos, and recent check stubs. While a check written to a hitman would clinch it nicely, no one would be stupid enough to leave such a thing lying around. What I looked for was anything with a baby connection—adoption forms or a receipt for baby supplies or the scribbled number of a local judge. When nothing suspicious popped up, I headed for the stairs.

The pin-neat bed and light layer of dust on the sports trophies told me the first bedroom belonged to Trent.

I glanced in the en suite bathroom, then moved on. The next hall door led to a walk-in closet with more towels and linens than we kept for the whole lodge, but no baby supplies. On to the main bath, where I checked for baby shampoos or diapers.

Across from the bathroom was another bedroom, this one belonging to a teenage girl. Trent's sister. Again, I performed only a basic survey, in case a stray infant toy had been dropped behind the bed or in the suite. Nothing.

I looked more carefully in the guest room, in case they were using it as a makeshift nursery. No crib, no baby linens, no empty bottle kicked under the bed. And no baby smell.

The door across the hall was closed. I touched the handle, then noticed the master suite at the end of the hall.

This room must belong to the younger brother. I'd have more luck with the master suite, so I moved on for now.

In Frank and Lauren's bedroom, I checked all the places someone could stash notes and receipts and scribbled phone numbers. No sign of a baby or anything connected to babyhood or adoption. I pulled a chair to the closet and looked on the top shelf.

Finally, standing on the chair, looking at stacks of dusty photo albums, I had to admit it. There was no baby here. My brain popped back with "yes, but you could check bank records, phone records..." I was grasping at straws, unwilling to relinquish my one and only idea. I should have thought it through—

A noise cut me off in midthought. Not a car in the drive or a key turning in a door lock. A toilet flushing.

Fourteen

Rule one of breaking and entering: check the goddamned house for people.

The first tingle of alarm quickly evaporated. I wanted answers? Here was my source. I knew the Draytons had Destiny. What better proof than a confession? The toilet flush had come from downstairs. Either Lauren had returned, or she'd never left. As I crept to the hall doorway, I pulled out my gun. Then I concentrated on listening.

Footsteps padded across the hardwood floor. I ran a quick mental inventory on my knapsack. None of my supplies could be used for binding, but I'd seen bandage rolls in the main bathroom. They'd do.

A squeak came from below. A chair being reclined. Perfect. Lauren was relaxing, probably with a book or magazine, enjoying her morning coffee. I could slip up behind, put the gun to her head, and she'd never see me. I'd take the bandages, but only as a last resort. With someone like Lauren, the cold steel of a gun pressing against the back of her neck would be enough.

I took three steps toward the main bathroom.

"Mom?"

My heart slammed into my throat and I stopped so fast my shoe squeaked on the wood.

"Mom!" A racking cough, then a muttered, "How long does it take her to pick up medicine?"

The younger son, home from school, sick. No problem. He'd still know what happened to Destiny. I'd just—

The image flashed in my mind. Pressing the gun to the head of a teenage boy.

My God, what was I thinking?

I took a deep breath.

Destiny wasn't here. If she was, I would have found something. She wasn't here and the Draytons probably didn't have anything to do with her disappearance, and I'd been ready to hold a teenage boy at gunpoint to prove it.

I crept back into the master bedroom and looked out the window, which overlooked the back of the house. There was a two-foot-wide overhang between floors, more architectural than structural, and I wasn't sure whether it would hold my weight.

I removed the screen then slid through the open window, grasped the window sill, and lowered myself until my feet touched wood. Still gripping the ledge, I tested my weight on the overhang. Next I maneuvered the screen back into place. An imperfect job, one I hoped would be blamed on the cleaning staff.

Footsteps stomped up the stairs. I ducked beneath the sill, listened. A door slammed as the boy retreated to his room.

I crouched on the overhang and looked at the ten-foot drop. If I broke my ankle, it'd serve me right. I hit the ground hard, but straight, then I hightailed it back to my truck.

An amateur's mistake. I'd been so busy laughing at the Draytons' lack of security I hadn't taken the most basic precautions.

Sure it had been a sound lead. But even if I could

believe Frank Drayton would hire a hitman to kill his granddaughter's teenage mother, I had to consider the *kind* of hit it had been. Professional. That required someone like Jack or me, and to get us you needed top-notch, Mafia-grade criminal connections. When your average Joe hires someone to off a lover or business partner, he ends up with semicompetent drug-addled morons.

I remember a case from the eighties. Helmuth Buxbaum. I once went on a Sunday-school trip to his house, to swim in the indoor pool. A true pillar of the church. When his wife started interfering with his nightlife of cocaine and hookers, he decided to get rid of her. So, for twenty-five thousand dollars—a decent sum, I might add—he got himself the Beavis and Butt-Head of hired killers. They arranged for Buxbaum to be driving past with his wife while they feigned car trouble. He'd pull over and they'd shoot her. First time they tried it, Buxbaum pulled over right on schedule. So did a helpful OPP officer.

They tried it again. Using the exact same plan. Ten hours later. With the same car. On the same highway.

That time, they managed to kill Buxbaum's wife. And guess what? The OPP officer had called in the earlier stop, as per procedure. Didn't take much to put two and two together, and come up with three complete idiots. Buxbaum, the killer, and the getaway driver were caught and convicted, though the getaway driver admitted he recalled little of what happened that day because he'd been dead drunk. Yes, drunk. On a hit. These are the kind of criminal masterminds the average millionaire businessman can hire.

Who could have hired a pro to kill Sammi? Who

would? That question put me right back at square one. Why would anyone who didn't have a direct interest in Destiny's welfare kidnap her and kill her mother?

I was in a motor sports shop getting parts for the ATVs— my alibi for the trip into the city. When I realized I needed the exact specs, I took out my cell phone, which I'd had switched to "answer only" during the break-and-enter, and saw I had four calls and two new messages from the lodge.

If Emma just wanted me to grab something, she'd call once. Last year, I'd been in town when we'd had a small fire, from a guest throwing his cigarette into a brush pile, and Emma had only called twice. Four times meant… Hell, I couldn't even imagine what it meant.

I hit speed-dial so fast my fingers punched the wrong button and I had to try again. Finally the call went through, straight to voice mail, meaning someone was on the line. I jammed the end and redial buttons in rapid succession. Too fast for the phone apparently. With a growl of frustration, I slowed down, only to get the busy signal again.

I disconnected and flew through the keys to retrieve my messages. The first began with at least five seconds of silence. My heart jammed in my throat, picturing Emma in the midst of a heart attack, struggling to speak. Then, "God-fucking-damn it."

A click as Jack hung up. The second message began right away, Jack again.

"Nadia? Where are you? Fuck." Click.

The last two calls had come after those. Jack, I was sure.

Shit.

Did I really expect him to buy the "I ran into town early to grab those parts" excuse?

To be honest, I hadn't even factored Jack into the equation. Like I hadn't factored in the possibility of someone being in the house.

Last night, I'd been furious at his suggestion that I was obsessing over Sammi, that in my determination to find her, I'd get sloppy, maybe do something stupid... like fly off chasing the first lead that came to mind, and break into a house mid-morning without checking for occupants.

I called the lodge again. Emma answered. I hesitantly inquired after "John."

"I think he's outside on the porch," she said. "Do you want to talk to him?"

"No, no. That's fine. If he asks, just tell him I'll be back in an hour. What I really called for was that part list. I forgot it in my room. Could you ask Owen what we need again?"

As I parked, there was no sign of Jack. I took the parts to Owen in the shop, talked to Emma, and learned that the first batch of guests had paid for early check-in and were expected for lunch. Still no Jack.

Half of the weekend's guests had specifically requested shooting lessons, which meant probably three-quarters would want them—others would hear their stories at meal times and decide they wanted to give it a shot... so to speak. So I could hide out at the range until lunch, checking equipment.

There are two paths to the range: a shortcut through the woods and a scenic route past Crescent Lake. I took the latter to run a quick inventory on the boathouse, this being our first full house since spring thaw. Two lifejackets had been chewed by mice, and replacements were already on order at Canadian Tire, but unless every guest decided to join the sunset canoe ride, we'd be fine.

When I reached the junction between the main path to the range and the lake route, there was Jack leaning on his crutch, blocking my way.

"Where were you?" he said.

I was tempted to say "the boathouse," but knew that wasn't what he meant, and he wouldn't appreciate having to expend more words to get the proper response.

"Following a lead," I said as I brushed past him.

"What lead?"

I considered speeding up. With his injury, I could easily outrun him. But speed wasn't Jack's style at the best of times. I could escape him all day, and I'd wake up tomorrow morning, sit down to breakfast, and have him plant himself across from me, asking the same question.

I eased back. "Whatever you're hiding out from, it's bigger than you're letting on, isn't it?"

His face screwed up in an unspoken "Huh?"

"I won't press for details. The point is that if you need me here, I'll stick around as much as possible. Yes, I am a little preoccupied, but I've got your back."

He stared at me, dark brows creasing over a deep furrow. "You think . . . ?" His lips worked, as if he hadn't yet figured out how to finish the sentence. "No one's coming after me, Nadia. It's not…" He rubbed the back of his neck. "It's not like that. You want to know? I'll explain later. But watching my back?" He shook his head. "I'm trying to watch yours. Only this—" He knocked his crutch against the cast. "Slows me down."

"I don't need your help, Jack. Let's—" I pulled my hands from my pockets and leaned against a maple tree, the bark cold under my fingers. "Let's cut through the bullshit, okay?"

"Bullshit?"

"The only reason you're here is because you needed a place to go, and I was the only one offering. So now you're stuck, and you feel obligated to at least pretend everything's the way it used to be. Maybe you think that'll make the situation more comfortable, but it doesn't. You're a paying guest; you don't need to make nice, okay?"

"Make nice?" The words rolled out awkwardly, as if he didn't recognize them. A soft sigh as he repositioned his crutch. "Been a while since I called. But—"

"You were going to. When, Jack? This week? Next?"

He rubbed his mouth. In the silence that followed, I inhaled through my mouth, the air suddenly too thin.

You stupid twit. You were still hoping, weren't you? Still praying it was all a big misunderstanding.

"I would've called," he said finally. "Wouldn't just… leave."

"You don't owe me anything, Jack, especially explanations. But don't insult me by pretending, okay? There was never any obligation, and I always knew that someday you'd stop coming around."

"Didn't—" He shifted his stance, moving the crutch in

front again. "Didn't stop coming around. Just...Stuff came up. My stuff. Nothing to do with you. Didn't think you'd—" A roll of his shoulders. "Didn't think."

My face heated and I raked my hair back, trying to cover my blush without turning away. I sounded like a spurned lover.

In the first year, months had often passed without word from Jack. But after that, he'd called or stopped by at least once a month.

Jack lived a solitary life. Always had, as far as I could tell. If a job came up that demanded all his attention, he'd give it all his attention, never stopping to say, "Oh, I should check in with Nadia." Whatever hang-ups I had about rejection and abandonment, I'd better learn to keep them to myself, or I *would* scare him away.

"I should—" I straightened and brushed bark bits from my hands. "I was going to check the range before my guests arrive. I have a lot of sign-ups this weekend. You can go on back to the house or down to the lake, enjoy the peace and quiet while you can."

I made it three steps.

"What happened?" he asked.

I stopped.

"Today. Something went wrong."

I didn't turn, just gave a tight squeak of a laugh. "I screwed up. Big surprise, huh? I stayed up all night, thinking about Sammi, and about..."

"Amy."

I kept my voice even. "I decided I knew who'd taken Destiny, flew off half-cocked, and screwed up. Just like you expected."

A sharp intake of breath, cut off at the midpoint. "What'd you do?"

"It was like Wilkes in that alley. I saw my target and that was all that mattered."

His hand closed around my arm. "We'll fix it, Nadia. Just tell me—"

I shook my head as I turned. "There's nothing to fix. I broke into Destiny's dad's house, certain his parents had killed Sammi to get their granddaughter. I didn't take proper precautions. Their younger son was home from school. A stupid, amateur's mistake."

His fingers trembled against my arm as he exhaled and released me. "That's it, then?"

"What did you think—?" I stopped, pretty sure I didn't want an answer. "Yes, that's it."

"So this kid saw you—"

"I'm not *that* careless. I got out before he knew I was there."

"Before you could case the place."

"No, I did that. No sign of a baby in residence."

One brow lifted. "So your big mistake? Going into an occupied house? That's it?" A short laugh as he shook his head.

"Hey, that's embarrassing enough."

"Kinda like this." He waved at his foot. "Didn't fuck up the job. Still feel like an idiot."

"Can I ask what happened?"

"Rather you didn't."

"Ah . . ."

"I'm kidding. Tell you later. Right now? Got a range to get ready."

Fifteen

Jack helped me check the guns and put away the "non-civilian" equipment—the human-form targets, exotic guns, and gadgets I reserved for my military and law-enforcement guests. As we worked, I told him my theory about Destiny's grandparents. He didn't think I should be so quick to dismiss it, nor did I need to be so quick to pursue it. If the Draytons had Destiny, she wasn't in any danger, and the longer I waited, the more likely they were to appear in public with their new granddaughter, saving me the work of proving they had her.

I considered contacting the Peterborough police and notifying them about Sammi's disappearance, maybe suggest the Draytons had Destiny. But I knew how the department would treat an anonymous, proof-free tip like that, particularly an accusation against one of the most powerful families in the region. They might not ignore it, but I'd get a much better response if I had some proof, so that's what I was going to get.

I couldn't chase down that lead—or any others—for a while, though. With a full house, I was bound to the lodge for a few days, which would give me time to clear my head and come up with other ideas.

Our lunch guests were a quartet of widows who would look to Owen for most of their recreational needs, wanting nothing more strenuous than bird-watching. I'd taught many a seventy-year-old to shoot—both guns and

rapids—but these four made it clear they were here to relax and commune with nature.

After lunch, Jack suggested we retire to the range. A
good idea, one that would help *me* relax. Marksmanship
requires concentration, and I couldn't do it while thinking about dead teenage girls and kidnapped babies.

I'd taken up the sport after Amy's death. It was my father's idea—maybe because he realized how badly I
needed to feel in control.

In distance shooting, I found my talent and my salva-
tion. It took hard work—memorizing ballistics tables,
learning to accommodate changes in climate and envi-
ronment—but if I put in the effort, I could guarantee
success. Life isn't like that.

We took rifles to the outside range, a thousand-foot
strip of meadow with targets.

I usually practice in the offhand—standing—position,
because that's the one I'm most likely to encounter on the
job. But Jack's ankle gave me an excuse to lie down in the
more stable prone position.

Though Jack preferred simple, close-contact hits,
sniping is a skill every decent hitman needs, and he always took advantage of the opportunity to learn more
from me. It was the one way I could repay him for all his
advice.

He tried a few shots at the farthest target, but missed
the mark entirely, and challenged me. He knew I could hit
it—I wouldn't have it there if I couldn't—but when he
watched through the binoculars as I hit the bull's-eye, he
shook his head.

"Fucking amazing."

"Under controlled circumstances and on a perfect day. I wouldn't dare try that far on a hit."

"Don't be so quick. Shouldn't grandstand, sure. But if it's the only decent shot? On a boat maybe? Never dismiss it."

"I suppose so . . ."

"Can't always have absolutes, Nadia."

I nodded. He pulled his rifle back to reload.

"Gun like this?" he said. "Makes even me look good."

"You like that one? I picked it up used from someone who'd fired no more than a few dozen rounds with it. It's a Sako .308—almost as old as I am, but it's in A1 condition. It shoots 1/2 MOA already, so I've avoided the temptation to tinker." I laughed. "I know that means little or nothing to you, but it's a sweet piece."

"It is." He slid the rifle back into position. "Speaking of sweet . . . Ever heard of a corner gun?"

"Oooh, yes. It's not actually a gun, but a device that holds a pistol. You can put a Glock in the end, fold it ninety degrees, then aim using an attached videocam to shoot around a corner. Now that would be sweet. Strictly government sales only, though."

"Want one?"

"Seriously?"

"Felix."

Felix—less colloquially known as Phoenix—was a political assassin, a quiet, professorial man with a passion for high-tech gadgetry.

"If he has one, I'd consider buying it, but I suspect it's way out of my price range."

"Got one for you. At a stash. Check it out. Probably

shoots worth shit. But . . ." He shrugged. "Can't dismiss it. If it works? You can show me."

In other words, he'd give me the gun if I'd test it out, train on it, then teach him how to use it.

"Got some other stuff, too," he said.

"Toys from Felix?"

"Yeah. Always pushing 'em on me. Can't be bothered. Take what you want. Got some surveillance stuff, too. Cameras and shit."

I sat up sharply. "The photographer—" I stopped. "Sorry. That made me think of Sammi again."

"Go on."

"Remember I mentioned that photographer who'd taken pictures? They were shots of Destiny, not Sammi, right? I should get more details from Tess." I checked my watch. "She's usually at the liquor store after four. We can always use more beer, maybe some extra wine. I'll make a run into town later and—" I clipped the word off and shook my head, then lowered myself to the ground again.

"She work tomorrow?"

"All day, but it can wait—"

"Go then. Schedule around it."

I wanted to protest that I could wait until Sunday, but knew by then I'd be ready to pack for my guests and valet their cars to the door. Postponing it to tomorrow would slow me down enough.

My next wave of guests arrived as Jack and I returned to the lodge.

Check-in time is four, but we don't stick to that. Those who arrive hours early, though, usually have the courtesy to acknowledge it and ask whether their room is ready. The Previls waltzed in at two, dropped their bags at Jack's feet, and told Emma she could serve them cocktails down by the lake.

The Previls, as I soon learned, were fraternal twin brothers who, when given the chance to celebrate their fortieth birthday any way they wished, had decided on a weekend wilderness retreat with their wives and two other couples. They started their visit by presenting an itinerary of everything they needed me for, half of which they hadn't requested pre-check-in. It included pretty much everything we offered, from canoeing to rafting to rock-climbing . . . for guys who'd showed up in golf shirts and looked as if they'd never set foot anyplace wilder than the eighth-hole rough.

Their wives took in their rustic surroundings with no effort to conceal their horror, and I had a feeling they'd spend most of the weekend nursing bottomless glasses of wine and consoling themselves with the thought that such martyrdom would surely earn them a weekend at the spa.

An hour later, the other two couples joined them. One of the men was a childhood friend. The second was an employee who I suspected had been promoted to buddy status for the weekend, probably as a substitute for a cash bonus. The employee and his wife seemed more polite than the others, though at this point, I'd seize on a half-hearted "thanks" as a ray of hope.

Jack retreated to his room with a mumbled "Need me? Be upstairs." I suspected if I *did* need help, it would take a lot of banging on his door to get a response. Owen slipped away with the widows for a nature hike. Emma had to cook dinner—though it was one time when I'd have gladly taken the chore for her. Instead, I took the Previl twins and their friends on a canoe trip, a deep-woods hike, and a brief visit to the cave system...all before dinner.

Jack was a no-show for the meal. Smart man.

The last guests had arrived before dinner. They were a young honeymooning couple who'd assured us they wouldn't be taking advantage of any of the activities, presumably having their own to keep them busy.

We eat family style, at two large tables. In warmer weather, there's the option of dining by the lake or on the patio. After twenty minutes of listening to the Previl wives chirp and twitter about the food—oh my God, is that iceberg lettuce? And *fried* chicken?—the widow quartet decided to brave the elements and have their dessert outside.

After dinner, I offered the first shooting lesson to the Previl party. As I predicted, they couldn't care less about *learning* how to shoot. But when it comes to the dangerous sports, I have a rule: you don't listen, you don't do it. Not that I can say that out loud. I just drag out the lesson until "Oh, would you look at the time..."

Next on the schedule was a night-forest walk that I'd promised the widows. The Previls were very put out, even when I explained it was too dark for anything else. When I firmly told them that I had a prior commitment, they wanted to know why "that porter guy" couldn't take them on an excursion. I pointed out "that porter guy" was on crutches, and was a guest, not an employee. They stalked off, muttering among themselves.

After the walk, I managed to sneak to my room for an

hour of downtime before the bonfire. I spent it on my laptop, searching for crimes similar to Sammi's murder.

I started by searching for homicides in Ontario that mentioned an infant. After skimming through several cases of child abuse and young mothers killing their new-born infants, all I could think about was how many couples would have loved to have those kids. Instead they were born to people who shouldn't be allowed within spitting distance of children.

I revised my search to recent Ontario homicides of teenagers that also mentioned an infant. Most were mishits, things like movies about homicide, teens, and babies.

Once I'd winnowed out those, I was left with only four cases of murdered teens. Three involved teenage mothers being killed by their boyfriends—open-and-shut cases of domestic violence in which the baby hadn't been touched. In the fifth, a teenage mother had been raped and murdered, her body dumped in a wooded lot. I plugged the girl's name into the search engine for more details.

After twenty minutes, I knew this case had nothing to do with mine. Besides the obvious differences of the rape and body dump, the eighteen-year-old had left a bar with a stranger, while her infant son was safely with her mother.

A rap sounded at my door, accompanied by Jack's gruff "Me." I started closing my laptop, lips parting to call "just a minute." Then I stopped myself.

Hiding my research from Jack implied I shouldn't be doing it. So I called him in. When his gaze went straight to the laptop, I braced myself.

"Looking stuff up?" he asked.

I explained.

"Good idea."

A soft exhale as I realized I'd been holding my breath. While I inwardly railed at the suggestion I needed Jack's approval, I did, if only to gauge whether I was slipping into obsession.

He offered to continue digging for me while I hosted the bonfire.

"I'm not late, am I?" A watch check before he could answer. "No, I have another half hour."

"Yeah. But those brothers? Getting a little eager. Started looking for the axe."

I leapt to my feet. "Why didn't you say so?"

A laconic shrug. "Got insurance, don't you?"

I glowered at him and raced out the door.

Sixteen

"Got some kind of message," Jack said when I returned after the bonfire. "Popped up on your screen. From 'back-doorman.'"

"Oh, that's—"

"Quinn. Yeah. Figured that out."

Last fall, in coming up with online names, that's what Quinn had picked—a private joke. I didn't think Jack had been paying attention, but I guessed I should have known better. Nothing escaped him.

"Did you, uh, respond . . ."

"Didn't know how."

Which was probably a good thing. Jack may have invited Quinn on the job last year, but only because he needed his contacts. Jack thought Quinn was too brash, too fervent, too open. Quinn found exactly the opposite faults with Jack—too somber, too cold, too secretive. The only thing they agreed on was that the other could be trusted and was good at his job . . . as long as he did that job someplace else, with some*one* else.

"So you gonna tell me? About that job?"

"Job? Oh right, the Toronto one I did with him. Give me a minute and we'll go outside. I just want to pop him a note."

I motioned for him to sit on the bed as I checked my e-mail. There was one from Quinn. I started a brief response. Then my messenger pinged. Quinn, noticing I was still online and trying again. I answered, planning to say I had to run, but he asked if I'd seen the latest on the "rapist killer" case and I said I hadn't and . . . the conversation snowballed from there. After about five minutes, Jack stood and cleared his throat.

"I'll be outside," he said.

"Hold on. I just—"

"No rush."

The door closed behind him.

Jack's online search had gone better than mine. He'd substituted missing for homicide, looking for cases of young women who'd disappeared with their babies. He'd had to wade through lots of custody disputes and suspected homicides, where the infant had likely been killed, intentionally or through abuse, then the body hidden and never recovered. Once the chaff was removed, he was left with three cases.

I took the names and searched. One case ended tragically, with a newspaper article revealing that mother and child had been found in a river—an apparent suicide brought on by postpartum depression. In the second, six months after disappearing, the mother showed up at a homeless shelter, then took off in the middle of the night, abandoning her baby. That left me with Deanna Macy.

I found multiple listings for her on missing-persons Web sites, but no resolution, happy or otherwise. With her dark hair and eyes, she was the physical opposite of Sammi, but like Sammi, Deanna Macy was a startlingly beautiful young woman. Coincidence?

I scanned through the details. Sixteen years old. Last known residence: a home for teen mothers, indicating little or no family support. The home was in Detroit—she'd been listed on Canadian sites in case she'd crossed the border.

At the time of her disappearance, her baby, Connor, had been a few weeks younger than Destiny. One evening Deanna and Connor had been taking the bus to see a friend. They never arrived. According to the bus driver, they'd never got on. The police were treating the case as a runaway, but the woman who'd notified the police was convinced otherwise.

The contact was Denise Noyes, with a Detroit-area phone number. From her emotional pleas, Noyes had to be a friend or family member. I didn't want to make this call from the lodge, so I'd do it tomorrow, when I was in town to see Tess.

Saturday started at 6 a.m. with my jog. The Previls had signed up, and while I was tempted to say, "I knocked and no one answered," I had to do my job—so I knocked... lightly. They answered. And they made their wives join us to share in a "romantic country run," which I'm sure would have been far more romantic if the guys hadn't spent the time commenting on my "form" and making indiscreet inquiries into the state of *my* romantic life.

After breakfast, I decided to get the biggest chore of the day over with—taking them shooting. Again, they joked all the way through my lesson, so I gave up. I couldn't keep stalling, but I could make sure we stayed on the inside range and only one gun was in play, as they took turns under my supervision.

I took a paper target from the bin.

"A bull's-eye?" one of the brothers—Ben—said. "Where are the people? Like what they use in the movies?"

"Sorry, I don't allow human-form targets unless you're a cop or someone who might need to shoot in the line of duty."

"And only if a perp does something dangerous, right?" said Ken, the other brother. "Like reaching for a tissue."

I'd shot Wayne Franco when he made the mistake of reaching for a tissue. It was a small detail, one people could hardly be expected to remember if they'd casually heard it seven years later. In other words, the Previls had looked up my story before coming to the lodge. Nice. It was nothing new, though, and while most people pretended not to remember who I was and what I'd done, I'd learned to deal with those who weren't so polite. As the twins guffawed over their joke, my expression didn't change.

"The bull's-eye is better for accuracy testing," I said as I wheeled it down the line.

"We want the paper men."

I clenched my teeth without tightening my lips, forced a bright hostess smile, and said, "Okay, then. But I'll warn you, the plain black-and-white can be harder to see."

They stood back, giggling and whispering like teenage girls as I set up the target.

"Who wants to go first?"

"You. Show us how it's done."

I nodded, picked up the gun, stepped to the boards—

"Pop him right between the eyes," Ben said. "That's your specialty, isn't it?"

I turned slowly. The twins and their old friend were

grinning. Their business associate pretended not to hear, absorbed by my first-aid poster.

"Come on," Ben said. "Between the eyes. Show us how it's done."

"You volunteering?" grunted a voice from behind them. Jack hobbled from the shadows and jerked his chin at Ben. "Go on. Show your friends how it's done."

After a full chamber—with only two nicks in the edge of the target—Ben complained I'd put it too far away. When Jack gave a derisive snort, the brother challenged *him* to try it. Jack eyed the gun as if it was a snake that might bite, then, after some ribbing, let me reload it, and took it awkwardly.

"Is there a safety or something?" he asked.

"It's a Glock. They don't have one."

"Huh."

He took one shot and missed the target completely, to the laughter of the brothers and their friend.

"Hold on," Jack said when Ben reached for the gun. "I'm getting the hang of it."

He took three shots, putting a perfect triangle through the target's heart. Then he passed the gun to Ken. When all four had had a chance to be humiliated by the "porter," they decided marksmanship wasn't really their thing.

"Done here?" Jack said to me as the men clustered, grumbling, near the door.

"Seems so." I fingered the hole where the target's heart would have been. "*He's* definitely done. Damned fine shooting."

Jack shrugged. "Close range. Good gun. Anyway..." He raised his voice, accent changing as he stretched his words into full sentences. "I need a lift into town, to pick up a prescription. I was hoping we could do that before lunch."

The men stopped and turned our way.

"What does she look like, a taxi service?" one said.

"No, that's fine," I said. "No taxis or delivery services around here, so I'd be happy to run you into town—"

"The hell you will," Ben said, advancing on us. "We have rappelling scheduled for—"

I didn't see the look Jack gave him, but it was enough to shut him up mid-sentence.

"There's been a change of plans," Jack said. "You're going rappelling later this afternoon."

"What the hell?" Ken said, staying where he was, willing to join his brother in voice but not in body.

I caught a glimpse of Jack's expression. There was no menace in it. Not much of anything really, just that steady, piercing stare. It was enough.

"You can't change our plans," the friend said, voice taking on a whine.

"I didn't. Your wives did. I was talking to them this morning, showing them brochures Nadia has for some art studios in the area..."

"Oh, shit," one brother breathed.

"Seems they want an arts-and-crafts tour, so they told Emma to reschedule the rappelling for after lunch." Jack's lips pursed, musing. "Or maybe not. They were saying something about checking out a bistro way over in Haliburton if it didn't look like you'd be done with the tour before lunch..."

The men were gone almost before he could finish.

I grinned at him. "I owe you."

"Fucking assholes. Shouldn't have to deal with that."

"It's part of the job," I said as I locked the equipment closet.

"They get worse? I'll take care of them. Got lots of woods. Never find the bodies."

When I pulled into the liquor store parking lot, Jack mumbled something about grabbing a newspaper and hanging out in the diner. I could find him there when I was done.

Tess was unloading stock. At seventeen, she was too young to work at the liquor store, but, since she wasn't at the till, potentially selling to her underage friends, no one complained.

The moment she saw me, she disappeared out the back door. I bought a token bottle of wine and followed her.

Tess hovered at the building corner, waiting. She waved me behind the building.

"What have you found out?" she asked.

"Nothing yet."

Those two words snuffed out the light in her eyes. "Oh, I thought maybe…" She shrugged and let the sentence drift off.

"I'm still looking. I'm thinking maybe she did go visit that photographer in Toronto."

Tess's chin jerked up, eyes glowing again. Guilt shot through me. It was wrong to let her think her friend was still alive, but I didn't have a choice.

"Did she know this photographer's name?" I asked. "Or the name of the company he worked for?"

"No, but she said he worked in Toronto and..." Tess paused. "Maybe you should take notes."

"Oh, uh, yeah. Sorry." I patted my pockets. In my business, you learn not to write anything down. I gave a wry smile. "Guess I'm not too prepared. Do you have—?"

Before I could finish, Tess darted through the rear door. A moment later she emerged, pencil and paper in hand.

"Okay. So he was from Toronto. He worked for a modeling agency that specializes in kids. For advertisements, she said. TV and magazines. She said he looked like a photographer. Like the guys in the AV club at school."

"A geek."

"Right. She didn't say anything specific, though. Oh, except that he didn't wear glasses. Like a grown-up AV guy, but without glasses. All the guys in our AV club wear glasses."

With each new bit of information, Tess grew more animated, excited to finally be able to help. As another pang of guilt shot through me, I told myself I *was* helping Sammi. Just not in the way Tess expected.

"She said he took a bunch of pictures of Destiny, plus two shots of Sammi holding her." Tess looked up at me. "Do you think that's important?"

"It might be. Everything you can tell me might be."

"He said Destiny was a beautiful baby. Just like her mom. I remember that because I asked Sammi if she thought he was hitting on her. She said no way, he was—oh, right, I forgot this. It might help. She said he was at least thirty. Old." Tess glanced at me and colored. "Uh, you know, old for her. Not, like, old in general."

"Trust me, some days, over thirty feels very old."

"That might help, right? An age? She said he didn't seem interested in her at all. I thought that was weird. Guys are always checking Sammi out. Even the old— older ones."

"So he didn't check her out? Or Sammi just didn't notice?"

"Oh, Sammi always noticed. But this guy was only interested in Destiny and he was all business, not even sneaking a look down Sammi's top when she leaned over. I guess that was good, huh? Not some pervert with a camera."

"Probably not."

Tess nibbled at a hangnail, then shook her head. "That's it. That's all she said. Just that one short conversation."

"It gives me a place to start," I said. "You have a good memory."

"Yeah? Well, if it helps . . ." She went quiet, the momentary excitement draining away. "You think she's okay?"

"I—I don't know, Tess."

She nodded, trying to hide her disappointment. "Well, okay, then. If there's anything more I can do . . ."

"I'll let you know."

She stepped away, then turned sharply. "I'll be off for lunch in a few minutes. I could show you where she met the guy. The exact spot in the park. You used to be a cop, right? Maybe you could take fingerprints or something."

"Um, sure."

"Meet you there in ten minutes?"

I nodded and Tess walked back into the store, her step a little lighter. Of course, I couldn't take fingerprints. Any evidence would have vanished, washed away by rain or obliterated by other park users. But it would make Tess feel better.

Seventeen

Tess showed me the bench where Sammi had been sitting with Destiny. I took notes and promised to come back after dark to do forensic work.

As she headed back to work, I cut through the park to meet up with Jack at the diner.

"Scene of the crime?"

The voice startled me from my thoughts and I spun to see him on a bench beside the cenotaph. He lifted his lit cigarette, with a grunt that probably translated to "want some?" I did. I haven't officially smoked in years, but I'm not above taking a drag off Jack's now and then, especially if I could use the nicotine hit to calm my swirling thoughts.

When I passed it back, he put it out on the bench, then stuffed the butt in his pocket. It'd been less than half smoked. Just an excuse to hang out in the park, then.

"Scene of the crime?" he repeated, waving at the spot through the trees, where he must have seen me with Tess.

A short laugh. "Something like that. It's where they met the photographer. Tess wanted me to check it out, maybe pull some forensic evidence, which I can't, of course, but I wasn't telling her that." I shoved my hands in my pockets, my gaze magnetized to the distant Ernst home. I told Jack what I'd learned. "Not much, but I'll give—"

When I stopped, he followed my gaze to Janie's place.

"There's a For Sale sign," I murmured. "That wasn't there when I broke in last week."

"That's her house?"

I nodded.

"Fuck." He shook his head.

I took three steps, squinting, as if there might be some way to mistake Benny Durant's neon-yellow realtor signs.

"For sale . . ." I whispered, walking closer.

Jack followed. "Not gonna get much."

"The land's worth something, being right in the core. It's hardly downtown Toronto, but there's some value there. I know the town offered to buy Janie out a few years ago. They really just wanted to get rid of the eyesore. They offered her fair market value plus, by order of the White Rock Town Council, an additional payment of five hundred dollars."

"Generous folks," he said, stepping up beside me.

"Oh, they are. Janie told them where they could stuff their offer."

"Don't blame her."

"Then from what I heard, she blackmailed the mayor for twice that much by threatening to tell his wife about the special services she paid His Honor to avoid property citations."

"That the same mayor I saw in the diner?"

"Looks like he got hit in the face with a brick?"

A twitch of a smile. "Yeah. Doesn't seem much of a Romeo."

"You haven't seen Janie. My guess, she takes what she can get and, if she can turn a profit, calls it a bonus. She's none too bright, but she's got a keen sense of self-preservation and not an ethical boundary in sight." My gaze traveled over the house. "If *your* daughter disappeared, would you decide that's a good time to pack up and move?"

He shrugged. "Don't have kids. Suppose you might. Memories and all that."

"I can't see Janie moving to avoid reminders of her daughter. But even if there is some hidden wellspring of maternal love there, would she take off so soon? After a few months maybe. But *days*? When Sammi could still call? Show up on her doorstep?"

I looked at the house again. Jack said nothing, just waited.

"You'd almost get the impression she knew Sammi wasn't coming back." I glanced over at him. He stared straight ahead.

I scanned the businesses along the street. "Benny should be in the office today. That's the realtor. I'll go see what he can tell me about this. You can wait—"

"I'll come."

"You wanted to keep a low profile—"

"I'm coming."

He meant he wanted to keep an eye on me, make sure I kept my emotions and my imagination in check. That smarted, but not as much as *knowing* I needed that check.

I headed for the sidewalk, leaving him to follow.

Benny Durant sat at his big oak desk in the window, an extra-large take-out coffee at his elbow, a copy of *Maclean's* in his hand—probably with a less salubrious magazine tucked inside it.

Durant was a good ol' boy who'd lived here all his life and chased away competition with the ferocity of a junkyard dog. Friendly and affable, he had a smile for every-one and a "special deal" for all his "friends." Though he was canny enough to take advantage of a client's real es-tate naiveté, he always stopped short of an outright swindle.

I'd bought the lodge from Durant, and was happy enough with the deal to send him a steady stream of peo-ple looking to make the area a permanent vacation desti-nation with a new cottage. Few of those leads translated into sales. That, too, was typical for a town like White Rock. People spend a week, and are seduced by wilder-ness life: the clean air, the endless lakes, the peace and quiet, the friendly people. They start thinking they'd like to purchase a piece of this paradise.

Then reality rears its ugly head. The nearest Wal-Mart is how far? Ethnic restaurant? Movie theater? *Hospital?* No high-speed Internet? No cable? *Party* lines? Not to mention black flies, power outages, and winter storms. Many a new resident has left after the first winter, upon discovering that our gorgeous country roads rarely see a snowplow and their urban SUV just isn't going to make it through that three-foot drift. But Durant still gets enough sales from my referrals to put me on his good side.

I didn't even get as far as the door before his head popped up, like a hound on a scent. When I opened it, his gaze shot to Jack, fairly salivating at the prospect of fresh meat.

"Nadia Stafford," he boomed, sliding the magazine into a drawer, then standing and offering his hand. "Did I hear you're booked solid this weekend?"

"I am."

"That's amazing. So early in the season, too. Seems people are finally discovering our little hidden gem." A wink at Jack. "That reminds me, I'm running low on your brochures. Got them right out here, front and center." He pounded a meaty fist on the stack. "They're a hot ticket. If you could bring more by . . ."

"I'll do that Monday."

"Wonderful. I love promoting great local businesses, and it's easy these days. Our economy is booming. Yes, it is." His gaze was fixed on Jack, the spiel clearly for his benefit. "So, Nadia, what can I do for you today?"

"It's about the Ernst place. I saw it's for sale."

He straightened, fairly quivering now. "It is indeed. A rare and lovely property." A small laugh. "Well, the *property,* that is. The land. The existing structure could be removed. I already have a quote from Ed Baines for plowing it down."

I imagined Baines's bulldozer ripping through Sammi's home, reducing it to rubble, her treasures buried at the bottom, to be hauled to the dump. Every trace of her obliterated.

I opened my mouth, but my next question wouldn't come. Fortunately, Durant picked that moment to wave at Jack's crutch.

"Had a little accident, did you?"

I expected Jack to respond with an abrupt "Yeah." But he launched into a story about tripping off the deck chasing a runaway barbecue. By the time he finished, Durant was howling with laughter.

"Did you rescue the steak?"

"Sure. I took it to the emergency room and had my meal there."

"You probably needed it, considering how long they expect people to wait these days. Criminal. Just criminal."

"So, is Janie really leaving?" I cut in. "This isn't one of her games?"

"Oh, no. I wouldn't do that to a client." He glanced at Jack. "So you're interested . . . ?"

"One of my guests is," I said.

Durant nodded. "I know how Janie can be, so when she said she'd sell, I handed her a check and had her sign the preliminary paperwork on the spot. I own that property now. She'll be cleared out by Tuesday."

"How did you finally convince her?"

He laughed. "I'd love to take credit, but it was all Janie. She came to me Wednesday wanting to know how fast she could get the money and leave town. I guess with Sammi disappearing and all . . ."

"Is that what she said?"

"Well, no, but the timing can't be a coincidence."

No, it can't.

"Still, it seems a little hasty," I said. "With Sammi gone barely a couple of days."

"You know Janie. She gets her mind made up. If Sammi does come home, her mom's still around, just over in Bancroft."

"Bancroft?"

"She's got a boyfriend there, I heard. And that's the forwarding address she gave."

"In case Sammi came back?"

"Well, no, she didn't say that. For legal work, though I'm sure she meant I could pass it on to Sammi. I didn't put up the sign until I was sure she'd cashed the check."

He winked at Jack. "Gotta put my client's interests first. As of now, that place is free and clear."

We walked back to the truck in a comfortable silence, Jack letting me puzzle it through, knowing I'd share when I was ready.

If Janie knew Sammi wasn't coming back, then the obvious answer was that she'd killed her. But I'd seen the way Janie's hands shook. She'd barely be able to aim a gun, much less execute such a perfect shot. Her criminal background—running with a biker gang—was all in the distant past. Would she still have connections? Be able to buy a hit?

But to what purpose? Why kill—?

A figure stepped from the pharmacy, bag clutched to her chest. I blinked, certain I was seeing wrong. I wasn't.

I veered onto the road and broke into a jog. Janie's gaze skittered my way. She hugged the bag tight and walked faster. Jack must have figured out who she was. He called my name in a tone that warned me to get my ass back there before I did something I'd regret.

I kept going, bearing down on my target.

"Doing a little shopping with your windfall?" I grabbed the bag from Janie.

"You crazy bitch!" she shrieked, clawing at me.

I looked inside and pulled out one of two rye bottles. "Doesn't look like medicine."

"Doug and I have an arrangement," she said, naming the drugstore clerk. "He gets them for me. There's no law against that."

"Crown Royal? Little rich for your budget. You must have got a pretty penny for your shack."

She snatched the bag back. "None of your business, cop."

"What about Sammi? What's she going to do when she comes home and finds her house gone?" I stepped closer. "Unless you know she isn't coming home."

"Wha—?"

"You sold your house a day after she disappeared. What do you know? Where's Sammi?"

Fingers clamped around my arm. "Nadia..."

I tried to pull away, but Jack held fast and leaned down to my ear. "You're drawing a crowd."

A quick glance around showed he was right. Every Saturday shopper within earshot had stopped to gawk.

I turned back to Janie. She was eyeing Jack, her lip curling.

"A cripple?" she said. "Little old for you, isn't he? Guess that's the best a psycho cop can do, huh?"

Jack tugged my arm.

I resisted, but lowered my voice. "If you know where Sammi is..."

"You'll what? Shoot me?"

Jack yanked hard enough to pull me off balance. One final glare at Janie, and I let him lead me away.

Eighteen

Jack drove back to the lodge. I was so furious, I wouldn't be able to see the road clearly.

As soon as we'd walked away from Janie, I'd realized the question wasn't "Why kill Sammi?" but "Why take Destiny?" It had taken every ounce of restraint not to tear back there and throttle a confession from her.

I'd seen those two bottles of premium rye whiskey. I'd seen the satisfied look on her face. And I'd remembered my Internet search last night, thinking about all the people who'd killed their babies when so many others wanted them desperately. Would do anything to have a child. Would pay any price.

Janie had sold Destiny.

She and her new boyfriend had hatched the scheme using her old contacts, or maybe his—it was a sure bet any boyfriend of Janie's had paid more than a few visits to the wrong side of the law. They'd had Sammi killed and sold the baby.

Janie couldn't flaunt her new wealth in White Rock, especially right after her daughter and granddaughter vanished. The smart move would be to sit tight until everyone forgot Sammi, then move. But Janie wasn't smart. She had money and by God, she was going to spend it. So she'd raced over to Benny Durant, eager to sell.

I could barely sit still, fidgeting with my seat belt, waiting until we were beyond the town limits.

"I think Janie killed Sammi and sold Destiny."

I waited for Jack to wince. To tell me that was ridiculous and I was overreacting.

He drove for a couple of minutes in silence, then said, "Yeah. I was thinking that."

"So you agree it's plausible."

"Plausible. As in *possible*. Not a sure thing. Need—"

"Evidence. I know that. I may not have any detective work in my past, but I've already learned my lesson about jumping to conclusions. So if it did happen like that, what would be your theory?"

Silence for another kilometer. "Hate to think anyone'd do that. Daughter. Granddaughter. But obviously she doesn't give a shit. Meets a new guy. He plants the idea. All she sees? Open bar. Lets him set it up. Takes her share."

"So now we need—"

"*You* need to do your job. Take care of your guests."

I released my death grip on the seat belt. "Right."

"Let me work on this. Plan something. Gonna need to move before she does. Monday, right?"

"If she stays that long. We can guarantee she'll be home tonight, enjoying those bottles, but she may decide, come morning, to clear out early and start enjoying the windfall."

"Yeah." He turned to watch a stray dog at the roadside, saying nothing until we'd passed it. "Gonna have to be careful. Half the town saw you yelling at her."

"Sorry."

He shrugged. "We'll work it out. Get your answer. Then? She's guilty? Do what you gotta do."

*   *   *

I spent the afternoon rappelling. Being busy helped keep my mind off Janie Ernst, and I was almost thankful for the Previl party's constant barrage of demands. Almost.

After the rappelling came cave exploration. Then dinner. Then a sunset canoe ride, cut short when Ben wouldn't believe me when I said canoes, unlike rowboats, could tip. Fortunately, I was in the third canoe with the Previls' associate and his wife—the "nice couple," as I'd come to think of them. Unfortunately, when Ben plunged into the icy water, he grabbed the first thing he could reach, which happened to be the side of Ken's canoe.

So we had two wet and sheepish brothers, and two wet and furious wives, one of whom demanded to know why the water wasn't warmer, as if heating it was my responsibility.

Owen helped me bundle the four into warm towels. Then we discovered a handy new use for the hot tub. I even broke out the hard liquor, though I warned them against drinking too much while in the tub.

Once they were reasonably happy, I fled into the house on the pretext of making coffee. I found Jack in the kitchen, filling a thermos with that same beverage. Mugs were tucked into a basket resting beside it.

"Ah, you heard the commotion, did you?" I said. "I was just coming in to make some for them. I'll grab the real cream or the wives will complain."

"Fuck 'em. This is for you. Missed dessert."

I had—I'd been too busy warming, then cooling, the wives' pies. Jack had once again taken his meal in his room, but Emma must have told him.

"Come on." He hefted the basket. "Get away while you can."

I took the basket, restarted the coffeemaker for Emma, and followed Jack down to the lakeside gazebo. As I laid out the dessert he'd packed, and poured the coffee, he checked out the structure, commenting on the heater, the sliding screens, and the cushioned wicker table set.

"Nice," he said.

"Thank you."

A muscle in his cheek twitched. He knew I wasn't thanking him for his kind words about the gazebo. I was thanking him because his money *bought* the gazebo. He'd argue it was my money, earned on the job last fall, but the point still hung there, a subject that made us both un-comfortable—me for taking his money, and him because he didn't like me knowing who'd financed the job.

He braced for more, but I let it slide. I had more im-portant things on my mind.

"Are we going to Janie's tonight?" I asked when we were halfway through our pie slices.

"Been thinking..."

His tone made my hand tighten around my fork.

"Interrogating an old drunk?" he went on. "One-man job."

"Sure. If you'd rather stay here, get some sleep, go ahead."

"You know what I mean."

I took a mouthful of pie, chewed, and swallowed be-fore answering. "Do you really think I'm that out of con-trol, Jack?"

"Think this case is hitting where it hurts. You feel bad for the girl. Pissed off because no one cares. Reminds you of Amy."

"The only people I'm thinking of are Sammi and Destiny, and getting justice—"

"All right. But still? Tearing you up. Too close to home. If Janie did this?" He shook his head. "Never pulled a hit for free. But I'd do it for this. And I didn't even know the girl. You did. All I'm saying? You need to step back. Before you do something you'll regret."

We finished our pie in silence.

"So what's the plan?" I said finally.

He studied me before moving his plate aside. "Go alone. Make sure she doesn't see me. Change my accent. Tell her I was sent by the boy's parents."

"The Draytons."

"Yeah. Get details before I go. Say they heard Destiny's gone. Want her back. Play it out a bit. Threats don't work? Draytons are offering to buy the baby."

"Skip the threats and head straight for the cash. Greed is the way to Janie's heart. Offer more than she would have gotten, then promise to stage it as a kidnapping, so her partner won't suspect anything and she'll get the whole wad."

He sipped his coffee. "You're good with that?"

I set my plate on his, then fiddled with a stray piece of broken wicker, sticking it back into the weave. "Remember how we played it with Cooper in Kentucky? We didn't want him seeing you, so you stayed offside, giving me backup while I took him down and interrogated him."

"You want to do that? You stay offside?"

I nodded.

"All right." Another sip. "She confesses? You want her gone? Have to go prepared."

I stared out at the lake, watching a loon bob on the

waves. If Janie had Sammi killed, did I want her dead? No. That was too easy. I'd rather see her rot in jail and burn up in headlines as a woman who killed her own daughter for profit. That might not hurt right away—her hide was too thick—but maybe after she dried out, she'd feel something.

"If we get a confession, I'll figure out a way to set the cops on her," I said. "Knowing Janie, she's left a trail so wide even the local idiots shouldn't be able to screw up a conviction."

"If you change your mind..."

"I won't." I looked at him. "But let's not take any body-disposal supplies, in case I'm tempted."

I continued going through the motions, hosting the bonfire, closing the house for the night, staying up another half hour in case guests needed anything. Normally the extra wait is just a precaution in case of emergencies. Most guests respect my need to get to bed if I'm going to be up at six for the jog. Not so with the Previls, who needed towels, fresh pillows, glasses of water...I was just waiting for them to request a tuck-in and bedtime story.

Jack had moved the truck earlier. So at two, we snuck off in silence. Everything went fine until we reached Janie's house and found the windows dark and her truck gone.

We stood in the shadows, watching the house.

"Guess those bottles were a victory celebration for two," I said. "She must have gone into Bancroft to see her boyfriend."

"We shouldn't follow."

"I wasn't going to suggest it. But as long as the place is vacant, let's take a look."

Jack hesitated.

"We can check for evidence that she killed Sammi or sold Destiny. And, while we're at it, I'll see whether Sammi left anything about that photographer. Maybe a business card."

The last part tipped the balance. Proof that I wasn't single-mindedly focused on my Janie theory. Proof that I was still in control.

We took a quick look around, in case Janie was passed out on the sofa or bed, and somehow had remembered to turn out the lights first. Then we split up. Jack took Janie's room. I returned to Sammi's.

I meticulously searched the tiny bedroom, right down to unwrapping every gum wrapper in the trash, in hopes of finding a phone number or name scribbled inside. I was pulling Destiny's baby book off the shelf when a flurry of photos and paper scraps rained down. Two of the pictures landed face up. One was of a party for Destiny, with three candles in a cupcake, Sammi grinning as Kira held a homemade Happy 3 Months banner. In the other, Sammi sat in a Muskoka chair, holding a sleeping baby, scowling, clearly warning whoever was taking the photo that they'd better not wake Destiny. I stared at them both for a moment, then picked up the second— the Sammi I knew best—and gingerly pushed it into my pocket.

I scooped up the handful of scraps and flipped through them. Sammi's penmanship was atrocious, her spelling phonetic. On the first, she'd written "First dentist appointment 3-4 years." On another she'd scribbled "Chicken pox vaccine 12 months (safe?)."

I read through several more. Each held a tidbit of child-rearing information, a tip someone had told her or she'd heard on TV. Scraps tracing the path of a young woman's desperate desire to be a good mother.

Then I found what I'd been looking for. On one scrap Sammi had written four words. Jordan Fifer Model Agency.

I put that into my pocket and tidied up the book. As I did, my gaze fell on Sammi's treasure box. I reached for it, the sudden urge to take it, too, to bury it with her body. Ridiculous, of course. Sentimental tripe. Not like she'd be needing it anymore. And if Janie had her daughter killed, I had every intention of tipping off the police and making sure Sammi's body saw a real grave. Finding her treasures buried with her would suggest Janie regretted her decision, and I wasn't giving her that.

The box had to stay. But whatever happened, I'd make sure Tess got it out before the place was bulldozed.

Now—

Jack wheeled into the room. "Clean up. Gotta go. *Now*."

"Wha—?"

He grabbed my arm before I got the word out, and led me into the hall.

Through the living room door, a stockinged foot protruded from behind the sofa, unseen when we'd been heading into the bedrooms.

I crept forward, gaze fixed on the dingy white sock. Soon a tattered jean hem came into view. Then a second foot. Then Janie herself, passed out drunk.

My gaze traveled up her body, past the stick-thin legs encased in dirty denim. Past the flabby belly protruding from under the shirt shoved up around her rib cage. Past her arms, oddly folded across her chest, fingers bent, as if in a "fuck you." A *final* "fuck you." I knew that as soon as I saw her head, askew, eyes still open, tongue protruding from swollen lips, bruise on her cheek.

"Beat the crap out of her," Jack said. "Neck's broken."

I supposed I should feel some twinge of pity, but the only emotion that rose was a surge of outrage that someone had robbed me of my best shot at finding out what happened to Destiny.

I returned to the bedroom to put everything back in place. When I came out, Jack was crouched beside Janie's body.

"Couple fingers broken. She have rings?"

I paused, recollecting. "Costume stuff, but yes. A few."

"Bottle's over there." He jerked his thumb at an empty Crown Royal bottle on the carpet. "One missing, looks like."

I walked over, staying away from the window, and found two empty glasses and two bottle caps. "So he swipes her cheap rings and an open bottle of rye, shoves her behind the couch, and takes off…in *her* truck. Something tells me we aren't dealing with a pro."

A snort that was almost a laugh. "Yeah." He straightened. "I'll watch the front. Get out the back. Stand guard for me. Be there in five."

Nineteen

The murder of Janie Ernst was so sloppy, you'd almost think it *was* a pro, setting the scene to frame her boyfriend. No guy could possibly be that stupid, right? Come over for a Saturday night victory drink, leave his DNA all over the empty glasses, kill his girlfriend for her share of their profits, then drive home in her truck.

Sadly, the IQ of the average thug isn't really all that high. Add booze into the mix, and it drops even farther.

The question wasn't "whodunit," but whether we could get to him—and the answers I needed—before the cops found Janie and followed the four-lane highway of bread crumbs he'd left behind.

When I suggested going after the boyfriend right away, Jack brought up another reason to act fast—one I'd rather not have been reminded of. The killer may have left a trail a blind man could follow, but when the White Rock cops found Janie dead, they'd come knocking on the door of the person seen fighting with her earlier that day. Sure, they'd eventually get back on the right track...but only after they'd done what they could to make my life miserable. And once that happened, there'd be no way of getting to Bancroft to find Janie's boyfriend—not without a police cruiser or a reporter on my tail.

I tried not to picture Don Riley and his crew on my doorstep, the satisfaction on their faces, the rumors they'd spread, the business I'd lose just from those rumors. I tried not to imagine the press getting hold of it.

Even if I wasn't a viable suspect, they'd love the excuse to disinter the story of Nadia Stafford, killer cop.

If only I'd resisted the urge to confront Janie.

"Well, that'll teach me" really didn't seem adequate.

We headed for Bancroft. It was a thirty-minute drive straight up Highway 28. We already had our interrogation gear on us, so we were set. The boyfriend's address would have been useful, and it rankled, knowing it was right in Benny Durant's office. But no matter how careful we were, it was an extra risk, especially after I'd been asking Durant about her property that same day.

So we were driving to Bancroft in hopes of finding Janie's truck. It was a small town, just a little bigger than White Rock. Still, even at four thousand people—and shrinking—that was a lot of driveways to search. And hunting for an old pickup in these parts was like searching for a new Mercedes in Toronto.

We started with a tour of the bar parking lots. Now, if you ask me, a guy who just killed his girlfriend shouldn't be heading out for beer, but Jack thought it was a strong possibility, and the more I considered it, the more it made a weird kind of sense.

I knew all the bars in Bancroft, since White Rock didn't have any, and I needed all the alternate venues at hand—addresses, directions, music variety, clientele type—for my guests. In Bancroft there were two, and one was attached to a restaurant.

We found Janie's truck at the other, a hole-in-the-wall called Charlie's. And we found her presumed killer, slumped over the steering wheel, dead drunk.

"Fuck," Jack muttered.

"You can say that again."

"Sure that's her truck?" Jack asked. We were parked at the end of the lane.

"Yep. See that dent in the front bumper? Get close enough and you'll see fur caught in it, from Mrs. O'Malley's late Irish setter, Red. Beautiful dog. Dumb as a post, but beautiful. This winter, Mrs. O'Malley found Janie passed out drunk in a snowdrift, got her inside, warmed her up, and called the doctor. Later, she suggested Janie needed help and tried to find a program for her. So Janie ran over her dog and left the fur in the bumper as a reminder to anyone else who might try to 'interfere' in her life."

"Should've left her in the snowdrift."

"I won't argue. And this is the woman we let raise Sammi. Isn't that what child services is for? Did anyone even call them when she was little?"

"Probably too scared to interfere."

"I've known Sammi since she was twelve. I wasn't afraid of Janie, but I still didn't do anything."

"By that time? Too old. Wouldn't want to leave."

"How do I know that if I never tried?"

"Gave her a job. No one else did."

"Too little, too late. No wonder she hated me—hated all of us." I undid my belt. "Okay, back to work. So how are we going to interrogate a guy who's passed out dead drunk in a truck in a public place?"

"Could be tricky."

"A master of understatement, as always."

*   *   *

I peeked in the passenger-side window. The man inside was in his fifties, with dyed black hair that he probably wore in a comb-over, but was now sticking straight up. He had his face planted on the steering wheel, every snore making that rooster comb quiver. We wouldn't need to *see* him wake up. We'd hear it.

The passenger door was locked. The driver's side wasn't, but I couldn't risk that slap of cold night air waking him when I opened it. I slid the slim jim in and jostled the passenger door open. Then a low whistle from Jack stopped me. I glanced over as a drunken couple wobbled my way, arms wrapped around each other. I dropped and rolled under the truck.

The woman's giggles twittered across the quiet lot. "Can you believe that place? It was like something out of a honky-tonk movie."

"Or a meeting spot for Rednecks Anonymous," the man said.

They roared with laughter, pleased by their incredible wit. More giggles. More jabs about the "rubes," who'd probably treated them with respect, served them full-strength drinks at reasonable prices, fed them an unlimited supply of peanuts and pretzels, and peppered them with suggestions for the best hidden fishing spots and scenic lookouts. I could rail against the stereotype, but the truth is that more than a few residents are just like me, with a high school education, driving a fifteen-year-old pickup, and only wearing makeup on special occasions. Doesn't make us worse; we just have a different set of values.

Apparently, though, all that crisp fresh air and undiluted booze was bringing out Mother Nature in this citified couple. Or maybe it was just all the drunken stumbling, grabbing each other for support. Before they were halfway across the lot, their giggles gave way to moans, their jibes to whispers of "oh, baby," proving they weren't any more articulate than our local high school dropouts.

The wet sound of sloppy kisses tempted me to do a little moaning of my own. *Move along, people. I'm sure you have a perfectly good bed in your fancy inn. Undress out here, and you're going to freeze.*

"Hmm, is that an open pickup bed over there?"

I had a mental flash of Janie's truck...and missing tailgate.

No. Please, no.

Two pairs of feet stumbled my way.

"Wait," the woman said. "There's a guy in there. Sleeping, I think."

"Then let's give him a thrill. Show these country bumpkins how it's done."

No. Please...

The truck jolted as they banged into the back. Rust rained down. The woman's feet disappeared as her partner lifted her onto the bed. A pair of panties landed in a puddle. He stayed standing, presumably just hiking up her skirt.

The bed rocked once. Twice. I wrapped my arms around my head and squeezed my eyes shut against the rust shower.

Three. Four.

It stopped. Shit, they'd woken him up. I braced for a shout or, worse, the engine starting.

"Good?" the woman panted.

"Yeah, babe."

That was it? I hadn't even had time to regret what I was missing.

They staggered off, leaving her panties still floating in the mud puddle. Once the couple had driven away, Jack gave an all-clear whistle. I crawled out and glanced in the truck cab. Our target was still snoring.

I prepped my materials, then took a deep breath. That brief rocking might not have woken him, but it could have started the process. I counted to five, then threw open the door and lunged across the seat, gag going around his mouth, turning his face away from mine before his eyes opened.

I didn't need to bother. I had the gag tied, the blindfold on, and the guy pulled flat on the seat and he kept sleeping. If it wasn't for the now-muffled snores, I'd have thought he was dead. It was only when I tried to bind him that he woke, flailing and elbowing me in the gut, knocking my wind out. Tight quarters for a takedown. Even tighter when Jack got in the passenger side to drive us out of there before someone noticed the struggle.

There were a few moments of chaos as I got the guy's hands and feet bound while trying to keep him off Jack's lap. Jack got kicked and elbowed a few times, including one in a place that probably smarted, but he didn't say a word, just drove from the lot.

By the time we reached the road, I had our guy fully restrained and on the floor at my feet. Then I sat up, face toward Jack, as if talking to him. The streets were empty, but if anyone did notice us, they'd see only a couple heading home. I didn't say a word, though. I wasn't giving our guy any sign that he was dealing with a woman. If he took that story back to White Rock, I'd have Don Riley on my doorstep in a flash.

When we neared the town limits, which didn't take long, I pulled out the man's wallet. Peter Weston. I showed it to Jack, so he'd have the name, then stuffed it back in the wallet and tossed it behind the seat.

Jack pointed to a sign announcing Eagle's Nest lookout. I shook my head. It was a great location—a thickly wooded hill with a winding road going up—but on Saturday night, even this late, we couldn't be sure local teens wouldn't be using it for more than sightseeing.

It didn't take long to leave the town lights behind. Out here, civilization is just a hole carved from the wilderness, the thick woods always at the outskirts, waiting patiently to reclaim their territory. In more than a few places up here, that's exactly what's happened. Our ghost towns are nothing like the empty buildings and dusty streets of the old West, but just village ruins overtaken by Mother Nature, the footprint of man growing fainter with each year.

Jack drove a couple of kilometers from town, then he headed down side roads until we found a lot with a For Sale sign so weather-beaten it was almost illegible. There are plenty of good building lots up here. This just wasn't one of them. Maybe the forest was too dense to clear, the ground too rocky, the lakes too far, or—the kiss of death—it was too near a potential native land claim.

Jack drove up a rutted lane and parked behind a curtain of brush. I hauled Weston out and dragged him deeper into the woods as Jack cleared a path with his crutch, the harsh thwacks betraying his frustration at leaving the heavy work to me.

Once I got Weston in place, facedown in the undergrowth, I retreated, staying close enough to hear but too far to be tempted to jump in with "extra persuasion."

Jack reached down, grabbed Weston's hair, yanked his head back, and ripped off the gag. Weston only moaned and mumbled something about his head.

"Out celebrating tonight, Peter?" Jack said. "Feeling a little extra flush?"

"Ow, my head. My head hurts."

"Answer the question, Peter."

"I don't know what you're talking about. My head—"

"Janie Ernst."

Weston went rigid and, after that, it didn't matter what he said. We knew we had Janie's killer.

"I don't know no—"

"You were involved with her. You were seen coming out of her house tonight, right before one of my associates went in and found her with a broken neck, shoved behind the sofa."

It took Weston at least ten long seconds to muster up an appropriate exclamation of shock and dismay. Then he stopped short.

"Are you guys cops?"

Jack gave an ugly laugh. "You wish. Have you ever heard of the Rock Machine?"

"S-sure. A biker—um, I mean motorcycle club. Janie used to run with them back in the day. But they were swallowed up by the Banditos and the Angels." Again he stopped. "Are you guys from—"

"Let's just say Janie's relationship with our organization isn't as far in the past as she led you to believe."

"That bitch! That cold, sneaky bitch. She was holding

out on me. Said she didn't have any money coming in, but she did, didn't she? She was working for you guys."

"If she was, you can see how her untimely death might cause us some concern."

"I didn't have nothing to do with—"

This time it was the swish of a switchblade that cut Weston short. His head jerked up, turning wildly, as if he could see through the blindfold.

"What's—" he began.

Jack bent and pressed the knife tip into the back of his neck.

"Hey!"

Jack dug it in farther. "Feel that?"

"Y-yes."

"Know what happens if I go another half inch?"

"N-no."

"You'll be paralyzed."

"P-par—"

"Not permanently. Just for a day or so. Full paralysis, though. Won't be able to move a muscle." A pause. "Do you know what lives in these woods? Black bears, wild dogs, coyotes, maybe even a wolf or two, wandered on down from Algonquin. Plus you've got your smaller predators like martens, weasels, rats, and the birds—the hawks and the vultures. Normally, humans are too big a challenge, but if you've got a few nice cuts leaking blood, and you're just lying there, not moving, they'll take a nibble. They won't bother killing you first. They'll just feed, while you lie there, unable to move, blink, scream..."

"I killed Janie, but it was an accident. I just got so mad at her, holding back, that I went a little nuts. I started whaling on her, and next thing I know, she's dead."

"Holding back. You mean she wouldn't give you her share from a job?"

He squirmed. "Well, no, it wasn't a job, so it wasn't really my share, but it'd been my idea. So I was entitled to a little advance, right?"

"So where'd the money come from if it wasn't a job?"

"From the house."

"Selling the house?"

"Right."

"That was your idea?"

"Right. With that kid of hers gone, Janie kept moaning about how she wouldn't have any money coming in. She didn't have a job . . . or so she said, though I guess she forgot about working for you. The bitch."

"The house . . . ?"

"I said she should sell the place to that real estate guy who keeps bugging her, then move in with me. It was my idea, so I thought she should give me a little cash, you know, as a thank-you."

Jack glanced back at me. For a moment, I couldn't respond, seeing my theory—my only theory—shatter around me. Then I motioned for Jack to push, but didn't need to—he'd already returned to Weston.

"What do you know about Sammi Ernst's disappearance?"

"The girl pissed off. Left her mom in the lurch. Ungrateful brat."

Jack pressed harder, but it was clear Weston knew nothing of Sammi's fate and, apparently, neither had Janie, who'd been scrambling to make up for the lack of rent money.

"So you went to ask for a few bucks, had a drink, got into a fight, and accidentally killed her."

"Exactly. I swear that's how—"

"I believe you."

Weston slumped. "Thank God."

"And now you're going to take that story to the cops."

"What?"

Jack leaned down, knife digging in. "You think my employer wants the cops nosing around in Janie Ernst's past?"

"No, but—"

"You said it was an accident. You were drunk. Hell, you were so drunk you took her truck."

"Mine's not running so well," Weston whined.

"Point is, you're looking at manslaughter, tops. Even if you do time, you'll be out before you know it, and back to your life." He bent farther. "Which you aren't going to have if you don't turn yourself in."

Weston audibly swallowed.

Jack twisted the switchblade. "Remember how I said you'd die if you didn't tell me the truth? Well, if you *don't* tell the cops, you're going to *wish* I'd killed you."

"O-okay. I'll go see them in the morning—"

"You'll see them tonight. If you want manslaughter, you're damned well going to want to prove remorse. And you want to prove you were drunk while the booze is still swimming around your blood. You'll go to them tonight and, as for me, I was never here, right?"

"R-right."

"And just in case you think of running? Remember who you're dealing with. This isn't some pissy local gang.

Wherever you go, we'll find you, and when we do, it'll be too late to change your mind."

As Weston babbled promises, Jack tossed Janie's keys into the undergrowth. Then he untied Weston's hands, leaving him to get the blindfold off and his legs freed before he found the keys. That meant we'd have a lengthy head start, which we'd need, considering we had to walk all the way back to town for my truck.

There was no way I was making Jack limp for five kilometers. Of course, I wasn't stupid enough to *offer* to get the truck—I just waited until we got back on the main road and took off, his muttered curses fading behind me.

When I returned, I drove right past Jack, who'd stepped into the ditch when he saw lights. But I caught his wave through the mirror and turned around.

I took the long way out, circling Bancroft so I wouldn't be seen passing through twice in a few minutes. Not that there was anyone around, but I wasn't taking chances.

"That stuff about paralyzing someone," I said. "It's bullshit."

A faint smile. "Are you sure?"

"Ninety-nine percent."

"Would you risk it?"

"I guess not," I said with a laugh. "I'll have to remember that one. Anyway, about getting him to confess? I hadn't thought of that, but it'll make things much easier if no one comes banging on my door."

"Thought so."

I glanced at him. "Thanks."

A shrug. "Easy enough."

Ten kilometers of dense forest passed in silence, then I said, "So I was wrong again."

"Both of us were. Got the killer right. Just the wrong motive." He rubbed his leg above the cast. "The wrong motive for Janie. Maybe not wrong for Sammi."

"You think someone else killed her to steal Destiny."

He nodded.

Twenty

At breakfast Sunday, the Previls informed us that they'd require a picnic lunch, served in the lakeside gazebo—preheated, if you please—followed by two more hours of rappelling.

When Emma reminded them of the noon checkout time and offered to make that a lunch to go, they told us to tack on the late-departure charge, because they weren't leaving before five. I could only muster a twinge of pique, as if three days in their company had anesthetized me.

But that didn't stop me from telling Emma to add a late-departure charge plus a fee for the extra rappelling lesson. I couldn't be too hospitable...or they might come back.

While I was tempted to take a run into town to get the "news" on Janie, Jack said it was better if he did that and I stayed clear. He was right, of course.

At lunch, while the Previls and their guests were in the gazebo, I used Jack's phone to try calling the contact number for Deanna Macy, following up on the Detroit girl's disappearance. No answer.

Jack took off after that to get a pack of cigarettes from town. While he was gone, I went online to look up the Fifer Agency. When I didn't find it in Toronto, I widened my search area, but it didn't do any good. Outside the greater Toronto area, you don't find a whole lot of model agencies. There were a couple in Ottawa and a few more in southwestern Ontario, but nothing with a name close to "Fifer."

I pulled up a list of Canadian modeling agencies. Nothing. The site linked to general photography studios, so I tried that. And there I found Pfeiffer Photography Studio, specializing in children.

I clicked on the link to the studio Web site. There was no "Jordan Pfeiffer" listed. No Pfeiffers at all. The agency was owned by a woman named Francis Lang. Working under her were four photographers. One of them was Jordan McDermott.

The note had read "Jordan Fifer Model Agency," which had been shorthand, I guess, for "Jordan at the Pfeiffer Model Agency." If this photographer had been making it up, it was unlikely he'd come up with a combination that just happened to exist. So it seemed legit.

That meant he probably had nothing to do with Sammi's murder. He'd likely been passing through cottage country, seen Destiny, and decided to shoot a few rolls. She *was* a beautiful baby. Maybe he'd taken her picture for his portfolio.

I couldn't see how this tied into my baby-selling theory, but I had to strike every question off my list. Once the Previls and their guests left, the lodge had no one booked until tomorrow night. I could visit McDermott in the morning and be back before check-in time.

Jack returned from town with the news that Janie was dead, "breaking" it to me in private, then letting me tell Emma and Owen. Janie's boyfriend had confessed to accidentally killing her in a drunken fight. Everyone was fine with that. It seemed as if no one had thought of Sammi, and wondered how to get the news to her. It was as if she'd been gone for months, already forgotten.

At nine-thirty the next morning, Jack and I were sipping coffee in the parking lot of a strip mall on Lakeshore Boulevard, waiting for the Pfeiffer Studio to open. I didn't keep disguise materials at the lodge, but by raiding the lost-and-found chest, I'd been able to whip up my favorite disguise—me with thirty-five pounds' worth of extra padding.

Most witnesses are savvy enough to realize a criminal can easily alter things like hair color or style, eye color, facial hair. But when it comes to weight, they see it as an inalterable physical trait, like age or height. Add bags under my eyes and a weak pair of prescription glasses and, to a target who made his living photographing the unique and remarkable, I'd be utterly forgettable.

The studio—in the next strip mall over—opened at ten. At nine thirty-five, a middle-aged woman arrived and unlocked the door. Over the next forty minutes, four other people arrived, three women and a man. On the Web site, McDermott was the only male employee listed, so I paid close attention to him.

At ten-fifteen, I slipped in behind another woman dragging a screaming preschooler. The woman who'd opened the studio flew from behind the counter, a coffee mug of suckers in hand. While she mollified the youngster, I asked, "Is Jordan McDermott in?"

Without turning, she jabbed a finger toward the back

hall. I shot one longing look at the suckers, then hurried off before she thought to ask whether I had an appointment.

In studio 1, two women were wrestling with a toddler who really didn't want to wear a suit and tie. I passed studio 2. Beyond it there were three office doors. The first stood open and bore McDermott's name in bright balloon letters. Inside a dark-haired man rifled through the filing cabinet.

"Mr. McDermott?"

When he turned, I knew this was not the guy who'd met Sammi. Jordan McDermott was one photographer who was clearly on the wrong side of the cameras. It would take a hunchback and facial reconstruction to make this guy anything but drop-dead gorgeous.

When he turned, I smiled a welcome. He returned it with a stone-faced once-over, assessing and dismissing me in an eye blink. My ego boost for the day.

"Mr. McDermott." I extended a hand. "Liz Bowles, *White Rock Times*. Do you have a minute?"

He resumed filing. "I do, but we aren't hiring."

"Hiring? Oh, no, I'm not a photographer. I'm a journalist."

McDermott closed the filing cabinet and moved to his desk. "From where?"

"White Rock."

He waited.

"Cottage country," I added.

"Oh." A slight twist of the lips. "The Muskokas."

"The Kawarthas, actually."

"What can I do for you, Miss..."

"Bowles. Call me Liz."

Not likely, his eyes said with another glance at my midriff.

I beamed a small-town smile. "Not a big fan of black-fly country, I take it?"

He rewarded my smile by picking up a sheaf of papers from his desk, turning to the filing cabinet, and presenting me with a lovely view of his back. He then proceeded to file as if I'd already left.

"You should get up our way sometime," I continued. "This time of year, it's absolutely gorgeous. We have some great vacation getaway deals, too."

I watched his body language for any reaction, any tensing of the muscles. Instead, he gave a soft snort. "I'm sure it's beautiful, but I've already taken my spring vacation. To Venice." He glanced at me. "Italy."

"Wow. I bet it was gorgeous."

McDermott turned to nod, and I detected the faintest thaw in his cold front.

"It was quite nice, yes," he said. "Of course, one really should see Venice in June, but my fiancée had a photo shoot, so we had to settle for April."

"She's a model? Wow. You must have just got back home."

"This week."

"That must be tough. Coming back here after a week in Venice."

"Three weeks."

I widened my eyes. "Wow. Our readers are going to flip. A Bancroft boy, dating a supermodel, and jetting off to Venice."

McDermott's brows arched. "Bancroft?"

"You're from Bancroft, aren't you?"

He snorted. "Hardly. Born and raised right here in Toronto, thankfully."

"Oh, my God. I am so sorry, Mr. McDermott. I'm looking for a Jordan McDermott, son of John and Hazel from Bancroft. He's supposed to be a photographer in Toronto and someone gave me this address."

"I see," McDermott said, cooling fast. "Well, then I would suggest you double-check your sources. I have work to do."

Every once in a while, you get lucky and everything goes smoothly. Of course, I guess if things had gone really well, McDermott would have been moonlighting as a hitman and confessed to killing Sammi, but nothing's ever that simple.

If Sammi had tried to double-check the information, she'd have discovered that a man named Jordan really did work for Pfeiffer Photography in Toronto. Had she attempted to contact him, she would have learned he was on vacation.

Whoever had taken those pictures had put a lot of effort into his story. Exactly the kind of attention to detail you'd expect from a professional killer.

As we drove, I told Jack what we'd found. Then I tried Denise Noyes again. She answered on the third ring.

"I'm calling about Deanna Macy," I said. "I got your name off one of the missing-persons Web sites."

"Yes?"

Noyes invested the single word with such joy that I winced.

"I'm sorry," I said. "I don't have any news for you."

"Oh." Her voice drooped.

"I'm calling because my niece has disappeared, in circumstances similar to Deanna's. She vanished with her six-month-old daughter. The police say she's run away—"

"But you know better, don't you? You can tell. The police—I guess they've heard that story a million times, they stop listening after a while." Her voice shifted, as if she was settling into a chair. "I'm glad I decided to come home for lunch today. I forgot some tests I'd marked over the weekend."

"Are you . . . a friend of Deanna's?"

"Her sister. Well, half sister. Our dad got around. I was from his first marriage. Deanna was from number four. He's on six now. I'd be lying if I said Deanna and I were close. I didn't know she existed until I bumped into her at a family funeral a few years ago. Helluva way to meet, huh?"

"I bet."

"She's half my age, so we didn't exactly do the sister thing, but I could see she was in a bad place, her mom dead, our dad long gone, Deanna living with her nana, who didn't much want her around. I've done okay for myself, so I tried to help out, but she wasn't comfortable with more than the occasional lunch date. After the baby, her nana kicked her out. I offered to let Deanna stay with my husband and me, but I think she didn't want to intrude, so I helped her find the group home. It wasn't ideal, but she seemed to like it there."

"Which is why you don't think she ran away."

"I know she didn't run off because if she had she wouldn't..." Another pause. A sharp intake of breath. "I'll be blunt. I don't mean to speak poorly of Deanna. She was doing the best she could but, if she'd left, she wouldn't have taken Connor. If she'd wanted to start a new life, it wouldn't have included him. She was having a hard time. She wanted to be off with her friends, going to parties, dating..."

"Like any sixteen-year-old."

"Exactly. When she became pregnant, I strongly suggested adoption. Maybe too strongly. I might have made her feel like I didn't think she could care for a baby and she wanted to prove me wrong."

In the silence, I could hear Noyes's self-recriminations and hurried to change the subject. "I saw Deanna's picture. She's a beautiful girl."

"Isn't she? And Connor? He was gorgeous. People used to stop Deanna in malls and tell her Connor belonged on TV."

"Did anyone ever take his picture? Offer to make him a model?"

Noyes paused. "No. Why?"

"A few weeks before my niece disappeared, a man took photos of her baby. He claimed to be from a modeling agency, but I was suspicious. You hear so much about perverts—"

"Yes!" Noyes fairly shouted the word. "Oh, God, yes! I knew it. I knew it. I told the police, but they brushed me off—" She inhaled, controlling her excitement. "A few weeks before Deanna and Connor vanished, she took him to a Christmas parade. This man said he was from the *Free Press* and wanted to take Connor's picture. Deanna was thrilled. She thought her baby was going to make the front page."

"But he didn't."

"Not the front page, not the back page. I know photographers don't use every shot they take, but when Deanna told me the story, I didn't like it. She said he took a whole roll of pictures, mostly of Connor, but some of the two of them together. That's too many takes for a simple human-interest shot."

"Did Deanna get his name?"

"She didn't ask. Too excited, I'm sure."

"Did she tell you anything about him?"

"She said he looked like a photographer. Clean-cut. Nicely dressed. Homely." A laugh. "That's not the word she used, but you know what I mean."

"Unattractive."

"Yes. She said he was around my husband's age. Thirty-five or so. Oh, and he had very nice teeth. Very straight, very white. She made a point of saying that. As if no one could be a pervert and practice good oral hygiene. Does this sound like the man your niece met?"

"She didn't say anything about his appearance." I hated to lie, but I couldn't have Noyes phoning the police with added information. "I don't know if there's a connection, but I'm going to keep after our local police. Would you like me to keep you updated?"

"Even if there's no connection to Deanna, let me know

if your niece turns up. And hang in there. I know it's hard, but there's always hope, right?"

God, how I wished that were true. But there was no hope for Sammi, and I was pretty sure there wasn't for Deanna, either. I could only hope there was still some for their babies.

Twenty-one

When I got off the phone, I drove in silence and stopped at the first coffee shop we spotted. We went inside, found a quiet table, and I told Jack my theory.

There's a black market for every valuable commodity, including infants. Years back there'd been a scandal over one set of twins being sold multiple times. I recalled none of the specifics, but what did stick in my mind were the photos of the deceived adoptive parents. In their faces, I'd seen all the raw pain and grief of any victim touched by violence.

Though I had no experience with the adoption system, I knew it wasn't like driving over to the Humane Society and saying you'd like a kitten. There were too many parents and too few babies. What if you had a blemish on your personal history? I could be married to a minister and they'd turn down my application.

I'd heard of international adoption, but if you were hell-bent on having a healthy Caucasian baby, how far would you be willing to go? How much would you be willing to pay?

Sammi and Deanna were both marginalized teenage mothers, girls that everyone would assume had just run off. Sammi had an alcoholic, abusive mother. Deanna's grandmother had disowned her. To anyone who did a routine background check, it would seem there was no one to miss either of them.

Both were beautiful young women with beautiful

babies. Healthy girls, healthy babies. Both had their pictures taken within weeks of their deaths. Sales photos.

See how beautiful and healthy this baby is? See the mother? See how she's smiling? She's so happy her baby will go to a good family.

I could not—would not—believe that the people who'd adopted Destiny and Connor knew what had happened to their babies' mothers. I hold out too much faith in the human race for that. The smiling photos of mother and child would go a long way toward persuading buyers of the teen's sincerity. The parents would pay the money, sign phony documents, take the child, and be reassured that they'd never have to worry about the mother contesting the adoption.

Why not just pay the mothers off? From what Noyes said, it wouldn't have taken much to buy Connor from Deanna. The girls had been killed because it was the easiest thing to do. It avoided haggling over price, let the seller keep all the money, and eliminated any chance of interference. They'd been killed because they were disposable.

"What I need to do now is research black-market adoptions. Not that I know where to start looking."

I scrubbed at an ancient coffee ring, my napkin shredding as the stain clung to the melamine.

"Wanna move?" Jack said. "Table over there's clear."

"For a coffee stain? I'll live. It's just . . . it's like seeing a crooked picture. It gnaws at me, especially if I'm already edgy." I rolled my shoulders, then laid a clean napkin over the mark. "There. Now, I need to figure out—"

"Stick with what we know. Black-market babies? No. Hitmen? Yes."

I reached for my coffee, then decided I really didn't need more caffeine. Just thinking about guys out there, killing kids for their babies, was enough to have me perched on the edge of my seat, toes beating the floor, gaze sliding to the door.

"Hit was good." Jack grimaced. "Don't mean that way. Good as in—"

"—professional, I know. It was a clean hit and a decent b—" I couldn't bring myself to say body dump. "—burial. We aren't talking about some thug who'll graduate to contract killer if someone offers him five grand. This guy's a serious pro, meaning we're dealing with a restricted pool of suspects. Not small enough to just go knocking on doors, though..."

"Leave it with me. You look after your business."

We made it back to the lodge by midafternoon. I'd told Emma I was dropping Jack off in Peterborough on my way to Toronto, giving him a break from being cooped up at the lodge. As for why I'd gone to Toronto, Emma knew it was related to Sammi, presuming I was still trying to find her.

I found Emma in the laundry room, folding linens.

"Did you see anyone as you were coming in?" she asked.

"Are we expecting early guests?"

She shook out a pillowcase. "We had one, but only for about an hour before he took off."

"Decided this wasn't quite what he had in mind?"

"No, that wasn't it. At least, I don't think it was." She folded the case, ironing out the creases with her rough hands. "Does anyone know you're looking for Sammi, Nadia?"

I nearly dropped the sheet I was lifting. "What?"

She waved for me to calm down. "It's probably nothing. At worst, the Draytons have hired a PI to look for their grandbaby, and I wouldn't say that's a bad thing. They have the money; they should be looking, not you."

"Someone was asking questions about Sammi?"

"No, nothing like that. If you weren't checking into Sammi, I'd have figured him for someone Mitch brought up, took a shine to you, came back on his own..." Mitch was a Toronto homicide detective who came up a few times a year. "Though, God knows, if that's the case, I could have just told him not to waste his time. You cloister yourself like a nun, blind to perfectly fine men like Mitch, who'd be up every weekend if you gave him one iota of encouragement—"

"This guy..."

"Nice fellow. Big strapping sort, short hair, clean-shaven, polite. Could have been one of our regulars—cop or firefighter—but I didn't recognize him. He checked in, took his bag up, then came down and started poking around."

"Poking around?"

"Checking things out. He saw some of the photos, and he pointed you out, wanted to know whether that was the Nadia Stafford who owned the place. Seemed like he already knew the answer. He asked whether you were around, and when I said you weren't, he wanted to know when you'd be back. I offered him a coffee or a beer, said I could get Owen to take him on a tour of the property, but he wasn't interested. Wandered around for about an hour. Next thing I know, he's at the desk, ringing the bell, bag in hand, telling me he got a call and has to leave. He needed directions to the nearest gas station. I tried giving him his money back for the booking, but he wouldn't take it."

"He paid cash?"

She nodded. My heart felt like it was pounding against my windpipe, cutting every breath in half. I shook out the sheet, letting it snap like a sail as I hid my reaction behind it.

"Did he give a name?"

"Ryan Brown."

"Doesn't ring a bell." Two common names—a good sign it was fake. "Did you happen to see what he was driving?"

"Little silver box. Looked like a rental."

"Huh."

I folded my sheet in half, and was scrambling for an excuse to take off again, when hands grabbed the bottom corners and brought them up for me. I glanced over the quartered sheet at Jack.

"Thanks," I said.

"I forgot your stuff."

"St—?"

"The supplies for the range you asked me to buy. I completely forgot. I'm sorry. If you don't mind me borrowing the truck, I can run into town and see if the hardware store carries them."

I checked my watch. "I'd better go. I know where it's stocked."

I finished folding the sheet, stacked it with the others, and met up with him in the front room.

"You heard?" I asked.

"Yeah."

"I'll pick you up at the door."

Twenty-two

For a professional killer, the line between caution and paranoia can be hard to find. One could argue that it doesn't exist at all. Every hint of threat is worthy of investigation.

It's not like robbing the corner store or dealing drugs behind the lodge. If I'm caught, I'll never see the outside of a prison. That's the cost of a job that pays the equivalent of a constable's annual salary for a couple of four-day stints in New York every year.

Jack thought Emma's initial reaction—that it was some guy who'd visited with his buddies and now was coming back to see me—was a possibility. I didn't. You don't express interest in a woman by driving from God-knows-where and checking into her hotel for the night. That kind of thing only happens in movies...and to other women.

It could be the first scenario Emma had raised—a private investigator looking into Sammi's disappearance, hired by the Draytons. He'd want to question me, as Sammi's employer, but I'd publicly expressed concern, so I'd be a willing source, meaning there was no need to check into the lodge. Maybe he didn't know that. Or maybe he thought my concern was actually ass-covering.

If he knew about my background, that could make me a suspect. Yes, there's a huge difference between killing a lowlife who raped and tortured a teen, and killing a teen employee with a bad attitude, but to some people murder is murder.

* * *

Jack insisted on driving. On my own roads, I instinctively regulate my speed. As Jack had proven the night I found Sammi, if he wasn't on a job, he had no such compunctions.

He pushed the truck up over 130, which wouldn't be so bad on a four-lane highway. On a winding dirt road barely wide enough for two cars? It was a struggle to keep my eyes open.

I knew the service station Emma would have sent him to, and their "full service" was far from "fast service." Sure enough, about two kilometers past it, as we neared the highway turnoff, I spotted a silver compact.

I didn't get a chance to open my mouth before Jack stomped on the accelerator, slamming the words back down my throat. The truck roared forward, engine shrieking, tires hydroplaning over the dirt, and I decided that, target in view, I could safely close my eyes.

When the truck went into a skid, my eyes flew open, certain we were heading for a tree. Instead I saw the silver car. Jack swerved into the car's path and slammed on the brakes, forcing it to stop. He wrestled out of his seat belt, cursing under his breath. When he got it free, he ducked for a look at the other car and went completely still, one hand still holding the seat belt. Then he spat a string of oaths with a venom that made the others sounds like endearments.

"Gonna kill him. Swear I'm gonna fucking kill him." He swung toward me. "Stay here."

"What's—?"

He was already out the door, slamming it so hard the

truck rattled. I wasn't letting him confront anyone without backup. I waited until he'd stumped off without his crutch. Then I got out.

The other man was getting out of his car. His head was down as he unfolded himself from the too-small vehicle, and I saw only the top of his head, dark blond hair cut military-short. He wore slacks and a sports coat, nothing fancy, but a cut above the department store wear my dad and his colleagues bought. His white dress shirt was open at the collar, tie probably stuffed in a pocket.

Leaves dancing in the wind overhead cast moving shadows over the man's face, leaving me with only fleeting glimpses. But it was enough to recognize him.

"Quinn," I whispered.

I broke into a grin and started forward. Then I stopped, hand going to the truck bed, gripping it, the chill of the metal creeping up my arm.

Quinn. At my lodge. Looking at my picture.

Is this Nadia Stafford? The owner?

Seemed like he already knew the answer, Emma had said.

Quinn. Who'd seen my police college nightshirt. Who'd caught a glimpse of me out of disguise. Who'd sworn he'd never use that information, never try to find out anything about me.

My heart thudded so loud I could barely hear Jack, his voice so harsh he sounded like a stranger, words coming as fast and hard as blows. He stood a few inches from Quinn, who'd backed up against the car. Quinn, who never backed down from Jack, who always pulled himself up to his full height, making use of those extra inches in every confrontation.

I took another step.

Seeing me, Jack wheeled. "I've got it. Get back in."

Quinn turned. "Nadia..."

He barely breathed my name, but it floated over as clear as Jack's sharp words.

I turned back to the truck.

"I can explain."

Jack snorted. "Or sure as hell gonna try."

I glanced over as Quinn straightened, jaw tensing with a flare of that old antagonism as he pulled himself straight.

"I screwed up, okay? I admit——"

"You do? Fucking wonderful. You admit it. Apologize. Everything'll be fine."

"You condescending——" Quinn bit the sentence short and turned to me. "I——"

"——fucked up," Jack said. "Yeah. You did. I warned you. Use what you saw? Deal with me."

"I didn't *use* anything. I meant I screwed up by coming here. Look, can I just talk to Nadia—Dee—?"

"Here it's Nadia," I said. "This is my home."

His chin dipped. "I know, and I'm sorry. I thought—well, I guess I wasn't thinking——" He looked at Jack. "Can you give us a minute—?"

"No."

Quinn paused, as if struggling not to be drawn into a fight. He sidestepped toward the front of the car, closer to me. I stayed where I was, tucked in the open doorway of the truck.

"This is what I wanted to tell you in Toronto," Quinn said. "That I know."

"How?" Jack said.

A brief glower at the interruption. Then Quinn continued. "A couple months ago, some of us were talking in the office about a case in Tennessee. A detective shot a dealer point-blank. I guess he'd had a few run-ins with the guy, and nothing would stick, so he just...had enough. Anyway, we were talking about that, and what makes cops snap, and one of the guys said it's always men, that you never see a woman doing that."

The hairs on my neck rose.

"Then someone says no, he remembers this case in Toronto with a woman cop, and the other guy says bullshit, and he says come here and I'll look it up. He Googles it and..."

"Finds me."

Quinn nodded. "He called us over to read the article. I saw the name, the particulars, but it didn't mean anything until he scrolled down and there was a picture."

He shoved his hands into his pockets, head down. "I didn't know what to do, Dee...Nadia. I thought maybe I should act like I'd never seen it. But what if, later, you found out I knew all along? You'd never forgive me and I wouldn't blame you. I knew I had to tell you. I started with the ski trip idea, then thought, great, I treat you to a nice getaway and hit you with that. No way. Then the Toronto job came along. Professional setting, close to home if you wanted to walk away. But then..."

"You got called back."

"And I couldn't just drop that bomb and leave. But all week, it's been driving me nuts, so when I had to be in Montreal tomorrow, I decided to take an early flight, make the drive...And when I got there, I realized it was my worst idea yet."

"So you left."

He nodded.

"That's your story?" Jack said.

A muscle in Quinn's cheek twitched as he pivoted Jack's way. "Yes, Jack, that's my *story*."

I headed toward them. "Jack..."

"Can you prove it?" he said.

"No, Jack, I can't fucking prove it and you know that. You want to hook me up to a polygraph? Or better yet, put a gun to my head and see if I'll crack."

"Quinn..."

At least *he* acknowledged me, glancing over and nodding, then rolling his shoulders and smoothing his tone as he said to Jack, "It would be nice if you could look at our history and agree that I've never been anything but honest and fair. But that's obviously out of the question, so at least give me credit for having a healthy sense of self-preservation. You don't like me. You don't like what I am. It makes you nervous. And seeing me getting close to your protégée *really* makes you nervous. But whatever ethical code you play by, it says you need an excuse to kill me. So do you honestly think I'd give you one?"

Jack snorted, but said nothing. Quinn fished the keys from his pocket.

"I'll take off now, and give you guys time to think it over and decide...whatever you're going to decide." He opened the door. "I'll e-mail you in a week or so, Nadia, and—" He stopped, fingers drumming against the window frame. "Or, I guess, I should wait for you to get in touch with me."

"I will."

He nodded, trying for a smile, but not finding it. He

pulled the door wider. Jack's hand shot out and slapped it shut.

Quinn wheeled. "Oh, for God's sake, Jack. You won't even let me make a graceful exit, will you?"

"You owe her."

"Owe—?" He ripped a wallet from his pocket, yanked out his driver's license, and waved it. "You mean this? Tit for tat? Do you think I wasn't going to tell her who I am? Maybe I just wanted to do it in private, but if that's too much to ask for..." He held the license out, the edge falling from his voice. "Here, Nadia."

I shook my head. "I don't need that. Jack, please, just let him—"

"He owes you. Not information." He plucked the license from Quinn's hand and tossed it through the open window. "She needs help. Working on something. Needs to dig up old cases. Compare—"

"No. He doesn't need to—"

"I will. I'd be glad to," Quinn said. "Anytime you need my contacts or my research, you only have to ask, like I've said. Why don't we find someplace to grab a coffee—"

"Can't," Jack said. "She's got guests coming. Responsibilities." He glanced at me. "After dinner?"

I nodded and we arranged the meeting.

Twenty-three

I had trouble getting away. One couple who'd booked a twilight canoe ride decided over dinner that they'd love to tour the range first. They weren't pushy or demanding, but it's hard to say no without a good excuse.

Jack came to my rescue, saying he knew I wanted to check out a downed fence section, so he'd give the range tour. After dinner, I gathered my fence-mending tools and headed out.

I'd told Quinn to meet me at the service lane near the back of the property. I could have driven there, but it was a warm evening and I needed the walk. When I got to the spot almost ten minutes early, he was already there.

He sat on a log with his back to me. He'd changed into a T-shirt and jeans, the shirt tight over broad shoulders, muscles tense. He stretched his legs, crossing them at the ankles, then pulled them in. One hand drummed the log. The other peeled bark from an old birch. His legs went out again. Back in. As nervous as a twelve-year-old waiting in the woods, not sure his "date" will show.

"Trying to kill my trees?" I asked.

He turned so fast he slid backward, awkwardly catching himself before tumbling to the dirt. A sheepish laugh as he stood, brushing the earth from his hands.

"I thought you'd be coming that way," he said, pointing at the path he'd been watching. "Which is probably the opposite direction to your place, isn't it?"

"It is."

"Lousy sense of direction."

Silence fell, then hung there, awkward. He made a show of looking behind me.

"No chaperone?"

"Not tonight."

"I'm not sure if that's a good sign or bad." He peered into the woods. "If you see a little red dot of light on my forehead...?"

"I'll let you know."

He shoved his hands in his pockets. "Man, Jack was pissed. Not that he didn't have a right to be, if I'd done what he thought I did, hunting you down."

I leaned against the tree he'd been picking at. "Remember when we first met? Accidentally bumping into you and Felix when Jack had been deliberately keeping me away from you guys? Well, he wasn't just being his usual...overcautious—"

"Paranoid."

I smiled. "*Paranoid* self. He hadn't wanted us meeting because of my background and your job. He was afraid..."

"Of exactly what happened. That somehow I'd figure out who you were."

"After that run-in, Jack decided keeping me hidden would only raise more questions. There wasn't much chance you'd heard about my case, much less would remember me even if you had. But, now, he feels responsible."

"I can see that."

I sat on the log. As Quinn lowered himself beside me, he pulled his ID card from his pocket, upside-down.

"If you really don't want to see this, I understand. But I'd like you to."

I took the license and read it: home address, date of birth, and his real name.

"Quincy?"

"Don't laugh."

"I'm not."

"If you try any harder *not* to, you'll give yourself an aneurysm."

I sputtered. "Okay, sorry, it's just ... you don't look like a Quincy."

"I haven't been one since kindergarten, when my teacher misread the list, called me by my middle name, and I decided to stick with it."

I looked at the card. "Robert."

"Rob, usually, but yes."

"So Quincy ... Quinn."

"Not the most original nom de guerre. Jack grumbled about the stupidity of picking it, but it was kind of a personal thing. First action flick I saw as a kid had a hero named Quinn, and then I heard the song 'The Mighty Quinn,' and so ..."

"You went through a phase of wanting to be called Quinn?"

"It was more of an alter ego. Like when you play games, and you need to call yourself something? I was always Quinn, who, let me tell you, was way cooler than Robbie."

"I'll bet."

"Of course, I grew up and I'm *totally* over that now."

"I suppose you'll want me to keep calling you Quinn."

"Up to you." A sly look my way. "But I won't complain if you do."

I laughed, my gaze on the card still in my hands. When

I looked up again, his face was right there, above mine. I blinked, and he pulled back.

"So this job you're working," he began.

"Job? Ah, right. The reason we're out here. It's not a job. More of a . . . private investigation."

I told him the story. In his face, I saw everything I'd felt: concern, dread, grief, rage, then disgust and fury at Sammi's fate. Sometimes, reading a newspaper article and feeling grief or outrage for a victim I've never met, I think there's something wrong with me. Seeing that in Quinn's face was a vindication.

"I'm sorry," he said when I finished.

"I didn't know her that well. Can't even say I liked her very much."

"But you helped."

"I don't think I—"

"You did."

Even without knowing about Amy, Quinn understood what consumed me—fear that I'd failed Sammi.

"I want to help," he said. "I can research similar disappearances."

"Which could risk your job."

"Nah, I'm an old pro at covering my tracks. I'll get whatever you need. I just wish I could do more, that I could stay and help."

He put away his license. Then we sat there, the silence turning awkward again.

"I guess you have a long drive to Montreal," I said finally. "And I should be getting back. Jack was taking my guests on a tour of the range."

Quinn choked on a laugh. "I hope they're behaving themselves. And if not, I hope they paid you in advance."

"It probably didn't last long enough for anyone to give him trouble. Locker. Guns. Ammo. Targets. Seen enough? Good. Done."

Quinn started to laugh, then stopped. "Did you say 'range'? You have a shooting range?"

"An impulse buy when I first got the place and had a bit of money left over, from my buyout and such. One of those things you later regret splurging on, but you're kind of glad you did. It's a nice feature for the lodge, too."

"I'll bet. I saw those pictures inside—boating, caving, rock climbing, rafting . . ."

"The rapids are off the property. Strictly amateur fare. But we have a decent caving system and the lake's nice."

"Man, that's sweet." He shook his head. "Wish I could come up— I mean, *theoretically*. I know I can't."

"We could work something out, some story, like I'm doing with Jack."

"So, Jack, it's his foot, I'm guessing. He's here to recuperate. How'd he—? No, let me guess. He won't tell you what happened."

"He could, but then he'd have to kill me."

We laughed as I stood.

"Anyway, if you ever want to come up, midweek off-season, there's often no one here. It's a great business, but not exactly profitable."

He looked out at the darkening forest. "So that's why you . . . do the other work."

"I can't lose the lodge. Not after— Anyway, you're welcome anytime."

We said good-bye and I started to leave. I'd made it almost to the road, when his footsteps thundered behind me.

"Nadia?"

When I turned, he was right there, so close I smacked into him and his arms went around me, as if to steady me, then I saw his face coming down to mine, so sudden I didn't realize what he was doing until his lips were on mine.

For a second, I didn't respond. But the feel of his mouth, of his arms around me, the smell of him, woke the memories from last fall. Good memories.

I needed this. After one failed relationship since killing Wayne Franco, I'd stopped dating, maybe even passed over into avoidance. No, there was no *maybe* about it. I'd burrowed into the safe cave of avoidance and made it my home. Here was my chance to climb back out. With a guy I liked, one who knew my biggest secret and apparently didn't give a shit. A guy who could never demand commitment or even a standing Saturday night date. The perfect solution, and damned if I was going to be a coward and turn it down.

So I kissed him back. I could feel my body respond, a yearning building into hunger.

But last fall it had been different. Safe. I'd known it couldn't go anywhere. Just fooling around with a sexy guy.

Now the "sexy guy" was Quinn. A friend. Someone who wanted more than a one-night stand.

I might need this, but could I take this chance? Risk losing a friendship for a relationship that might not work out? Maybe I was a coward, but I needed his friendship more than I needed any romantic relationship.

I'd stopped kissing him. I didn't even realize it until he pulled back, looking down at me, confusion and disappointment clouding his eyes.

"I blew it, didn't I?" he said.

I looked up. "No, it's not you—"

"It's not you, it's me. I really like you, but this isn't a good idea. I still want to be friends." A wry, almost bitter smile. "Am I getting close?"

What the hell was I going to say? This was the conversation I'd imagined, only I'd thought it would come from him. Now I could see his feelings hadn't changed. He'd kept his distance in Toronto because he wanted to tell me what he knew first. The honorable thing to do.

"Is it because I know who you are?" he said. "If that bothers you— Hell, I'm sure it bothers you. But it was an accident and I'd never use it against you, Nadia—Dee—" His hand went to his mouth, rubbing his lips. "Shit. You'd think getting past the secret identities would help, but it really doesn't, does it? Just makes things even more complicated."

And there I saw my way out, my excuse to take more time, to not have to make a decision, and, coward that I was, I leapt on it. "It's—it's a shock. I just— Things cooled off between us, and I know we said we were going to back off, but after Toronto, when you didn't seem interested, I thought that was it. Now with this…I just need some time."

A slow smile that lit up his eyes and made my insides twist with guilt.

"I understand," he said, then leaned over and brushed his lips across my forehead. "I won't rush you, Nadia. I want this to work. I really do."

Twenty-four

I found Jack with the guests at the lake, helping Owen prepare for the canoe ride. I apologized for being late, but he brushed it off and kept helping. He even seemed ready to join the excursion, until he found out he'd have to kneel, which wouldn't work with his cast. So he stayed on the dock and had a beer with Owen.

After the trip, one couple wanted to do some dock-sitting of their own, and the other opted for the hot tub. If a couple wants the hot tub, I don't offer to join them. So I took advantage of the break to head to my room and do some research on black-market adoptions. Jack came along, still nursing his beer.

"Saw you didn't take the truck," he said as he closed my bedroom door behind us.

"I like to walk."

"Yeah. On deserted roads. No cell phone. No gun."

"Um, part-time professional killer?" I whispered as I took out my laptop. "I think I can look after myself."

"How? You armed? You need a—"

"Don't say it."

"—dog. Need one. You'd like one, too."

"What I'd like isn't a priority as long as I'm running an inn. If you have any ideas what I could search on, let me know."

He grunted and sat on the edge of my bed. I spent the next hour researching the baby market.

Babies aren't exactly a commodity you can sell on eBay. A quick search brought up an old *Time* magazine article. In it, the writer wondered whether a recent spate of child kidnappings represented an actual crime wave or media hysteria. He imagined editors looking at stories of war and drought and political corruption and saying, "What, no kidnapped kids this morning? Well, find some." If half of those stories were true, you'd be afraid to set foot outside with a stroller.

So how did you sell a baby? Private adoption is illegal in Canada, but I found plenty of sites for it south of the border. Most were likely legitimate, charging only administrative costs. Still, I suspected some were a cover-up for baby-selling, but how to tell? And what I was looking for wouldn't advertise openly. It would be a very small operation—one hitman specializing in finding and killing teen mothers, then selling their babies.

Jack helped me dig deeper into the underground sites. That was really Evelyn's forte, but he'd picked up enough to know how to bypass her, which is always a bonus. Tell Evelyn what we were after, and she'd want in—not because she gave a shit about dead teenage mothers, but because it was something shiny and new. Then she'd add it to my chit as a favor owed. If Quinn found more cases like Sammi's, we'd need Evelyn's encyclopedic knowledge of hitmen, so we were keeping our requests to a minimum.

We found nothing. We'd have to wait for Quinn.

What was I going to do about Quinn? I lay in bed, thinking of that.

I should have taken the excuse he offered, not to postpone a decision, but to let him down easy. *I'm sorry,*

Quinn—I just can't take the chance now that you know who I am. But I couldn't close that door. Part of me still wanted to make this work. I'd responded when he kissed me. I'd wanted more. So what if my heart didn't pitter-patter? If I didn't get all weak in the knees? That was romantic nonsense and I'd always been practical about these things.

I'd never fallen crazy in love. Never even fallen crazy in lust. From the time I'd started dating, I'd picked guys that I liked and enjoyed spending time with. So why this sudden need to feel more? That smacked of an excuse, setting hurdles for Quinn that he could never leap.

By my own self-imposed standards, Quinn was perfect. Someone I liked and liked being with. Someone who understood me.

I remembered all the conversations we'd had last fall and online since. The endless discussions of justice and mercy, like the ones I'd heard around my father's poker games through my childhood. Quinn and I didn't always agree, but we were on the same wavelength. We understood each other in a way that I think we both craved.

In Jack, I'd found someone who accepted the worst in me. The killer in me. But that was only one half, and the other part—the cop—he'd never get. He couldn't understand the battle between the cop and the killer, how the two sides attracted and repulsed each other, magnets unable to separate, unable to fit together. In Quinn, I found someone else waging that war. Now, he knew what I'd done. And he was fine with it—so fine he hadn't deemed it worthy of comment.

His biggest concern had been coming clean and reciprocating. But as I lay in the darkness, my mind wandered into that nebulous realm between waking and sleeping, where emotion overshadows thought, and suddenly was horrified by how easily I was taking this. A federal agent knew I was a hired killer...and I was okay with that?

What if it didn't work out? What if I decided not to get involved with him, and his revenge was to turn me in? What if he was caught and threw me to them instead— the unstable ex-cop hitwoman who'd seduced him into a life of crime?

The deeper the night got, the deeper my worries ran.

Did I think I'd seen his real license? We could buy the best fakes around. Quinn himself was probably a fake— not even a real hitman.

I'd never seen him pull a hit. The one time I'd done a job with him, *I'd* taken out the target. He'd set me up. He was an undercover cop, building a character I wanted to see, luring me in so he could get to the big fish, to Jack.

A cute, sexy, funny lawman who rode rapids and rappelled mountains in his spare time. The perfect guy wrapped in the perfect package. And he wanted *me*? How deluded could I get?

I got up, pulled on jeans and a sweatshirt, and headed downstairs.

Shadows swathed the lower level. Moonlight dappled the floor like a cobblestone path. I followed it into the kitchen, leaving the lights off, my eyes having already had hours to adjust.

Crossing to the cupboards, I saw a figure by the window and bit back a yelp of surprise. It was Jack, his back to me as he leaned against the window frame with one hand, the other clutching the neck of a beer bottle. He stared out the window, lost in thought, oblivious.

I took a slow step back, retreating. He turned.

"Come in."

"No, you're—"

"Come in." He grabbed his crutch from the wall, leaving the bottle on the sill, then limped toward the cupboards. "Which one?"

"I can make—"

"Sit. Which one?"

I told him and he found the canister of hot chocolate mix—my "can't sleep" beverage of choice, dating from childhood when my father would fix it for me as he worked on cases into the wee hours. Cocoa and candy—I'm sure a shrink would have something to say about my choice of comfort foods.

Jack abandoned his beer and fixed a second mug. As he made the hot chocolate, I poured cookies onto a plate.

"Should talk outside," he said.

I agreed, and we gathered our jackets and shoes, then headed out.

As we approached the gazebo, I eyed it uncertainly. It looked so ... confined. Like being back in my room again, staring at the four looming walls, inhaling stale air.

Jack glanced my way, then nodded toward the dock. "Sit out? Seems warm enough."

"Sure."

I sat on the edge, my feet dangling a few inches from the water, the warm mug cupped in my hands. For a few minutes, we just stayed like that, the quiet broken only by the munching of cookies.

"Couldn't sleep?" Jack asked finally.

I nodded.

"About Quinn?"

I lowered the mug to my lap, my hands still wrapped around it. "When he left, everything seemed fine. But once I crawled into bed...I don't know. Thoughts seem to roll around in my head with no place to go, like tumbleweeds getting bigger and bigger. The next thing you know, I'm totally convinced Quinn is an undercover agent setting me up to take you down."

"He's not."

"I know. If you had any doubts about that, you'd never have gotten near him."

He eased back, shrugging. "Might. But he's clean. Evelyn's checked him out. So have I. Ever changes his mind? Decides to flip on me? On you? Remember what I said last year. He flips..."

"You'll flip harder."

"His story? About finding you? I believe him. Ever seen Quinn lie? Like a fucking five-year-old." He shook his head in disgust. "Looking you up when he promised not to? Then making up a story? Nah. Quinn's a lotta things. Not sneaky. Not sly. Doesn't have what it takes."

"He's an open book."

"Noticed, huh?" Another shake of his head, more bewilderment than disgust now. "Should make him a lousy pro. But the thing about Quinn? He doesn't kid himself. Knows what he is. What he isn't. Works around it."

"I know I'm overreacting, but I lie down and...anxiety dreams, I guess. Even when I'm still awake."

Jack sipped his cocoa, giving no sign he understood. I suppose he'd exorcised all his demons years ago...if he'd ever had any.

"So, is everything going okay here, at the lodge?" I said. "I know it's not exactly four-star accommodations—"

"It's good." He took another sip. "Reminds me of summer vacations. When I was a boy. Cabin we used to go to. Nothing like this. Belonged to a friend of a friend. For a bottle, anyone could use it. A shack. No running water. No electricity. No forests and lakes. Just bog land. But for us kids? Fucking paradise."

He shifted, laying his mug aside as he eased back, braced on his arms. "Spent days tramping around. Brothers and me. Build forts. Swim. Goof off."

"Sounds nice."

"It was. 'Cept when I'd get lost. Happened sometimes. Brothers took off. I couldn't keep up. Forgot I was there."

I laughed. "You weren't any noisier than you are now, huh? So you must have been the youngest, then."

I meant it as a casual comment, but hearing it, I realized it could sound like a question—an invasion of Jack's closely guarded privacy—and I was about to hurry on when he said, "Yeah. Four of us. All boys. I was youngest."

"Do you—?" This time I managed to stop myself.

"What?"

I shook my head. "Nothing. Just . . . I'm used to making conversation with guests, so I start blathering and prying. Sorry."

"Ask."

"Really, I—"

"Ask."

"I just wondered whether you ever go back and see them."

"No one to see. Brothers. Parents. Gone."

He could have just meant they were no longer in Ireland, but I could tell from his tone that wasn't it.

"I'm sorry."

He shrugged. "Been a long time. Gone before I left."

He reached for another cookie, realized it was the last, and broke off half.

"Quinn? *He's* got family. Parents. Some siblings. Nieces, nephews, what have you. Part of what I was saying. He wouldn't flip. Family. Friends. Job. Community. He's got too much to lose."

"More than we do."

"Exactly."

Twenty-five

Quinn called late the next morning. He said he would send his results through the anonymous e-mail accounts we used, then call Jack's cell and tell him the message was there, to keep me from racing off to check my e-mail every five minutes.

His timing was perfect. One couple had already checked out, and the other had left for lunch reservations in Bancroft.

Quinn had found another case similar to Sammi's and Deanna's. Two months ago, in Michigan, another pretty teen had disappeared with her infant son. Like Deanna, she'd been in a group home.

"It seems the killer started with group homes," I said to Jack as I read. "But he ran into a problem with this second one. The girl was the grand-niece of a city alderman, who insisted on a police investigation. A cursory investigation, Quinn says, and already shelved, but I bet it gave our guy a scare. He realized that living in a group home doesn't necessarily mean you don't have any family, so he started being more careful. And he decided to cross the border.

"A week before Sammi disappeared, a girl in Barrie complained about a guy matching our description wanting pictures of her and her baby. The police fluffed it off as a random pervert. Barrie's an hour north of Toronto. He switched to Ontario. Maybe he thinks our law enforcement isn't as sophisticated. Or he's afraid of the cases being linked."

"Could be."

MADE TO BE BROKEN

Jack's tone was no more laconic than usual, but it was like a spritz of ice water, reminding me to slow down.

"No bodies have been found yet," I said. "The second girl disappeared on a walk, like Sammi. He seems to prefer quiet, private kill sites. But that could just be a response to circumstances. After he kills the girl, he's stuck with a crying baby. As great as it is to have similar cases, I'm not sure how much they'll help in narrowing down *who's* doing the killing."

"Got some ideas. Run past Evelyn."

Jack consulted Evelyn. I wasn't thrilled with that, but it was the fastest way to narrow down the list. From her, he got the names of two hitmen possibilities, with the more likely one having moved to Toronto recently.

"Great," I said as I cleaned up after the sunset canoe ride. "This week looks slow for guests, so I can take off and—"

"I'll do it."

My hands tightened around the paddle I was lifting into its berth. Something pricked my hand. I stared at the welling blood.

"Nadia?"

"Hmm?"

"I'll go after him."

"N-no." I fumbled the paddle into place and swiped my hand across my jeans. "You can't, not with your foot. I'll—"

"No, Nadia."

"I can—"

"Shouldn't."

I swiped my fingers again, harder, wincing. Jack caught my hand and lifted it into the dim light of the boathouse.

"Got a sliver."

I balled my fist. "I'll be careful. I'll do proper reconnaissance work and make absolutely certain this is the guy. You can come if you want, and I'll let you make the decisions. I just need to see this through."

"You will. It's him? I'll call. Bring you in. He's all yours."

I opened my fist and stared at the blood, my heart hammering. As much as I wanted to find Sammi's killer myself, he was right. Scouting didn't require my personal touch, and it was better if I stayed put for a little while.

When my hand started curling again, he pulled my fingers flat.

"Only making it worse. Come on. Get it fixed up."

Jack went to Toronto alone. When the guests opted out of the bonfire, I drove him to Peterborough and let him take my work car from there. He promised he'd check in with updates a few times a day. He called the next morning, then afternoon, then evening. He didn't have much to say, just, "I'm looking," "Found him," "Following him," "Cased his place." The calls were a waste of his time, and I knew he was only doing them for my sake, but I wasn't sure what would be more frustrating: his single-sentence updates or none at all.

As for the person he was following, I knew only that he was male. Before he'd left, Jack had sidestepped my questions with "tell you later."

Finally, Thursday afternoon, I heard the words I'd been waiting for: "It's him." Then, "Need you here."

"In Toronto? Sure, I can be there in—"

"No. On the move. Heading your way. Can you meet up?"

"You're coming back?"

"He is."

It took me a minute to decipher his shorthand: Sammi's killer was heading out of Toronto, coming this way. On the move. After another girl.

For a moment, words wouldn't come. All I could see was Sammi's corpse, streaked with dirt, staring up in outrage.

"You there?" Jack said.

"He's on the trail, you mean. Of another—"

"Maybe just hunting."

Hunting...

I took a deep breath. "Right. Okay. Um, so where—?"

"On the 401. Heading east. Just passing—" A pause, as if looking for signs. "—Oshawa."

"So should I—?"

"Get ready. Tell Emma you're leaving. Wait for my call."

The next ninety minutes seemed like nine hundred. Finally Jack called again. He was outside a restaurant in Kingston. His target was inside.

"Might be nothing," Jack said. "Different job. Meeting a client. Still... Thought you'd want to head out. Catch up."

"I do."

* * *

Two hours later, after quickly assembling a disguise, I was there. For the last thirty minutes, the target had been parked outside a community center, reading a newspaper.

I'd left my truck in a grocery store lot a block away, and joined Jack in my work car parked beside a church. From there, we watched the target as he waited in his compact car, tucked between a minivan and an SUV.

Even with the binoculars I'd lent Jack, I couldn't see the man. He had a newspaper stretched across the steering wheel, either reading as he waited or just wanting to look as if he was.

"Work name, Rainman," Jack said. "Real name, Ron Fenniger."

"You know him?"

"Not personally. Evelyn checked him out years back. Possible protégé. Seemed promising. Didn't last."

"Where was he putting his money?"

"Up his nose."

An old story, and a common trajectory for professional killers. They start as garden-variety criminals, then discover they have a knack for killing—good reflexes, steady nerves, and the ability to blend. They realize how much money there is to be made in contract hits . . . but it's like a lounge singer suddenly pulling in twenty grand a gig with no idea how to spend it. They find places—women, booze, dope, gambling, all the usual vices.

That's when it falls apart. The reflexes, the nerves, the ordinariness that made them a good hitman disappear. So they have two choices—retire fast, or find themselves on the other end of a gun, facing an associate hired by someone who deems them a liability.

As Jack explained, Fenniger had begun his crash-and-burn, then leveled out, learning to keep his drugs and work separate. But someone like that would never be top-tier again. He'd made a couple of small mistakes, enough to keep a middleman from recommending him to a big client. He could only pull in top-tier money if he didn't mind taking risky jobs with subpar clients who'd turn him in at the first sign of trouble.

According to Evelyn, though, Fenniger had withdrawn his name from the pool with one middleman, who figured he'd retired. But it seemed he'd just found a way to bypass the middleman, going into business for himself, with clients who wouldn't care how good a hitman he was, because as far as they knew, they were hiring a baby broker.

"Do you think he's meeting with one of those clients now?" I asked.

Jack shrugged. "All I know? Moving too fast. Three girls in four months?"

"The pace doesn't seem to be causing him any trouble. As far as Quinn can tell, none of the missing girls are still being investigated."

"Lotta money. But lotta work."

"You think he's getting greedy and overextending himself. Could be. It probably seems like fast, easy money in an untapped market. I doubt he could keep it going for long, though. Is that what you mean? I should back off and let him hang himself?"

"Nah. This rate? Could kill half dozen girls by then. You don't want that."

I didn't miss the pronoun. *I* wouldn't want that. As for Jack, well, I'm sure Jack wasn't keen on the thought of a hitman targeting young mothers, but left to himself, I'm not sure he'd do anything about it.

"Are you saying you'd rather not be involved? Because you don't have to—"

"Not saying that. Just ... thinking."

The community center side door opened, and out streamed a conga line of teenage girls and baby strollers.

And Fenniger began to hunt.

He was as accomplished as any predator, zeroing in on the best prey even as the door closed behind the last girl. He targeted four with his camera. All were Caucasian. All pretty—though that wasn't a difficult criterion at an age when youth itself makes most girls attractive. But he winnowed out the cute girl with glasses and the beautiful overweight one, both of which could suggest a hereditary condition that might not sit well with prospective baby buyers. Ignored, too, was the blond with the upscale, shining new megastroller, who probably came from a more affluent section of town.

Fenniger made no move to leave his car, just surreptitiously snapped photos, camera lens resting on top of his paper, as if he was still reading. When one of his choices lifted a dark-skinned baby from the stroller, to adjust his hat, his number of candidates dropped to three.

His favorite seemed to be a strawberry blond with a quick smile. When she headed toward the sidewalk, his reverse lights came on ... until an older model sedan pulled into the lot, a middle-aged woman jumping out to help her daughter get the baby into his car seat.

His next choice headed to a bus stop across the street with two other girls. Fenniger eased the car into the spot behind his. It lacked the cover of the minivan and SUV, but would be easy to slide out of quickly when the bus arrived.

As he watched her, he pulled at his lower lip, head slightly tilted, gaze sliding now and then to option three, a girl with dark curls swaddling her baby against the chill as she cooed at him.

I knew what he was thinking. Option two wasn't as pretty as three, but she was blond and fair, whereas three seemed to have Mediterranean blood, and could be a tougher sell. Yet three was alone while two laughed and chatted with her friends, more vivacious, probably more popular, with more people to miss her. And number two hadn't so much as glanced in the stroller since leaving the building, while three couldn't take her eyes off her baby. Which would be the happier, healthier, better adjusted child? More important, which would provide those important "happy mother and child" photos?

I knew what he'd decided. When the dark-haired girl bundled her baby into his shabby stroller, he turned his car off, then got out. He spent a couple of minutes fussing with things in the vehicle, working out the kinks from sitting while giving her time to get a head start.

"Yes, I'm following," I said when Jack glanced my way. "I'll leave a big gap. With that stroller, she's not going to break into a sprint and disappear. Even you could probably keep up."

"Want me to? I follow direct? You circle the block?"

I shook my head. "I'd rather you wait here in case he comes back for the other girl."

I waited until the girl reached the first street corner, with Fenniger tailing twenty paces behind, then I got out of the car.

Twenty-six

I followed Fenniger for three blocks. The origin of his nom de guerre quickly became apparent. At least an inch shorter than me, skinny, with a pinched face, he looked like a community theater actor trying to imitate Dustin Hoffman in *Rain Man,* right down to the shuffling walk.

The girl finally turned into a three-story walkup. I was a few paces from a bus shelter, so I veered in there, where I could stand around without looking obvious.

Fenniger went about ten feet past the doors, then backed up, straining to see a street number. Finding it, he nodded, took an envelope from under his jacket, and hurried into the building. Playing delivery guy—an easy way to get in.

Five minutes later, he came out, having seen where the girl went, whether she let herself in, and whether a roomie answered her knock.

He scanned the street—low-income housing on one side and storefronts on the other. Then he crossed and went into a tiny Tim Hortons coffee shop, probably settling in for a longer stakeout.

I called Jack.

"I need to find a better place to hang out," I said. "I see another coffee shop a few doors down but it looks dead. Might be closed. The Tim Hortons is packed. I could probably—"

"No."

"I'll head to the other one, then, and call you when I'm settled."

The coffee shop wasn't closed, but I suspected it soon would be. A shame, really. One step inside and you knew the place had been there forever. The faint smell of cigarettes, worn into the walls long before antismoking bylaws. The grooves in the floor from chairs being pulled in and out, day after day, year after year. Yellowing newspaper articles on the walls, trumpeting the triumphs of countless Little League and soccer teams the owner had sponsored.

But now, only the most steadfast customers remained, all the other regulars probably circling the block guiltily to get their daily double-double at Timmy's. Can't say I've ever understood the appeal. The coffee's decent enough, but the rabid devotion the chain inspires is enough to make one suspect there's something more addictive than caffeine in those beans.

With only a few tables in use, I easily got one by the window. Five minutes later, Jack walked in. I waved him over.

"What can I get you?" I asked. "I'd have grabbed it, but I wasn't sure whether you'd want decaf, too." On a job, any stimulant was a no-no, but this wasn't really a job.

"Decaf's good."

Juggling hot coffee and a crutch was a recipe for first-degree burns, but that didn't keep Jack from insisting he could manage. That crutch, though, meant I could move a lot faster, and I sprinted for the counter, leaving him muttering behind me.

So we sat, drank coffee, watched out the window, and talked. Or *I* talked, about my plans for a meadow picnic area. Intentionally boring conversation. Had anyone been inclined to eavesdrop, he would have given up after about ten seconds... or fallen asleep. Jack seemed interested enough, asking questions and making comments. He always seemed interested in my plans for the lodge. Maybe because he knew it was one topic, other than guns, that I could blather endlessly about.

After an hour, Fenniger left... to relocate to a restaurant farther down, presumably for dinner. We took his place in Tim Hortons and dined on sandwiches.

As dusk fell, the girl and baby left their apartment. I gathered our trash, preparing to follow. But the restaurant door stayed closed. Had Fenniger been caught unawares on a bathroom break? Or with the bill unpaid? Or had he slipped out the back?

We were about to leave when Fenniger finally emerged. The girl was a block ahead, but he didn't hurry to catch up, instead fussing with his wallet under the shadow of the storefront overhang. Two minutes passed. Then he crossed the street, and disappeared into her building.

"Recon work," I said.

Jack nodded.

"Should we...?"

Another nod. I wiped our crumbs from the table, then followed him.

I hoped Fenniger was breaking into the girl's apartment. Instant interrogation room. An occupied building in early evening wasn't ideal, but we could make it work.

Unfortunately, Fenniger chose to get his information from a more direct source. As we waited in the foyer, out of sight, we heard him stop a boy who sounded about twelve, naive enough to answer a stranger, old enough to answer intelligently.

Fenniger put on a good show. He was looking for his niece, whom he hadn't seen in a few years. She was a teenager, dark hair, baby... Oh, right. Tina in 2B. Tina? No, his niece's name was Katrina. But he'd heard friends called her Trina. Or maybe that was Tina...

Using leading questions under the guise of making sure his Katrina was this Tina, Fenniger fished for the details he wanted, soon learning that Tina didn't have a boyfriend, rarely had friends over, and was never visited by anyone over twenty. The boy said she kept to herself, and he didn't know her well, but if Fenniger was her uncle, maybe he could help her out, because she seemed really nice, and he'd heard she was behind on the rent. Another marginalized teenage mother, estranged from her family. Perfect pickings.

Fenniger ended with a few general questions about Tina's appearance, and finally admitted that, no, this definitely wasn't his niece. Too bad.

Mission accomplished, he left... and returned to Tim Hortons. Before Jack and I could decide on another place to hole up, Fenniger emerged, large coffee in hand, supporting my theory of addictive properties.

He headed back toward the community center. Jack went for the car as I followed on foot. At the center, Fenniger got into his car and pulled away. We fell in behind.

"A junkyard?" I said, squinting into the darkness at the jagged metal mountains crossing the landscape.

"Auto wreckers."

"Whatever. The point is—"

"—why's he stopping? No fucking idea. Maybe his car-buretor broke. Needs a replacement."

I couldn't tell whether he was joking. I never could.

I peered out at a half dozen heaps of parts on a lot blanketed with rusting corpses. The whole place might be seven acres. Around the front, at the end of the rutted dirt laneway, we'd spotted a tiny building, probably an office, much too small for a house. The only lights came from it, a pair of security floods attached to the roofline.

Whatever the reason, I could only pray that Fenniger got out of that car and walked into that vacant lot, with the nearest neighbors a half kilometer away . . .

A flare of light as Fenniger opened his door. For a sec-ond, he stood illuminated in the glow. Then he eased it shut, trying to be quiet, the click still loud enough to carry through our closed windows. A moment of dark-ness. Then a second ball of light, smaller, as he flipped on a flashlight and headed for the fence.

I smiled. "Talk about a lucky break."

"Not luck. Wait long enough? Chance will come. Just gotta be patient."

"Evelyn's right. You are an optimist."

He met my grin with a level look. There was no rebuke in it, but no smile, either.

I rubbed my hands over my face, pushing back the lick of giddy excitement. "Okay, I'm fine."

"Never said you weren't."

"You don't have to—it's all in the look."

I massaged my neck, working out the kinks from a long day of sitting, while trying to forget that my prey was walking straight into a trap as perfect as any I could have set.

Too perfect?

What if Fenniger was the one *setting* it?

That slowed my thumping heart.

"Do you think he could have made us?" I said. "If he knows we're tailing him, this is the perfect place to get us out and separated."

"Yeah."

"Yeah?"

"Thought about that. Was going to mention it."

"When? As I'm running after him? Were you going to shout after me, 'Oh, by the way, this could be a trap'?"

"Nah. Hate shouting."

I shook my head as Fenniger scaled the eight-foot fence.

Jack continued, "Could *always* be a trap. Any stakeout. Any chase. Any hit. You think you're in control? Never count on it."

Fenniger was at the top now, dimly silhouetted against the overcast night sky. There were two lines of barbed wire across the top. As Fenniger cut it, Jack cracked down his window. I arched my brows.

"Dogs," he murmured, meaning he was listening for guard dogs.

I suspected the barbed-wire fence was the only security. The cars inside didn't look like they'd have enough salvageable parts to make even fence climbing worthwhile.

Fenniger hit the ground with a thump. No thunder of running paws answered. Not a bark, growl, or whine, either.

"Toolbox?" Jack whispered as he put the window up.

I pulled it from under my seat and checked for wire cutters as he outlined a plan.

When he finished, I laughed softly. "An oldie but a goodie."

"Think you can manage?" he asked.

"I do believe I'll be a natural."

I turned off the dimmer so we could open the doors without the lights going on. I waited for Jack to step out, then crawled across his seat. The fewer doors opening, the less noise.

We searched for a good spot to scale the fence. Clipping the barbed wire at the top was a noise we couldn't eliminate, so we'd make our cut under a tree, where I couldn't be seen.

After last night's warm evening, the temperature had dropped again in typically unpredictable spring fashion. I could see my breath hanging in the air. Cold always seems to make every noise louder, as if the sound waves bounce off the frozen surfaces. More likely, it's just the absence of competition—on nights like these, most living things hole up.

I helped Jack over the fence—one time he didn't pull the "I can handle it" routine. Then we stood in the dark patch under the tree. After a moment, I picked up the faint scratch of metal on metal—the wind rubbing parts together deep in the yard. A furious rustle erupted to our left. Rats or other night animals. A rhythmic plinking from the direction of the building would be rain gutter runoff or fluid dripping from a car. A cow lowed in the distance. A dog answered, a trio of hopeful barks trailing off in a mournful howl.

Jack's fingers brushed my hip, and he directed my attention to a faint glow behind the wreck mountain closest to the office. The light bobbed, then swung across the building. Fenniger's flashlight.

Was he heading for the office? Junkyards and auto wreckers were popular businesses for both petty criminals and crime organizations—a legitimate business on a big piece of property in an isolated location.

There was unlikely to be anything of value in the office, but Fenniger wasn't a thief. More likely there was a drop box here where he could pick up weapons, fake ID, or other equipment he'd bought.

Only a guess, of course. He might be moving closer to the building to lure us in. Or he might be searching the parts heaps for that carburetor he needed. As Jack would say, it didn't matter. Consider the possibility his target was the office, consider the possibility it wasn't, and give neither the dangerous weight of expectation.

Twenty-seven

I motioned to Jack that I'd loop around the two interven-ing junk piles, letting him take the straightaway along the dark fence. Again, he didn't argue. With his cast, he was in no shape to creep through a minefield of rusting metal. He was in no shape to be hunting a killer at all, but there was no sense trying to tell him that.

I picked my way through the part-strewn strip be-tween the fence and the first heap. As I circled behind it, the going got tougher. In the city, "darkness" means you have to squint to read signs. In the forest, you're almost guaranteed a "can't see your hand in front of your face" black. But in a rural area? Conditions can change by the minute. With a full moon and stars, it's brighter than any city street. Once those astral illuminations sneak behind the clouds, though, every source of light makes a huge difference. By the fence, the office floodlights had been more than enough. But when I passed behind that first mound, the building disappeared, and so did the light.

I waited ten seconds, hoping my eyes would adjust more, my racing pulse reminding me that with each pass-ing moment, I could be losing my best shot at Fenniger. I gave up, started forward, and knocked my knee against a tire. The rubber absorbed the sound, but it was lesson enough—better a dim light than a loud crash. I turned on my penlight, holding it under my hand, the beam lighting only the ground at my feet. Then I continued through the automobile graveyard.

There was an eerie unnaturalness to the place that

made my hackles rise. It looked like something from a postapocalyptic nightmare, the wrecks like mutilated corpses, front ends hacked off, tops peeled away, empty headlight sockets staring blindly. The stink of gasoline and rust and vinyl blocked any natural scent. The wind carried only an icy, metallic chill that seared my lungs. When I rounded the last heap, the office light opened up a landscape of fields and fences and barns—a natural view that eased my nerves.

I turned out my light and crept along in the shadows. Finally I had a clear view of the building. Fenniger was less than ten feet ahead, stepping away from the very parts heap I was using for cover. I stopped. He kept going, cutting across the dozen empty feet between us and the office door.

I eased forward for a better view. To the left of the door was a lit window. Did that mean someone was inside? If so, Fenniger was exposed now. Either he was taking a huge chance or he expected to find someone there. Not a blind pickup but a meeting.

I should have considered that. Jack would have.

Damn.

A second party meant a potential witness.

Unless . . .

I lifted my gun, my fingers automatically adjusting their position as I analyzed my target. Shoulder shot. The right— No, his left hand was poised by his open jacket, ready to grab his firearm. I shifted my target.

A single silenced shot. Take him down. Drag him away from the building before whomever he was meeting knew he was there.

And I expected him to take the bullet without a peep?

Shit.

Maybe there was no one inside, and the light was just on for added security. If so, I could follow him inside— an even better place for an interrogation.

If he *was* meeting someone, I'd just need to be patient, like Jack said. Let him do his business, wait for him to leave, and when he was far enough away, grab him, gag him, and drag him to the back of the lot.

Still, I hoped the light was just—

Fenniger raised his hand. The knock rang out through the silent yard.

Damn.

Don't expect. Don't even hope. View all options with equal dispassion. Easy for Jack to say—the guy who viewed *everything* with dispassion.

At the clank of an opening dead bolt, I realized I'd made another mistake. When Fenniger's back was to me, I should have scampered to the car wreck ten feet to my right, where I could hide and see whoever opened the door. Now I'd be running right across that person's field of vision.

The door opened. I could tell only by the light flooding out. For all I knew, there were a half dozen people inside.

"Shit," a voice rasped from within. "I told you—"

Fenniger's hand swung up, as if to shove his contact back inside. I withdrew into the shadows, shuddering with frustration.

The harsh spit of a silenced shot stopped the speaker midsentence.

Not a meeting, but a hit.

As I pulled farther back into the shadows, metal

clanged far to my right. I spun. A figure vanished behind a wrecked car.

Jack.

Goddamn it, he shouldn't be out here. One whack of his cast against a car . . .

Had Fenniger heard? Stupid question. He'd just pulled a hit—he'd be straining to hear so much as a mouse scampering through the debris.

Fenniger was poised in the doorway, frozen while bending to check his mark. Still hunched over, he backed up, then swung to the side of the door, pressing himself against the wall, out of the light.

He surveyed the darkness. I stood still, holding my breath. After a minute, he decided it was only an animal. Twenty more seconds, and his shoulders dropped, gun sliding down a few inches as he relaxed. A few moments and . . .

Another clank. Softer, but this time, Fenniger homed in on it in a split second. He edged along the wall. Then, gaze and gun trained on the spot where he'd heard the noise, he pushed his mark's corpse inside with his foot while closing the door, shutting out the light. Back still pressed to the wall, he sidestepped to the corner of the building. His free hand swung up, flashlight flicking on. As the beam pinged off cars, a scuffle answered—Jack scurrying to better cover.

Shit, shit, shit! He should have stayed in the car. Goddamn him, if he blew this because he was too damned proud to admit he couldn't handle it . . .

"Five seconds," Fenniger's voice rang out. "Show yourself or I start shooting. Five. Four. Three—"

I fired. Just as I did, Fenniger stepped away from the

building, and the bullet destined for his shoulder only grazed it.

He veered toward me, shooting on instinct—the same instinct that had me diving for the ground instead of trying for a second shot. I hit the dirt in a tumble and rolled out of it, flying to my feet, gun swinging up, finger already on the trigger . . .

He was gone.

I swallowed a curse that came out more like a growl, then dashed for the wreck ten feet away—the one I should have been behind earlier. I peered through the broken windows. From here, I could see the whole building, and the swath of empty yard around it. No sign of Fenniger.

I took a deep breath, quelling my frustration. He'd run when I'd gone into my tumble, meaning he hadn't had time to get far. No farther than the back of the building. As I eased around the car for a better look, the clatter of gravel from behind the office confirmed my suspicions.

I smiled and readjusted my grip on the gun.

Surrounding the office was a twenty-foot open patch of land. Behind it was the fence. Just beyond that was a windbreak of evergreens, and a great place to hide, but to get to it, he'd have to cross that open ground and climb over the fence. Twenty feet to be seen. Twenty feet to be shot. He wouldn't risk it. Not yet.

Something tapped the back of my calf. I looked down. Nothing. A second hit.

Jack stood behind the car, tossing pebbles to get my attention. Once he had it, he approached, silent now. If only he'd been that quiet earlier.

I turned my attention back to the building.

Jack touched my hip and leaned down to my ear. "You okay?"

I nodded. "He hit a mark. Did you see it?"

As he paused, I knew he must not have. I glanced back at the building. Still no Fenniger. When I looked back at Jack, he motioned for me to keep watching, and leaned down, his warm breath thawing my frozen earlobe.

"Go around. I'll cover. Signal. Take him down. Pick up the plan."

I nodded.

Twenty-eight

While Jack covered me, I made the short dash, and moved quietly around the heap. I lifted my hand to signal that I was going to run, as he'd asked.

Still, it was a slow trip along the wall, step by step, gun ready. I was about three paces from the back when a clang reverberated through the yard, from the far side of the building, where Jack waited.

Signal . . .

He hadn't meant for me to signal him before crossing. The missing pronoun was "I" . . . as in "I'll signal you with a distraction that'll draw his attention to the opposite side of the building, so you can get around the back corner unseen." Damn him. One of these days, I was going to be the first hitman killed by verbal shorthand.

I dashed to that corner. One quick peek. Sure enough, Fenniger was at the far end of the building, looking in the direction of the noise. I wheeled silently around. As the toe of my sneaker was about to touch down, I remembered the crunch of gravel that had given Fenniger away. I looked to see a six-inch border of it along the foundation, and slid my toe to the dirt beyond.

Fenniger leaned out, around the opposite corner, hunched over. He glanced left, probably gauging the distance to the fence. A muttered "shit" as he realized it wasn't any better an escape route than it had been five minutes ago.

He rolled back onto his heels, straightening, flexing his gun arm. His free hand reached up to rub a kink from the back of his neck. When he pulled his fingers away, I pressed my gun barrel into the vacated spot.

He went rigid. Then his elbow shot back. I grabbed his arm, wrenched it behind his back, and peeled his fingers from the gun. He shifted his weight, putting all of it onto one leg and lifted the other to kick back at me. I slammed the weight-bearing leg out with a knee to the back of his. He went down, and I let him, arm still behind his back, guiding his fall.

"So predictable," I said as I dug one knee into the small of his back, gun back in place at the base of his skull. "You make it too easy, you know that?"

He struggled. I pushed his arm up and he grunted in pain.

"You like killing pretty girls, Ron?"

He went perfectly still, and I swore I could hear his heart thumping against his rib cage.

Facedown on the ground? Arm a half inch from breaking? Gun to his head? Nothing he couldn't handle. But an attacker who knew his real name? That was a problem.

"Ronald Fenniger," I said. "Aka Rainman. Still putting your profits up your nose, Ron? Or are you making too much to snort these days? Got yourself a sweet little business enterprise there. Killing teenage girls and selling their babies."

"You want in?"

I'd been doing well until then. Keeping my cool, playing my part. But at those words, a white-hot ball of rage exploded behind my eyes. Fenniger let out a high-pitched squeal of agony, and his arm went limp. I looked down to see it bent backward, the forearm almost perpendicular with the upper arm.

Then the icy anger slid away, leaving something warm and blissful. I lifted his broken arm, then dropped it and smiled.

"That's gotta hurt," I said.

"You bitch." Spittle rained on the dirt as he twisted under my knee. "You fucking—!"

I grabbed his hair and yanked his head back. He gagged, choking on his own curse.

"Ever snapped a man's neck, Ron? They say if you know how to do it, one wrench is all it takes." I pulled his head back another inch. He gurgled, but his eyes were slits, hiding his fear. "As fast as a CNS shot, with none of the noise and none of the mess. You don't even need a weapon. How cool is that? But it's not something you can get right on the first try. You'd need practice, and I bet you'd have trouble finding people willing to volunteer."

I eased back, knee digging into his spine. "That's the problem with postindustrial society. People just don't volunteer the way they used to. That sense of community, of helping a neighbor in need...people just can't be bothered. A girl and her baby go missing? If it's the wrong kind of girl, no one cares. They barely even notice."

I entwined my fingers in his hair, leaning forward again, weight back on my knee. "And you've taken full advantage of that, haven't you? Well, I'm going to give you the chance to make amends by volunteering for a worthy cause." I yanked his head back another inch. His eyes bugged, mouth working. "What do you say, Ron? Spend the last few minutes of your life helping a colleague further her education?"

"Let him go." The words rippled through the air, wrapped in a sigh.

Fenniger's hair pulled tight against my fingers as he struggled to see the newcomer.

"Come on, girl." Jack walked up behind me. "Get off him. You've had your fun."

"I'm not done yet."

"Yes, you are." A few seconds of silence passed. "Did you hear me?" His words came sharper now, that laconic, almost bored tone evaporating.

"He killed those girls. Shot them and took their babies."

"Yeah? And it's none of your fucking business, is it? You're here because I brought you in. My job. Now get the fuck off him."

I shifted, rising just enough to take the pressure off Fenniger's back. Jack's fingers closed on my shoulder.

"Hey, watch the hands. I'm getting—"

I propelled myself up, as if being yanked off, flying to the side, and landing hard with a squawk of outrage. Jack's good foot slammed into Fenniger's back as he tried to get up. Pinned again, Fenniger settled for straining to look over his shoulder at me as I pushed to my feet, brushing myself off, cursing and snarling.

Jack's gun pressed into the base of Fenniger's skull. "Eyes forward."

When Fenniger didn't look away fast enough, Jack smacked the barrel against his skull, knocking his face into the dirt.

"Bastard," I said to Jack.

"Just how you like it. Now go park yourself around front and watch for trouble." As I turned to go, he lowered his voice. "I'll make it up to you later."

"Think so?"

A growl of a chuckle as he slapped my ass. "Know so. Now get going."

I headed the way I'd come, behind Fenniger. Jack watched over his shoulder and gestured for me to stand near the corner, where I could watch the proceedings and still see anyone drive into the lot.

When I motioned that I'd broken Fenniger's arm, and mouthed an apology, Jack only nodded, unconcerned.

"What a piece of work," Fenniger muttered when he figured I was gone.

"Watch your mouth," Jack said.

"Hey, no disrespect. I bet she's worth it." A dirty old man chuckle. "She sure looks like she is. Hot little bitch with a temper to—"

"Watch. Your. Mouth."

Fenniger fell silent, struggling to find his footing now, thrown off balance by the edge in Jack's voice. After all, this was the good cop, the one who'd understand him, who'd rescued him from the bad cop. Had Fenniger realized how quickly—eagerly even—he'd fallen for the hackneyed routine, he'd have been horrified. But no matter how many times they see it in cop shows, perps still snap it up. It's the survival instinct. When faced with danger, we run for shelter, whether it's a solid building during a storm or a sympathetic face during an interrogation.

For a minute, Jack let Fenniger dangle in fear that he'd misread the signs, that Jack was not the reasonable colleague he'd believed. Then he said, "My partner takes issue with your new line of work."

In the silence that followed, I could have laughed, imagining Fenniger struggling as hard to interpret the meaning of Jack's full sentences as I did with his three-word ones.

Jack let him flounder in uncertainty some more, then said, "She doesn't like you killing teen moms."

"Oh, right. I-I can see that, her being a woman—"

"I don't much like it, either."

I swore I heard Fenniger suck in the rest of his words. I grinned as I flexed my hands, trying to still the giddy bubbles in my stomach. It was all but over. Now I could just sit back and watch Jack work.

After another thirty seconds of uncomfortable silence, Jack said, "But business is business. I suppose it'd be a lucrative way to make some fast money."

"It is," Fenniger said, words tumbling out. "If you want, I could cut you—"

"Not interested."

Reel him in. Let him drop. Keep him off balance, searching for equilibrium.

"Can I at least ask who I'm dealing with?" Fenniger said.

"No."

An audible sigh of relief. If Jack gave his name, even his street name, that would mean Fenniger would never get the chance to use it against him. By withholding it, calling me "girl," and getting pissy when Fenniger looked my way, Jack was suggesting that while he might intend to kill Fenniger, the matter was still open to negotiation. That was essential—a man who's about to be executed has no reason to talk.

"I suppose it'd be a decent gig, though," Jack said. "If you could stomach it. I can't blame a guy for that. I've done stuff..."

I'm sure Fenniger was barely breathing, eyes screwed shut as if he could mentally swing the pendulum his way. Thoughts of escape wouldn't enter his head. Jack was a pro, at least as good as he was, plus armed, physically bigger, and with a psychotic partner. Fenniger's only escape would come through cooperation. There was no cowardice in that, no loss of face...or so he'd keep telling himself.

"Shit like this?" Jack continued. "Not my style. But business is business, and you take what you can get. If you don't take the job, someone else will."

Ah, hitman justification at its finest. I'd used that one a few times myself.

"The sick fucks are the ones who put out the contracts," Jack said.

Fenniger's nods punctuated every word, though he probably didn't even realize he was doing it.

"Something like this?" Jack said. "Who dreams this shit up?"

My fingers stopped drumming against my thigh and I squinted into the darkness, as if I could see Jack's expression, though he had his back to me. What was he doing? We'd discussed what we needed from Fenniger. First, confirmation of the hit. Second, the name and location of the people who'd bought Destiny. I had no idea what I'd do with the latter—probably nothing—but if I didn't ask for it, I'd be waking up at 2 a.m., certain Destiny had been sold to a Satanic cult or something.

Parents...buyers...That's where he was heading—giving Fenniger an "out" by blaming them. The muscles between my shoulders tightened. Letting this bastard lay the responsibility on people whose only crime was desperation? But Jack was right. It provided Fenniger with an excuse for giving them up.

"That's who I'm interested in," Jack said. "You? You're just a means to an end."

"Okay," Fenniger said, head still bobbing. "So you want to know who hired me?"

"Yeah, that's what I want to know."

Silence.

Damn it, Jack. He's not that bright. Prod him. Dangle the buyer as his scapegoat and he'll—

"They made contact through the broker. A guy named Honcho."

"I've heard of him. Headhunter, right?"

A headhunter was a broker who took contracts based on a price, with only the barest of details: number of marks, deadline, international versus domestic, political versus personal. Then, he offered it to his hitman contacts, who'd get the specifics directly.

The broker would argue that he's providing an invaluable service by tightening the security between client and pro. He's really just covering his butt. Any advantage to the hitman is more than wiped out by the liability of accepting a job based almost exclusively on price. That's the best a second tier has-been like Fenniger can get while still making enough to finance his drug habit.

So I didn't doubt he was doing other work for this "Honcho" guy. But to blame him for this job, one he'd created himself? Low. Risky, too, presuming Jack would follow up.

And yet...maybe Fenniger was more clever than I gave him credit for. If Honcho didn't know the details of the jobs he gave Fenniger, how would he know he hadn't given him one for killing teen moms?

"So Honcho sets up the meeting..." Jack prompted.

"Byrony Agency."

"What?"

"That's the name of the company. Or, at least, the name of the office the client works at. I don't know if it's legit or a cover, but after the meeting, I followed him back and that's where he went. Byrony Adoption Agency in Detroit. Moron walked away from the meeting and never even looked over his shoulder. Complete amateur. Got the bright idea to hire a hitman to help him steal babies, and had no fucking idea how to go about it. I had to hold his hand through the first two."

So this hadn't been a one-man project. It hadn't even been Fenniger's idea. The way he was now spitting details, I knew he wasn't dreaming up a story on the fly. He gave us a description of the client, a play-by-play of their meetings, and the address where he'd dropped off Destiny. With the first two babies, he'd taken them to the client in a park, but after the second hand-off caught the attention of a passerby, the client decided they'd do this more privately. With Destiny, he'd given Fenniger a suburban Detroit home address, met him there, and taken her.

The scheme had been orchestrated by this Byrony Agency. They found the parents and they sold the babies, while Fenniger juggled the roles of scout, killer, and delivery boy. Earlier, Jack had said it was a lot of work, considering his pace. This is what he'd meant. It was too much work for one man.

Why the hell hadn't I seen that?

Because I hadn't allowed myself to consider the possibility. I'd been completely focused on my goal, and that goal was one man. Like Drew Aldrich. Like Wayne Franco. Like Wilkes. One perpetrator. One target. That I understood. That I could stop.

An entire organization . . . How could I stop that?

Forget it for now. I had to concentrate on the immediate situation. The immediate resolution. The immediate vengeance.

By the time Jack finished, I'd found my focus again.

"Dee?" he called.

At that word, Fenniger's head jerked up. In that second, as he heard Jack say my name, he knew he wasn't walking away. He started to struggle, to protest, to promise, to threaten. The words passed by me, meaningless. All I heard was the rich undercurrent of fear.

I thought about Sammi, her fear and rage in those final moments, and I slowed my pace, dragging it out until I hoped his panic outweighed anything she'd suffered.

I stood in front of him, and let him see me, and he knew that meant he wasn't walking out of here alive. And I prayed that in that last second, maybe he thought of Sammi and the other girls, maybe he thought "so this is how they felt."

Then I lifted the gun and pulled the trigger.

Twenty-nine

My first body dump. Jack seemed shocked when I said so, but after a moment's thought, he realized that with my specialty, it wasn't surprising. Half the reason for calling a mob hit was to warn others. A corpse in a subway car said "Screw us over, and we'll get you, anytime, anywhere" far better than a former ally missing, presumed dead.

Even last fall, the two bodies I'd left behind had stayed pretty much where they'd fallen. Hauling a hitman out of a motel would have been more dangerous than leaving him there. The second guy I shot was the killer we'd been chasing and we needed the authorities—and the public—to know he was dead. My body disposal know-how was pure theory.

Jack was the one who found a place to hide Fenniger—the still functioning trunk of a wreck. The police might find him when they investigated the death of his mark in the office, but we weren't giving them any help.

I'd hauled Fenniger to his resting place, Jack carrying his legs as best he could. As I arranged the corpse in the trunk, Jack returned to the site to double-check for any traces we might have missed.

"Did you look over where I was standing?" I asked. "The ground's hard, and I'll be trashing my shoes, but I should check—"

Jack grabbed my arm as I passed. "Got it."

"What about the mark?"

"Dead. Checked."

Still holding my arm, he started toward the fence.

"But there's a chance it's someone connected to this Byrony Agency—"

"It's not."

"How do you know?"

"I do."

He led me to the part of the fence Fenniger had scaled.

"Shouldn't we use the section we cut?" I said. "I can see headlights—"

"Couple miles away. Get over."

I hooked my gloved fingers in the fence links, then heard a sound that made my head jolt up.

"Is that a siren?" I whispered.

"No."

His answer came quickly—too quickly. He'd already heard it, and that was why he was hurrying me over the fence.

I hefted myself up, toes finding purchase. The wail came again and I instinctively stopped, head swiveling to follow it. If there was one sound I knew, it was a police siren. And this wasn't it.

It came again, and my gut went cold. I dropped to the ground and broke into a sprint, heading for the building. Jack lunged, catching my arm and wrenching me back.

"It's not—" I began.

He grabbed my shoulders and swung me toward the fence. "Climb."

"It's not a siren, Jack. It's a baby."

"Yeah."

I heard the voice inside the office again. Raspy. I'd presumed it was a man, but it could have been a woman.

Fenniger had indeed been in Kingston to kill another girl and steal another baby—it just hadn't been the one we'd thought. He'd been scouting that girl earlier as a potential future target while waiting until it was late enough to come here and kill the one he'd already targeted on an earlier trip, as he'd done with Sammi.

I pushed back from the fence, struggling to duck out of his grasp.

"Nothing you can do," he said.

I managed to turn around and face him. "There is a baby in there, and I am not going to walk away and hope someone hears it. My God, how could you—"

His arm swung up. I instinctively yanked back, but he only lifted his hand. In it was a cell phone I didn't recognize.

"Fenniger's. We get away. Call 911. Toss it."

Fenniger's cell phone? Jack didn't just happen to grab it before we dumped him. He'd seen who was behind that door. That's why he'd gone back to check, and that's why he'd been dragging me away, before I heard the baby.

"You didn't accidentally make that noise earlier, did you?" I said. "You thought I saw who he killed. You were distracting Fenniger before I did something stupid—"

"Over the fence, Nadia. Now."

"I want to—"

"The longer we wait? The longer that baby cries."

I paused, then grabbed the fence links and hoisted myself up.

We made the trip back to my pickup in silence. When I didn't speak, Jack didn't push. Maybe he thought I was in shock. I guess I was.

I forced myself not to speak, not to move, not to think

on that drive and later on the way to the lodge, after we dropped off my work car in Peterborough. When we got home, Jack accompanied me up the stairs, said good night, and waited while I went into my room.

I closed my door and leaned against it, tracking his footsteps, fearing he'd head back downstairs. But the familiar thump of his cast went toward his room. The door opened, then closed.

I peeked out. A dim glow came from under his door. I pulled back inside, waited five minutes, then checked again. His door frame had gone dark. I crossed my room, opened the window, and slid out, my toes finding familiar grooves in the wood as I climbed to the ground.

Only when my feet touched the frost-covered grass did I realize I was still wearing socks. I'd left my shoes and coat in the back hall.

I could get them now, but I doubted my hands were steady enough to pick the lock. I was already shivering. I set out along the path and, within a few steps, my feet were too numb to feel the chill.

When I was far enough from the lodge, I stepped off the path and sat at the base of a big maple, leaning back against it, knees hugged to my chest.

Blaming myself for Sammi's death was irrational. Yet I still felt guilty, that nagging sense that I should have been nicer to her, should have offered her a room at the lodge, should have somehow *sensed* Fenniger was in town.

If her ghost was here now, I'd say, "I got him, Sammi. I killed him for you," and she'd only roll her eyes and call me a loser for bothering. I couldn't save her. I could only avenge her death and prevent another.

Only I hadn't prevented another. Tonight, I'd stood twenty feet from another Sammi. One I could have saved. And I'd failed.

I could have taken Fenniger down as he'd perched on that fence, before ever setting foot in the wrecking yard. Or as he'd walked to the door, his back to me. Or before he'd knocked. Or even once I'd heard someone answer.

Instead, I'd watched him open the door, watched him shoot her, then left her, maybe still alive and bleeding to death, as I toyed with Fenniger behind the building, taunted him and tormented him and gorged on his fear.

Why hadn't I shot him before that door opened? Because I needed to question him and satisfy myself that I was killing the right man. So I wouldn't wake in a cold sweat, convinced Sammi's real killer was still at large, and that Destiny had met some horrible fate.

Me. All about me.

Just like with Amy. I'd thought only of myself. Of getting untied. Of getting away. Of getting to safety. I'd heard her screams as Aldrich raped her, and I'd run the other way.

I'd done what I'd been taught—run for help. At thirteen, I was no match for a twenty-four-year-old man. Stay, and he would have killed us both. Run, and I gave Amy a chance. I'd heard it all. Over and over. My father. Amy's parents. A parade of therapists. No matter how many times they said it, no matter how many times *I* said it, I couldn't feel it.

There was always an unstoppable voice, deep in my gut, that said I'd failed her.

And now I'd failed a girl in a wrecking yard office. A girl I couldn't even picture because I hadn't even seen her.

I'd found Fenniger and I'd had him in my sights, with the means and the will to end his life . . . and I hadn't.

I just hadn't.

I sat there, huddled against the tree trunk, rough bark scratching my back as I shivered, staring out into the darkness until I stopped shivering, until I couldn't feel the cold.

"Nadia?"

I jumped.

A slow look around. Nothing. I was about to settle again when a voice floated over, barely louder than the sigh of the branches overhead. When I strained to hear, I caught the distinct sound of my name again.

Jack. He must have gotten up, unable to sleep, checked on me, and found me gone. I pushed to my feet.

"Over here!" I called, as loudly as I dared.

Tree branches creaked. A mouse scampered through the brush. Waves slapped against the canoes.

I squinted, trying to see a flashlight beam through the trees. I should have been able to make out the lodge lights from here, but I must have been in a particularly dense pocket, because every way I turned I saw only darkness.

"Nadia . . ."

A woman's voice skated around me. I spun following it and tripped, hands smacking the tree trunk as I caught myself.

"Nadia . . ."

A pale shape darted through the trees. I took two steps, then tripped in the undergrowth. Another two, east—I was sure it was east—but the brush only grew thicker, no path in sight.

Another flicker through the trees, followed by a girlish laugh that raised the hairs on my neck. I stopped and rubbed my arms.

"Nadia?"

A man's voice, sharp and clear. Definitely Jack. As I turned toward it, a light bobbed through the forest.

"Over here!" I called.

The light steadied, then jiggled again, as if moving, but coming no closer. I set out after it, tripping and bumbling through the undergrowth, unable to find the path. Finally, the trees and brush began to clear and, ahead, I saw not a flashlight, but a bare bulb over a cabin door. Branches swayed in front of the light, making it seem to move.

I squinted at the building, trying to see past the glare. I must have crossed my property line. My neighbors had a few cabins they rented "informally," and I'd heard they were in rough shape, like this one. But as I stared, my stomach started to dance, breaths coming sharp and shallow.

I knew this place. I'd been here—

"Isn't this Bobby Mack's cabin?" a girl's voice said behind me. "My dad says he uses it to dry pot, but they can never catch him."

That voice. Oh, God, I knew that voice.

"Amy," I whispered.

"You're not going to tell on me, girls, are you?"

Another voice I knew, couldn't forget, and my spine froze as I spun, searching. That bare bulb lit the forest edge and the patch of clearing in front of it. Empty forest, empty clearing.

"That depends on what you're going to give us to keep

quiet," Amy's voice rang out, the teasing lilt making Aldrich chuckle.

"Oh, I think I've got something," Aldrich said.

"Amy..." My voice. A whisper at her ear, too low for Aldrich to hear. "I think we should—"

"Shhh, it's just pot, Nadia. Don't be a spoilsport. We'll have fun."

I blinked and saw the door right in front of me. I reached for the knob and turned it slowly. The door swung open. I stepped inside.

The door slammed behind me. I jumped, spinning as the bolt whammed shut. The sound echoed in my ears.

"Gawd, it reeks," Amy said, gagging for effect. "Don't you guys ever clean this place?"

I inhaled. Mildew, rotting wood, and mouse droppings. Take-out wrappers and beer bottles littered the wooden floor. In the corner, a blue heap. A sleeping bag. I stared at that bag, heart beating faster.

"You girls go on in. There's a couch in the next room."

Footsteps. A pause. Then a sharp click. I lifted my head to see a padlock, swinging against the wood.

"You girls ever smoke grass before?" Aldrich called as his voice receded.

Amy's laugh rippled through the room, as if it was a silly question. I followed the sound and her voice as she answered, but the farther I walked, the farther they seemed to float away. The floor suddenly dipped. I grabbed for the wall, but it shimmered, my hand sliding through the wood.

A whisper. So soft I swore it was only the leaves against the roof, but the sound drummed in my skull, a steady beat becoming words.

"Gotta get up."

I followed the voice back to the front room. Dark now, the only light the faint glimmer of moon through a window. In the corner, a girl crouched on the open sleeping bag, her face hidden in shadow, only her legs visible. Bare legs smeared with blood. More trickled from a cut on her neck. She was unwinding a rope from her ankles.

"Gotta get up," she whispered.

She dropped the rope and picked up something white, glowing in darkness. Fabric. She turned it over in her hands, over and over, and the shape became clear. Panties. One leg hole torn through, and she kept turning it, as if confused by the new configuration, trying to figure out how to put them back on.

"Gotta get up. Gotta get up. Gotta get up."

The mantra repeated under her breath, hands shaking as she kept turning the underwear over.

"Amy?"

She stopped and looked up, and I braced myself to see my cousin one last time. But the face that rose into the moonlight wasn't Amy's. It was mine.

Thirty

I backpedaled. Arms encircled me. When I screamed, a hand clamped over my mouth. I bit down, catching a fold of skin. A gasped curse, the hand instinctively jerking away, but then slapping back, too flat to bite, though I tried, kicking and flailing, the arm around me hugging me, arms pinned to my sides.

"Nadia."

I jabbed my elbow back. A grunt, but the arm only clasped me tighter. I kicked, foot making contact.

"Nadia!"

A wrench. I flew off my feet, the world toppling into darkness, then, in one bright second, slamming into focus. I was staring at a life jacket, the orange so harsh I blinked. After a moment, I managed to pull my gaze away from that blaze of color and look around. Life jackets hung on hooks. Oars and paddles leaned against the wall. A faded Boating Safety poster, with phrases highlighted and extra rules written in spidery strokes. My handwriting. My boathouse.

The overhead light beamed down, as bright as the life jacket. A cold breeze blew in from the open door. The hand over my mouth had vanished, but the arm still held me. I looked down, catching sight of a broad, square hand as it moved to my shoulder.

A squeeze. "You okay?"

I turned and looked up at Jack. A hard blink, my brain still foggy.

"You had a nightmare," he said. "About Amy."

"I thought I was..." I swallowed, rubbing my throat, and looked around. The boathouse... "How did I get here?"

"Sleepwalking. Wasn't sure at first. Then..." He shrugged. "They say someone's sleepwalking? Don't wake them. Not sure why. Didn't want to chance it. Just followed."

"You heard me from the house?" I stiffened and swung toward the open door. "Did I wake Emma? The guests—did they hear—?"

"No one heard anything. That's why I..." He looked at his hand and I thought I saw a red mark on his palm.

"Did I bite—?"

"Nah." He shoved the hand into his pocket. "When you screamed. I tried to block it. Knew you wouldn't want..." He nodded in the direction of the lodge. "Anyone hearing."

"I-I saw the cabin. The one where he took us. Amy and me. I saw..." I stared at the spot where the sleeping bag had been, then shook it off. "Sorry. Sleepwalking, huh? I've never done that." A harsh laugh. "Something new to add to the repertoire. Oh, happy day."

I stepped away, but my gaze swung back to that spot under the life jackets.

"What'd you see?" Jack asked.

"Hmm?"

He gestured at the floor, that shadowy corner from my dream, now just a bare spot, brightly lit.

"Myself," I murmured. "Or me, as a girl. It just... threw me. I thought it was Amy. She was getting dressed. Trying to escape, I guess."

"You."

"No, not me. Amy."

"Thought you said—"

"It looked like me, but it was Amy or what I imagine, after ..." I swallowed, rubbed my throat again. "I've had the dream before. I've never sleepwalked during it, thank God. I dream I'm in the cabin again and I see Amy. She's trying to get dressed after Drew Aldrich...." I shook my head. "It's what I picture, but I know it didn't happen like that. She didn't have time to do anything. The coroner figured he strangled her while he raped her, probably trying to subdue her when she fought back. The dream is my guilt talking, I guess."

"So it's Amy you see?"

"Yes, it's Amy." I heard the exasperation in my voice and tried to squelch it. It was like anytime you explain a dream to someone—it makes perfect sense to you, and zero to everyone else. "Usually when I dream it, I see Amy. This time, it was me. You know how dreams are. Last week, I dreamed I came downstairs, and instead of finding Emma serving breakfast to my guests, it was my mother. Now *that* was a nightmare."

I headed for the door. "Anyway, I apologize for waking you—yet again."

"You didn't. I was still up."

"So how did you find—" I stopped, hand on the door frame. "You followed me from the house. You knew I wasn't going to bed."

"Think I'm stupid?"

"Jack, you don't have to—"

"Wasn't sleeping anyway. Let's get you a drink. And shoes."

*   *   *

I tried, with increasing insistence, to persuade Jack that I didn't need him to sit up with me. At one point, I even threw up my hands and headed for the stairs, saying I was going to bed and he could suit himself. He only retrieved my sneakers from the back hall, handed them to me, and said he'd be waiting outside my window.

So I humored him.

We returned to the lake, this time in the gazebo with the heater blasting.

"I'm handing the case over to the police," I said.

"Huh."

He stirred his cocoa, submerging a mini marshmallow and watching it resurface. Not quite the response I'd expected. He probably thought it was stress and exhaustion talking, and come morning I'd be right back at it, bashing my head against the wall pursuing "justice."

"They've got a body now—the girl at the wreckers. Quinn can advise me on how to link that, anonymously, with Sammi's disappearance and nudge them to her body."

"Huh."

"It's time for me to admit I'm not the right person for the job. That I'm being selfish by claiming I'm doing it for Sammi."

"When did you say that?"

"It was implied."

"Huh."

"Anyway, we both know the real reason. The same reason I shot Wayne Franco. The same reason I was so quick to join you to go after Wilkes, and equally quick to take chances catching him. By killing these guys, I think somehow I can set the balance straight. Selfish and pathetic."

A slow nod. "Yeah. Guess so. Killing Franco? Wilkes? Fenniger? Oughtta be ashamed of yourself."

I bristled, hands tightening around my mug as I lifted it. "You don't need to be sarcastic."

"And you don't need to be stupid."

I sputtered chocolate, then swiped my hand over my lips. "Stupid? I'm confessing—"

"That it's all about you? You don't give a shit about the victims? Yeah. That's why you're shivering in the forest. Running from ghosts. Right after that girl died. Must be coincidence."

I smacked the mug down, table shaking from the impact. "She died because I was too wrapped up in my revenge, my . . . absolution, to even realize she was there."

"No. She died because Fenniger decided she'd die. He didn't know we were tailing him. Didn't speed up because of it. Just followed his schedule. And we happened to be there. *That* was the coincidence."

"I could have taken him out before he got to that door."

"So now you're beating yourself up. Because you can't foresee the future." He shook his head and fingered a cookie, turning it over, thumb running along the edge. "You wanna blame someone, Nadia? Blame me. I could see her. Door opened. Girl was right there. But the angle? Wrong. Shoot, kill both. Tried to move. Get a better position. Too late. Fucking foot slowed me down. Maybe I should have taken the shot. So go ahead. Blame me."

"I'm not trying to blame anyone. I went after Fenniger because I didn't trust the police to do their job."

"You still planned to tell them. After you got more—" He rubbed his mouth. "Go on."

"I didn't trust them, and now I realize maybe that's just an excuse, which is why I'm stepping aside."

"You want out? Fine. Talk to Quinn and turn it over. If the cops fuck up and don't see the connection? If the trail goes cold and the case gets shelved? There's gonna be a lotta long nights in this forest. If you sleepwalk down by the lake again, make sure you don't wander in. I won't be here to save you."

"God, you can be a jerk." I pushed away from the table, spoon falling with a clatter. "Maybe you're grumpy because I'm keeping you up after a long night. Maybe you're sick of dealing with my shit. That's fine. But don't forget that I *never* asked you to deal with it. I came out here to handle it alone. You followed me. You insisted on coming back out now. You wanted me to talk. So here I am, talking, sharing this . . . epiphany with you, and what do I get? Sarcasm and mockery."

"What epiphany? That you like killing bad guys? That it makes you feel good? Tell me something I don't know. Something *you* don't know."

"I've always known—"

"Of course you have. You never pretended otherwise. Now you think you went too far. Not by killing Fenniger, but by wanting it too much. So you think that by wanting it, you got that girl killed? That's not an epiphany, Nadia. It's idiocy."

Teeth gritted against a retort, I scooped up the spoon and dropped it into my mug. Instead of a satisfying clang, I got a soft splash, and cocoa spray on my white sweatshirt. I grabbed the mug, turned to go, and smacked into Jack, standing right there, blocking me.

"You wanna quit? I don't mean this job. The life. You wanna stop taking hits?"

"I can't. The lodge is never going to turn a profit—"

"You want money? I've got money. Make me an investor and you'll never have to pull another job. But I won't offer because you wouldn't want me to. Money's just the excuse."

I stiffened. "It's not—"

"At first? Sure, it was about the money. With the Tomassinis, part of it still is. You wouldn't kill Mafia thugs for free. You don't get enough out of it. For that, you need the real sons of bitches. Franco. Wilkes. Fenniger. That does the trick. If you didn't find out about the girl, you'd be enjoying the best sleep you've had in months."

"And what does that say about me, Jack?"

"That you like killing losers. So?"

"Forgive me if I don't think you're the best person to judge the moral and ethical rights and wrongs of killing people."

He shrugged, taking no offense. "It's what you gotta do. You don't kid yourself and call them good deeds. But you know they aren't bad ones, either. Ask the girl in the walk-up. See if she'd rather you'd turned this over to the cops. Maybe, Fenniger dead, you can say 'good enough.' For now. Pretty soon? You'll be looking for the next Fenniger. He doesn't come? You'll take Evelyn up on her offer. Let her find you jobs. Maybe you're right. It's all about Amy. One day, you'll be done. Or maybe it's not about Amy. Not anymore. It's not what you gotta do. It's what you are."

"I—"

"Give this to the cops? Chance it'll go the way you hope? Ten percent. Chance you'll blame yourself when it doesn't? One hundred." He met my gaze. "Your choice."

"I hate you."

The corners of his lips twitched. "That's okay."

As I looked up at him, I knew I didn't mean "I hate you" at all. What I felt for Jack . . . I couldn't put a name to it. It was a swirl of emotions that smacked too much of need.

Jack was there for me as no one had been since my father died. He was there to watch over me and listen to me and challenge me, and pick me up and dust me off. That meant more to me than I could ever express, than I ever dared express.

I wanted this relationship to mean just as much to him. But as hard as I tried to read more into his caring, his protection, his gifts, I had only to look into his eyes, blank mirrors that reflected nothing but my own feelings, and I knew it just wasn't the same for him.

In me, he'd found someone to look after, someone to teach, someone who'd care for him in return when he needed it. Mentor and protégée. Teacher and student. That's all I was going to get, so I'd damned well better accept it.

I stepped back. "I suppose I should . . . take it a little further, at least build a case, since I already have the leads from Fenniger. As for what to do with them . . ."

"Got some ideas." He motioned to the table. "Sit. Finish your chocolate."

Thirty-one

No one had signed up for morning jog. Considering I'd been up until four, I decided I could let myself slide for a day. Our four guests had asked for breakfast at nine, so I was showered and downstairs at eight to help Emma. When I entered the kitchen, she sent me right back out, with coffee and cinnamon rolls for "John."

"He's up?"

"For the past—" A glance at the microwave clock. "—hour. He's out working on those ATV things again."

"What?"

She waved, showering me with flour. "Four-wheelers, minitrucks, whatever you call them."

"I know what you meant. I just . . . John?"

"He's been tinkering on them with Owen. Or he was before his trip to Toronto. Now he's back at it. He went out about an hour ago, and asked me to send you around when you got up."

I took the tray, with steaming mugs and warm buns for two, then headed to the shop around back. I was glad Jack had found something to keep him occupied while I was busy, though I suspected his involvement was limited to handing tools to Owen.

When I stepped into the shop, though, there was no sign of Emma's husband. Jack sat awkwardly on the cement floor, cast stretched out, parts scattered in front of him.

"Emma wasn't kidding. You are fixing the ATVs."

"Hope so. Not so sure." He lifted two parts, turning

them over as if trying to figure out how they fit together. His scowl was so unlike him that I had to laugh.

"Yeah? Won't be laughing when I fuck up. Make them run in reverse." He pushed to his feet and tossed the parts on the workbench. "Who am I kidding? Been too long."

"You know this stuff?" I said as I set the tray on the bench.

"Used to. Thirty years ago. Gonna be a mechanic."

"Seriously?"

He shrugged. "Was just a kid. But yeah. That's what I wanted to do." He picked up the part, as if drawn back in spite of himself. "Dropped out of school. Got an apprenticeship. Lasted a year. Then . . . things changed. Only mechanical work in my future? Rigging a mark's car so it won't start." He started to reach for the coffee, gaze still fixed on the parts, then murmured. "Fuck, yes." He scooped them up. "Should have seen that."

Coffee forgotten, he lowered himself to the floor and reassembled the pieces as I searched about for an old cushion. I started to sit, tray in hand, but he waved me to the door.

"Done here. Nicer outside."

We headed out.

"Called Quinn this morning," he said, squinting into the morning sun.

"Already? Thanks."

He motioned me to the dock, where we could talk and see anyone approaching.

"He'll work on it. Wants to come by. Talk."

"Talk?"

"About the case. Thinks it'd be easier. Safer. In person."

A roll of his eyes as he sipped his coffee. "I mention he's crap at excuses?"

"So he doesn't really think it'd be better to chat here, he just wants to come over because..."

A look that said the answer should be obvious. "The company."

"Ah. Okay, so he wants an excuse to pop around before he heads home, and you told him no—"

"Nah."

"Fine, you told him 'nah.'"

Another look, this time accompanied by a soft sigh as he leaned back in the Muskoka chair. "I mean no. I didn't tell him no."

A sharp shake of my head. "Is it just me or is this conversation degenerating?"

"Just you. Told him fine. Come by. Might be easier. Cop shit? He's the pro. Could use him."

"So you told him it was okay to come by so the three of us could discuss the best way to build a case that can be handed over to the police."

"Said that, didn't I? He's stuck in Montreal for the weekend. Said that's fine. No rush. You've got guests, responsibilities. He'll be here Sunday night. Meantime, this—" He tapped his cast against the deck. "—is going."

"I thought you had another two weeks."

"It's fixed."

"So now you're a doctor as well as a mechanic?"

He pushed the last chunk of cinnamon bun into his mouth, talking around it. "They say ten weeks? Probably half that. Covering their asses. Afraid of getting sued."

I thought of asking whether it hurt, and suggesting it might if the cast came off early, but Jack would no more take that into consideration than he'd admit he was in any pain now. "It's just two more weeks, and you're getting around pretty well—"

"Like last night? Hitman with a crutch? Clomping around on a cast? Fucking bad joke. And dangerous. It's coming off. You wanna help? Appreciate it. Otherwise? Point me to the hacksaw."

I managed to persuade him it could wait until Sunday. He grumbled, but agreed.

I will admit to pangs of panic at the thought that Jack expected me to shelve the case until Sunday. But, having only last night sworn I wanted nothing more to do with the investigation, I could hardly complain at a forty-eight-hour delay.

As we headed in for breakfast, though, Jack told me Quinn would be expecting my call at four. I wanted to start discussing the how and when of handing the case over to the police, and while it could have waited until Sunday, I appreciated the excuse to do it earlier. Just as I appreciated Jack's suggestion that I join him in the shop before the weekenders arrived. Mechanically, I'd be no help at all, but it gave me an excuse to hang out with him . . . with the shop radio tuned to the Kingston stations for news of last night's murder.

It was like sneaking chocolates to a dieter—feeding me little bits to keep my resolve up. I felt guilty about that, but it didn't keep me from accepting the tidbits, and being grateful for them.

* * *

The dead girl was sixteen-year-old Mina Jackson. And, far from being stumped by the murder of a teenage mother at an auto wreckers, the police—or at least the media—had no end of suspects and theories . . . none of them being "a hitman whacked her to steal her baby."

Mina had lived in that office, courtesy of her boy-friend, Nate Hellqvist, owner of Hell's Wreckers. Nate had rung up more than his share of enemies, all of whom might send a message by killing his girlfriend. There was the bookie he owed fifty grand to, the gang cohorts he ratted out in a plea bargain, and, of course, his wife, who was a little annoyed with the whole "teenage mistress and baby" arrangement . . . and whose doting father had "re-puted mob ties." No wonder Fenniger picked Mina. People might notice she'd disappeared, but it wasn't likely that any of them would care. Even Hellqvist would prob-ably presume she'd had enough and run off.

With the ever-growing list of motives and cast of sus-pects, all centering on Nate Hellqvist, Mina herself would be lost in the soap opera, mere collateral damage. As for the baby, Hellqvist apparently didn't want him, which, all things considered, was probably the best thing that could happen to the kid. If Mina had any family, the reports didn't mention it. Her four-month-old son was currently in the care of children's services, which would find a suit-able foster family.

If I informed the police that Mina died in a botched professional hit and kidnap scheme—completely unre-lated to her personal situation—the cops would toss the theory in with the rest of the crazy-person leads. I wished we *had* left Fenniger's body out for the police to find. I considered tipping them off now, but then attention might turn to who had killed *him,* and Jack wouldn't want that.

When I spoke to Quinn, he agreed. With a half dozen more likely scenarios to explain the one death we could prove, we had little hope of getting the local police on the right track. They couldn't afford to devote valuable time investigating claims of a connection between three missing girls—two in another country—and one almost-solved murder.

Hell, I could send them a PowerPoint presentation with interactive maps leading them to Sammi's body, the Byrony Agency, and the house where Fenniger said he'd delivered Destiny, and it wouldn't make a difference... except that they'd probably consider the sender the murderer of Sammi Ernst, concocting this wild "black market baby" scheme as a cover-up.

That wasn't insulting the intelligence or competence of the police. When I used to dream up elaborate solutions for my father's unsolved cases, he always quoted Sherlock Holmes: "We balance probabilities and choose the most likely. It is the scientific use of the imagination." When I was older, I'd shoot back Heraclitus: "A hidden connection is stronger than an obvious one," to which he'd only laugh and tell me that, given the choice between the words of the world's greatest fictional detective and some dead Greek philosopher, a cop was going with Mr. Holmes every time.

To woo the authorities, I needed more evidence, and I knew where to start collecting it.

"I have a couple days off coming up," Quinn said when we finished. "Compensation for my lost weekend, and the day off I'd requested after my Toronto visit. Jack gave me the okay to swing by and chat but ... well, already being in Canada, no one would think it odd if I decided to spend my days off up here ... or in Michigan."

"You mean to help me with this?"

"If that'd be all right with you."

"Absolutely."

A moment of silence. "While I'd love to say that's all that counts, I'd better let you run it past Jack first. When it comes to us, he seems to be warming to the idea." A laugh. "Or, I guess 'warming' is optimistic, but he seems resigned to it. Elbowing my way into a case you two are working, though, might be pushing my luck. And overstepping my boundaries. And invading his turf. While I'd normally say 'screw him if he doesn't like it,' I don't want to put you in the middle of our fights."

"I'll talk to him."

Thirty-two

Jack agreed. It wasn't an enthusiastic or even speedy agreement, but if I'd said, "Quinn wants to know if he can join us for a few days" and Jack said, "Sure, sounds like fun," I'd have been running inside for the thermometer, certain his broken ankle had somehow become infected.

His first word was, predictably, "Fuck," followed by a string of profanity-peppered mutters. I said it was totally up to him. He said he'd think about it. Sunday morning, he agreed. He wasn't certain we needed a third pair of hands, but Quinn's expertise would be invaluable, especially in building a law-enforcement-ready case.

As it turned out, though, that assistance would have to wait awhile longer. A complication in whatever case Quinn was working had him delayed in Montreal, and he had no idea when he'd get away. Jack didn't seem terribly broken up about the delay. In a damn fine mood, actually, though he credited it to relief at getting his cast off... with his foot still intact.

Monday morning. Detroit. Jack twisted in his chair, legs squealing against the linoleum, then grimaced as he tried to wedge his fingers under his pant leg without whacking his chin on the tabletop. After a few seconds of furious scratching, he straightened, wincing as his spine cracked.

"You're starting to regret removing that cast, aren't you? Did you use the lotion I picked up last night?"

"Yeah. Probably rubbed off by now."

"If you had a purse, you could carry it around with you." I nodded toward a middle-aged man with a pleather fanny pack sheltered by the belly spilling over his waistband. "How about I get you one of those?"

A muttered profanity. I reached into the tiny paper bag beside my elbow and popped a Swedish berry into my mouth. I struggled not to tap my toes and wriggled, trying to get comfortable, the plastic chair rock-hard against my tailbone. I'd spent the weekend on the go, hosting a full slate of activities, but I still couldn't relax and enjoy this quiet cup of coffee. Unfortunately, for now, progress meant sitting still.

I peered out the window, through the morning sun, at our target—a door across the road. The offices of the Byrony Agency, the private adoption firm where Fenniger's contact worked.

"Thank God for coffee shops, huh? It's the one place you can sit for an hour or two, and as long as it isn't too busy and you keep ordering coffee, no one bugs you. There's only one drawback." I lifted my mug. "The coffee. Emma makes decaf in the evening for me—I hate drinking caffeinated after dinner, like I need anything to keep me up at night. Hers is fine. Places like this, though? I swear they make the pot when they first get in and leave it stewing until it's empty." I took a sip and made a face. "I'm probably torturing myself for no reason, too. All we'll be doing is looking."

"Yeah. But you don't need the caffeine. That sugar's enough."

"Hey, don't forget who bought me the candy."

I popped another berry. As I chewed it, I watched the plain smoke-gray door across the street. The Byrony

Agency was one of two key addresses Fenniger had given us. The second was the house where he'd dropped off Destiny. That one, we'd check out later.

When I'd envisioned the adoption agency, I'd pictured two possibilities, polar opposites. One, a sleek suite in a fancy high-rise. Two, a barred, unmarked door in a syringe-strewn alley. The truth seemed somewhere in the middle. The office was in the business district of an upper-middle-class Detroit suburb, on a street of historic buildings that had probably once been a village downtown core. Now it was a mix of restaurants and specialty shops topped by offices—legal, accounting, insurance...

An intense Web search on the weekend had revealed little about the Byrony Agency except that it was licensed to provide private adoptions in the state of Michigan. That definitely wasn't what I'd expected. Though it didn't have a fancy Web site like some of the others, the Byrony Agency seemed to be legitimate.

Private adoption had been legal in Michigan since 1995, as long as it was conducted through a licensed agency or adoption lawyer. From Detroit-area Web sites, I got some idea of the process and the costs.

Prospective adoptive parents needed to provide everything from a home study and criminal record check to doctor's reports and tax statements. Once approved, they could expect to wait about two years for a child.

They could be charged only for direct expenses incurred by the agency and the birth mother, topping out at about ten thousand dollars. International adoption could be more than twice that. Less than a third of the ten grand typically went to the mother, and only to pay the additional costs of pregnancy—doctor's bills, counseling, additional food and clothing. So, in killing the birth mother, the Byrony Agency could see a profit of about three thousand dollars. For that, they couldn't even hire a crappy hitman.

Clearly then, the buyers had to be special cases. Those who couldn't pass the background checks, those who were unwilling to wait years for a match, those with very strict requirements for race, gender, and coloring—getting a baby that "looks like Mom and Dad"—above all, clients willing to pay very dearly to see their cradle filled.

So was this a special service offered by the agency? Or a single greedy employee making deals on the side? Finding out wouldn't be easy.

We'd left the lodge Sunday night after our two remaining guests went to their room. They'd be gone today and we had no more bookings before Friday. I'd told Emma I was pursuing Sammi's case, and might be gone for a few days. I'd check in daily, and make sure I was back by the weekend. As for "John," he had a nibble on a job in Toronto, so I'd be dropping him off there.

We'd been watching the door to the Byrony Agency since eight-thirty. Four employees had gone inside—two women and two men, both of whom, from our angle, had matched the description Fenniger gave of his contact.

At nine-thirty, the first couple arrived. At 10:15, they left, their steps slower, the husband's hand against the small of his wife's back as she stared down the street with empty eyes, clearly having had their hopes dashed. Even if I'd never wanted a child, I could imagine what it would be like to be told I didn't qualify to be a parent.

In a few hours, when their shock and disappointment had time to crystallize into despair, would they get a phone call? "Hello, it's Joe from the Byrony Agency. I was just reviewing your file. While you don't qualify for regular private adoption, I'm in charge of a special project we're testing here at the agency, and I think I might have some good news for you."

He'd offer a few more words of encouragement, enough to make them eagerly agree to the first meeting. After feeling them out over several sessions, he'd feel confident enough of their answer to make the offer. Their special needs could be met by special girls who wanted to get their lives back on track and, more important, hand their babies over to parents whose devotion would be unquestioned, parents willing to pay more than the price of a used car for a child. Provide this girl with the money she needed to go to college, to move away, to restart her life, and she would give up her child and all rights to that child, make the clean break that she was certain was in everyone's best interests.

One baby, at premium cost. A healthy, beautiful, well-adjusted baby with pictures they could see in advance. The mother paid and gone from their lives forever. Officials bought off to provide legitimate adoption papers, with no fear of future repercussions.

How closely would the prospective parents examine such a deal? One glance at the faces of that couple leaving the office, and I knew the answer. With their dream within reach, they wouldn't *dare* look too closely.

About five minutes after the first couple left, a second arrived.

"They seem to have a steady flow of clients," I said. "Or prospective clients, at least."

Jack nodded.

The couple paused at the door, double-checking the name on the plaque, consulting a PDA, then flipping through papers in a folder.

"Their first visit, I bet," I said.

"Probably."

"Bet they get a lot of that."

"Probably."

I watched the couple go inside. "I imagine it wouldn't be very hard to—"

"No."

"May I finish the idea before you shoot it down?"

"Don't need to. Gonna suggest making an appointment. Playing parents. Long shot."

He sipped his coffee. I waited, giving him the chance to expand on that. Futile, of course, but I always do, just to be polite.

"What's a long shot?" I asked.

"Getting the offer. Won't do it for everyone. Gotta be just right. Try it? Big risk. Little chance of payoff."

"I wasn't thinking we'd play prospective parents and hope they'd offer us a black market baby. I'm not *that* deluded. But if you have a better idea for getting inside and taking a look at the office, the layout, the security setup, the staff..."

"Huh." Another slow drink of coffee. "Good idea."

"I do get them, on occasion."

Thirty-three

Jack expected I'd want to wait for Quinn, so I could play this ruse with a husband closer to my age, but Quinn's acting skills were minimal. As Jack said, he preferred to play things straight. A small role with little stretching, yes. This required far more. It required Jack.

Besides, Jack's age seemed more an advantage than a liability in this scenario. A middle-aged guy with a younger wife still in her "I want a baby" time of life would be smarting from his inability to provide one. Even if the problem wasn't his, people might presume he wasn't as virile as the thirty-five-year-old prospective daddy she could have married.

The waiting time would be a factor, too. Tell that thirty-five-year-old he has to wait three or four years to get a baby, and that'd be fine. For a guy we could pass off as closer to fifty-five, he'd start having visions of walking his child to school in a mobility scooter.

Calling to make an appointment using phony names was risky. We had no idea whether the agency would research couples that were only asking for preliminary information, but we had to presume they might at least run a basic name check.

We needed a genuine cover. For that, Jack suggested getting Evelyn's help again. While he was adamant there would be no cost to me—it would go on his chit, which was overpaid—I knew Evelyn wouldn't go for that. Neither would I. I kept my accounts just as carefully tabulated, and would pay them back.

This time, though, Evelyn demanded her payment in advance.

"She wants something," Jack said, as he returned to the rental car from a pay phone.

"Dare I ask?"

"To see you. Before you go home."

"Uh-huh. And the purpose of this visit is to hit me up for—no, don't tell me. She's found another vigilante job that might tempt me more than the last."

"Yeah. Had it for a while. Kept pestering me to tell you. Said I would. Eventually."

"What's the job?"

"Not telling me."

He started the engine.

I put out my hand. "Go ahead and call her back. If I refuse, I'm only postponing the inevitable, and we need that appointment. Besides, given the choice, I'd much rather deal with her in person—with you there."

He nodded and shifted into reverse.

"You already told her to go ahead, didn't you?"

"Yeah."

We'd just finished lunch when Jack got a call from Evelyn. He didn't answer it. Just checked the number, then went to find a pay phone. His cell phone was, of course, a prepaid throwaway, and fine for basic security, but "fine" wasn't good enough for Jack. Detroit was a big city, where a pay phone call was far more anonymous than it was in White Rock, so he was mixing it up.

Fifteen minutes later, he tossed my notepad onto my lap. One of the pages was covered with shorthand details of the identities we were about to assume. In the top margin, he'd written and circled 4:45.

"Dare I hope this is an appointment time?"

"It is."

"For tomorrow? Wednesday...?"

"Today."

"Today?" My voice squeaked as I checked my watch. "Four hours from now? How did you manage to get one so quickly?"

"My admin assistant."

"Ah, Evelyn. You know, you really don't give the poor woman enough credit. She's just a sweet old lady who *lives* to help you, Jack. And for what? Just the simple satisfaction of staying useful in her twilight years."

A snort, followed by a few choice epithets.

"Let me see how well my Evelyn radar is working today," I said. "You didn't ask her to set it up. She did it on her own, to prove how useful she can be... and to sneak a hidden charge onto my bill."

"If I didn't ask her to do it, we don't owe. She knows that. She's grandstanding."

"Are you suitably impressed?"

"I'm not her target."

"Don't worry. When I see her, I'll be sure to thank her for the speedy appointment, and to display the appropriate lack of awe."

He laughed sharply as he pulled out of the restaurant lot. Identities in hand, we needed to find suitable outfits to hang on them. Time to go shopping.

* · *

We were assuming the identities of Debbie and Wayne Abbott. Thirty-three and fifty-one years old respectively, the Abbotts had been married four years. It was his second, her first. Neither had children. He owned a successful construction company. She taught third grade.

A lovely couple, I'm sure. Rather private individuals, it seemed. According to Evelyn, their phone number was unlisted, and the only reference she could find on the Web was to Abbott's company, which didn't include photos of the owner. I'd double-check all that. I didn't mistrust Evelyn—at least, not when there would be no advantage to endangering us with false information. I'd check simply because I could.

The Abbotts lived in upstate Michigan. When Evelyn called the Byrony Agency, she'd explained that her boss and his wife were finishing a weekend getaway in Detroit where someone had mentioned their agency and recommended them. The Abbotts had to be home tomorrow, but was there any chance they might be able to speak to someone briefly?

At the mall, I went for smart casual—an Anne Klein blouse and slacks ensemble, and pumps with no special designer name attached. I chose a wig of short, dark blond hair, and added a tan from a winter sun getaway. Elegant small-frame glasses, pearl earrings, and a gold watch completed the look of the casually stylish schoolteacher who'd married into a bit of money, but hated to flaunt it.

The outfit rang up quite a bill, particularly the jewelry. It was more than I liked to spend on a pro bono job, but I'd brought money from my hidden stash, and I could easily take the watch and earrings home and add them to my costuming collection in New York. The rest of the ensemble I might be able to reuse on this job, but after that it was garbage.

As always, the male half of the act got away with a much cheaper outfit. Jack bought washout white hair color, meant for kids to add funky streaks, but equally suitable for adding more silver to his dark hair. He used my fake tanner, and bought cheap blue contacts. Expertly applied scar makeup from a joke shop added an ugly mark on his chin for interest. For clothes, he went for the kind of golf shirt, casual pants, and loafers combo that said "working-class guy turned entrepreneur."

Neither was a grade-A disguise, but they'd do.

Thirty-four

At four thirty-five, we stepped through the very door we'd been watching that morning. It was a simple door, with a simple lock and dead bolt. A security system or camera was a definite possibility, but once inside, alone in a semidark stairwell, we had time for a thorough search. No alarm system. No camera. No need for them in a business like this.

To reach the office, we had to climb a set of old, narrow stairs that smelled of must and rotting wood, underlain with the faint "soaked into the walls" stink of urine. The stairs were slick with age and poorly lit. I didn't dare touch the handrail.

I wondered how many prospective parents never got past these stairs, struck by the uncomfortable feeling they were about to ascend into a squalid office manned by a sweaty beef-jerky-chomping guy named Sal, who had a sports book on the side. If a couple had any twinges of guilt over private adoption, any fear that it wasn't the legitimate business they'd been led to believe, they probably turned around right here.

But if they made it up the stairs, past the shadowy landing, and through the wooden door, all their fears would evaporate. It was like stepping into the reception area for an upscale preschool.

The reception desk was large, made of rich wood, with no hint of the corporate or industrial about it. The walls had been painted beige with just a hint of pink for warmth. Framed watercolors adorned the walls, all in soft, warm tones. Two armchairs waited, big and inviting, each flanked by a table with magazines, but with nothing between the chairs, letting the anxious or excited couple stay close, whispering or holding hands.

A glance at the magazines showed not a single parenting one. Nor were there any pictures of children—even the watercolors were all landscapes. No need to remind clients of what they lacked. And yet the general air still suggested a business that catered to children—maybe just that lived-in homeness that you couldn't help associating with family life.

The receptionist looked like a primary schoolteacher—early forties, with dangling, whimsical cat earrings, slacks, and a wool sweater decorated with bright geometric shapes. She even had that nursery school patois down, that cheerful singsong that's so reassuring to a child, but grates on anyone over the age of ten.

"Oh, you must be the Abbotts! I bet you're *so* excited. A little nervous, too, hmm? Don't be. Everyone here is *so* great. You're just going to *love* it."

I peered down the hall behind her, expecting to see a circle of preschoolers singing "If You're Happy and You Know It." As she led us into that hall, I was transported back thirty years, to my first day of school, that sudden terror that maybe I wasn't ready for this. Fortunately, I had someone to hold my hand and guide me forward, someone I trusted, someone who'd stay with me, and watch out for me. Or I did today—Jack's hand engulfing mine, his firm grip reassuring me we could pull this off. Thirty years ago, I hadn't been so lucky. Mom had pulled up to the curb and pointed me toward the door, annoyed that Dad had been called into the station when he'd planned to take me to my first day of school. I'd made her late for her weekly bridge game.

Inside the office, we were introduced to our "case coordinator." Conrad Soukis was one of the two employees who could pass for Fenniger's contact. The description, sadly, fit an entire legion of men best categorized as "middle-aged pencil-pushers." Soukis was roughly Jack's age, but with none of his edge, none of his physical power, none of his—I hate to say it—virility. Average height, receding hairline, scrawny but with a paunch, and the bland, pasty face of someone who spent his days basking in the glow of a computer screen.

Soukis sat us down and started with a description of the agency's services. He sped through them, probably recognizing the look that said he wasn't telling us anything we didn't already know. Then it was time to find out more about us, our expectations and our situation.

We wanted children—that much was obvious. We'd been trying since our marriage. At first, I'd blamed the difficulties on passing thirty, moving farther from my prime childbearing years. But last year, a barrage of fertility tests revealed the real problem: my husband's low sperm count.

When Jack and I devised the plan, I'd been perfectly willing to take the medical blame for the Abbotts' inability to reproduce, but as Jack pointed out, "low sperm count" was a simple concept that didn't require an in-depth explanation, and he knew a way he could use it to our advantage.

So we played our stereotypical roles. The teacher wife

did all the explaining, being very careful to couch the fertility issue as "our" problem while her silent, rough-mannered husband struggled not to squirm, clearly uncomfortable with the subject and with the disappointment of being to blame for not giving his younger wife the baby she longed for.

I talked about my situation—how I'd always imagined I'd have children, and became a teacher out of love for little ones, but as my twenties slipped past, I'd come to accept that the "minivan and 2.5 kids" lifestyle wasn't in my future.

"Then I met Wayne," I said, beaming at Jack. "At first, I figured if we did get serious, kids would be out of the question. If he'd wanted them, he'd have had them with his first wife. But I wanted *him*, not a baby-maker. I wouldn't have even raised the issue, but then—" Another broad, loving smile. "—*he* did, and he wanted a child, so it was perfect."

Jack nodded. "My first wife, she didn't want kids, which was okay. I was busy with my business and, besides, it wasn't—" He cleared his throat. "—it wasn't a good marriage. I didn't want to bring kids into it. This time—" Another throat clearing, obvious embarrassment at discussing his marriage with a stranger. "It's different."

Soukis moved on to our requirements. As for gender, we had no preference. Same with age, so long as the child was under a year. But race? That was another story.

"It doesn't matter to me at all," I said. "A baby is a baby." I snuck an anxious look at Jack, who nodded a "same here," but without conviction. "But where we live . . . that's the problem. Wayne's business is there, so we

won't be leaving anytime soon, and the town is very...
racially homogeneous."

"White," Jack said.

"As someone who works with children, I know first-hand that it doesn't matter how accepting the parents are. If the surrounding society isn't as accepting, it can be very difficult for the child. So we'd need to have a, uh—" I dropped my gaze as if in shame. "Caucasian baby. Otherwise, we'd have pursued international adoption."

"That will make it harder," Soukis said.

My gaze dropped another fraction as I added a mournful "I know."

Jack reached over to squeeze my hand.

Soukis asked a few more questions, then explained the next steps. If no complications arose in the background check and home study, we'd be put on the waiting list, but with our "requirement," it would probably be a three-year wait, maybe longer.

I let my disappointment seep out while Jack squeezed my hand and whispered words of support and reassurance. Then he asked me to give him a moment alone with Soukis, just to run over some of the financial details again. He stayed behind in the office, and shut the door all but a crack, so I'd hear their voices.

As I left, I realized our late-day appointment came with a huge bonus. The agency's workday must have ended at five and, being a Monday, no one was keen to stay late, so by 5:15 the office was empty.

I started in the reception area. My gaze kept sliding to the dual temptations of the filing cabinet and computer, but I needed more time with them. I concentrated on figuring out how Jack and I could safely break in.

I zoomed through the front room, having already gotten a decent overview when we'd been admitted. No alarm system. No camera. Just a regular lock and dead bolt, like the street-level door.

I quickly moved on to the office. I could hear Jack and Soukis, their voices muffled and low, but still audible.

"Deb doesn't know about any of that," Jack was saying. "I'm not hiding it from her. There's just no reason to bring it up now, right? Ancient history. The credit stuff, well, it comes with the territory, starting a business. The assault was a bar fight that got out of hand when I was a stupid kid. And the DUI ten years ago...I wasn't a kid, but still stupid, you know? The divorce and the stress at work...It's all in the past and none of it has anything to do with Deb, but I'm worried it's going to hurt our chances of adopting a kid."

"It could."

"Shit."

"In fact, I hate to say it, but it almost certainly will."

Their voices faded as I moved into the farthest office. There were four offices in total—five employees, including the receptionist. None of the doors had locks. The filing cabinets did, but they'd be easily picked, the sort that only stopped someone casually trying to peek inside.

The computers would be the biggest stumbling block. I could download e-mail and data files onto a flash drive, but that was the extent of my knowledge...and I was pretty pleased with myself for knowing *that* much. If the operating system was password protected, I was screwed. I'd have to check with Evelyn and see whether she knew a way to bypass it to grab files. Another charge for my tab.

The voices surged louder as I moved to the office across the hall.

"I get their reasoning," Jack was saying, "but I'm not the same guy now. Deb's the best damned thing that ever happened to me. She'd make a great mom, and if she can't have a kid because of me, first because of this... sperm thing, and now because of shit I did before I met her..." His voice trailed off.

"I understand."

"Do you?" Despair tinged Jack's voice. "I love that woman. The only thing I want is for her to be happy. I'll do whatever it takes to see that happen. Do you get that?"

"I'm not sure..."

"Hell, I don't know what I'm asking. Just, you know, some way to grease the wheels."

"If you mean anything illegal..."

"Not that. I wouldn't—" A short, embarrassed laugh. "Yeah, I would. Hell, there's not much I wouldn't do to make her happy, you know? But this is a completely legit business and I get that. I just thought, you know, sometimes there are ways... around stuff."

Their voices fell again as I hurried back to the main room, knowing Jack's talk was coming to a close. He'd planted the seeds. If they bore fruit, it wouldn't be tonight.

Five minutes later, we were back on the street.

"Any nibbles?" I asked.

"Hard to say. Seemed sympathetic."

"How could he not be? I knew what you were doing and I *still* felt bad for you. A perfect play. The right pitch.

The right tone. Just an ordinary guy who loves his wife and wants her to be happy. If Soukis is involved, I bet you'll be getting a call."

"Doesn't matter. Just a side play. Main point—"

"—was getting an inside view of the setup and security. The biggest obstacle will be getting through that street-level door, where anyone can see us breaking in. The only windows are up front, and the fire escape is there, which is just as risky—if not more so—than coming through the front door. But we'll come up with something, and after that door is open, it'll be a cakewalk. I'll give you the details over dinner."

I swung around the corner, my fingers grazing the streetlamp. "I was thinking steak before our stakeout, if that's still something you like."

"Always."

"Good. I saw a place a few blocks over. We should probably drive, with your foot—"

"I'm fine. Warm enough. We'll walk."

I nattered on about Jack's great performance for the first block before stopping myself. "Sorry. I *really* don't need any more sugar today, do I?"

"Things are going well. You're happy. Nothing wrong with that."

"Thanks. Oh, and for a more tangible thank-you, I picked up something at the mall."

From my purse, I pulled a pack of his special brand of cigarettes. His eyes lit up, probably the same way mine had when he'd handed me candy this morning.

He reached for it.

"Not so fast," I said. "It comes with a price. You'll get

them after the stakeout, and I'll get a story. You still haven't told me how you hurt your foot."

He nodded, gaze swinging to look down the road. My cheeks heated and I thrust the package at him. "I'm kidding. Like I said, it's a thank-you for—"

He didn't take it. "I'll tell you. Said I would."

"You don't have to if it's—"

"Tonight. After the stakeout. Cigarette and a story. Gotta warn you, though. Not very interesting. Just damned stupid. And embarrassing."

"Those are the best kind. If even you can screw up now and then, there's still hope for me."

Thirty-five

We had a great dinner. Jack once told me that growing up he'd dreamed of being rich enough someday to have steak every night. He'd tried it, following his first job, and gave up after a few weeks, but a steak house is still his restaurant of choice.

So finding one was a way to put him into a good mood, relaxed, even voluble ... or what passed for voluble with Jack. After a quick rundown of the security—couched in terms appropriate for a public setting—conversation turned to the more personal ... or what passed for personal with Jack. He told me a story about an old job—also modified for the setting and containing no information to identify the target, location, or even time period, but entertaining nonetheless.

We had dessert at a patisserie three doors from the coffee shop where we'd staked out the Byrony Agency. We went in at 10:30 p.m., which seemed late for dessert, but I'd noticed earlier that the place was open until midnight, presumably to catch the postshow crowd from the theater down the road. Before the show got out, the place was nearly empty, and we easily got a window seat.

I ordered a chocolate torte. Jack got apple pie. I teased him about that—faced with a display of elaborate desserts, he picked something he could have any night at the lodge. When it arrived, he seemed a little annoyed by the attempts to fancy it up with caramel crackles, whipped cream, and chocolate drizzles. After a few bites, he pronounced it decent enough, but not as good as Emma's...and he left the broken crackles and blob of cream on the side.

As the shop started to fill with the theater crowd, two women entered the Byrony Agency. Cleaning staff. By 11:45, as we were settling the bill, they were already leaving, being either superefficient or figuring, with the empty office, no one would know how long they'd stayed.

We took our time. The staff, unlike the cleaners, seemed in no rush to get home, and when we left at 12:10, they'd done no more than dim the lights as a subtle hint to the remaining diners.

As I stepped onto the sidewalk, my gaze scanned the opposite side of the street. Dark and quiet.

"Fuck."

I followed Jack's glare to a homeless guy on the coffee shop steps.

"He's just catching the stragglers from the show," I murmured. "When the shop clears and closes, he'll leave. We can't move until then anyway."

We tucked ourselves into an alley. Twenty minutes later, the last of the dessert shop staff locked the door, the click echoing. Through the reflection in a store window, I watched the homeless man stand, stretch...then retreat farther into the alcove and curl up in its shadows.

"Fuck," I said.

Jack grunted his agreement.

We waited, hoping he was just resting or that a passing cop would roust him. But the man stayed in his corner, the sidewalk stayed empty, and the street saw a car only every few minutes.

"If he's asleep, maybe we can..." I shook my head. We couldn't risk it.

We waited until a distant church bell rang twice, and my nose and toes had gone numb. Then Jack shook his head and motioned me toward the car. We weren't getting into the Byrony Agency tonight.

"Three hours to Evelyn's," Jack said as we climbed in. "This time of night? Probably less."

"You don't need to come up with distractions for me, Jack. Yes, I'm disappointed, but we knew this wouldn't be an easy break-in. We'll try again tomorrow night, with backup plans for dealing with the guy, if that's his regular spot. If we're lucky, we'll have Quinn. I'm sure he can play cop and send him on his way."

"Wasn't a distraction. Just saving time. Getting it over with. Unless you're tired..."

"Even if I was, I don't think I'd sleep."

"Good." He opened the door and got out. "Take first shift. Head to 94 west."

There was no rush so we stopped for washroom breaks, leg stretches, and coffee runs, taking turns at the wheel. I'll admit I'd hoped one of those stops would be a cigarette break, so I could hear Jack's story. I wasn't as interested in knowing how he'd broken his foot as in the simple fact of his telling me, trusting me enough to share a story that was, as he said, embarrassing. But he didn't suggest it, and I started to feel a little silly about our deal, maybe even rude, asking for a personal story before I gave him the cigarettes. So at the last driver switch, thirty minutes from Fort Wayne, I opened the hatch and slid the pack from my bag to his.

We arrived at Evelyn's just before six. Jack parked at the usual strip mall around the corner. If it seemed like we'd stay longer than a couple of hours, he'd move the car to her garage.

As we climbed her steps, I asked what time she expected us.

"Doesn't."

"She doesn't know we're coming? We're showing up, unannounced, on her doorstep at six in the morning? That's not very nice."

"Yeah."

I laughed. He knocked, then waited ten seconds and knocked again.

After another minute came the faint sound of footsteps on the stairs. Now she needed to check who it was. There wasn't a peephole. In this neighborhood, populated with upper-middle-class retirees, I'm sure there were lots of peepholes. But Evelyn would never get one installed for fear she'd be mistaken for something a lot worse than a cautious retired criminal: a nervous little old lady. And, besides, peepholes? This was the twenty-first century. For Evelyn, nothing short of a wireless, motion-detecting, autotracking closed-circuit camera would do.

Locks sounded. I counted off all three, then waited for a sharp command to the dogs. It came, followed by the scrabble of their claws on the stairs as they headed back up to bed.

The door opened. Evelyn stood there, wearing a pale yellow linen shirt and gray slacks, the shirt slightly cock-eyed, the only sign the outfit had been hastily pulled on. She raked her hand through her white bob and fixed Jack with a killer glare.

"What the hell are you doing here?"

"Visit," he said. "Owed you one, right?"

"Not at five o'clock in the goddamned morning."

"Six."

"Get the hell in here, before I catch pneumonia."

Her sharp eyes followed Jack as he entered, sliding down to his feet. "I thought you had another two weeks in that cast."

"Changed my mind."

"And yes, I tried to stop him," I said. "But it was help or let him do it himself and risk hacking off more than the cast. Apparently, it was hampering his ability to help me with the case. *My* case, may I point out, which I was perfectly happy to investigate alone while he rested."

She snorted and took my jacket. "Rest and Jack are two words that don't belong in the same sentence. Holing up in a backwoods shack isn't for him—as lovely as it may be." Her look said she doubted *lovely* was the word. Evelyn had made it clear from the start that her opinion of my primary occupation wavered between "how quaint" and "my God, why would someone actually choose to live like that?"

She continued. "He was probably climbing the walls...though not as frantically as he was in that motel room. Much longer in *there* and he'd have chewed off his cast." A glance my way. "How bad was it?"

I remembered the state of Jack's motel room. "Let's just say a mild case of cabin fever had set in."

"Mild, my ass."

She led me into the living room, where Jack had already claimed his usual end of the love seat. He jerked his chin, telling me to take the other, which I would have done anyway—my only other options being the two hard-backed postmodern pieces or Evelyn's armchair.

"I told you he'd follow you home," she continued as I crossed to the love seat. "I'm sure he put up a token struggle, of course. Probably went something like this: 'I'm fine. Nah. Fuck, yeah. I'm fine. Go on.' Then he let you get...oh, about as far the parking lot before he limped out after you, deciding maybe, since you'd come all that way, and since you were offering, he might as well go with you. He offered to pay, too, didn't he?"

Jack tensed, preparing for Evelyn's inevitable crowing about how well she knew him.

"Pay?" I lowered myself onto the love seat. "Damn, I gave in too fast, didn't I?"

"I'll pay," Jack said. "Just didn't want to mention it."

"Oh, I'm kidding. You know I wouldn't take your money."

The briefest flicker of consternation glimmered in Evelyn's eyes. If I felt any guilt at lying just to prick her ego, it was wiped out by the equally quick flash of gratitude in Jack's.

"Coffee?" he asked, pushing to his feet.

"Yes, please."

"You might as well round up breakfast while you're in there," Evelyn said.

A grunt. As he disappeared through the kitchen door, his voice rolled back to us. "Update her, Dee."

In other words, don't give her a chance to make her offer until he was in the room. I told her about our appointment and thwarted break-in.

"So we'll try again tonight," I said. "If Quinn's here, he can roust the guy and stand guard."

"Quinn? What's Quinn got to do with this?"

When I fell into silence, she twisted to look toward the kitchen.

"Did you forget to mention something, Jacko? Or someone?"

He appeared with two coffees. I mouthed "I'm sorry" while Evelyn still had her back to me. He shrugged, crossed the room and handed me my mug.

"Go on," he said. "Tell her."

"Tell her . . . ?"

"Everything."

Meaning I should go all the way back to how Quinn first became involved—his unexpected arrival at the lodge and the reason for it. Jack gave Evelyn her coffee, then returned to the kitchen.

"Jesus Christ," Evelyn said when I said Quinn knew who I was. "And you didn't skin that boy alive, Jack? You're getting soft."

"Honest mistake," Jack called from the kitchen.

"You don't think it is?" I asked.

She sipped her coffee, considering. "Quinn's too much the Boy Scout to do anything that underhanded. And he's smart enough to know that if he did, Jack *would* skin him alive."

I told her the rest, how Quinn was now helping and due to join us soon.

"And Jack's fine with that?" she said, brows lifting. "Quinn sniffing around? Wriggling into your case?"

"He's not thrilled about it, but we could use Quinn's law-enforcement know-how and if he's offering—"

"Oh, I bet he's offering. Since day one, that boy's been panting after you like a junkyard mutt smelling his first bitch in heat."

"Colorful..."

"But true."

I eased back into the seat, cupping my mug. "Whatever Quinn's motivation, we gave Jack the final say, and he agreed."

"Making Jack now, officially, the first professional killer ever to aspire to sainthood via martyrdom."

"I know hanging out with Quinn isn't Jack's idea of fun, but all he has to do is say no—"

"Hear that, Jack?" Evelyn swiveled, leaning over the side of her chair to yell toward the kitchen. "All you have to do is say no."

Silence returned.

"So, back to the break-in—" I said.

"Dee? Would you be a sweetie and feed the girls for me?"

"Uh, sure..."

"Their food is on the basement landing and their

bowls are outside. You'll need to take them out and watch them. Make sure Scotch gets her share. Ginger's been bullying her again."

"Okay..."

"I'll help Jack with breakfast."

Thirty-six

When I fed the dogs, I noticed their water bowl had a pair of flies doing the backstroke. So I dumped it and looked around for an outside tap, but couldn't find one. I glanced at the back door. Evelyn had obviously kicked me out so she could talk to Jack, presumably give him shit for letting Quinn onto our case.

Ginger stopped eating, looked at where her water bowl had been, then up at me. When I didn't return her bowl, she lapped rainwater from a groove in the deck.

"Okay, okay," I said. "But if she gives me shit for interrupting, I'm blaming you."

I opened the screen door and lifted my hand to knock. Then I glimpsed Jack's shoulder and arm through the dining room doorway. He was shrugging, talking to Evelyn in the living room again.

I decided knocking would be more of an interruption. Just slip in and get the water. They'd hear me filling the bowl, so I clearly wasn't eavesdropping. It wasn't as if I'd been ordered to stay outside.

I stepped in, prodding Ginger back out as I quietly closed the door.

Evelyn was talking. "Bad enough you don't give that boy a smack upside the head."

"Boy?" Jack snorted.

"I don't care how old he is, he sure as hell doesn't act it. He's like a teenager, chasing after Nadia, barging in on your investigation."

Yep, arguing about Quinn. I headed for the sink.

"Didn't barge in. I invited him."

"That's my point, you dumb fucking Mick. You're not just letting him poach on your turf—you're opening the gate and inviting him in."

Evelyn had a point. Me working alone with Quinn was one thing. Bringing him in on this meant I was exposing Jack to an unnecessary risk.

I reached for the tap.

Evelyn went on. "Why don't you just hand him a bouquet of roses and a box of fucking condoms while you're at it, Jacko?"

"It's not like that," Jack said.

"No? Nadia is yours, and it's about time you had the balls to do something about it."

Did Evelyn think Quinn was trying to shoulder Jack aside as my professional contact? Had Jack mentioned the Toronto job, leading her to think Quinn and I were partnering?

"Don't start," he said.

"Why not? You obviously won't. You were taking your time. Fine, I understand that. God forbid you should commit yourself to anything before you've checked out every angle, made absolutely sure the water is warm and safe. Then Quinn leaps in with a splash that sends you flying out of the fucking pool. But still, you're not worried. Big splash, full of sound and fury, signifying nothing. By the time you blink, it'll be gone. She'll go home, forget him, and there won't be so much as a ripple to show where he'd been. So now—" A pause. "Where are you going?"

"Glass of water. Making me thirsty."

His footsteps sounded on the dining room floor. I

glanced at the door. I couldn't make it and I wasn't about to be caught eavesdropping. I reached for the faucet again.

The fast clicking of Evelyn's pumps on the hardwood, then Jack's footsteps stopped.

"Not so fast, Jacko. We *are* having this conversation, and this time, you aren't running."

"Not running. Walking."

"As fast as you can."

He snorted. "Nothing to discuss. You get these ideas. These fancies—"

"Fancies? Oh, yes, I would *love* to see you shack up in some backwater hovel, go Grizzly Adams, and raise a passel of brats. Nothing would make me happier. Maybe I can even visit now and then, play Grandma Evie—"

A wheeze that took me a minute to recognize as stifled laughter. Jack's laughter.

"You think that's what I want?" he asked.

"I don't know what the hell you want, Jack, and I don't think you do, either. The only thing you do know is you want *her.*"

My heart thudded so hard I couldn't breathe. I'd misheard. Misunderstood. Misinterpreted—

"It's not like that," Jack said.

"No?"

"No."

I relaxed my grip on the faucet and exhaled. Okay, that's what I wanted to hear, wasn't it? Wasn't it?

"So last year, when you set up that Helter Skelter killer hunt for Nadia, it was just because you like her as a friend?"

"Didn't set it up for her. Needed to shut him down. Bad for business."

"True. And, while you were acknowledging that and thinking something should probably be done about him, you couldn't help thinking how much she'd like to be the one to do it, how it might be good for her, exercise those vigilante yearnings, while showcasing you in a better light, and giving you two time together..."

"It wasn't like that."

And it *hadn't* been like that. In all those days together, he hadn't given any sign of treating me differently than he would a male partner. We'd shared the same motel rooms, for God's sake. He'd seen me in my nightshirt. Not so much as a lingering glance.

"Nadia tells me you two have been out of touch all year," Evelyn said.

"Been busy—"

"The hell you have been. You don't think I know your schedule, Jack? Even when you don't tell me what you're up to, I know. You've been no busier than usual."

Okay, that stung...

"Do you want me to tell you what happened, Jack?"

"Not particularly."

"You found out this thing with Quinn hadn't fizzled, as you expected. He was still in contact with her. They were trying to make something of this. And why the hell not? They're about the same age, cop backgrounds, part-time hitmen, vigilante leanings, plus all that sports crap they're into. You couldn't have found Nadia a better match if you tried. And you knew, whatever you said or did, you didn't have a hope in hell of competing. So you backed off to lick your wounds."

"Do you really think I'd do that? If I can't have her, I don't want to have anything to do with her?"

"Whoo-hoo. Full sentences. I must have touched a nerve there."

"Fuck off. It's not like that. Her and me. I'm just saying—"

"That you hadn't left her for good. I never said you had. You just wanted to withdraw long enough to get used to the idea that you'd lost your chance. Lick your wounds, suck it in, and bounce back to being her friend and mentor, and be happy with just that."

"I am happy with *just* that. It's all I want."

"Is it? Or is that what you're telling yourself because you think you never had a shot in the first place? You'd better wake up fast, Jack, or she's going to settle for Quinn, and let me tell you, it's settling, because it's not Quinn she—"

I wrenched the tap on full blast, heart pounding.

Out of the corner of my eye, I saw Evelyn storm into the kitchen. I kept my gaze on the bowl. As good an actor as I was, a blush is something you can't hide, so I waited until the bowl was full, shut off the tap, then turned—

"Oh!" I jumped as if just noticing her, water cascading over the edge. "Sorry. The dogs needed water and I couldn't find an outside tap."

She eyed me. After a moment, she harrumphed and stalked to the coffee machine, clearly unable to tell whether I'd overheard.

"There's one beside the deck," Jack said.

My jump that time was genuine. I wheeled to see Jack.

"The faucet. By the deck. I'll show you."

He took me outside and showed me the tap, around

the far side of the deck. I wasn't likely to need it again, but it made a good excuse to get out of the house while Evelyn had her coffee and cooled her heels.

I filled a second bowl of water for the dogs. Then I tossed a ball for them, Jack leaning against the deck, taking a turn if the ball happened to roll past his feet but otherwise just watching.

"See? You do like dogs," he said as I took a break to scratch behind Ginger's ears.

"Guilty. But you already knew that. And I still don't need one."

"Good breed." His chin jerked toward the German shepherds. "Guard dog. Smart. Even-tempered. Sticks around property. Run with one? Wouldn't even need a lead."

I shook my head, picked up the slobbery ball, and threw it again. We stayed outside for ten minutes, saying little, the silence comfortable. He seemed to assume I hadn't heard what Evelyn said. And as for what Evelyn had been about to say when I turned on the tap . . . ?

I tried to tell myself I had no idea what she'd been going to say. I turned it on because I was worried about being caught eavesdropping. And because I wanted to rescue Jack from her pokes and jibes.

But I knew what she'd been going to say. That I'd be settling for Quinn because I wanted someone else. I wanted Jack.

The very thought should make me laugh. At the very least, I should brush it off, the way he'd done when she said he was interested in me. *Zero for two, Evelyn. Your romantic radar is a million miles off course.*

Instead, the very thought made my heart pound so hard

I could barely breathe. And what filled me wasn't outrage. It was fear—stark, heart-stopping, mind-emptying fear.

Fear that she was right. And, as those first numbing blows of terror subsided...the ice-cold knowledge that she was right. Absolutely right.

I said I wanted more from Jack. I wanted him to care more. I wanted to interpret his attention and his gestures as meaning more. More *what*? I'd tried not to think too much about that, just stick a vague label on it—more depth to our relationship, more emotion, more...something.

When Evelyn accused him of having more than a friendly interest in me, it felt like when I was twelve, and Amy told Colin Forbes I liked him. I'd been horrified and hopeful at the same time. But when Colin said he liked me, too, and I realized he'd meant "as a friend," it was the same as hearing Jack's denial, a small squeeze of disappointment, but mostly relief. My first thought had been that I was disappointed because of simple ego, and relieved because I didn't want to deal with an unwanted attraction. Now I understood the truth.

I cared about Jack more than I should. I needed him more than I should. I thought about him way more than I wanted to, in ways I definitely didn't want to. Even to consider a romantic relationship with Jack terrified me. But, apparently, I didn't need to, because the point was moot. Whatever I felt for him, he didn't reciprocate. And my overwhelming reaction to that was relief.

Breakfast was typical fare at Evelyn's—more gathered than prepared, with bagels, fruit, cheeses, and store-bought muffins. We moved on to discussing angle two of our plan. As Jack had put it, with Fenniger dead, the agency was in the market for a hitman.

"I finally got hold of Honcho yesterday and spun my story, setting up Dee to replace Fenniger," Evelyn said. "I told him I've got a new protégé. Damned good, but with limited work experience. I said I'm getting too old for hand holding and baby steps, but this one doesn't need it. Doesn't need to be coddled, either. Whatever the hit is, however messy, this protégé can take it and sleep through the night."

I cast a small glance at Jack, but he was kind enough not to snort in derision.

"I said this protégé is charming and sociable, which, believe me—" She looked at Jack. "—can be hard to come by in this business. This one's not only a people person, but can play it so sweet and sincere you'd hand over your baby while you used the restroom. Easy on the eyes, too, which is always a plus. The only issue I skirted was gender."

She peeled and sliced a banana. "Now I'd say a woman would be perfect for the job. Some guy wants to snap pictures of a pretty girl? Instant perv alert. But no one's going to consider that with a woman. The problem is that Honcho, being a man, isn't going to think that way. He'll think no woman would agree to murder a girl and steal her baby. As if our ovaries would leap through our guts and stay our trigger fingers. Sexist morons."

One banana slice, skewered on a knife end, slowly chewed and swallowed before she continued. "So he'll presume male, which is fine for now. The 'charming and good-looking' part would be a plus for any guy trying to lure in a teenage girl."

"And all of this matters...how exactly? It would be a great setup, *if* Honcho knew the details of the job."

"Of course he knows the details. With Honcho, it's ass-covering deluxe, Dee. If he understands the job, he can find the right guy, please the client, and minimize the chance of the pro backing out. The pro thinks he's covered by the middleman not knowing details, which is great, but also means he can't complain or negotiate. Hell, even the client probably doesn't realize how much Honcho knows. He's a sneaky bastard. He'll weasel out just enough to piece it together for himself."

I glanced at Jack.

He shrugged. "He might. Couldn't say."

"Well, I can," Evelyn said. "Absolutely and definitely. As I told him all about my protégé's credentials, he tried being cagey, but I could hear drool hitting the receiver. Fenniger has gone AWOL, fucking up a job and pissing off a client. Honcho is desperate—he just can't let on he is. He told me he might have something and he'll call back tomorrow. Now he's trying to flush out Fenniger, figuring he's just gone on a bender. When he can't find him, he'll call before he loses the contract completely."

We were finishing breakfast when Quinn phoned to say he was on his way. We'd meet him in Detroit at four and launch the third wave of attack. Three ideas, three paths, one of which we hoped would lead to the information we needed. It was more complicated than I liked, but all of us were under time constraints and couldn't afford to follow one avenue to a dead end before starting the next.

We took our coffees and moved into the living room as I mentally prepared to deal with the reason I'd been summoned—Evelyn's offer.

Evelyn and I had started our courtship dance last fall. Actually, she'd taken the first step almost three years ago, sending Jack to check out this intriguing new possibility she'd heard about from her former employer and good friend, Frank Tomassini. The invitation was never delivered. Jack met me and decided I'd make a better project for him. So he'd returned to Evelyn, told her it didn't work out, and kept seeing me on the sly. Then, last fall, she'd met me, decided I hadn't been irredeemably spoiled by Jack's tutelage, and begun her campaign of seduction.

She'd started by impressing me with her knowledge and her vast network of contacts. Then she'd wooed me with offers of vigilante work, and promises of a long, storied, and moneyed career pursuing only the cases that would scratch my itch. I'd played coquette, listening to her offers, but wary of the price tag. Mentor and protégée was no marriage of equals for Evelyn. She'd demand unswerving loyalty—even servitude—and slowly encroach on my regular life until there was nothing left but the job.

I hadn't refused her outright. I knew she'd be useful, but feared I'd end up the one used. What she was offering was exactly what I wanted, and while I felt I had the maturity and stubbornness to keep my life intact while enjoying her jobs, I was still wary.

All the while, Jack had stood to the side, the third party in this proposal, supporting and advising me, while letting Evelyn know that even if I accepted her offer, he wasn't stepping aside.

And now, she was back with something new to tempt me.

"Have you ever heard of the Contrapasso Fellowship, Dee?"

"Ah, fuck."

She shot Jack a glare.

"Contra...?" I began.

"Contrapasso. It's from Dante's *Inferno*."

"Right," I said. "The punishment fits the crime. The idea that whatever sins you committed will dictate your suffering for eternity. Fortune-tellers walking backward blind. Adulterers stuck together. Sometimes the punishment is ironic, sometimes not."

Evelyn tried to hide her surprise and, maybe, dismay that I wasn't rendered clueless by her literary reference. I'd been taking college courses for a few years, for a diversion, not a degree—at this rate, I'd be fifty before I *got* a degree. I'd read the *Inferno* last year, so it was still fresh in my memory. But if Evelyn wanted to think I spent my free time reading Dante, let her.

"Yes, that's it," she said. "Ultimate justice, you might say, which supposedly is the goal of the Contrapasso Fellowship."

"Goal?" Jack made a rude noise. "The goal is entertainment. It's a story. One of those..." His lips pursed as he searched for the word. "Urban legends."

Evelyn fixed him with a look. "And that means it can't be true?"

He met her gaze. "That'd be the definition of urban legend."

"And it's not true because . . . ?"

"Because it's not. I've been on the street how long? Never run into this 'Fellowship.' Never met anyone who did. All friend of a friend shit."

"So, having never personally encountered proof, it must clearly not exist?" She turned to me. "Have you noticed this about Jack, Dee? He deals only in tangible fact. If he can't hear it, see it, or touch it, it isn't there. It doesn't matter if it's dead obvious to the rest of the universe. If he can't prove it, it doesn't exist."

I sipped my coffee and waited for her to get back on track.

She threw up her hands. "Why am I asking you? It's like asking the skunk if he's noticed those other black-and-white vermin smell funny."

"I have no idea what this Contrapasso Fellowship is or isn't, but Jack's right. I won't chase rumors. If it exists, great. I'd love to hear about it."

"If it didn't exist, why would I bring it to you?"

"One, to get me chasing a rumor that interests you. Two, it's like the old joke about the guy asking a woman if she'd go to bed with him for a million dollars. You want me to work for you. I say I'm not interested. You offer me something incredible, and I accept it, which proves that I will work for you. You just haven't found my price."

A low rumble from the other end of the love seat. I turned to see Jack laughing.

"Oh, you liked that, didn't you?" Evelyn snapped. "You poison her against me, then get a good chuckle out of it?"

He dismissed her with an eye roll. She scowled, but

there was no more anger in it than a mother cuffing her son for being cheeky. Evelyn once called Jack her favorite protégé, and he'd countered by saying he was just the only one still talking to her. I think there was some truth in both. Jack was her best and most successful student. But he was also probably the only one who saw through her, and didn't judge what lay beneath. He said, "I won't feed your ego and I won't take your bullshit, but if you want me to keep coming around, I will." And that was more valuable to Evelyn than the loyalty of any bootlicking sycophant.

I turned to Jack. "What do you know about this Contrapasso Fellowship?"

"Him?" Evelyn squawked. "He doesn't even believe it exists. You're stacking the deck, Dee."

"I want to hear the legend first. Then you can tell me what parts of it you've heard are true. If Jack's willing…"

"Sure." He moved to the edge of his seat and took a muffin from the plate.

"Oh, God, this is going to take forever," Evelyn said. "Let me refill my coffee, and you can call me when he works up the energy to speak in full sentences."

She stood, glancing at Jack, as if still willing to hang around if he showed any signs of getting to the story soon. He took a bite of his muffin and chewed slowly. She stalked off into the kitchen.

Once she was gone, he put the muffin back on the table. "Contrapasso Fellowship? Revenge for hire. Kinda like what Quinn does. Only free."

I knew Quinn didn't always collect a paycheck, but didn't say so—to Jack this would be a mark of incompetence, not integrity. I could point out that Jack himself wasn't collecting a paycheck for this job we were doing, but he'd say it wasn't the same thing.

"Pro bono vigilantism?" I said.

"Anonymous, too. Send them a newspaper clipping? They investigate. Decide whether it deserves attention. Then they pick the punishment. Something fitting the crime."

"They administer their own brand of justice."

"Nah." He propped his injured foot onto Evelyn's glass and silver table. "Judge and jury? Yeah. Executioners? No. Get others to do that. They foot the bill."

"Vigilante philanthropists, then."

"Pretty much. Why? Everyone's got a theory. Rich folks who lost kids. Retired judges watched juries let too many assholes off. Even heard one about it being cops. Steal drug money to finance it."

"So it's bullshit, isn't it?"

"Seems to be." His lips parted again, then he rubbed his mouth.

"What?"

"Nothing."

"You were going to say more. You've heard something, haven't you?"

"Nah. Just . . ." He paused, his gaze studying mine with that quiet intensity that said he was trying to get inside my head. "Hear Evelyn out. If there's anything to it? Check it out. I'll help."

Thirty-seven

"Well, I blew that," I said as I backed the car from the parking lot.

"Nah."

"Nah? She kicked us out of the house without a word about the Contrapasso Fellowship. She's furious."

"Sulking."

I glanced at him as I merged with morning traffic.

"If she's really angry?" he said. "You'll never see it. Acts angry? Just that. An act."

"And she's sulking because..."

"Wrong reaction."

"I thought you said she was sulking."

A look, mild exasperation. "*Your* reaction. To her news."

"Ah. I didn't respond appropriately. She tells me she's uncovered a legendary group of philanthropists who'll presumably pay me very well to avenge horrible crimes, and I should have reacted by, oh, I don't know, kissing her feet and pledging undying devotion."

A small twist of a smile. "That'd have worked."

"So now she's punishing me for my lack of excitement by making me wait."

"Pretty much."

We drove out of the city in silence. Then I said, "I do want to hear about it."

"I know. You will. Just..."

"Be patient. Let her come to me, and when she does, show moderately more interest, enough to satisfy her ego without stroking it."

"Yeah." He ratcheted back the seat, stretching his bad leg. "Probably more than that."

"Give her a stronger reaction, you mean?"

"Nah. Her getting pissy. More than sulking. She's back-tracking. Dotting her i's. Crossing her t's."

"About what?"

"This fellowship thing. I questioned it. We demanded proof. Wanted facts. Gonna make damn sure she has them."

"To present a more solid case and avoid the risk of embarrassing herself by admitting she can't back up what she knows. But, naturally, she couldn't just say that, and admit you might be right to question her sources. Instead, she'll blame me, kick me to the curb as an ungrateful bitch, and make me stew for a while, worrying that I've blown a once-in-a-lifetime opportunity while she scrambles to check her facts."

"Pretty much."

I shook my head and adjusted my seat belt. "I know she has a lot to offer, Jack, but I really hate the games. I'm no good at them."

"Wouldn't say that."

"Maybe, but I don't like them."

"I know."

I looked over. "I never get that with you. We have our disagreements and our misunderstandings, but I never get the sense you have a bigger agenda, or that you want anything from me except exactly what you ask for up front. I appreciate that."

He nodded and bent to scratch his foot as I turned on the cruise control.

* * *

At eleven, I was slowing the car in front of the house where Destiny Ernst now lived. Or where we hoped she did. This sprawling two-story matched the Troy address where Fenniger said he'd delivered her. Whether Destiny was here remained to be seen.

Fenniger had no reason to lie, but just because he'd brought Destiny here in the dead of night didn't mean she'd stayed. Still, we were dealing with ordinary citizens, the kind of people so far removed from the criminal mindset that if they bought a hot stereo, they'd drive five blocks out of their way to pick it up . . . but would call the seller using their personal cell phone.

My research had shown that the house was owned by Kenneth and Leslie Keyes, a systems analyst and his advertising executive wife. A childless couple, but still within their childbearing years. A call to Leslie's workplace revealed she'd quit about a month ago, shortly before Sammi's death. Rearranging her life to accommodate her new baby? We couldn't jump to conclusions.

Getting proof wasn't going to be easy. It was a tough neighborhood to stake out. Our small rental, so inconspicuous in an urban setting, stood out here in the land of SUVs, Volvos, and Audis. I pulled in behind some weird SUV station wagon cross, then stretched a map over the steering wheel.

"Can you see the house okay?" I asked without looking up.

"Yeah."

"If anyone walks by, start bickering."

"Bickering?"

"You know. 'I told you to make a left back there.' 'Well, you're the idiot who wouldn't ask for directions.' '*I* don't need directions.'"

"Got it."

"We've got about fifteen minutes before someone peering out a window makes us for private investigators. What can you see?"

"Car in the lane," Jack said. "Sedan. Foreign make. Got one of those . . . baby signs in the back."

"Baby on board?"

"Yeah. Yard's clear. No toys, strollers, shit like that. Got a light on. Looks like—" A pause. "Someone just passed the window. Woman, I think. Probably living room. Where the light is. Upstairs? Got curtains in the left window. Bright yellow. Frilly."

"A nursery . . . or someone with god-awful decorating tastes."

"Yeah."

He continued to watch.

"So are we going to execute phase two when Quinn gets here?" I asked.

"Yeah. Otherwise? Never gonna be sure."

"Will he be okay with the acting gig?"

"Playing cop? Better be. Seemed fine with it. Anything changes? You're in. Rather not, though."

"It'll work better with you two, and it's better to mix it up now that the Byrony Agency has seen you and me together."

I checked my prepaid cell for the umpteenth time, still hoping we might get a call from the Byrony Agency, with a special adoption offer for Debbie and Wayne Abbott. It was a long shot, but if it panned out, it would be better than the avenues we were pursuing now.

"Anything?" Jack asked.

"No."

He reached behind the seat, grabbed a parcel he'd picked up at the courier depot, and tossed it onto my lap.

"Are those the expedited goodies from Felix?" I asked.

"Yeah."

I peeked in and pulled out one package.

"Bugs?"

"Yeah. Ever place one?"

"No."

"Want a lesson?"

I smiled. "Please."

We left without seeing any definitive signs of a baby in residence. With only fifteen minutes to stake out the house, we would have been extremely lucky if we had. The cool, dreary, and overcast day wasn't "push the pram around the block" weather. Probably not even "take the baby shopping" weather if you were a new and nervous mom.

Jack took over the driving and went in search of a shopping mall for our bug practice. The Web site for Troy, Michigan, had bragged that it was in the second most prosperous county in the U.S. and, while it was only the twelfth biggest city in the state, it was the second "biggest" for property values. So it was no surprise that when we located a mall, it was high-end. The valet parking gave it away.

We drove right past it before I saw the signs for Saks

Fifth Avenue. By then we had to make a left to get back, which sounds a whole lot easier than it was, because we were on a divided highway, which meant the notorious "Michigan left"—to go past the light, make a U-turn in a designated lane, double back, and quickly cross traffic to make a right to where you originally wanted to go.

On a Tuesday afternoon, the mall patrons were mostly Martha Stewart devotees checking out bronze Buddha knickknacks that would look so nice next to their five-thousand-dollar leather sofas. It was a world removed from my reality and, from the way Jack looked at the thousand-dollar Mont Blanc pens—as if searching for the button that would release a cache of uncut diamonds—it was a *universe* away from his. It was, however, the perfect place to play "hide the covert listening device."

While neither of us looked like anyone who'd pocket a thousand-dollar pen, we didn't look likely to buy one, either, so while salespeople weren't watching our every move, we did stand out. Therein lay the challenge.

Still, that wasn't enough for Jack. He had to up the ante by turning it into a real game with dares and rules, the basic premise being that one of us would pick an increasingly difficult location, then the other would lay the bug, retreat, listen, then recover it.

We went about ten rounds. After I managed to retrieve it from the men's washroom, Jack declared my training was complete . . . the declaration roughly coinciding with the moment that I started eyeing the Victoria's Secret changing rooms for his turn.

* * *

At three, I was in our hotel room, taking a much-needed bath. When I got out, I realized I'd forgotten to bring my clothes into the bathroom. I was going to have to get used to these coed living arrangements again. Fortunately, I was alone, Jack having left on a supply run.

So, towel haphazardly wrapped around me, I stepped from the bathroom and caught a glimpse of a tall man in a ball cap. I backpedaled into the bathroom, looking for a weapon, gaze settling on a can of hair spray.

"Dee," Quinn called.

"Jesus Christ," I said, peeking out. "How the hell did you—?"

He brandished a key card. "I passed Jack as he was leaving. He gave me this, muttered 212, and drove off."

I put the hair spray back on the counter. He stayed there, a foot from the bathroom door, his gaze traveling down me as I realized how small the towel was. It covered everything it needed to cover, but not by much. From his expression, though, he didn't mind. I could have closed the door. Or asked him to step outside while I got my clothes. But I didn't.

After this morning, I understood what was keeping me from taking what Quinn was offering. I'd been holding out hope that somehow I'd missed the signs and Jack felt the same way I did, and if I opened the door to Quinn, I'd be slamming it on Jack.

Well, that door had been slammed. And not by me.

With that possibility gone, I felt once again a shuddering sense of relief. Now I could take what both men were offering, and be happy with it.

Quinn stepped toward me, then leaned against the bathroom doorway, as if waiting permission to cross the threshold. Waiting for me to make the first move. And I wanted to make that move. Yet I stood there, clutching my towel, looking as sexy as a headlight-stunned deer.

I'd read about things like this—meeting your lover in a towel, doing a little tease—and it always sounded sexy and fun. I could certainly see how a guy might appreciate it. But it was like reading about the customs of another culture—I had no idea how to proceed.

Fortunately, the fact that I hadn't run away yet was encouragement enough for Quinn. He covered those last few steps slowly, giving me every opportunity to say no. Then he stopped in front of me, fingers running down the edge of the towel.

"Are you done with your shower?" he asked. "If you aren't, I've had a very long drive. I'm sure I could use one."

"Actually, I had a bath." As the words came out, I mentally smacked myself. Bad enough I didn't know the steps to a dance of seduction. Surely I could follow someone else's lead. I stepped closer, moving against him as I looked up. "But a shower would be nice."

I lifted on tiptoes to kiss him, but he motioned for me to wait. Then he peeled off his cap and wig and turned away, taking out and discarding his contacts. When he turned back, he looked like he had at the lodge, the dark blond brush cut and light green eyes.

"Better?" he said.

"Much."

I reached for the back of his head, his short hair bristling against my fingers, and pulled him down into a kiss. He tried to swing me against the wall, but my foot slipped on the wet floor. He caught me, but awkwardly, and ended up on one knee, holding me before I hit the floor.

"Um, okay..." He struggled not to laugh, cheeks coloring. "So much for graceful."

"The trick is to pretend this is where you were heading the whole time."

I wriggled from his grasp and lowered myself to the floor, then wrapped my hands around the front of his shirt and pulled him down.

His hands went to my thighs, shoving the towel up over my hips as he pushed between my legs. I undid the buttons on his shirt and slid my hands over his chest, feeling his muscles move. I broke the kiss, and traced a trail down his neck with my lips, tasting him, teeth grazing his skin as he arched up, grabbing my hips and thrusting.

He slid his hand between us, finding the edge of the towel. Wriggling to give him room to pull it off, I knocked over the wastebasket. He gallantly pretended not to notice, and peeled the towel—

The doorway darkened, a figure wheeling in, gun barrel swinging my way. I let out a yelp. Jack stood there, gun drawn, eyes widening, lips forming a silent "Fuck," as he tore his gaze away.

"Jesus-fucking-Christ," Quinn swore, scrambling to cover me as I squirmed from under him. "How the hell—? I thought you gave me your key card."

"Gave you Dee's," Jack said. "Forgot to leave it. I said that."

"You *muttered* something. It's hard enough to figure out what the hell you mean even when I *can* hear you—"

"Can I get dressed now?" I said as I scrambled up, Quinn moving in to block me while I pulled the towel into place. "Please?"

"And can you lower that gun now?" Quinn said. "Please?"

Jack had looked away, but kept the gun poised, aimed at a spot where Quinn would probably rather not be shot. Jack turned, careful to keep his gaze away from me. He glanced at the gun. Glanced at Quinn. Paused. Then holstered it.

"Outside," he said. "Let Dee dress."

Thirty-eight

I dressed as fast as I could, then fled past them in the hall, murmuring, "I'll be in the lounge." I sat on a bar stool, longingly eyeing the rows of liquor bottles as I sipped my Coke.

Being found making out on a bathroom floor is, I suppose, cause for some blushing. Sure, I was thirty-three and single and we'd had every expectation of privacy, thinking we had the only key—but I'd always been very private in my sex life, so, yes, I'd been embarrassed.

Yet having *Jack* find me making out on a bathroom floor took the humiliation to a whole new level. Last fall, he'd made it clear what he thought of Quinn's flirting with me on a job. Unacceptably unprofessional. Now that he'd been generous enough to put aside personal feelings and agree to let Quinn in on this case, exactly how long had it taken before we were rolling on the floor?

Jack was pissed. And I didn't blame him one bit.

"Is this seat taken?"

I looked up at Quinn. He'd changed into a new disguise for the evening—a somber jacket and tie ensemble straight from his suitcase, dark contacts, and dark hair.

He waited until I nodded, then slid onto the stool next to mine and ordered "whatever she's having."

"You found me," I said.

"That's my specialty."

I smiled. "I heard something like that."

His brows rose. Then he said, "Jack, right? I should

have figured he'd tell you." He took a Coke from the bar-tender. "So everything's okay? At least you're smiling."

"I'm fine. Just embarrassed."

"Kind of like having your parents walk in on you when you were sixteen?"

I sputtered a laugh. "Exactly like that, now that you mention it."

We sipped our drinks in silence.

"Can I talk to you?" He jerked his chin toward the booths.

I nodded. He led me across the nearly empty lounge to the farthest booth and we slid in.

"About what happened upstairs. I was pushing hard," he said. "Again."

"No, I—"

"You said you needed time. I knew that. I just..." A crooked smile. "Thought maybe I could speed the decision-making process along. Talking is good, and I'm damned good at it, but in some cases words aren't really my best friend. I'm more of an... action guy."

I laughed. "And damned good at *that*."

He laughed, but spots of color touched his cheeks, and as he nodded, his gaze dropped, as if that could hide his blush. Sitting there, looking at him, hands wrapped around his Coke, eyes downcast, that fascinating mix of confidence and uncertainty, I wanted to slide over and touch him. I wanted to kiss him and tell him that what-ever he felt for me, I felt the same back.

"I think—" I began.

"No, let me guess," he said, eyes lifting to mine, that half-smile still playing on his lips. "You like me, but you think this isn't such a good idea. Not just here and now, which is a *really* bad idea, but in general. Maybe it could work, but it probably wouldn't, and you think we should just stay friends."

"Um, no. I was going to say 'I think we should go upstairs before Jack gets even more pissed off.'"

A sharp laugh. "Damn. I wasn't even close." He wiped condensation from his glass, hands still around it. "Still, maybe that isn't what you were going to say but ..."

I took a deep breath. He tensed at the sound, bracing himself.

"The truth is that I have no idea what I want right now," I said. "Sadly, that's a damned good statement on my life in general these days. I know I'm making too big a deal out of this. We're single. We're adults. Go for it, have some fun, see what happens. But ... It's been a while since I've had a relationship. Hell, since I've dated, if you want the full embarrassing confession. And, you know what? I'm okay with that. I've gotten used to it. I'm past—"

"—the point of looking for someone."

I nodded. "Which isn't to say—"

"—that you don't want to be with anyone, just that you're not so eager you'll jump at the first decent offer."

I laughed. "Keep that up and I'll think you *can* read minds."

"No, I'm just good at diagnosing a condition I've been living with myself." He pushed the glass away. "Have you ever been married?"

I shook my head. The one time I'd approached engagement, it had ended with Wayne Franco. My boyfriend had stuck by me during the fallout, but the moment I suggested maybe it would be better for him if we took a break, he fled like a lifer seeing a hole in the prison yard fence.

"Well, I was. College sweetheart, didn't work out, nothing ugly. It just...faded away. Old story. Anyway, it wasn't so bad that it soured me on women, just left me determined to find the right one. That was..." His eyes rolled up as he calculated. "Eight years ago. After two years of looking and not finding anyone, I slowed down. Then I had to deal with friends and family setting me up on dates. After two years of that, I said enough is enough. Between my friends and my job and my moonlighting, my life is full."

He stopped. Before I could say anything, he went on, "So, I guess what I'm saying is, I'm not waiting for you to make up your mind so I can move on to the next woman on my list. I want you. But if you aren't ready, I'm not going anywhere. If someone else comes along, for either of us..." He shrugged. "We'll deal with it. No hard feelings. No expectations."

What could I say to that? It was the perfect solution... and no solution at all.

The trip back to Troy seemed to take triple what the clock said. I sat in the backseat and carried on some semblance of a conversation with Quinn in the passenger's seat.

We talked mainly about Montreal. How was his trip? Did he do any sightseeing? Had he been there before? Nothing related to his purpose for being there, just completely neutral conversation, but when I tried to include Jack by asking whether he'd ever visited, his sharp "no" told me I'd overstepped a boundary, and I withdrew into silence.

Jack was disappointed with me. I'd been unprofessional and, to him, there was no worse crime. If I was following Quinn down that road, then maybe I wasn't someone he should work with.

The situation probably wasn't that dire yet, but on that endless, uncomfortable drive, it felt like it was.

Jack stopped at a car rental agency. Quinn went inside to get a vehicle matching his specifications—full-size, neutral color, no obvious rental stickers. Jack stayed behind with me, making sure I knew how to use the wireless earpieces.

"Don't bother with the bugs. Concentrate on these." He waved the earpieces and the transmitter. "You want to add anything? Ask a question? Change our tactics? Just say so."

I nodded.

"No need to whisper. Just talk normally."

"Okay."

"Sure? Last chance for questions."

"I'm sure."

He opened his door.

"Jack?"

He glanced over his shoulder at me.

"I'm sorry."

He shut the door. "Nothing to be sorry—"

"Yes, there is. You're here, helping me with my investigation, taking risks for me, and I'm goofing off with Quinn—"

"Doesn't matter."

"It does and I'm sorry. I'm also sorry for asking you

about Montreal in front of Quinn. I didn't mean anything by it. I was just trying to make conversation."

He released the door handle and twisted in his seat, frowning as if trying to remember what I was talking about.

"Oh. That. Those damn left turns. Concentrating on them. Wasn't really listening. Montreal, right? Been there a few times. Had a job once. Middle of a fucking snowstorm."

I smiled. "They get those."

"In October?" He shook his head. "Wasn't prepared. Get right behind the guy. Pull my piece. Fucking gun's frozen."

I choked on a laugh. "A gun can't—"

"You telling the story? It was cold. Fucking cold. Did I mention that?"

"No, just the fucking snowstorm, which I'm sure, combined with the fucking cold, froze your fucking gun."

"Fucking right. Where was I? Right. Gun fails. But the guy hears something. Turns around." He shook his head. "Wasn't pretty." He squinted through the windshield. "Huh. There's Quinn. Better go."

He reached for the door handle. I grabbed his sleeve over the seat, then stopped, unsure, but when he turned, I saw the glitter of amusement in his eyes.

"How'd you pull the hit if your gun was supposedly frozen?" I asked.

"Grabbed an icicle."

"A what?"

"Icicle. You know. Long, sharp piece of ice ..."

"Bullshit."

His brows shot up in mock offense, the eyes under

them still dancing. "Don't believe me? Right in the neck. Perfect weapon. Melts. No evidence."

"No way."

"You don't sound so sure."

I searched his eyes but, as always, there were no answers there. He gave a dry rasp of a laugh and grabbed the door handle, then looked back over his shoulder.

"Okay?"

I smiled. "Thanks, Jack."

Fifteen minutes later, Quinn pulled a beige Crown Victoria into the Keyeses' driveway. He got out, stretching his legs as if it had been a long ride, then peered over his shades at the house. The sky was overcast, but with some disguises, you can get away with wearing sunglasses, just like you could get away with an earpiece that wasn't completely hidden.

As Quinn surveyed the house, Jack got out and adjusted the holster, making sure it would "accidentally" show if his suit jacket swung open. Again, just part of the disguise, not necessarily an accurate one, but sometimes expectation is more important than realism.

They proceeded to the door. A tiny woman with a dark ponytail answered their knock. From my vantage point down the road, I could only make out her size and hair color. Their voices, though, were clear, courtesy of the two-way earpieces.

"Leslie Keyes?" Quinn asked.

"Yes?"

"John Turnbull and Derek Walker, federal agents

with the Department of Intrastate Regulation and Enforcement."

Quinn machine-gunned the words, nearly too fast to distinguish, but bolstered with a weight of authority that dared you—ignorant layperson—to suggest there was no "Department of Intrastate Regulation and Enforcement." He flashed a badge and a card, emblazoned with a logo mishmashed from several legitimate federal agencies.

When I'd expressed skepticism—after I'd stopped laughing—Quinn swore it worked. He'd been using the badge and ID for over a year, and never been questioned. The moment people heard the words "federal agent" from a big, solid-jawed guy in a suit and shades, the rest flew past in a jumble as they mentally scrambled to figure out what they'd done wrong.

Leslie Keyes certainly bought it, saying, "Yes, yes, of course" when Jack asked if they could come inside and ask a few questions. I watched the door close, then steered out to find a safer place to sit and listen.

Thirty-nine

Leslie led Quinn and Jack into the house, seating them in what was presumably the living room. A faint rattle crossed the transmission, then Jack's low laugh.

"I don't want to sit on this. Some little guy wouldn't be too happy if I broke it." Another rattle as he laid the toy on the table. "Boy or girl?"

"Boy. My friend's son. They were over yesterday. He must have left that there."

From the tautness in her voice, she was lying. Yet her response wasn't what we'd expected. Presumably, the Byrony Agency would have made the adoption as legal as possible. Legal enough to pass a federal inspection, though? Maybe she wasn't sure.

"Don't call her on it," I said. "Play it out."

"But you do want children, correct?" Quinn said. "That's why you engaged the services of the Byrony Agency."

A moment's silence, then, "Yes, we did. Is that what this is about? We're no longer with them, and we paid our bills—"

Quinn laughed. "We aren't bill collectors, ma'am."

"No, no, of course not. I just meant—"

"We're here on a routine check of the agency's procedures," Jack said.

"The agency? Have they done something wrong?"

"No, as I said, it's a routine check."

"Why?" Quinn cut in. "Did you have concerns about them?"

"Concerns? Not at all. They were wonderful. We just decided to pursue other options. But we'd recommend them, and we have. A great agency."

I said, "Okay, take it down a notch. She's already spooked and you don't want to push her into full-blown panic."

Jack took over. "Like I said, it's a routine check only. Private adoption can be a very tricky area, Mrs. Keyes, and we have to be absolutely certain no one—from the birth mothers to the agency to the prospective parents—misuses the system."

"Prospective parents? You think *we* misused the system?"

"At the moment, our investigation focuses entirely on the Byrony Agency."

In the moment of silence that followed, I could picture Leslie, looking from one "agent" to the other, not believing their "routine check" line. That was fine. We didn't want her to.

Quinn and Jack took turns asking about her experience with the agency. Most of the questions were mundane—how much advance notice was she given before the home visits, did she have any difficulty understanding the forms. But every now and then they'd toss in a zinger like, "Did anyone ever offer you additional services for an additional fee?" before swinging back to the general queries.

After ten minutes, I swore I could hear her heart pounding against her ribs. Then, as they reached the end, I *did* hear a sound—the distant fussing of a baby.

"Ignore it," I said quickly. "Unless the baby starts crying, pretend you don't hear anything. If it's Destiny, she'll fuss for a while before wailing. Finish up and get out of there. If she cries, you'll have to call Keyes on it, and I'd rather you didn't."

As Quinn finished the questions, Jack asked to use the washroom. In the silence that followed, you'd think he'd just demanded permission to conduct a full search of the premises.

"There's one right here on the main level," she said finally.

A low chuckle. "In a house this big, I hope so."

A few flustered words. Obviously, she'd mistaken Jack's request for a ploy to go upstairs, maybe investigate the gurgling and whimpering. That wasn't his intent at all. He just wanted to lay a bug.

While Jack was gone, Quinn asked the final questions, then chatted with Leslie, saying it seemed like a nice neighborhood, a great place to raise kids, he hoped that worked out for her and her husband... All benign small talk, but the woman was probably convinced she heard a note of sarcasm behind his words, that he knew she already had a child.

When Jack returned, she bustled them to the door.

"Oh, I left a card on the table," Jack said. "In case you need to contact us."

She thanked him and hurried them outside. By the time she realized the card wasn't on any table, they'd be gone.

The guys drove over and parked near me at the minimart. Quinn hopped in my passenger side, as Jack made his way, at half the speed, from their car to mine, across the minimart parking lot.

"Has she—?" he began.

I motioned Quinn to silence, nodded, and turned up the volume as Leslie took that critical next step—placing a call to her husband. Jack hadn't had time to bug the phone, so we were limited to her side of the conversation. First came the rush of words, as she explained the visit from "the FBI" . . . having apparently completely blocked everything after the words "federal."

"They found Miranda's rattle and I know I shouldn't have lied—we have the papers—but I wasn't taking the chance, Ken. I won't lose her—"

A moment's pause.

"I'm not panicking," she snarled, sounding a lot less flustered than she had with Jack and Quinn, her protective instinct taking over. "They asked a lot of questions about the Byrony Agency, like whether they'd offered us anything different or special, but they didn't specifically say—"

A sharp intake of breath as he presumably cut her short.

"Damn it. Right. Okay I'll meet you—"

Pause.

"I'll be right there."

A click as the phone returned to the cradle.

"He told her to shut her mouth," Quinn said. "Probably thinks the phone's bugged."

Jack watched the house through binoculars as we listened to footsteps pattering up the stairs, a baby crying, then Leslie quieting her as she came back down.

More noise, then the slam of the front door.

"Who's got the most experience tailing?" I asked.

"Probably Quinn," Jack said. "Switch."

We hoped Leslie was heading to see whoever had sold her the baby. Instead, she drove to an Applebee's down the road and met a man, presumably her husband, who hugged her and took the baby carrier. They went inside. Talking in a public place. Smart.

"Too bad we couldn't get a bug into her purse," I said.

"Did," Jack said. "But she left it behind."

Leslie carried only a diaper bag—probably having been too rushed to grab her purse. Damn.

I followed them inside, hoping to get a seat near enough to overhear their conversation. No such luck. Though it was still early for dinner, the place was filling fast.

I did manage to walk near the table, after Leslie had taken the baby from her snowsuit and hat. If asked earlier, I'd have said I'd never recognize Destiny—all babies looked the same to me. But the moment I saw that baby I knew, without a doubt, that Miranda Keyes was Destiny Ernst.

I retreated to the car, where we waited for close to two hours before the Keyeses finally emerged, hand in hand, Kenneth carrying the baby seat.

"Did he convince her she's overreacting?" I murmured. "Or that he'll take care of it?"

"Could go either way," Quinn said.

"Maybe I was wrong, getting you guys to back down.

Maybe you should have pressed harder. Been more specific. More threatening." I glanced at Jack. "Okay, I'll stop fretting."

"Never said that."

"You don't need to."

We watched them get into their separate cars.

"So who do we follow?" I asked.

"Dad," Quinn said.

It didn't matter. They went to the same place. Home.

Jack and I spent the next hour monitoring the house as Quinn returned the rental car. Then Quinn caught a cab back, and we waited two more hours. Leslie put the baby to bed, the couple talked about their respective days, watched a pretaped episode of *Desperate Housewives*, and, at ten-thirty, headed off to bed without a single exchange about their visitors from earlier.

Quinn yawned. "Wake me up if they start having sex."

I cuffed him across the chest.

He opened one eye. "We probably wouldn't even notice anyway. Something tells me that bed doesn't see a lot of action. This has to be the most boring evening I've ever eavesdropped on. Are we done yet?"

Jack nodded.

So much for our hopes that the Keyeses would contact the Byrony Agency, spilling the details I needed to prove they'd bought their new daughter. There was still some hope from that quarter, but they were sleeping very soundly for a couple that believed their new baby was about to be ripped from their arms.

On then to the break-in portion of the evening. We stayed away until nearly midnight, only to discover the dessert shop was long closed, the theater presumably closed that night. And, with the actors taking the night off, our homeless guy was, too.

We arrived just as the cleaners were leaving. Twenty minutes later, we went in.

Forty

Jack had decided he'd stand guard, since Quinn and I had more experience conducting searches. He did, however, provide locksmith services, while Quinn and I stood at opposite ends of the block, whistling when the coast was clear, and ready to whistle again if a car approached. But the night was quiet, and the streets empty, and we stayed silent. By 12:25, we were in.

We started by downloading files. After Evelyn booted us out, I couldn't very well ask for tips on bypassing computer security, but Quinn knew how, and even gave a quick demonstration, promising more later.

Once the e-mail, accounting, and word processing files were on a flash drive, we moved on to the locked filing cabinet. A key in the receptionist's desk meant we didn't even need to pick the lock.

Quinn took the top drawer and I took the bottom, working together.

"Damn it, this isn't easy wearing latex," Quinn muttered. "The pages all stick together."

"You don't usually need to be discreet, do you?"

"Discreet . . . sometimes. But avoiding prints, no."

I thumbed through another folder. "I'm trying very hard not to put the pieces together, you know. Figuring out what federal agency you're with."

I tried to make my voice light, teasing, but in the moment of silence that followed, I cursed myself for mentioning it. When I glanced up, his expression was puzzled.

"You don't know? You said Jack told you my specialty

was— No, I guess I misinterpreted that to mean Jack had told you who I work for. I thought he would—tit for tat. I'll keep you guessing…" His wide lips curved in a grin. "At least for another hour or two. After we're done here, we'll see how close you are."

I finished with my drawer—all very old records—then pulled out the next one and set it on the floor.

"Man, all these files," he said. "All these couples wanting kids. Hard to believe."

I laughed, keeping it quiet. "I take it you don't want any…or don't want more."

"More?" He paused. "Shit, I keep forgetting. We've been talking online for six months and we couldn't even do the 'first date basic info exchange.' No, I don't have any kids. As for wanting…I'm not saying no, just…"

"It's not in the forecast. Same here."

He exhaled, as if correctly answering a quiz question. "I've got a passel of nieces and nephews. I love being an uncle. Taking them to movies and minigolf and baseball games. Even coach their teams. But when it's all done, and I've tired them out and loaded them up with soda and ice cream, I get to drop them off at home."

"That's the way to do it."

"Everyone's always trying to set me up with nice divorcée moms. But just because I like kids doesn't mean I want my own, you know?"

I pulled out a thick folder. "I hear you."

"Have you got nieces and nephews?" he asked.

I shook my head as I returned the folder. "I've just got the one brother and he hasn't reproduced yet…at least not as far as I know. We aren't close."

"Really?"

I shrugged. "We never were and then...what happened with me, it was tough on him and my mom, so that pretty much nailed the coffin shut." When Quinn looked confused, I said, "The shooting. It got ugly afterward, with the media. Huge embarrassment for them."

"Embarrassment?" His voice took on an edge. "You made a mistake. Hell, I wouldn't even call it that, except the part about getting caught. But your family should have been the first ones to step up and—" He shook his head. "Sorry, I just mean..." He shrugged. "Their loss anyway."

I smiled. "Thanks."

"So—" Another head shake. "Sorry, I'll shut up and work. We'll have plenty of time to talk later. It's just..." He met my gaze. "There's a lot to say."

"I know."

He nodded and returned to the files.

We didn't find anything in the paper files, though we did copy the employee records. There would probably be more in the computer files.

By the time we got out, it was almost two, but no one was ready to call it a night. So when we passed a plaza advertising both an all-night liquor store and take-out pizza until three, we pulled in. Quinn went for the liquor store, Jack into the pizza parlor, and I kept the car warm. Quinn returned first, with a twelve-pack of beer.

"Even got Labatts," he said as he climbed in. "Just for you."

"Having tried American beer, you have no idea how grateful I am."

He grinned. "I'm tempted to ask 'how grateful,' but I did say I'd cool it, didn't I?"

"You did."

"Damn." A dramatic sigh. "So, changing the subject, have you picked an agency yet?"

"Ag—? Oh, your job. I know you've done fieldwork—searches, stakeouts, tailing suspects. Given how much help you were with the Wilkes case, keeping us abreast of the FBI investigation, the most obvious answer is FBI. But Jack said something last fall that made me think that wasn't it."

"It's not. I could help because I have a lot of contacts, in a lot of different branches—friends really—and no one thinks twice if I'm nosy or curious, because that's normal for me."

"Next, I considered DEA, which would fit, especially with the cross-border visits, but it doesn't feel right."

"It isn't."

"CIA, NSA . . . Maybe ATF."

"No on all three."

"Homeland Security?"

A bark of a laugh. "No, thank God."

"Postal Inspector? Fish and Wildlife?"

He gave me a look.

"Hey, I'm running out of options. I know there are a bunch of military law enforcement agencies, and those would be federal, but I'm going to guess no to all of them."

"You'd be guessing correctly."

I leaned back in the passenger seat, racking my brain. In Canada, we had a handful of federal law agencies. In the U.S., there were dozens.

"USMS," Quinn said.

"What?"

He sighed. "Even when I give the acronym, it doesn't help. What did Jack say my specialty was?"

I thought back. "Oh, right. Finding people." A pause. "Border patrol? Coast Guard?"

A deeper sigh. "No respect, I tell you. The oldest federal law agency in the country, and we always get forgotten. Or, worse, discounted as glorified bounty hunters."

"Marshals. USMS—United States Marshal Service."

"It was the 'glorified bounty hunters' that did it, wasn't it?"

"Sorry."

He fixed me with a mock glare. "I'll have you know the marshals do a lot more than apprehend fugitives. We're not only the oldest law agency, we're the most versatile. Just check our Web site. Says so right there."

I smiled. "I stand corrected. But fugitive apprehension *is* what you were doing in Canada, right?"

"Montreal, yes. I got a lead about someone your RCMP is also interested in. Toronto was a training seminar."

"What were they teaching?"

"*I* was teaching." He caught my look. "What, I don't strike you as instructor material?"

I glanced over at him and considered it. "Actually, yes. I can see it. But not full time."

"Agreed. They've been pushing me to do more, but I'm digging in my heels. I might have the personality for teaching—curious, outgoing, reasonably patient. But I love field—"

He stopped and lowered his head to peer out the windshield. Jack had paused, pizzas in hand, at the front of the car. I rolled down the window.

"We're decent," I said.

"Just checking," he said as he walked around. "Windows looked steamy."

"Just talking. We're good at that, in case you haven't noticed."

His grunt said he had. I got out, took the pizzas from him, and crawled into the back with them, letting him drive.

We returned to the hotel, where Quinn started checking the files on his laptop. We didn't sit around in anxious silence, though. Maybe it was the lingering buzz from the break-in, or maybe we were just giddy from the late hour. Whatever the reason, Quinn and I were both in talkative moods, tossing anecdotes back and forth, mostly related to break-ins—outrageous or incompetent thief stories we'd heard on the job.

There was a lot of one-upmanship and laughing as we downed the beer and pizza, and I wouldn't have blamed Jack if he walked out and found a quiet, sane place to wait, but while he didn't contribute to our stories, he seemed content to listen, eat, and drink.

Nowhere in those files did we find a receipt for the sale of one blue-eyed, blond-haired baby girl from Ontario. Nor was there a ledger file with fifty grand paid to Ronald Fenniger for "services rendered" and a hundred grand from the Keyeses for "goods received." A paper trail would have been nice, but unlikely.

We had the employee files, both on paper and on disk,

and they'd open a new avenue of investigation. Was anyone in financial straits? Or enjoying a sudden surge in wealth? Did anyone have a criminal record? Or complaints lodged against them regarding adoption practices?

We had the client files, too. The Keyeses' one was interesting. They'd been on the waiting list for about six months, after a prolonged background study where a few red flags had arisen. She'd spent time in rehab for prescription drug addiction. He had two kids from a prior marriage, and a history of defaulting on child support payments.

The problems, though, seemed to have been worked out. Leslie had been clean for three years and the addiction had been to painkillers after a serious auto accident. Ken blamed his child support problems on a "miscommunication" with his wife, who'd even written him a letter of recommendation, assuring the agency he'd repaid her. So they'd been placed on the waiting list, but from the notes, I suspected they'd have been waiting awhile. Then, two months ago, the Keyeses had withdrawn, their bills paid in full. A note on their file said they were pursuing other options.

If we could find more files with a similar pattern—problems with the intake process, proven financial means, and a recent departure from the agency's prospective parent list—we might find the other babies.

Forty-one

When we reached the end of the files, our energy drained fast. We only had the one room—renting a second hadn't crossed anyone's mind until it was too late to bother.

Even as we slowed, no one actually mentioned going to bed. We just started winding down and settling in. Quinn checked his business e-mail while I tidied. Jack stretched on the bed, and got messages from his voice mail while I used the washroom—brushing my teeth, washing up, putting on my nightshirt but leaving my jeans in place. When I came out, Jack had his eyes closed, still on top of the covers, and Quinn was at the desk answering e-mail. I crawled into bed, shedding my jeans once I was under the covers. I was asleep before the lights went out.

I woke a few hours later to the soft whistle of deep breathing. I looked over to see that Quinn had crawled into bed with me. He was being circumspect, lying a foot away, and he was dressed—at least in a T-shirt.

I watched him sleep, the streetlight between the curtains casting a pale mask over his eyes.

This afternoon, when he'd come to the hotel, I'd decided I was going to take the plunge. Stop pissing around with "should I or shouldn't I," stop waiting for the stars to align and the firecrackers to pop and the tiny violins to start playing. So what if Quinn didn't make my heart pitter-patter? He could make other parts of me pitter-patter, and that was more than I could say for any guy who'd shown an interest in me in a very long time.

I'd made my decision. I started following through. I'd *liked* following through. Even now, thinking of that kiss brought a blast of delicious heat. Yet the moment he'd misinterpreted my discomfort over being caught as reluctance, and offered to give me more time, I'd ducked out the chicken door.

If I had any lingering romantic notions about Jack, I had to get rid of them—fast—or eventually I'd do something to totally embarrass myself, and send Jack away for good.

I was ready for romance. I was definitely ready for sex. I wanted Quinn as more than a friend. I wanted to keep Jack as a friend. The answer to all this was lying right beside me, and damned if I was going to dither and fret another six months.

Tomorrow I was telling Quinn that as much as I appreciated his patience, I didn't need it. I was ready.

The next time I woke was from a dream in which I was on a game show, about to win a trip to Egypt, if only I could remember the name of the guy in the Inferno whose contrapasso punishment was eternally eating the brain of the coconspirator who'd betrayed him. The show's buzzer kept malfunctioning, going off before my time was up, and I was about to complain when I realized the buzzing sounded like Jack's predictably banal ring tone.

I pulled myself from the dream as he was slipping out the door, phone to his ear. A moment later, he returned.

"Everything okay?" I whispered.

"Yeah. Go back to sleep."

I did.

I woke again as the daylight streaming through that crack between the curtains hit my eyes. As I shifted, Quinn's eyes opened. He reached over and pushed a strand of hair off my face, tucking it behind my ear, his fingertips gliding over my cheek.

"Good morning," I said.

His lips curved in a drowsy, sexy smile. He started to say something, then a sharp rap at the door had me jumping back so fast I pulled the covers with me.

"Got it," Jack grunted.

I looked past Quinn to see Jack sliding out of bed. He stood, rolled his shoulders, then stepped over, peered into the peephole, and let out a profanity.

"What the fuck is this?" he said as he opened the door.

"Just repaying your ungodly early visit from yesterday." Evelyn's voice preceded her. "Is Dee bunking down—?"

She stepped in and noticed me, sitting on the edge of the bed. Then she saw Quinn rising on his elbows, and cocked her eyebrows, gaze traveling from us to Jack.

"Well, that's one solution," she said.

"The cheapest one," I said, stifling a yawn. "But, no, I'm not making the guys squeeze into one room to save money. We were up late and never got around to renting another."

Quinn got up, and I saw he was wearing only his boxers and T-shirt. He stretched, then grabbed his pants.

"Sorry," he said. "We're a little casual around here."

"Oh, don't rush on my account."

I glanced over to see Evelyn admiring the view as much as I'd been, and taking far fewer pains to hide it.

I fished my jeans from under the bed. "Coed sleeping arrangements are always tricky."

"Not if you do it right. Of course, if you do it right, there's no need to worry about clothes."

I shot her a look.

She sighed. "Youth really is wasted on the young."

"How'd you find us?" Quinn asked as he sat back on the bed.

"I can find anyone."

"Called last night," Jack said. "Wanted the hotel number. Said she had to fax something."

"I needed to talk to Dee."

"The phone works."

"And I had business in Detroit, so I decided to make a trip of it."

"What business?"

"None of yours."

Jack snorted, not buying it, but when he opened his mouth to call her on it, I shot him a look that asked him not to.

I said, "If it's about what we started to discuss yesterday, let's let the guys get showered and shaved while we go grab coffee and talk. I'm interested in hearing—"

"Oh, I'm sure you are." She flashed a smile that set my teeth on edge. "We'll get to that. Eventually. Probably."

I turned to Quinn. "Up for a jog, then? I've missed the last couple of mornings, so I'm heading out. You're welcome to join me."

He grinned. "Love to." He crossed the room and opened his suitcase. "Even brought sweatpants. I've been trying to get out a few times a week. I'm not up to your five miles yet, but I don't get your quiet country lanes. Or your clean air."

I tossed the grin back. "So that's your excuse?"

"Absolutely."

I took my duffel and headed for the bathroom, then stopped, leaned out and looked at Evelyn. "Catch up later, then?"

Her lips tightened. I smiled and closed the door.

For the first half of the run, I said little, feet pounding the pavement hard, knocking thoughts of Evelyn from my mind, letting myself get caught up in Quinn's chatter instead, commenting just enough so he knew I was paying attention.

Having now finally passed that first-date exchange of information—"What's your job? Ever married? Any kids?"—seemed to open the floodgates for Quinn. He talked about his family. They seemed close. Enviably close, and I was happy for him.

Mostly, though, he talked about his job, including a couple of cases he was currently working. While he avoided identifying details, he still gave me more than he should have. I knew that was intentional. It was his way of saying he trusted me, and he knew I didn't quite trust him yet, so here was a bow-wrapped package of confidential information, proof he had no plans to flip on me.

By the halfway mark, Quinn's chatter had banished Evelyn from my mind, and I began to share my own story, starting slow, with my family and my dad, and how I grew up, then moving into what I knew he really wanted to hear: how I shot Wayne Franco and what happened afterward.

For the first time in seven years, I told my story to someone who understood. Really understood. I'd had people say, "I see how that could happen." I'd had some— cop friends—who said it and meant it. I'd had plenty of people who tut-tutted at the media for ruining my life. I had people who were outraged at it and fired off letters on my behalf. But the one thing I never had was the one thing I needed most, and Quinn gave it to me.

He understood what it meant to me to lose my job. Others said it was a shame, but I'd only been an officer for a few years, and I got a good buyout, so no harm done, really. Quinn understood that, for me, the end of my career was more devastating than all the front-page photos in the world. I'd grown up to be a cop, and now I wasn't, and I don't think I'd ever stop feeling the loss, ever stop grieving.

The more we talked, the more I realized that Evelyn had been right. You couldn't find a better match for me if you tried. And if I screwed this up, I'd never forgive myself.

When we were a block from the hotel, I stopped at the mouth of an alley. Quinn got a few more strides in before realizing I wasn't beside him and circling back.

"You okay?" he asked. "Did you—?"

I wrapped my fist in his sweaty shirt front and walked backward into the alley.

His eyes danced. "I meant what I said. No need to rush. I'll give you all the time—"

"I've had more than enough," I said, pulled him to me, and kissed him.

Forty-two

I unlocked the hotel room door with my card.

"Breakfast is served," Quinn called as he slid his tray onto the table. He took mine, laid it beside the first, gestured for Evelyn and Jack to dig in, then swung around to face me. "Flip for first shower?"

"You go ahead. I'll talk to Evelyn."

He sailed toward the bathroom. Halfway in, he spun. "Dibs on the strawberry cream cheese. Anyone else wants it, they gotta arm wrestle me when I get out."

Jack glanced over at me. "Good run, I take it?"

"I think the exhaust fumes go to his head."

"Bouncy, chipper hitmen," Evelyn murmured. "I despair for this generation."

I pulled the coffees from the cardboard tray. "The cream and double sugar is Quinn's. Black for Jack, cream and sugar for Evelyn..." As I handed them out, her blue eyes bored into mine.

"So we're done playing games, I take it, Dee?"

I forced a smile. "I never started."

She eased into the armchair, stirring her coffee. "Getting confident, aren't you? Of course, it's easy when you have a bulldog at your back, ready to snap my hand off if I look at you the wrong way. With that kind of backup, even the most timid mouse isn't afraid to bare her teeth."

I turned to Jack. "Could you give us a moment?"

"Yes, Jack, please. I think Dee wants to try standing on her own feet. Should be amusing."

He looked at me, and I knew he didn't want to go. It didn't have anything to do with defending me against Evelyn. I'd never complained to Jack about anything she said or did when he wasn't around, never hesitated to take her on. To suggest I hid behind him, though, was sure to put me on the defensive.

I should refuse to play. But I couldn't.

After a moment, he left, though clearly not happy about it, and telling me to ring his cell when we were done.

I waited until he was gone, then turned to Evelyn. "Let me put this bluntly—"

Her lips curved, teeth flashing. "Oh, I hope you do. But I doubt it. That wouldn't be polite."

I moved to sit on the edge of the bed. "I hate the games, Evelyn. I don't understand them. I don't want to play them. I think you know that and you get a kick out of seeing me off-balance. I don't want to do this anymore."

"All right, then. Let's speak plainly. I have a proposition—"

"And I'm not interested." I shook my head. "No, obviously that's a lie. You know I'm interested. If I say yes, I'm not putting an end to this game—I'm only launching a bigger, more elaborate one. I'm doing fine with the Tomassinis. I might like something better, more satisfying, but I don't need it."

If I thought I'd gain some points for honesty, I was deluded. Evelyn only narrowed her eyes as she studied my face.

"This isn't open for negotiation, Dee. If you think you can set boundaries—"

"I'm not negotiating."

"If you think I'll come back in a few months, offer it again—"

"God, you don't get it, do you?" I got to my feet and strode across the room. "I'm not playing a game. I'm not trying to win concessions or string you along. I don't want this job or any other job you have to offer. The price is too high."

She sipped her coffee, then settled back in her chair. "Speaking of price, I do believe you still owe me..."

"Yes, I do. You've helped me out with this investigation and I know you expect more than my sincere appreciation. But don't use that as leverage to get me to consider your offer. You need a pro who's willing and committed. If you want to settle up now, fine, let's settle up. What do I owe you?"

She crossed her ankles, eyes rolling back as if thinking. "A job would do it. I think I have one. A cartel wants to send a message to a former associate by killing his family. Wife, couple of kids." She met my gaze. "That's my price, Dee."

I turned away before she had the satisfaction of seeing my reaction. "Then I guess you'll need to find someone to do it and send me the bill."

A moment's silence, then a small laugh. "You couldn't afford it. Not pulling penny-ante jobs for the Tomassinis. Your charming inn takes all that." She flashed her teeth again. "You wouldn't want to lose it..."

When I laughed, she blinked. And, yes, I took some pleasure in that, as small a reaction as it was.

"I hired you for a few days of research, Evelyn. The bill for those services can't possibly be enough to warrant selling my lodge. I'll ask around, get a reasonable price, double it, and pay you back. I should have enough stashed away and, if I don't—" I flashed her smile back at her "—this is one obligation I'll work my ass off to relieve."

The bathroom door banged open. "All yours, Dee." Quinn grinned. "Unless you need someone to wash your back."

I managed a smile for him. "Another time. Get your breakfast while it's warm. And could you call Jack? He stepped out for a smoke."

When I emerged from the bathroom, I fully expected Evelyn to be gone. Fully hoped, too. But she was still there, in the chair where I'd left her, nibbling at a bagel.

"Honcho called," Jack said. "Evelyn mention that?"

"The middleman? Great. We can—" I bit the word off, clipping my tongue. "Actually, no, I think we should back-burner that idea for a while. Play out the others first." I turned to Evelyn. "Sorry for making you stop by for nothing. I would have called and said so, but I wanted a clearer picture of what we got last night. Anyway, we're good for now."

"I'm not so sure about that," Quinn said. "It'll take a while to dig through those files and get anything from them—"

"And you don't have the time. I know that. You can head home whenever you want to. I'll take it from here."

Quinn blinked, taken aback and, from the look that flashed behind his eyes, a little hurt. "I didn't mean that. I've got a few more days and—"

"I know. I'm sorry. I'm tired and it's making me snippy." As I walked by him, I passed him a wan smile.

"But I've used enough of Evelyn's help, so I'm going to drop that angle."

As I fixed myself a bagel, I could feel Jack's gaze boring into the back of my skull.

"All set then?" I said as I turned, my voice more brittle than I wanted. I forced myself to look around the circle of eyes. Evelyn's glittering with amusement. Quinn's clouded with confusion. Jack's steady piercing stare.

Evelyn broke the silence. "If you can get the job, Dee, you'll wrap this up. No question. I started this and I'll be happy to finish it for you."

"I can't afford it."

"Can't afford—?" Quinn began, then turned his surprise on Evelyn, having obviously figured, like him and Jack, she was doing this just to help me out, which proved he didn't know her very well. "Shit, if that's it, I've got—"

"No, please."

Quinn came up beside me, hand on my elbow, voice dropping. "Let's go outside and talk about this. Honestly, I can help and I'd be glad to."

"I can't." I met his gaze. "Please."

"Oh, for pity's sake, Dee," Evelyn said. "It's free, all right?"

"No, it isn't."

Quinn leaned down to my ear. "Let me help. I've got some money and, for something like this, I'd be more than happy to use it."

"Listen to the man, Dee," Evelyn said. "He'd be *more* than happy to help you out. And Jack, too. He's not quite so quick to jump in—never is—but he'll pay me for you. Money, quid pro quo, whatever it takes, he'll pay it. All these men tripping over themselves to help poor, sweet Nadia—"

I spun on her so fast, Quinn jumped back, and whatever Evelyn saw in my face, it made *her* pull back, eyes widening just a fraction. I tore my gaze away, shutting down as fast as I could, eyes moving to the door, avoiding everything in between.

"I'm sorry," I said. "Let me— I'll just walk it off. Give me a few minutes."

Jack found me behind the hotel, sitting on the curb of the delivery lane. He walked over without a word as he knocked a cigarette from the package. I managed a weak smile.

"Found them, huh?"

"This morning. In my bag. Thought you were holding them. Waiting for my story."

I flicked a pebble off the curb. "I'm sorry for making a scene in there."

"That's a scene? Piss-poor one."

Another tiny smile as he lowered himself to the curb.

"Is Quinn freaked out?"

"Confused. Worried."

"Which is exactly what I was trying to avoid. I just couldn't figure out how to tell Evelyn I didn't want her help without him wondering why. It's my best chance of shutting this operation down, which should be my main priority."

"Main priority should be you."

I shook my head, watching the match flicker as he lit it. "No, it shouldn't, not with something like this. But I need to cut ties with Evelyn. I can't play her games anymore. I know I should stick it out, toughen up, learn to roll with the punches and toss a few back. Maybe running away doesn't make me the kind of pro you want me to be—"

"Don't want you to be anything. Just you." He lifted the cigarette, inhaled, exhaled. "So you turned down her offer?"

"I told her I couldn't take the games...which only made her think I was playing one."

A snort carried on a puff of smoke. "She demanded debt repayment. How much?"

I thought of her first words. The family. I'd never tell Jack that, but he must have seen something in my eyes, because his jaw tightened, muscle spasming.

"What'd she ask for?"

I shook my head. "We settled on cash. She suggested I couldn't afford it. I said I would. But the point is, Jack, that I absolutely cannot afford to add to that bill...and I don't just mean the monetary value. If I agree after I've said I won't take anything more from her, then it's right back to the scenario I mentioned yesterday. There's no sense claiming I won't take anything from her, because she knows I will and it's just a matter of price."

"She found Honcho. She contacted him. She accepted the offer. All she's gotta do now? Give you the time and place. Already has that. Might say she doesn't—"

"Which puts me right back where I started, Jack. She'll keep playing her game and I'll keep buying in."

"Not you. Me. From now on? She talks to me."

I rubbed my legs, trying to work the frustration from my voice. "Which *again*, Jack, plays into her hands. You heard her in there, jabbing me because I have you and

Quinn helping out. The poor little damsel in distress. The chick who thinks she's a big tough hitman... and hides behind the real ones. That's not who I want to be."

"Course not. Think she doesn't know that? How many times you think *she* got that shit? Starting out? She hooked up with men, too. No choice. What happens? Dismissed as a wannabe. A groupie. Evelyn's been there. Knows how much it hurts. Knows how mad it'll make you. Knows how hard it is to prove you aren't."

He took another drag off the cigarette, then handed it to me. I accepted.

"This whole mess?" he continued. "My fault. I screwed Evelyn over. With you. Don't regret it. But then we needed her. I made a decision. Probably the wrong one." He took the cigarette back and inhaled, expelling the smoke before going on. "Yeah, the wrong one. Not much doubt about that. Rest of the debt? Mine. Only fair."

"Jack—"

"You care what she thinks of you?"

"No, but—"

"It's set then. We make the meeting. Evelyn goes home. You're done with her."

He passed the cigarette back and I took it.

Evelyn did not go home. She insisted on staying to see the contact through. Was she being a responsible go-between and protecting her reputation? Or just having fun pushing my buttons? I didn't care. At that moment, I had two main concerns. One, preparing for this meeting with the Byrony Agency contact. Two, convincing Quinn I wasn't an irrational bitch.

Fortunately, task two was simple. He was confused, nothing more. We went out for a walk and I explained a version of events that skirted the more "interpersonal" issues, like Jack and Evelyn's clash over my mentorship, which would only confuse him all the more.

I also left out any mention of the Contrapasso Fellowship offer. He'd be as excited at the prospect as I was trying hard *not* to be. There are guys who go vigilante because they like killing people and it gives them an excuse they can live with. Quinn wasn't one of them.

Evelyn once said the difference between us was that, for Quinn, the drive to see justice done came from the head. For me, it came from the gut. She had only a casual interest in his cerebral vigilantism. What she wanted to mold was my fire, my passion.

Maybe, but I suspected if I told him about the Contrapasso Fellowship, he'd want in, and I wasn't ready to deal with that—either his hurt when she refused him or the guilt of getting him entangled in her web if she accepted.

What I *did* tell him was that Jack had gotten Evelyn involved in Sammi's murder case by asking her to find a hitman who matched our profile. The expectation was that, because she owed him plenty and they were close, she'd do it with no obligation to me. Today I'd found out otherwise and, spooked, I'd reacted by wanting nothing more to do with her "help." The story made sense to him, so he let it go at that.

Forty-three

Before I left to meet the client, Jack took me aside for a few words of advice. I tried not to notice the roll of Evelyn's eyes.

We walked behind the hotel again, to the delivery lane, and again he pulled out his cigarettes.

"Still want that story?" he asked as he lit one, cupping the flame against the wind.

"Only if you want to give it to me. And if it won't reveal anything that could compromise your privacy."

He waved me to our spot on the curb and sat beside me. "Nah. Wouldn't care." He exhaled the smoke through his nose. "I trust you. Happened after the job anyway."

He took another drag, then passed me the cigarette before continuing. "Backyard hit. Went down fine. Getting out? No problem. Big yards. Estates. Full of trees and shit. Had my path mapped out. So I'm moving. Not running. But moving. Then there's this wall. Maybe..." He lifted his hand about three feet off the ground. "Knew it was there. No surprise. So I'm coming to it. Lots of time. Could stop. Climb over. But no. Gotta jump it."

He took the cigarette back and inhaled, letting the smoke swirl out as he shook his head. "So I jump. Don't clear it. Foot hits the wall. I topple over. Face-plant into the fucking tulips."

I swallowed a laugh, but not before some of it escaped.

Jack waved the cigarette at me. "See? Told you. Boring and embarrassing. No close call. No fancy trick. Tripped over a fucking garden wall."

"So you miscalculated. That's easy enough to do."

He took another drag. "Nah. Didn't miscalculate. No excuse but age. Mind's willing. Body says 'fuck that.'" He tapped the side of his head, ash tumbling to the grass. "Up here? Still thirty. Top of my game. The rest?" A slow shake of his head. "Starting to disagree. Young man's game. I'm on the side of the hill that goes straight down."

"I don't think you're ready to be put out to pasture just yet, Jack."

"Fifty next year." He slanted a look my way. "Since you'll never ask. But pasture? No. Not yet. Still, gets me thinking. Remember Saul?"

I nodded. Saul was a hitman I'd met last fall, a colleague of Jack's who'd retired only after he'd bottomed out.

"Seeing Saul? I feel . . ." He toyed with the cigarette, rolling it between his fingers. "Not contempt . . ."

"Disdain?"

"Yeah." He handed me the cigarette, like a prize for guessing right. "Disdain. Guy held on too long. Reputation went to shit. Forced to retire. His own fault. Got no time for that. Tell myself 'not me.' But then . . ." He shrugged. "Maybe it's ego. Bigger than I like to admit. Gotta slow down. Not retire. Just slow down. But like Evelyn says, I'm not good at sitting around."

I handed him back the cigarette and he smoked it to the end, then ground it out against the curb and dropped the butt into his pocket.

"So, when I'm helping you on this job?" he continued. "It's like the rest. Me coming around, teaching, giving you advice. It's not that I think you can't handle it. It's just . . . something new. Different. Interesting."

He rubbed his thumb across his lips, silent for a moment. "Like those ATVs. Not saying you *need* me to fix them." He glanced at me. "You know?"

"Actually, I do need you to fix them. Owen's been tinkering with them since we got them at auction last winter, and I think they're in worse shape than when he started."

"Yeah. Maybe. But you know what I mean."

"I do. But if you want to come back for a couple of weeks after this is done, get your fill of apple pie and get those babies running for me before the summer crowds start, I certainly won't argue."

"Then I'll do that."

I met the client at three, in a neighborhood park. I wasn't thrilled with a daytime meet. It meant there was no easy way to disguise the fact that I was female.

I dressed as a jogger, making it easy to bulk up. Also an excuse for oversized sunglasses and a hoodie pulled tight. Under the hood I wore a blond wig, with a few strands slipping out, as if by accident.

Because the hood covered my head, Jack wanted me to wear an earpiece. Quinn agreed. I was insulted. I reminded myself that they'd worn them to the Keyes house, but that had been *my* case, so it made sense that I'd want to have a say in the interview questions. To suggest I needed help meeting with a client, and having them both jump in, quick to presume I'd need it? That rankled. I won't deny it. So I refused.

I also refused their offers of backup. It was a public place and a midday meeting with an "amateur" client. There was absolutely no reason I needed my friends hiding fifty feet away, ready to pounce. Having them there would only increase the risk. People were more likely to notice male strangers hanging around a park. And the client might notice them, too.

Even having them there might make me act different. Same with the wire. Better to let me handle it while they waited off-site.

To my relief, neither offered any resistance. Quinn cast a sidelong glance at Jack and, seeing he wasn't arguing, presumed I was right. They agreed to wait in a coffee shop down the street, a phone call away if anything went off track.

I'd scouted the park before arriving. It was maybe three acres, all open. Stretched across the front was one of those bright red and yellow plastic playground structures that had replaced the wooden ones of my youth. Two older swing sets sat forlornly in the corner, one for children, one for babies, both with several of the swings wrapped over the top and a couple of others broken from their chains. Behind that was a brick box that I supposed housed equipment for the ball diamond.

I jogged around the block to work up a sweat so, to any onlookers, I'd seem like a real runner. Not that it mattered. It was a chilly midweek afternoon and the park was empty.

I headed for the bleachers—far enough from the playground that I could talk without whispering, should any parents show up. As I looked around, I realized I wasn't alone. A man stood behind the equipment building, wearing an overcoat, slacks, and dress shoes, his hands shoved in his pockets, shoulders pulled in as if against the chill.

Even if the guy hadn't matched Fenniger's description—thinning hair, narrow face, average height—I'd have known this was my client, and as much an amateur as Fenniger had said. I put my fingers in my mouth, and let out a low but sharp whistle.

The man jumped as if he'd heard a siren. When he glanced my way, I beckoned him over. He looked around, confirming I wasn't waving to anyone else, then squinted at me and, even from where I sat, I could see the faint hope in his eyes that maybe, just maybe, the woman on the bleachers was hitting on him.

I motioned again, more emphatic now. When he didn't move, I walked over.

"I-I'm waiting for someone," he said.

"Yes. Me."

A blank look.

"Through Honcho?" I prompted.

"Er, yes, right, but…" His gaze traveled down me. "I, um, think there's been a misunderstanding."

"Yes, I'm a woman. It's an equal opportunity job these days. If you want gender specificity, you have to request it on the order form."

He stared, a note of panic behind his eyes, as if thinking there really had been a form, and he hadn't gotten it.

"Is it okay?" I asked. "Does the job require a man?"

"N-no. You're fine. Maybe better, even. Sure. Okay. It just… threw me. So, I guess the first thing we do is—"

"Move over there." I waved back where I'd been sitting.

"Isn't here safer?"

"You look like Mr. Suburbanite waiting for his dealer ... and I don't look like your dealer."

A nervous twitch of a smile. "Right, right."

I led him to the bleachers. "No one's around, so just play it cool. You came home from the office early and found your wife had gone for her jog, so you caught up with her and now we're having a nice little 'how was your day, honey' chat."

"Right, right."

We sat through twenty seconds of silence.

"You have a job for me?" I said finally.

"Right. I need someone ... taken care of."

He put a tiny growl in the last words, as if trying out for a guest spot on *The Sopranos*. I bit my cheek to keep from smiling.

"That's what I figured."

A giggle. "Right, I guess so. Not like I'd be asking you to, uh—" He massaged his throat, unable to come up with anything witty. "The, uh, job. It's this guy."

I blinked to cover my surprise. Another moment of silence. When he didn't go on, I had to clarify.

"You mean the mark is a man."

"Right, right."

The first prickle of apprehension set my arm hairs rising. I resisted the urge to rub them down and kept my face neutral.

"Go on."

"It needs to be done tonight?"

"Tonight?" That time the surprise escaped. I covered it with, "Is he local, then?"

He nodded. "He has a house right here in Detroit. That's where it has to ... go down."

"Family?"

His eyes widened, lips parted in an O of horror.

"Is there going to be family in the house?" I went on. "Because that's a problem, and not one I intend to 'take care of.'"

A slow eye squeeze of relief. He'd thought I meant "do you want the family killed, too?" Further proof that the guy watched way too many crime dramas. That's not to say hitmen aren't asked to murder entire families—like the "job" Evelyn suggested—but it certainly wasn't a request so commonplace that they'd toss it off as easily as asking whether the client preferred a public hit or private.

"There isn't any family to worry about," he said. "He's divorced and lives alone."

My brain raced to figure out how this played into the baby scheme. A teen daughter maybe? Her baby so prized that they'd kill her father, too, the one person who might investigate?

"Any kids?" I asked. "Because they could be sleeping over, even if it's not his scheduled time—"

"No kids."

I stopped my fingers from tapping against the bench. *Move on and figure this out later.* "Okay, so this guy is the first mark, and then you need me to..."

My fingernails dug into the wood as genuine confusion filled his face.

"There's only one mark?" I said. "I was told—"

"Then someone's made a mistake," he said, his voice high, annoyance mixed with anxiety, ticked off that someone had screwed up. "I was very clear. I need—"

His cell phone rang. I waited for him to apologize and shut off the ringer. Instead, without even glancing at the display, he answered, covered the receiver, and told me to give him a minute. In other words, "get lost."

I would have complained if I hadn't been happy for the excuse to get away and collect my thoughts. I motioned that I'd jog around the block and be back in five minutes.

Forty-four

I set out, feet smacking the pavement, trying to jar free the ball of rage crystallizing in my gut.

Evelyn had set me up. This was a real hit that had nothing to do with the adoption murders.

I forced myself to consider the possibility it was a mix-up, that Honcho said he had a job for her new protégé and she'd jumped to the conclusion it was "*the* job." But Evelyn would never be that sloppy. Oh, I was sure she'd *claim* a mix-up, but Honcho had already said the "job" he had in mind was long-term, serial hits, with recon and researching work. This was not that job.

Could Honcho have tricked Evelyn? Tossed her protégé a separate hit to test me while he worked out the other one? And risk pissing off one of the biggest names in the business? Never.

Evelyn had set me up.

I thought I was a real hitman? Well, here was a real hit. And what was I going to do about it? Run crying to Jack? If I even mentioned it to him, he'd do it for me. How she'd laugh at that—the ultimate proof that I was a wannabe hiding behind the big guns. A little girl letting the men do her dirty work.

I inhaled the icy air, feeling it scorch my lungs and gulping more, dowsing the rage.

Evelyn set me up to prove her point. Now what the hell was I going to do about it?

Would I kill an unknown mark to prove I was a badass hitman? I rubbed my face and swallowed more cold air. I *wasn't* a badass hitman. Never claimed to be. Never wanted to be. What was wrong with being what I was? If Evelyn despised me for it, why did I care?

I didn't care enough to prove her wrong. But to let Jack kill someone so I could keep my hands clean? My stomach churned with disgust.

What was the alternative, though? Refuse the hit? Evelyn would never let me back out and tarnish her reputation.

Again, what was the alternative? I did it or I didn't. Kill an innocent—

Maybe he wasn't so innocent?

I shivered. So that's how I was going to play this? Tell myself someone wanted this guy dead so he'd probably committed a crime?

I took a slow, deep breath, clearing my head. I couldn't decide anything in the next five minutes. I'd get the details, investigate, and hope an answer would come—fast.

Back at the park, the client was off the phone and checking his watch with little lip purses of irritation as if I was the one now keeping him waiting. As I strolled over, he cast a pointed glance my way.

"My wife expects me home by six and I have an hour commute."

"Really? Then I'd suggest you don't answer your phone again. Actually, in general, I'd suggest you don't answer it again."

I smiled, but something in that smile made him inch back, perhaps reconsidering the wisdom of treating a contract killer in the same way he'd treat a filing clerk temp.

"I presume you have a name for me?"

"I have an address and a photo. That's all you need."

His inflection turned the last words into a question, though I knew that wasn't what he'd intended, and I considered pushing the matter, but his lips were pursed, prissily, like an IRS flunky questioning a mobster's tax return. Act tough and he might back down ... or he might get his back up. While I longed to hold the upper hand, if he had the address and my mark was the lone occupant, getting a name should be easy enough.

"Please tell me you at least have his schedule," I said.

"What?"

"If you want it done tonight, that means I don't have time for surveillance, meaning I can't get a feel for his daily routine."

"I want him killed at home, in his bed. He's in town, so he'll be there."

"All right, but understand that if he *isn't* there, in his own bed, alone, I can't do it. If I know his schedule, I can follow him from his workplace and ensure—"

"No, he'll be home. Alone. He doesn't have a girlfriend."

I thought of pointing out that this didn't preclude nighttime companionship, but the twitching of his lips warned me I was pushing him past nervousness into anxiety.

"So, presuming he's at home and alone—"

"He will be."

I met his gaze. "Please stop interrupting me. Now,

presuming he's there, you want him eliminated, using a method of my choosing—"

"I need the house—" He stopped, flushing. "I'm sorry. I didn't meant to interrupt, but this is critically important. I need the house torched."

"Torched?"

"Burned to the ground, with him in it."

I stared at him until he wriggled in his seat like a three-year-old needing to go potty. "That's a joke, right?"

"Of course not." His voice started squeaking again. "I have very specific requirements and I'm paying a lot of money to get what I want."

"Did you clear this with Honcho?"

His mouth set in that prissy line. "I don't need to tell him the details."

"Because he presumes you have the sense to request something that can actually be done."

"It can be done. I've heard—"

"Even with notice, I can't burn a house 'to the ground.' Ignoring that small fact, though, you're asking for an elaborate scenario that will take time and research. I don't go to a job prepared to honor all possible requests. I'm a hired killer, not the Piano Man." I paused, as if considering. "But if you give me a few days..."

"It has to be tonight."

Damn.

He went on. "Do it however you need to, but you must torch the place."

"And by 'torch the place,' do you still mean 'burn it to the ground,' because I don't think you're following me on that one. It can't be done."

"Why not?"

I sucked in a groan. This was like being back in my cop days, dealing with an irate citizen, accusing me of laziness and incompetence because I wasn't combing his BMW for hairs, prints, and DNA after someone smashed the window and swiped the laptop he'd left on the seat.

"Burning a house 'to the ground' takes an incredible amount of work, material, and, most important, time. It cannot be done in a residential neighborhood. The minute someone sees smoke, they're calling the fire department. I'm presuming you want something destroyed, so let's do this the easy way—tell me what you want removed."

That prissy line again, but before he could refuse, I held up my hand.

"I'm not asking what information you need destroyed, just what items I'll find them on. Files? Computer drives? CD?"

It took another ten minutes of wrangling before he finally agreed that torching the entire house might not be necessary. Then he handed me the photo and address, plus a contact number I was to call when I'd finished, so I could deliver the "proof."

I walked for a block, sloughing off the "hardened killer" facade and sliding back into myself. Then I called Quinn.

"Hey there," I said, hoping the poor connection would account for any tremor in my voice. "How are you guys holding up? Both still alive?"

"So far, though I've been on blind dates that were more comfortable. Fifty-seven minutes of awkward silence... and yes, I was counting."

"I take it Jack's not there right now?"

"He escaped about ten minutes ago, claiming he needed a cigarette, but he left his jacket behind, with the pack in it. Do you need him?" The scrape of chair legs against a hard floor. "I can probably track—"

"No," I said quickly, then hoped it wasn't too quickly. "I was just calling to check in and say I'm not coming back just yet. You guys can take off, and I'll catch up with you later."

"Something wrong?"

"Nothing serious. Seems I sprouted a tail."

"Shit."

"I'm not worried. Someone's just being careful, checking out the new hire."

He started giving me tips on how to lose a tail, which only made the lie cut deeper. I let him go on for a minute, then pushed in with, "Actually, I'm thinking maybe I should play this out. Let him follow me and see I'm just doing my research, as expected."

"Anything we can help with?"

"Maybe later. For now, I've got it covered. I'm going to shut off my phone, though, just in case. You guys can go your separate ways, get some dinner, relax. I'll call you . . ." I paused as if checking my watch and working out the timing. "Around nine, and we'll see how things are going then."

"Oh, speaking of calls, you got one—on the cell number you gave that agency. Jack took it. A guy there wants to speak to you two as soon as possible. It sounded like they took the bait."

Great. If only they'd done that a few hours ago . . .

"Dee? Still there?"

"Um, yes. Sorry. So what did Jack do?"

"He took the name and number. He said it wasn't the guy you two talked to, but it's one of the employees. Alex...Andrew...Anyway, we're going to check out his employee record again when we get back."

"Go do that then. I'm not sure how well this will play out. We may still need to make that appointment."

"All right. We'll wait for your call. Take care of yourself. If you need anything...?"

"I'll let you know."

There was no logical reason to turn off my phone if I was being tailed, and I only hoped they'd presume I thought it best and not question that. If I left it on, Jack would call the minute he got the message, and I'd never fool him as easily as I had Quinn. So off it went and, with it, my safety net disappeared.

Forty-five

I was reasonably sure I wasn't going to find evidence that my mark was an unpunished criminal I could justify killing. My client wanted him dead ASAP and all files in the house destroyed. That almost certainly meant the mark's only crime was having information the client didn't want getting out.

I kept telling myself there had to be a solution to this dilemma and, given time, I'd find it. But I suspected there were no easy answers—just tough decisions.

Where did I draw the line? What crimes did someone need to commit before I could justify taking a life? Where was the point where I could pull the trigger, and walk away with a clean conscience?

If I discovered my mark had an unrelated history of pedophilia but had apparently "reformed," could I kill him and tell myself he deserved it for the lives he'd ruined? What if he was a white-collar con man, bilking people of their life savings with shady investment schemes?

Where did I draw the line?

Would I know when I was about to cross it? Or was that something I wouldn't realize until I had?

These thoughts consumed me as I found Internet access and conducted a search on the address, my mind only partly aware of what I was doing, the rest snaking down these dark tunnels, balking at every shadowy corner, ready to turn and run, leave the question as I liked it best: unanswered.

I'd never had to consider where that line lay. The

Tomassinis only gave me contracts I could fulfill with a clear conscience. That was purely good business. They knew my limits, and to offer me an unsuitable job once would soil our working relationship.

So if I'd never had to question where the line was, I hadn't been about to hunt for it as a purely intellectual exercise. What I did—killing thugs for money—was best left as unexamined as possible, those vigilante impulses undefined, the very word making my skin creep, gut-level denial rising.

Quinn had the impulse worked out, had probably examined every facet of it until he understood what he did, why he did it, and how far he'd go. Had he ever crossed his line and, if so, how did he get back? Could you ever get back? Or, once crossed, did the line blur, move, fade?

Would it make any difference, hearing Quinn's experience? He wasn't me. He couldn't help me find my line or know what would happen if I crossed it.

Finally, with great effort, I put those thoughts aside. Whatever decision I made, I wouldn't be able to make it until I had some answers.

Getting a name from an address wasn't as tough as it should be. In about fifteen minutes, I had it. Andrew Payne. As I stared at it, I cursed myself for ten kinds of idiot, and thanked the heavens I'd insisted on having solid facts before taking action. Otherwise, I'd have made a first-class fool of myself, damaged my credibility with Quinn and my friendship with Jack, accusing Evelyn of double-crossing me when, on seeing that name, I realized she'd done no such thing.

Andrew Payne. Thirty-nine. An unfinished bachelor's degree in sociology, followed by a college diploma in social work. Divorced three years. Owned his current residence. Made fifty-five thousand a year. And no, I didn't get all this with his address. It came from his employment file . . . the one I'd read last night.

Payne worked for the Byrony Agency. He was the one employee we hadn't seen Monday. My client—while he fit that "middle-aged pencil pusher" profile of two of the Byrony employees—was neither of them. So who was he? Why did he want Payne dead?

I could come up with a logical scenario. My client *was* Fenniger's contact. He worked for the agency, in a contract position, doing their dirty work, which now involved getting rid of an employee.

Quinn said the man who called Jack wanting to meet us was a Byrony Agency employee. Alex or Andrew, he'd said. Andrew Payne was the only employee with an A name.

While it was tempting to jump to the conclusion that Payne was in on the scheme and about to offer us a baby through it, that wasn't the only explanation. He could have found out about it and was calling to warn us. If so, that would be a good reason why my contact wanted him dead.

I needed to know more. And the only way to get answers was to follow through on the job.

I called Quinn at eight-thirty and, to my relief, found him alone. I told him that my tail seemed to have disappeared, but I was wary of leading anyone back to them. Was everything okay? Jack had grumbled about my disappearing act, but nothing more.

He confirmed that the man who called was Andrew Payne. He'd only said he wanted to meet us, giving no hint about the reason, so both my theories were still in play.

They'd spent the evening investigating Payne and the other agency employees and clients, with Jack doing the legwork while Quinn and Evelyn worked their magic online and by phone. Quinn told me what they'd learned, but while some of it would have helped hours ago, none of it mattered now.

I claimed exhaustion from two nights with little sleep. I said I'd rented a motel room to convince my tail I was hunkering down, and I really was going to take that nap, crashing for a few hours, then coming back before morning.

At 11:20, after watching the news, Andrew Payne went upstairs, used the bathroom, and crawled into bed. At 12:10 he awoke to a noise, blinking at what looked like a person sitting in the corner chair where he'd laid his pants. At 12:12 his eyes adjusted enough to see the gun pointing at him, and he let out a yelp, skittering backward across the mattress.

"Stop," I said.

He did.

A moment's silence, then he asked, "What do you want?"

"Well, I'd probably ask you to stop reaching under the other side of the mattress, except, if you look closely, you might notice this gun—" I waggled it. "—looks familiar. You don't mind if I borrow it, do you?"

The whites of his eyes glowed in the dark as he retracted his roving hand. His gaze flipped to the nightstand.

"I took the Swiss Army knife out of there, too, though I doubt it'd do more damage than a thumbtack. You really have to keep those things sharpened, you know. Oh, and as you can see, I've removed the phone from the night table. So, having established that you can't reach any weapon or method of communication, how about moving back over here, where I can see you better?"

He didn't budge.

"That wasn't a request."

He inched to the middle of the bed.

"Good enough. Now, I've been sent here to kill you, Mr. Payne."

His mouth worked like a fish's, eyes bulging as he blew nothing but air bubbles.

"I-I have money," he said finally. "Whatever they're paying you, I can pay more."

"I'm sure you can. Selling babies is a very lucrative business, isn't it? Especially if you don't need to pay off the mother."

"N-no, you don't understand. It wasn't my idea."

He babbled on, sounding remarkably like Ron Fenniger in the moments before his death. It wasn't his idea, so while he'd taken part in the scheme, he couldn't be held accountable.

"Like I said, I can pay. Whatever they're offering, I'll double it. Triple—"

"Do you think we'd be having this conversation if I planned to kill you?"

"What?"

"This isn't a James Bond movie, Mr. Payne. In real life, if someone wants you dead, they aren't going to chat you up first, explain their motivations, whine about their lousy childhood forcing them to a life of crime. Kind of a waste of time, don't you think? Explaining yourself to a guy you expect to be dead in five minutes?"

He huffed a few breaths, cheeks puffing as he calmed himself. "Okay, okay, so it's about money, then."

"I'm not interested in money."

He blinked, trying to assimilate that concept.

"I want the people you're working for. Like you said, this was their idea. Tell me everything you know and, if it's enough to put them away, I'll walk out and give you twenty-four hours to decide whether you want to pack and run with the money or turn state's evidence and hand it over."

He nodded, working it through as his head bobbed.

"Remember, though, that I've built a decent case. That means I already know most of it. I just need proof. So if you lie, I'll finish the job, collect my pay, and get that proof another way."

"Okay, okay."

He licked his lips and seemed to consider asking for a glass of water, then thought better of it, and started his story. As it unfolded, I saw that, once again, I'd been wrong. Very wrong.

"Thank you," I said as he finished.

Payne let out long shuddering breaths of relief.

I stood, lowering the gun. "You're going to give me

fifteen minutes to download those files and leave. Then you can get up and decide what you want to do."

"O-okay."

"Fifteen minutes. Start watching the clock."

He rolled over to do that. I took three steps toward the door, then shot him in the back of the head.

Forty-six

I left Payne where he fell, facedown on the bed. I down-loaded the files from his laptop onto the drive I'd bought, then stole from the darkened house into the yard. Staying along the fence line, I cut through three yards and came out on the street behind an apartment building. The rental car was in the lot.

Once on the road, I called the client: Palmer MacIver, as I now knew him. He answered on the second ring.

"Done," I said.

"And you have the proof?"

"I wouldn't be calling you if I didn't."

A soft sigh rippled down the line. "Good. And the files?"

"Destroyed."

He gave me an address and told me to meet him there in thirty minutes. Along the way, I disposed of Payne's gun. Then, as I drove, I reached into my pocket and pulled out the item that was supposed to prove I'd killed Payne.

I lifted my hand over the steering wheel and turned the ring over, the silver glinting against my dark driving gloves. Payne's high school class ring. How this proved he was dead was beyond me. Maybe MacIver had always seen Payne wearing it, but what was to say he didn't take it off at night? What if he'd taken it off, and I hadn't been able to find it?

Amateurs. Probably saw it in a movie, like everything else about this job.

Speaking of which...When I saw where the address led, I let out a curse.

A cluster of warehouses. *Abandoned* warehouses.

I idled near the entrance, then shifted into reverse to find a place off-site to park. As I tramped back to the warehouses, I swore under my breath the whole way.

The problem with abandoned warehouses? They're abandoned. That means if anyone sees you near one at one-thirty in the morning, they'll remember it. They might even call the cops.

The yard held a quartet of warehouses, long narrow blocks illuminated by a haphazard scattering of area lights, the buildings themselves black against the night. Water slapped against the distant breaker and the air was damp and icy, stinking of Lake Erie. A ship sounded its horn, long and mournful, making me stop a moment, peering into the night.

A dog barked by the row houses a block west; just a lonely call for attention, no one paying it any. Between the houses and the warehouse yard was a cushion of industrial buildings in better condition and with better lighting, presumably still owned by someone who cared about security. The lights inside were all off, the parking lot empty.

I continued on, shoulders hunched against the lake wind, one hand resting on my gun. I could see no sign of a car near the warehouses, which I hoped meant MacIver had the sense to park elsewhere, but probably only meant he hadn't arrived yet.

I contemplated walking away from this. If MacIver's car squealed around the corner, lights on, radio blasting, I'd go...and be happy for the excuse. I didn't need anything from him. But skipping the meeting would let him know something was wrong, and I wasn't giving him and his coconspirators the chance to fold their operation and run.

I unholstered my gun. Unit three, MacIver said. The one nearest to me was marked with a dingy white four. Beside it was one, which made perfect sense. I continued on to the next, to find the number half missing, only a top loop remaining, which could make it a two or a three, but when I checked the last one, farthest out and behind the others, it bore a clear three.

I slid the gun under my jacket, keeping it at hand, but hidden. MacIver might come armed, and I didn't want to spook him. I'd already killed tonight and wasn't eager to do it again. But if I had to? I wouldn't regret it.

Earlier I'd pondered where I drew the line. Now I realized it wasn't that simple. Payne hadn't been a murderer, rapist, or pedophile—just a guy whose moral compass valued money over life. Someone who, when given the chance to join a plan to sell babies by hiring a hitman to kill their teenage mothers had apparently said, "Cool, sign me up!"

Payne's role at the agency had been exactly what we'd expected. He searched for wealthy and desperate couples with personal black marks that made adoption difficult. Then he contacted them. After a long interview process, he made them an offer. Only he didn't make that offer without approval. As it turned out, Payne was only a cog in this wheel, and a low-level one at that. Well paid, he took all the risks—contacting the prospective parents and playing point man with Fenniger—while others made the decisions.

Because he wasn't in charge, though, he insisted he couldn't be blamed. The scheme hadn't been his idea. He didn't pull the trigger. If he'd said no, they'd have found someone else. Classic criminal justification, just like we'd heard from Fenniger.

Did Payne deserve to die for that? No.

But did I have a problem killing him when he could tip off his colleagues? Or run and escape justice? No. And that's what it came down to: circumstance.

Half the marks the Tomassinis gave me didn't "deserve" death. What they deserved was to be locked up. But if that wasn't about to happen and the Tomassinis wanted them dead, I had no problem executing the writ.

Even those that I agreed had earned death—like Wayne Franco, like Wilkes, like Fenniger—I would have been happy to see behind bars for life. I remembered the moment when I went on the warrant to arrest Franco. It wasn't my warrant—I'd only been allowed in because of the extra work I'd done catching him. I'd gone with no thoughts of killing the man. I only wanted to see justice done, to relish that moment when he knew he'd been caught.

But when I saw no horror in his face, no expectation that his life was over, I remembered Drew Aldrich bouncing down the courtroom steps, grinning and hugging his supporters, free to live while Amy rotted in her grave. That's why I shot Franco. Not because he deserved it, but because I knew from experience that the only way to guarantee justice was to take care of it yourself.

But with MacIver, justice would be served without a bullet. If he didn't go to jail, he'd spend everything he had on legal fees. Even if he managed to bolt, his life would be lived on the run, as a fugitive. Good enough for me.

I drew up alongside the warehouse and paused under the filthy windows, searching the smoke-gray rectangles for any glint of light within. None. I checked my watch. I was five minutes early.

I circled the building. Just those two doors—the front door and the loading bay, side by side. As I stood by the door, I weighed the risk of breaking in versus the danger of hanging around outside. MacIver said to meet him inside. He probably expected me to whip out a state-of-the-art lock pick gun and open the door for him.

As I crouched to examine the lock, I noticed the plate was bent, with rust along the fold, meaning it'd been jimmied open long ago. The lock had probably been fixed, but I tried the handle anyway. The door opened.

I slipped inside, keeping my back to the wall, gun drawn as I took out my penlight. It barely cut a pinprick through the dark. I waited for my eyes to adjust, then stepped forward and banged my shin on something solid, but pliant. I shone the light down to see two stacked tires, invisible in the dark. To my left and right were virtual walls of tires, six feet high, transforming the entrance into a small black foyer.

Someone was using the warehouse to fence tires? It seemed a tough item to steal and awkward to resell, but as my light crossed the ones nearest me, I saw the treads were cracked and bald. Not reselling tires—illegally dumping them.

I picked my way across the tire-strewn entranceway and around the end of the "wall" twenty feet down. There, the unrelenting darkness lifted, as some light managed to sneak through the filthy windows. There were more tires in here, plus a stack of cans—paint, oil, and other toxins you couldn't toss in the trash. I shuddered to think what would happen if kids snuck in here, smoking cigarettes or playing with matches.

Headlights cut an arc across the dirt on the nearest window. I moved to it, but couldn't bring myself to wipe the glass, even wearing gloves. The lights swung my way as the car backed between warehouses one and two. Not an ideal parking spot. Better than pulling up to the front door, though.

I moved back to that tire-enclosed foyer and holstered my gun, but kept my jacket open for easy access. Jack always said a nervous client was more dangerous than a ruthless one. Lurking in the dark, even with a penlight on, probably wasn't the safest way to greet MacIver.

I opened the door as he hurried over. His eyes rounded and he frantically motioned me back inside as he scanned the yard. Sure, *now* he worries about looking suspicious.

I retreated into the building. A moment later, he slid in, shutting the door behind him.

"Do you have the ring?" he whispered.

"Yes." I resisted the urge to respond with, "Do you have the money?" He wouldn't get the joke and would probably think I'd seriously expected him to bring a briefcase of cash.

I handed him the ring. As he studied it with a flashlight, I studied him. Knowing now what he was, and how he was involved, put him in a whole new light, one that made my hands itch to fly to his throat, throttling him as I shouted, "How could you?"

Maybe knowing he wasn't in it for the money should

have made it better, but it didn't. All I could do was remind myself he'd see justice soon enough. Calmly, I asked about the wire transfer, which was going into Evelyn's offshore account. I didn't care about the money—she could keep it as debt repayment. But MacIver would expect that to be foremost in my mind, so I had to ask.

"I'll transfer it in the morning," he said as he lowered the flashlight.

"Why not tonight?" I asked.

"It's late. My wife is waiting."

With your new baby, I thought. But I couldn't say that, so I settled for, "Just have it in the account by nine. Now, you're right, it is late, so if that's everything…"

He rubbed the ring, as if calling forth a genie to help him think. "You shredded all the papers, right?"

"Yes, and I removed the hard drive from his desktop computer and took the laptop."

"Did you bring them?"

"Was I supposed to?"

He rubbed the ring harder. I aimed my foot and shoulder toward the door, hinting I wanted to be going, but the second I moved, he jumped back, as if I'd pulled a gun.

As I sucked in my annoyance and lifted my hands to say, "Look buddy, I just *moved,* okay?" I sensed someone behind me. Maybe it was a faint change in the light. Maybe it was a click so soft only my subconscious recognized it. Maybe it was just a sixth sense. But my body reacted, sending me diving for the floor, brain screaming "what the hell—?"

The *pfft* of a silenced shot cut the thought short.

Forty-seven

The bullet sliced through my jacket as I hit the floor in a roll. A second shot bounced off the concrete beside me. I came out of the tumble and shot forward, hunched over, head down, hand going for my gun. A third shot, this one so far from hitting me I didn't even see where it went.

I caught a glimpse of MacIver, still standing where I left him, his hands at his sides, eyes wide—not in shock that I'd nearly been shot, but that I'd avoided it.

I swung around as a shadowy figure spun, lifting his gun to take aim.

"Stop," I said.

He hesitated, gun still aimed down, lowered as he'd moved. He started to lift it.

"That goes for the gun, too," I said. "Move it and I'll shoot."

He adjusted his hands on the gun, as if considering his odds, only to decide they weren't in his favor. He let it drop an inch as he looked up, his face turning into the glow of MacIver's half-lowered flashlight.

"Hello, Ken," I said.

His brow furrowed.

"No, we haven't met," I said. "But I know who you are. Kenneth Keyes, proud papa to a new baby, just like MacIver here. Two new babies, courtesy of a pyramid scheme. How did you guys come up with that one? Sitting around the country club after a few holes, and someone says, 'Hey, I know how we give our wives those babies they want'?"

"We don't need them to give us anything," said a voice behind me as a gun barrel poked my spine. "I'm perfectly capable of getting what I need."

"Leslie," I said, striving to keep my voice neutral, hiding my surprise. "You hired a baby-sitter for the evening, I take it? Better keep this short, then. I hear they charge double after midnight. But I suppose when you've paid the big bucks to kill a girl and steal her baby, that's a minor expense."

The gun didn't even waver. Damn.

I inhaled through my teeth, telling myself it might not be a gun. For all I knew, she was poking me with a stick. But was I willing to bet my life on that?

These weren't cool and experienced criminal masterminds. They were suburbanites, panicked and ready to kill everyone involved to cover their tracks. That's why MacIver had told me this was a one-shot job. Spooked by Fenniger's disappearance and the "FBI" visit, they were shutting down all connections to their hitman—killing the guy who'd hired him, then the hitman who'd done the job.

Once the smoke cleared, they could get a new hitman elsewhere, which I was sure they'd do. It was a very profitable endeavor.

After coming up with the scheme to get babies for themselves, they'd recruited Payne to provide the documentation, and he'd convinced them they could sell babies to other desperate parents-to-be, who'd believe they were getting a child from a willing—and living—teen mother.

So they'd hired Fenniger to find girls and take pictures. If the child wasn't quite what they wanted themselves, he went to one of the paying parents. MacIver had taken Connor, the first baby. The second was sold to a pair of the "innocent" parents. Ken and Leslie held out for a girl: Destiny. There were two other couples in the scheme, still waiting for children; plus a half dozen more innocent prospective parents.

"Ted and Doug couldn't make it tonight, I take it?" I said. "Big poker game planned? Or since you guys have kids already, and the most to lose, they pawned off this nasty bit of business on you? Hardly fair."

"Shoot her," Ken mouthed.

"Payne isn't dead," I said quickly.

"What?" Leslie said.

"MacIver only asked for his ring. Do you think I needed to kill him to get it? He didn't even ask for proof that the files were destroyed."

MacIver's chin shot up, eyes bugging. "You didn't tell me to ask—"

"She's stalling," Ken said. Sweat trickled down his forehead. He couldn't tear his gaze from the gun pointed at his chest.

"Nervous, Ken?" I said. "You're praying Leslie shoots me before she finds out how badly you fucked up. I cut a deal with Payne. How else would I know your names? Your scheme? Know about that visit from the Feds?"

"Les, she's stalling." A note of pleading seeped into Ken's voice.

"You know what the problem is with hiring criminals? We aren't the most loyal employees. Right now, Payne is awaiting my call to say it went fine and his half of your hit money will be transferred tomorrow."

"*His* half?" MacIver sputtered. "Why would you pay him?"

"For the most valuable commodity of all: information. He gets his life and half your money, and I get all his files. He runs to Cancún. I blackmail you, and get an amazing rate of return on my investment. But, if he doesn't hear from me in an hour, he's going to run... with those files. One *advantage* to dealing with criminals though? If I double-cross you, I double-cross him, too. So how's this? I call Payne and tell him you paid me in cash, so we can make the transaction right now. He'll bring the files. I bring you..."

The pressure on my back eased as Leslie shifted.

"Les, don't listen to her," Ken said. "What's to say she won't just trick us again?"

"You'll be there to make sure I don't. Believe me, between money and my life, I'll take my life. I can always earn more—"

I fired. Ken gasped. I was already diving to the side. Leslie fired once, but the bullet went wild. I scrambled behind the wall of tires, skidded to the floor, then flipped around, on my back, gun raised, pointed at the edge of that tire wall.

"She shot him," MacIver breathed, the words coming in disjointed puffs.

"See?" I called, gun fixed on that tire wall edge, ready to fire at anything that came around it. "That's another problem with hiring professional killers. When things go wrong, people tend to die." I listened and caught the gurgling rasp of Ken's breathing. "Seems my aim was less than perfect, though. That gurgle you hear, Leslie? That's blood filling his lungs. I'd say he's got, maybe, fifteen minutes."

"You bitch! You fucking bitch!"

The brief sound of a struggle, MacIver holding Leslie back, trying to reason with her. I pushed to my feet, gun still on that spot, ears telling me they were both a few feet away.

Ken moaned. The shot, if I'd aimed right, had gone through his left lung, dangerously close to his heart, but not fatal. Not yet. Better to keep him alive and in mortal danger, dividing their attention.

"I'm going for help," MacIver said.

I sidestepped to the tire wall and backed up past a gap between stacks. Through it, I could see across the entrance and aim a gun, but Leslie had stopped MacIver and they were arguing.

I pressed my hands against one tire stack, testing it, but it would take all my weight to knock it over and I couldn't predict where it would land.

"We have to reason with her," MacIver was saying. "Come to an agreement."

"Reason with her? She shot Ken!"

"We—we'll pay her. Insurance. We factored this into the forecast, and we have enough—"

"To pay blackmail money to a killer? Start and you'll never stop."

They continued talking about me as if this tire wall was soundproof. I staked out the area, creeping about as my eyes continued to adjust.

"For God's sake, Leslie! Ken's dying. Who cares about blackmail? We'll just pay her to let us out of here."

Leslie's harsh laugh echoed through the warehouse.

"Let us out? Palmer, look around. We're ten feet from the door. *She's* the one trapped. Now, here's the plan."

Her voice lowered as she whispered instructions. I crept forward, straining to hear, but Ken's labored breathing drowned it out.

"No," MacIver said finally. "I mean it, Leslie. I've had enough of this, and I won't let Ken die."

His loafers slapped the concrete as he strode to the edge of the tire wall. Leslie called for him to stop, but his figure rounded the corner, stepping from the blackness into the gray gloom.

"I want to negotiate," he said.

I shot him in the forehead.

Forty-eight

"You bitch!" Leslie shrieked as MacIver crumpled to the floor.

"Did I mention the part about people dying?"

I flicked on my penlight, the weak beam illuminating MacIver's outstretched hand, still holding Ken's gun. Leslie stopped cursing.

"Yes, I knew he was coming around that corner to shoot, not negotiate," I said. "Did you really think I'd fall for it? Or just good enough odds...so long as someone else was taking the risk? That's how you operate. Get the guys to do the dangerous parts. It's easy, isn't it? We can slide into damsel-in-distress mode without even realizing it."

The barrel of Leslie's gun slid around the corner. I fired. She yelped and stumbled back, shoes scratching against the pavement as she recovered.

"The difference between you and me?" I went on, unfazed. "You do it intentionally. You tell them what you need, the ugly job that has to be done, say you're too scared to do yourself, and they jump right in to help."

"Would you shut up?" she said between gritted teeth.

"Why? Am I distracting you? I could talk all night, but Ken doesn't have that long." I paused. "Are you even thinking about Ken? What's little Miranda going to do without her daddy?"

"She's got me."

"Ouch, and you call *me* cold. He can still hear you, you

know, lying on that cold floor, dying. Think of all he's done for you. And this is how you repay him."

"Because he helped me get a baby? He sure as hell better. He robbed me of my own. Do you know what he did?"

"No idea, Leslie."

I mentally added "but, please, tell me" as I snuck along the wall of tires, trying to find a gap on the right angle to aim through.

"He knew I wanted kids, so when we were dating he said, 'Sure, we'll have three, four if you like.' Then on the honeymoon—the fucking honeymoon—he tells me he had a vasectomy after his second kid. But no problem. He'll get it reversed, just for me. Only it didn't work."

"Huh."

Through a gap I could see her elbow, but there was no way to fire a lethal shot without sticking my gun barrel through. I stepped back, staying in line with the gap, in case she moved this way.

"So I say, 'How about a sperm donor?' But no way, no goddamned way, is he having his wife pregnant with another man's baby. Adoption then. Fine, but it has to be a *white* baby, so his parents don't flip out."

Leslie finally moved . . . the other way. From the sound of her voice, she'd begun pacing as she worked herself into a righteous fury.

"And finding an agency that suits his needs? Well, that's my job. Even though I made more money, worked longer hours . . ." Her voice trailed off.

A blur of motion. Leslie's gun flew into the gap, firing. I'd swung to the side at the first sign of movement, my back slamming against the tire stack.

"You've got a real sob story there, Leslie. Poor little rich girl. Hubby's shooting blanks so she has to buy herself a baby. I'm crying for you. Really I am."

A sharp intake of breath. I kept my back against the tires, gun fixed on the end of the wall.

"Is Destiny worth it?" I asked when she didn't respond.

"What destiny? If you start some New Age bullshit—"

"That's her name, Leslie. The baby you bought. Destiny. Her mother's name was Sammi. Not that you bothered to find out."

A sharp bark of a laugh. "Oh, my God. Is that what this is about? Let me guess. You're her sister. Or aunt. No, Sunday school teacher, right?" The laugh took on a manic edge. "So my daughter has a hitwoman in her family tree."

"Are you worried about that? What's bred in the bone . . ."

I tried to read the play of light over the gap, telling me whether she was still there. Wheel, shoot fast . . . No, I couldn't take the chance.

"It's a good thing I believe in nurture over nature," Leslie said. "Otherwise do you think I'd go through all this trouble to get the daughter of a white trash whore?"

My finger clamped around the gun. "Sammi wasn't—"

"Oh, you know what she was, even if she was your sister or whatever. We went to school with girls like her. We'd see them every day. Empty-headed sluts who think of nothing but boys and partying. Too stupid to even take birth control. They get knocked up, go on welfare, and start pumping out babies like kittens, with no idea how to care for them, no interest in caring for them, because they have no interest in anyone but themselves."

"Did Destiny look neglected to you? Mistreated? Maltreated?"

She snorted. "Even a cat looks after its babies for a little while. Miranda was a novelty to her. Like a doll. That's what babies are to these girls. You've seen them, in the malls and the parks, running in packs, not a one of them over eighteen. Pushing their strollers like little girls with dolls. That's what gave me the idea. I was having coffee with a few other women—a support group we'd formed. There, at the next table, were three teenage girls, bitching about their babies, about how much trouble they were, about how they'd only had them because all their friends had one, like it was a goddamned fashion trend. The babies are right there, dressed wrong, fussing because they're ignored and uncomfortable, and here we were, four women who'd give anything to have those babies."

"Tragic." I'd taken a few steps as she spoke, but had reached an opening. I hovered on the far side of it. "So it's not fair. And that entitled you to find girls, kill them, and take their babies?"

"Are you telling me those babies would be better off with those mothers?"

By her voice, I knew she was far enough away. I side-stepped past the gap.

"We can give those babies everything," she continued. "The best care. The best schools. Stable, two-parent families."

"Er, you might want to check the definition of stable, Les. I'm pretty sure you don't fit it. And I'm pretty sure the two-parent part is out, too. Sounds like Ken's gone. Not that you care. You were willing to let him die to protect a baby that isn't even yours. Just like you killed her mother to get her. You couldn't come up with a better way?"

I readied myself to move again as soon as she spoke.

"Do you think anyone cares about those girls? Worthless little tramps, prancing around in next to nothing, shaking their asses at every man who walks by. Then, if he takes them up on their invitation, they cry rape."

A voice echoed through my mind. A neighbor, at Amy's memorial, whispering to her friend, saying almost the exact same words about Amy. As I struggled to focus, I missed the first part of Leslie's new diatribe.

"—accuses him of rape. Fucking bad judgment, sleeping with your fifteen-year-old student, but rape?" A manic laugh. "He couldn't handle it. Drove the car off an embankment. Killed himself and almost killed me. Then, as I'm lying in the hospital bed, I hear the little bitch is pregnant. She stole my fiancé, killed him, then has his baby. *My* baby."

"Destiny isn't that baby—"

"Do you think I don't know that?" The words were barely comprehensible, spewed on a stream of venom.

"I'm just checking, Les, 'cause I hate to say it, but you seem a bit nuts to me." A small laugh. "Oh, who am I kidding? You're full-blown fucked-in-the-head crazy."

"You're calling me crazy? You kill people for a living."

"Sure," I said as I reached the end of the wall. "But I *know* I'm not fit to raise a child."

"How *dare* you judge—!"

"Sorry, Leslie, but no matter what goes down here, you aren't keeping Destiny. I don't care how much money you have or how badly you want her, you aren't one-tenth the mother Sammi was."

She sprang around the corner, her face contorted with rage, gun raised. I slammed my fist into the bottom of her arm and the gun flew free. As she twisted to dive for it, I kicked her in the stomach. She howled, doubling over as she fell to the floor. I booted the gun out of her reach. She flipped over and grabbed for the one in MacIver's hand. I beat her to it, but as I bent to scoop it up, I stumbled, managing to grab MacIver's but drop my own.

I flew after it. She was faster, and snatched it as my fingertips brushed the metal. I staggered back, raising MacIver's gun.

"Stop," she said, smiling as she raised the gun to point at my head.

"Y-you don't want to do this, Leslie. I can help you. I can make sure you keep Destiny—Miranda, your baby."

"Sorry, but I can manage just fine on my own."

She pulled the trigger. Nothing happened. She pulled it again, face twisting. I took the cartridge from my pocket and dangled it in my free hand as I lifted MacIver's gun.

"Yes, it's empty," I said. "But thank you for putting your prints on it."

I shot her between the eyes. She toppled back, my gun still clutched in her hands. I took a deep breath, steadying myself, then crossed to MacIver and replaced the gun in his bare hand, putting it back as it had been.

"Not bad," said a voice behind me.

I spun, hand going to my holster.

Forty-nine

Jack closed the door behind him. "First thing? Before replacing his gun? Should have grabbed hers. Can't be unarmed. Not for a second. Better yet? Backup gun. Discussed that, didn't we?"

"How did you find me?"

"GPS. Put it on your cell phone. Figured that's one thing you wouldn't trash. Supposed to be a receiver, too. Piss-poor one."

"Probably interference from the cell."

"Gadgets." He shook his head as he walked over to look at the bodies. "Quick cleanup. Then go. You start—" He turned to me. "Am I *allowed* to help now?"

I tried to gauge whether he was angry or even annoyed. Impossible to tell, as always, so I said, "I'd appreciate it. Thanks."

There wasn't much to clean. I hadn't removed my gloves. Hadn't been hit by a bullet. Hadn't taken off my wig. My only concern was footprints in the dust that would suggest a fourth party to this lethal spat. A flashlight sweep of the floor, though, showed lots of prints, from lots of boots, presumably the people who'd been using the warehouse as an illegal dump site. I erased the most obvious of mine, and I'd discard the boots. Standard procedure.

As we were leaving, I looked back at the bodies.

"So you were outside listening?" I asked.

"Nah. GPS fucked up, too. Goddamned gadgets. Was at the mark's house. Lost you after that."

Was that the truth? Or did he just not want to take the wind out of my sails by telling me I'd had backup the whole time? As we circled through the shadows to the car, I decided it didn't matter. If he had been there, he'd stayed back, trusting me to handle it. That was enough.

Since I'd taken the rental, Jack had commandeered Evelyn's car, and parked it five blocks from the warehouse. He wanted the rental returned—another step in dissociating ourselves from the scene—so he followed me to drop that off.

Once in the car with him, I finally had the chance to explain what had happened. He'd figured out some of it, but was missing chunks, from the poor reception and from not being able to listen until he'd ditched Quinn, meaning he hadn't heard my playground meeting with MacIver.

When he found out, he cursed Evelyn. Not that he thought she'd done anything wrong intentionally. She just hadn't been careful enough, presuming that because it was clearly the correct client, then it had to be the correct job.

"Don't call her on it, okay?" I said. "I'm done with her and I want a clean break."

"Sure about that?"

"About wanting—?"

"Being done with her? That Contra-whatever lead?" His gaze bored into me as he idled at a light. "You're sure?"

As I stared down the dark street, I realized I wasn't.

That morning the answer had been clear. I wanted nothing to do with Evelyn. A sensible, cool-headed, logical decision not to deal with a woman I didn't trust. But now I wondered...

Was it really logical? Or was I just telling myself that to avoid the truth—that I didn't want to hear her offer, didn't dare take the opportunity to discover what I was, what drove me, where I drew the line...

"I-I'm not sure."

"Think about it." He glanced over. "But not indefinitely. Need to give her a deadline. A week. Can you do that?"

I nodded.

"And this...?" he said. "The case?"

"Well, obviously I haven't disbanded the operation. We've got two other couples who knew what was going on, and more who've paid them—including one that has a child they think is rightfully theirs. I have names for the two couples, but they'll likely run for the hills when Keyes or MacIver don't call back tonight to say everything's been taken care of." I took a deep breath. "But that's not my concern. I can't let it be. I've got my proof on the downloaded files. Time to turn over the evidence and back out."

"You okay with that?"

I took a few long minutes considering it, then said, "Yes, I'm okay with that."

Fifty

Two days later, I was back at Sammi's grave, sitting on the ground, knees pulled up, the setting sun casting an eerie yellow glow over the forest as I told her what had happened. I could imagine what she'd say about that, hearing it as clearly as if she'd been standing there, arms crossed, shaking her head.

Do you know how stupid you look? I can't hear you, you know. A total waste of your time, but I guess if it makes you feel better...

Yes, it did make me feel better. The case hadn't wrapped up as neatly as I would have liked, with every baby returned, every person involved facing jail time, and I needed this, to forget what hadn't gone right and concentrate on what had.

The case was in the hands of the police now. Quinn had advised me on how to compile and submit the evidence anonymously. We'd left Detroit that night, before the bodies had been found. There was no mention of those bodies in our report. Let the police find them and work out the scenario, preferably one that indicted their anonymous tipster only as a potential catalyst for the deaths—that the group had discovered they were about to be investigated, and in arguing over what to do, had turned on each other.

"There's always a chance they'll trace Destiny back to you and she'll go to the Draytons, but I knew you wouldn't want that, so I didn't point them your way."

Good.

"She'll go to a family in Michigan. Real adopters who've gone through a shitload of screening and are dying for a little girl just like her."

I imagined her muttering about city yuppies raising her daughter.

"They won't be as good as you would have been, but they'll be the next best thing. She'll have everything you ever wanted for her, Sammi. She got out, just like you wanted."

As for Deanna's baby, Connor, he'd had been found and gone to her sister, Denise Noyes. I didn't mention that. Sammi wouldn't have cared about the fate of some baby and girl she'd never met. I felt better knowing Connor had been found and Denise had both her answers and her nephew.

I squinted through the trees at the sun, then back to her grave—a leaf-covered pile lost in the forest. "I could find a way to direct the police investigation to you. To get you a real grave, in the town cemetery."

Oh, sure, just give the Draytons a road map to Destiny while you're at it. And for what? A place in the corner of the town cemetery? A charity case funeral? The smallest stone they can get away with? She snorted. *I'm fine here. Let them think we both got out.*

"That's what I thought you'd want." I pushed to my feet. "I brought you something. No, don't worry, it's not flowers. I always wondered why we leave flowers, whether the person liked them or not. When my cousin died, I used to leave magazines at her grave. She loved magazines. *Seventeen, Cosmo* when she could sneak it past her mom... They made me stop leaving them, saying it was littering the cemetery, but I think they just figured it was kind of weird."

Huh, really? Go figure.

"Yes, 'normal' and I have never been on close terms, as you probably figured out long ago. But I did bring something for you."

I reached into my jacket pocket and pulled out the photo of Sammi and Destiny I'd taken from her room. I knelt and started laying it on the ground faceup, then turned it over, facing her, and put a stone on top. I stood and brushed off my jeans.

"So ... I guess I just wanted to let you know how it all worked out."

Fine. Just don't expect me to say thank you.

I didn't.

Fifty-one

A week later, I was tearing across the south field on a newly repaired ATV. I'd never used the south field. The former owners had rented it to a misguided city transplant with dreams of organic tomatoes, who'd plowed the field only to learn that the soil wouldn't grow anything less hardy than potatoes.

When I'd moved in, I'd had dreams of a native wildlife meadow, but without the time or funds to cultivate the field, I'd settled for the north meadow as my picnic spot, leaving this five-acre plot a rough and rutted field choked with saplings. For ATVs, though, it was perfect.

I was ripping around the corner, sailing over a hillock, when Jack waved me in. He'd come back from Detroit with me, but now, with one ATV running and the other almost there, I suspected he'd be on his way before the weekend crowds arrived.

I raced the ATV over the ruts, hitting the brakes a few feet from Jack, then veering fast when I realized it wouldn't stop in time...and he wasn't getting out of the way.

"I think the brakes need adjusting," I said as I got off.

"Think the driver needs to slow down."

I grinned as I pulled off my helmet. "Never."

He motioned for me to follow him back to the lodge.

"Did Quinn call?"

Another head shake. Quinn had left that same evening

we had to head home, but he was keeping an eye on the case, letting me know how it unfolded.

Jack had helped me cobble together a story to explain how my "quiet evening resting at a motel" left four people dead and me holding a flash drive full of case-breaking details. That had surprised me—Jack helping me square things with Quinn—but when I'd joked about it, he'd only shrugged it off. If Quinn suspected there was more to the story, he didn't press.

Before we'd parted, we'd made plans for a few days in Toronto or Montreal. No date set yet—weekends were out for me, and weekdays were tough for him—but we'd work something out. And if we couldn't do it in the next month, I was going to take the bigger plunge and invite him here for a weekend instead. No more stalling. I wanted this and I was going to make it happen.

Now if only I could take as decisive an action with the Evelyn question. That one I still hadn't decided yet, and time was running out.

"So what's up?" I asked.

"Someone to see you."

"Oh, shit." I raked my hand through my hair and whacked the dust from my jeans. "Do I look presentable?"

"Don't think she'll care."

I squinted against the midday sun, seeing two figures on the porch. But it was just Emma and Owen, watching us. Emma was smiling. Even Owen looked impatient, as if waiting for me to get there.

"Okay," I said. "Let me repeat. What's going on?"

Jack motioned me to the other side of the building, where he'd left my truck after a run into town. I noticed a tall, narrow cardboard box propped against the lodge wall.

"What's that?"

He shrugged. The box looked like some kind of fencing. Why would we need...?

"Oh, no," I said. "You didn't. Tell me you didn't."

He slowed. "Want me to take her back?"

I hurried over to the truck. In the back, a pet carrier started quivering, a black nose pressing against the wire.

"I can take her back," Jack called.

I hopped into the bed, crouched beside the carrier and opened it. A white ball of fur torpedoed out, toppling me backward. The puppy lapped at my face, paws digging into my chest as she balanced on top of me. Jack glanced over the side of the truck. I turned a reproachful look on him.

"I said I can take her back."

I lifted the puppy off me and knelt, petting her. She was about the size of a terrier already, with huge batlike ears and massive paws that promised she'd grow into those ears soon enough.

"What is she?" I asked.

"German shepherd."

"Ha-ha."

"She is. White one. Thought that'd be good out here. Help people see you on the road. Easy to see her in the fields."

"And when those fields are covered in fluffy white snow?"

"Huh. Never thought of that."

I shook my head as I rubbed her ears. "I don't need a dog, Jack."

"But you want one."

"Nadia?" Emma called before I could answer him. She leaned over the porch rail, holding the phone. "It's your Aunt Evie."

"Fuck," Jack muttered. "Said a week. Waits exactly that. To the hour, I bet."

I motioned to Emma that I'd be there in a moment, and handed the dog over the side to Jack.

"Tell John to bring the puppy over," Emma called. "Owen wants to see it."

"And *she* doesn't," I murmured.

"Haven't decided, have you?"

"Not yet. I guess I'd better think fast."

As I climbed out of the truck bed, I looked around. At the lodge, the bright midday sun cresting over the roof. Towels flapped in the wind, hung to dry before guests arrived. The smell of soup and freshly baked bread wafted from the open windows. Emma laughed at something Owen said as he refilled the bird feeders, sneaking glances at the dog. I glanced at Jack, the puppy playing tug-of-war with his sleeve.

I looked around and had the overwhelming urge to say "good enough." This was good. This was right. This was me.

Stick with this. Sneak out a couple of times a year for the Tomassinis, and if it doesn't scratch the itch, just say "good enough."

Don't go deeper. Don't even look deeper. Tell Evelyn no.

And if I did that, did I secure my world? Keep it all sunshine and puppies? Or only make the darkness burrow deeper, fester deeper.

I took a deep breath, filling my lungs until they stung, then slowly let it out.

"Be back in a minute."

He nodded. "I'll be here. Whatever you decide."

I headed for the lodge.

EXIT STRATEGY

Kelley Armstrong

Nadia Stafford is an ex-cop – fired after she shot a child killer. She now works for one small mafia family: the way she sees it, no one innocent is getting hurt.

But then a serial killer starts murdering innocent people in the style of a hitman. The police investigation threatens to unmask several professional hitmen, including Nadia. So she bands together with five other hitmen, including her mentor, the mysterious Jack. Together they decide to hunt down the killer – but perhaps that's just what he wants. Are they walking into a devious and brilliantly planned trap?

BITTEN

Kelley Armstrong

Elena Michaels is your regular twenty-first-century
girl: self-assured, smart and fighting fit. She also
just happens to be the only female werewolf in
the world . . .

It has some good points. When she walks down a dark
alleyway, *she's* the scary one. But now her Pack – the
one she abandoned so that she could live a normal life
– are in trouble, and they need her help. Is she willing
to risk her life to help the ex-lover who betrayed her
by turning her into a werewolf in the first place? And,
more to the point, does she have a choice?

<u>STOLEN</u>

Kelley Armstrong

Elena Michaels is a wanted woman. She hasn't done anything wrong. Well, not recently, anyway. But ten years ago her lover turned her into a werewolf: the only female werewolf in the world, in fact.

And now, just as she's finally coming to terms with it all, a group of scientists learns of her existence. They're hunting her down, and Elena is about to run straight into their trap. But they haven't reckoned on Elena's adoptive family, her Pack, who will stop at nothing to get her back. They haven't reckoned on Elena herself, either, and that's a very big mistake . . .

DIME STORE MAGIC

Kelley Armstrong

Paige Winterbourne is a witch. Not that you'd notice – no warts, no green skin, no cute little wiggle of the nose whenever she casts a spell. No, most of the time she's just a normal twenty-three-year-old girl: works too hard, worries about her weight, wonders if she'll ever find a boyfriend. Okay, so she does have an adopted teenage daughter, Savannah, who wants to raise her black witch of a mother from the dead. And who is being stalked by a telekinetic half-demon and an all-powerful cabal of sorcerers. But other than that, Paige has a really ordinary life. That is, until the neighbours find out who she is, and all hell breaks loose. Literally . . .

INDUSTRIAL MAGIC

Kelley Armstrong

When Paige Winterbourne is ousted as leader of the American Coven of Witches, all she wants to do is hide under her duvet for a few months. But fate, of course, has other plans. A murderer is on the loose – someone with superhuman skills and a grudge against the supernatural community. When Paige learns that the killer is targeting children, she has to get involved.

Desperate to protect those she loves, Paige is thrown into a world of arrogant sorcerers, drunken necromancers, sulky druid gods and pretentious leather-clad vampires. Not to mention an apparently unstoppable supernatural psychopath hell-bent on revenge . . .

HAUNTED

Kelley Armstrong

Eve Levine – half-demon, black witch and devoted mother – has been dead for three years. She has a great house, an interesting love life and can't be killed again – which comes in handy when you've made as many enemies as Eve. Yes, the afterlife isn't too bad – all she needs to do is find a way to communicate with her daughter Savannah and she'll be happy.

But fate – or more exactly, the Fates – have other plans. Eve owes them a favour, and they've just called it in. An evil spirit called the Nix has escaped from hell. She feeds on chaos and death, and is very good at persuading people to kill for her. The Fates want Eve to hunt her down before she does any more damage, but the Nix is a dangerous enemy – previous hunters have been sent mad in the process. As if that's not problem enough, it turns out that the only way to stop her is with an angel's sword. And Eve's no angel . . .